SWEETBITTER SONG

www.penguin.co.uk

Also by Rosie Hewlett

MEDUSA

MEDEA

SWEET BITTER SONG

ROSIE HEWLETT

bantam

TRANSWORLD PUBLISHERS

UK | USA | Canada | Ireland | Australia
India | New Zealand | South Africa

Transworld is part of the Penguin Random House group of companies
whose addresses can be found at global.penguinrandomhouse.com.

Penguin Random House UK, One Embassy Gardens, 8 Viaduct Gardens, London SW11 7BW

penguin.co.uk

First published in Great Britain in 2026 by Bantam
an imprint of Transworld Publishers

001

Copyright © Rosie Hewlett 2026

The moral right of the author has been asserted.

This book is a work of fiction and, except in the case of historical fact,
any resemblance to actual persons, living or dead, is purely coincidental.

Every effort has been made to obtain the necessary permissions with
reference to copyright material, both illustrative and quoted. We apologize
for any omissions in this respect and will be pleased to make the
appropriate acknowledgements in any future edition.

Penguin Random House values and supports copyright.
Copyright fuels creativity, encourages diverse voices, promotes freedom
of expression and supports a vibrant culture. Thank you for purchasing
an authorized edition of this book and for respecting intellectual property
laws by not reproducing, scanning or distributing any part of it by any
means without permission. You are supporting authors and enabling
Penguin Random House to continue to publish books for everyone.
No part of this book may be used or reproduced in any manner for the
purpose of training artificial intelligence technologies or systems. In accordance
with Article 4(3) of the DSM Directive 2019/790, Penguin Random House
expressly reserves this work from the text and data mining exception.

Typeset in 12.25/16.5 pt Fournier MT by Falcon Oast Graphic Art Ltd
Printed and bound in Great Britain by Clays Ltd, Elcograf S.p.A.

The authorized representative in the EEA is Penguin Random House Ireland,
Morrison Chambers, 32 Nassau Street, Dublin D02 YH68

A CIP catalogue record for this book is available from the British Library

ISBNs
9781787637313 (cased)
9781787637320 (tpb)

For all the love stories erased by history

PART I
ANOTHER TIME

1

My mother cried when the King of Sparta first summoned me.

I could not understand why.

I remember staring up at her face, familiar features made foreign by emotions too heavy to grasp in my small hands.

Was it not an *honour* to be called to King Tyndareus' personal quarters? Should my mother not have been pleased, *proud* even?

The only way I could make sense of her tears was by assuming they were *my* fault. Perhaps she feared my 'sharp tongue' would get me into trouble, as it so often did with the other grown-ups.

'I will be good,' I told her, cupping her damp cheeks between my palms just like she always did when I was sad. 'I promise, Mama.'

Confusingly, my words only encouraged more tears to fall.

'Don't do this,' she begged the woman towering beside us.

This woman was a stranger to me, an unsurprising fact considering she was one of the king's personal attendants. Her kind rarely visited the lower parts of the palace where I had been born and raised. 'Slaves in denial', my brother called them. I did not know what he meant by that, though I laughed when he said it. Melanthius always liked it when I laughed at his jokes.

'It is already done,' the attendant said.

'She is just a *child*.'

'I am not!' I interjected. 'This is my ninth summer.'

Nine seemed an impressive number to me, far greater and wiser than eight, and only three summers shy of twelve, the divine number of the Olympians.

'The girl is old enough.'

I beamed up at the attendant, thrilled that she agreed with me.

She did not smile back. I wondered if she even knew how. She was all angles and edges, not an inch of softness to her. I imagined if we hugged, she would skewer me like a piece of meat. Though, the woman's eyes were by far the sharpest thing about her. They made the remnants of my supper squirm in my belly.

'Acte, please.' My mother tried again. 'Don't make her do this.'

Acte drew in a breath, her expression as cold and unreadable as the stone floor beneath our feet. Her stillness was strange to me, so different from the bustling bodies hurrying around us. Though night was setting in, the palace kitchens remained a hive of activity, a constant swirling current of slaves flitting about their tasks. There was a rhythm to this chaos – knives singing, pots bubbling, spoons scraping, fires spitting. It was the song of my childhood, warm and safe and familiar.

Behind Acte, I spied the water basins being filled and silently prayed the king's summons would relieve me of my washing-up duties. Whatever Tyndareus wanted would *surely* be more interesting than scrubbing dirty dishes.

'The girl has been summoned,' was all Acte replied. She sounded bored.

'Send me instead.'

I glared at my mother, furious she would suggest such a thing. How could she take away my chance of meeting our master, our *king*? I had never even seen Tyndareus up close before, having only glimpsed him from a distance on odd occasions, riding his stallions across the palace grounds like Ares, the great God of War himself.

Part of me suspected our master *was* a god. After all, it was said the princes and princesses of Sparta were the children of Zeus, so wasn't that proof enough that Tyndareus was the Thunder God in human form? Melanthius had said the Olympians liked their disguises.

'Send *you*? Don't be absurd,' Acte scoffed. 'You know Icarius likes them young.'

My mother's eyes flared with a rage I rarely ever saw.

'You know what he'll do to her.'

'As did you when you brought her into this world.' Acte's smile looked more like an upside-down scowl to me. 'Don't tell me you believed it would be any different for her.'

My mother froze, shoulders sagging as if a great weight had just been dropped upon them.

Acte stepped closer. 'Delay me again and I'll have you sent to the mines. Both of you. Understood?'

My mother stared at Acte for a long moment, until her eyes started glistening again. She swallowed a few times, as if she were eating something horribly stale, then crouched before me. Sighing, she took my hands in hers, callouses caressing my palms as she pulled me closer, enveloping me in her scent. She always smelt of warm flatbreads. It soothed me, that smell, reminding me of all those hours I had spent watching her work, caked in flour and barley.

'Everything will be all right, my heart,' she said. 'Obey the king and his brother. Don't give them any of that attitude of yours. Yes, Melantho?'

'Yes, Mama.'

'Whatever they—' Her voice caught, but she swallowed again. The corner of her mouth wobbled as she continued, 'Whatever they ask, you must do it. Yes? It'll be over quicker if you just obey. I promise.'

I did not like the way she spoke, voice thick and smothering. When she tried to pull me into a hug I scrambled away, feeling suffocated though I could not explain why. But my mother seemed to understand even if I did not, and so she kissed my cheek instead. Her lips felt shaky and cold, making me want to wipe my face immediately.

'You be brave for me.'

'Yes, Mama.'

Acte cleared her throat, and my mother touched my face one last time before rising to her feet. Then, she turned and walked away, her small, stocky frame melting quickly into the chaos around us. She did not look back, not once.

'Come.' Acte's bony fingers dug into my shoulder. 'The king awaits.'

Acte led me to another realm.

As I gaped up at the soaring ceiling held aloft by thick-ridged pillars, I was certain I had stepped into the hallowed halls of Olympus. Everything was so *vibrant*. The walls brimmed with vividly painted scenes, and the floors were scattered with curious, colourful shards glinting like spilt starlight beneath my feet.

All my life, my entire existence had been confined to the slave quarters, tucked safely away in the deep, warm belly of the palace. Now, it was as if someone had peeled back my reality, letting me peer into a world beyond my own, so distant from the hot, sweaty kitchens rumbling below. This world was cold and clean and beautiful and it radiated *power*. I swore I could feel it humming in the air, needling my skin.

As we walked, my eyes bounced between the giant statues, noting the faces of gods I had spent my life hearing stories about. Poseidon proudly wielding his three-pronged trident. Athena blazing in her battle gear. Zeus holding aloft a bolt of deadly lightning, face etched with a quiet, eternal dominance. They looked so real I half expected them to step down from their plinths to greet us.

'Is this where the Gods live?' I breathed.

Acte snorted. It was an ugly sound.

I didn't ask any more questions after that.

What struck me most was how *quiet* it was there. Even at night, the slave quarters were never silent; there was always someone whispering, bodies shifting, girls crying. Sometimes the adults cried too. This stillness felt heavy, splintered only by my scuffing sandals. I stared at my feet, and the spotless floors seemed to glint accusatorily up at me.

Did my skin always look so *dirty*?

The back of my neck felt warm as I glanced over my shoulder, worried

I might have spoilt this beautiful world. To my relief, there was no trail of filth behind me, but this did little to stop that hot, prickling sensation from spreading down my spine. It was a deeply unpleasant feeling, one I was yet to have a name for.

'What are you looking at?' Acte hissed.

'Nothing.'

By the time we arrived at our destination, I had no idea where we were. It was as if the palace had swallowed me whole, and I was now lost within the jaws of this ancient, glimmering beast. If Acte were to leave me, I feared I would never find my way back to my mother. I would be lost for ever, like the story my brother had once told me about the children locked in King Minos' labyrinth, left to be feasted on by the monster imprisoned there. The thought made my belly tighten as Acte ushered me through an arched stone doorway.

The room inside was the biggest I had ever seen, at least twice the size of the women's sleeping quarters, maybe even larger. Ahead, I glimpsed an enclosed courtyard, divided from the main room by moon-bathed pillars. I walked forward, drawn by the evening breeze rolling in, warm and sweet, laced with the flowers framing the courtyard. I drew in a grateful gulp, savouring its freshness. There was never any fresh air in the women's quarters. With no windows, and the door kept locked at night, the air down there was always hot and sticky. The kitchens were stuffy, too; sometimes it got so bad it made my head hurt. My mother told me I would get used to it one day, though I did not believe her.

I drew in another breath and lifted my gaze. The stars twinkled like morning dew dappled across the sky. Amongst them, the moon looked smaller than I remembered, curved like a farmer's sickle.

Acte yanked me backwards. 'What are you doing? Get inside.'

I glanced around me. 'Is this the king's bedroom?'

'No. These quarters are reserved for the king's brother. And he wouldn't like you *snooping*.'

'The king's brother, Icarius, King of Acarnania,' I stated proudly.

'They talk about him down below, say he visits every summer. That true?'

'It's none of your business, is what it is,' Acte said as she ushered me into the centre of the room. 'Wait here. Don't move. Don't touch *anything*. Don't even *breathe* too loudly. Or the Erinyes will come and pluck out your eyes.'

'The Erinyes only pluck out bad people's eyes.'

'And misbehaving slaves',' she warned.

Before I could reply, Acte turned on her heel and stalked out of the door.

The chamber somehow felt larger in her absence, the walls looming so high I feared they might topple down on me at any moment. Even so, I kept still, hands knotted behind my back, muscles drawn in so stiffly they began to itch.

I will behave, Mama.

Time trudged past and Acte's threat began to grow distant in my mind, unravelled by fingers of curiosity tugging at my thoughts. After what felt like a small eternity, I dared a single step forward. Pausing, I waited for the Erinyes to swoop down on their wings of vengeance and claw at my eyes. But only silence greeted me. I took a few more tentative steps and that silence held, the expanse of it like an open, beckoning palm.

Wondering if Acte had forgotten about me, I began to drift around the space. For a big room it had very little within it, the towering walls empty save for two giant crossed spears. To one side, there was a table littered with tablets. I picked one up at random, tracing my fingers over the swirly shapes etched into the wax, wondering what it must be like to be able to read such strange markings.

Nobody taught my kind to read. Especially not girls.

My eyes fell to an unsheathed sword lying beside the tablets, the blade winking dangerously in the moonlight. I went to touch it, wondering if it felt as cold as it looked, but my attention was caught by a table on the far side of the room. Here, an array of fresh, untouched fruit had been piled high – plump apricots, shiny olives, grapes sitting fat on the vine. Though, it was the tray of honeyed figs that drew me to the table, my mouth watering as I eyed their pink, glazed flesh. *Could I . . . ?*

I stuffed a fig into my mouth, swallowing so quickly I almost choked. Glancing around the empty room, I took another. This time I chewed slowly, savouring its rich, gritty sweetness on my tongue. Though we prepared this food daily for our masters, the meals we ate *never* tasted like this.

Before I could stop myself, I shovelled three more figs into my mouth, one after the other. My belly gurgled contentedly as I licked my fingers, eyeing the rest of the food, wondering what else I might try.

Melanthius will be so jealous when I tell him about this . . .

Someone cleared their throat, shattering the silence.

Shock locked itself around my muscles, a honey-coated finger suspended midway to my mouth. Turning stiffly, I found a girl watching me, eyes glinting like polished silver. She was standing in the doorway to an adjoining room, as still and silent as the shadows around her.

How long had she been there?

My mouth went dry as I watched her walk into the pool of moonlight reaching between the pillars. She looked only a little older than I, yet she was considerably taller with long, slender limbs.

She stopped a few feet away, and we stared at one another, seconds tumbling into minutes. I knew I should not have been gawking. I had been taught to keep my eyes on the floor when in the presence of our masters. But I could not help it . . .

The girl was the most striking thing I had ever seen.

She looked like she belonged in the realm of the divine, stitched from shadows and moonlight and secrets, all things beautifully mysterious. Her face was narrow and delicate, her eyes a peculiar shade of grey, like the great Goddess of Wisdom herself. Her dark hair was plaited neatly around her head, so tidy compared to my wild mane of rust-red curls.

I could tell from the gleam of her spotless, olive skin that she was not like me. Her clothing confirmed it, too, swathes of deep purple pinned at her right shoulder by a golden brooch. Only royalty wore purple – that's what Mother said.

I glanced down at my tattered tunic, marred with stains even older than I. It was far too large for me, hanging below my knees, and was the only item of clothing I owned, handed down by my brother and countless children before him.

'Are you the Princess Helen?' I breathed.

'What makes you ask that?' Her voice was deep, for a girl's, yet flowed with an elegance so unlike the accents of those I had grown up with.

'Mama says Princess Helen is the most beautiful girl ever born. She's the king's daughter.'

'Are you trying to flatter me, so I won't inform the king of your pilfering?' she asked. To my frown she added, 'Pilfering means stealing.'

'I know that,' I lied, crossing my arms. 'And I wasn't stealing nothing.'

'That's incorrect.'

'Is not,' I shot back.

Her lips twitched upwards. 'Your phrasing, I mean. You should either say you *were not* stealing, or you *stole nothing*.'

'That's what I said, didn't I?'

'You said you "wasn't stealing nothing". That's a double negative, which implies you were stealing *something*. Do you see?'

I frowned. 'You tryin' to trick me?'

If anyone in the kitchens had heard me speaking this way, I would have been struck. But the girl's face remained calm as she watched me, head tilting to one side. She reminded me of the cats I saw patrolling the storerooms, movements sleek, eyes clever.

Did that make me the mouse?

'I am not tricking you. I am simply trying to help you be a better liar.'

'I'm no *liar*.'

'Good. Neither am I.'

She smiled then, and it was unlike any I had ever seen before. It was not the quiet smiles of my father, or my mother's tired half-smiles. It certainly wasn't the silly, gap-toothed grins my brother offered. No, her smile was like a secret caught around her lips, making me want to lean in closer.

As if sensing this thought, the girl turned and walked away from me. I watched her graceful strides, gown swishing around her bare feet as she approached the table where the discarded sword lay. She ran an absent finger along the length of the blade.

'So, what *are* you doing here?' she asked.

'The king sent for me.'

'To eat his food?' She threw me a glance, her eyes brightening just like my brother's did whenever he teased me.

I tried to think of a smart response, but the girl made me feel like a worm pinned beneath a stick, wriggling and helpless and stupid.

'For the king's brother,' I said, lifting my chin a little. 'He *chose* me.'

Something changed in the girl's face then, like a shadow had fallen across it.

'Has the king's brother summoned you before?' she asked. I shook my head. 'Do you know *why* he has summoned you?'

'No,' I admitted, picking at a loose thread in my tunic. 'It made Mama cry, though.'

'It did?'

I shrugged. 'Mama cries a lot.'

'You should go,' the girl said. 'If you leave now, I can tell the king you were unwell, and I dismissed you.'

I frowned. 'Why?'

'Because you do not want to be here.'

'I do,' I shot back. 'And the king wants me here too. *I've* been chosen.'

A voice sounded from the hallway then, making us both flinch.

'I told you to bring the girl *after* the princess had been dismissed.'

'My sincerest apologies. I did not realize your daughter was still in your company, Master Icarius.' Acte's voice trailed behind, though she sounded different. Sweeter, softer.

My back straightened as two men entered the room. I recognized one of them immediately, for though he was wearing a simple, sweat-stained tunic and tattered sandals, the King of Sparta was unmistakable.

He reminded me of the oak trees bordering the palace grounds, thick and broad and gnarled. He looked older than I expected, his grey hair cropped short, face worn. His right ear had been claimed by a scar that sliced across his face, disappearing beneath his beard. He looked more warrior than king, though in Sparta they were often one and the same.

Beside the king was the man I guessed to be his brother, Icarius. He was tall and narrow, as if someone had taken the king and stretched him taut. Icarius wore robes of rich purple, like the grey-eyed girl, and his fingers were weighed down by jewels, chest glinting with golden pendants. Like the rest of him, his face was thin and pointed, chin dappled with a patchy beard. Unlike his brother, not a single scar marked his skin.

'This is her, your majesty.' I hardly noticed Acte as she scurried into the room. She looked so much smaller next to the king. 'Nine summers old. House-born. Child of the palace gardener, Dolios, and a kitchen slave.'

Tyndareus swept a cursory glance in my direction.

'Will she do?' he asked his brother. His voice sounded like the sky before a thunderstorm, thick and swollen.

Icarius drew uncomfortably close, looking me up and down with dark, sunken eyes. Nobody had ever looked at me like that before.

Be brave, be brave, be brave.

'She isn't the one I had last time,' Icarius said, features tight with an emotion I did not recognize. It looked a little like thirst, but harsher.

'We had to sell the last slave due to . . . complications,' Acte explained.

'Complications caused by your *seed*,' Tyndareus said pointedly. Icarius gave a dismissive huff. 'Perhaps you will be a little more careful this time, brother?'

Icarius' long fingers pinched my chin as he turned my face from side to side. He ran a thumb along my lower lip, pulling it down to examine my teeth. His skin tasted of sweat and meat grease.

'It won't be an issue, brother. This one can't have bled yet.' He tugged at one of my curls. 'Red hair. Unusual.'

'I can fetch another—' Acte began.

'No, no. This one will do.' Icarius grabbed my fingers, inspecting them. 'She's dirty, though.'

My cheeks felt hot as I snatched my hand away.

'If she's dirty, then have her cleaned,' Tyndareus sighed.

'There's fresh water in your room, Master Icarius,' Acte added.

Icarius straightened, still watching me as the tip of his tongue skimmed along his yellow-stained teeth. 'Yes, yes. She'll do nicely once she's tidied up.'

'Very well. I will retire and leave you to your . . . indulgences, brother,' the king said before turning to the grey-eyed girl. 'We are most pleased to have you with us for the summer, Penelope.'

Penelope. I knew that name. *Princess* Penelope.

'As am I, uncle,' she said, bowing her head.

'Clytemnestra is desperate for you to join her at the gymnasium, you know. A little training will do you good.' The king pinched Penelope's arm. 'Get some muscle on that bone.'

'I will train if you wish, uncle, and if my father permits it.'

'Good girl.' Tyndareus patted her cheek once, before exiting the room with Acte in tow.

In the following silence, I realized Icarius was still watching me. When I met his gaze, he leered closer, the pendants around his neck jangling.

'You are dismissed, Penelope,' he said.

I felt a sudden spasm of fear at the thought of being left alone with this man. I did not know what he wanted from me, but every inch of my body was screaming at me to *run*.

My eyes darted to Penelope.

'Does she have to?' I asked, but before the question even left my lips Icarius had grabbed my face again. This time his touch was harsher, nails biting into my cheeks.

'You will *speak* when *spoken* to, slave.'

His grip hurt, making hot tears sting along the bridge of my nose, blurring my vision.

Icarius rippled with disgust. 'Stop that.'

But the tears would not stop; they fell thick and fast as a sob swelled in my throat. Icarius let out a frustrated growl, releasing me.

'I said *stop that*, or I'll give you a real reason to cry—'

'Father.' Penelope's voice cut smoothly between us. She motioned to the table behind her. 'We were in the middle of a game. May we resume?'

'I said you are *dismissed*, Penelope.'

'But our game is unfinished.'

'Do you think because we are on Spartan soil you can behave like one?' he snapped over his shoulder. 'You are a princess of Acarnania, and Acarnanian women *obey*.'

Penelope bowed her head. 'Of course, Father. My apologies. I am merely surprised that you would accept defeat so readily.'

Icarius turned the full weight of his attention on to his daughter. Whilst he was distracted, I quickly rubbed my eyes with the heel of my hands, furious at myself. I did not even know *why* I was crying. I was no baby.

'You thought you were going to win?' he asked slowly.

'Yes, I believe the game was quite clearly mine,' she said.

Icarius' eyes flared, then he glanced back at me for a moment, considering.

'I will indulge you this once, Penelope, but only because I wish to teach you a lesson in *hubris*. Understood?'

'Of course, Father. I always enjoy your lessons.'

A jewelled finger jabbed into my face. 'You. Wait.'

I shrank against the wall as Icarius strode towards his daughter, taking the stool opposite her.

'It is your turn,' Penelope told him, her eyes flicking briefly to mine.

I did not know what game they played; I had never seen the likes of it before. A wooden board was set between them, divided into squares. They took turns tossing a small, dotted cube, then moving stone pieces around those squares. It seemed dreadfully dull to me, yet I found I could not look away, my eyes continually wandering back to Penelope's face.

They did not speak as they played, save for the occasional grunt from Penelope's father. Their silence felt stiff and uncomfortable, yet they seemed indifferent to it.

'An unwise move, daughter,' Icarius finally announced. 'Look here. Do you see your mistake?'

Penelope considered his move before making one of her own. She sat back, allowing her father to inspect the board. Something glowed inside me as I watched the smile fall from his lips.

'Does that mean I've won, Father?'

'Again,' Icarius demanded, rearranging the pieces on the board.

'As you wish,' she said, retrieving an elaborately decorated jug set between them and refilling his wine.

Icarius snatched the cup and drank deeply, then motioned for Penelope to refill it again.

'You.' He clicked his fingers at me. 'Go wash and wait for me in my bedchamber.'

I bowed, then hesitated. I had thought we were already *in* Icarius' bedchamber . . . Discreetly, Penelope tilted her head towards the adjoining room. I gave a small, grateful smile and headed inside, certain I could feel her eyes following my every step.

In the darkened room, I could just make out the shape of a giant bed, piled high with invitingly soft furs and blankets. Along the right wall was a small table, where I found a bronze water bowl and rag.

Carefully, I dipped the rag into the water and ran it over my arms and legs, watching my skin lighten to its usual freckled shade of pale olive. Once the water had turned cloudy and dark, I attempted to tackle my curls, using my fingers to untangle the knots. Eventually, I gave up the pointless battle and began to pace.

It did not take long for tiredness to set into my bones, weighing down my steps. My mind reached for my mother. We had never spent so long apart, and her absence ached like a bruise.

'Again!' I heard Icarius' voice reverberate through the walls.

I was not sure how long their games would continue, nor did I know what would happen when they finished . . . but I pushed that thought from my mind as I continued pacing.

As time wore on, and my legs grew sluggish, I decided to perch myself on the edge of the giant bed. I sat rigidly, ready to jump to my feet if I heard anyone approaching. But the bed was so soft and inviting, I could not help but sink a little lower, down and down, until sleep rose up to greet me . . .

'Wake up.'

I jolted upright. '*Mama?*'

'Shh. It's all right.' That voice came again as two grey eyes greeted me. 'It's Penelope.'

My cheeks warmed. 'I . . . I wasn't sleeping or nothing.'

She smiled. In her hand she held an oil lamp, the small flame illuminating her face with a honeyed glow.

'It's time to go,' she told me.

'Go where?'

'Back to your mother.'

'Now?'

'Yes. I shall take you.' She motioned for me to stand.

'What about Master Icarius?'

'He has dismissed you.'

I frowned. 'Did . . . did I do something wrong?'

Penelope's gaze was edged with something like sadness, but sharper. 'Not at all. Come, we must go.'

I followed her back into the main room where Icarius was slumped in his chair, snoring loudly. As we crept past, I couldn't help but stare. He seemed a lot less scary now, face smoothed by the soft hand of sleep, and I noticed his lips were stained a dark crimson.

'Father always falls asleep after too much wine,' Penelope whispered as she led me out into the hall, a small smile curling at the corners of her mouth.

We walked in silence through the passageways. Nyx had fully taken hold of the palace now, stealing away all its beautiful details. I found myself inching closer to Penelope, reassured by the oil lamp and her steady steps. She walked with such purpose, as if she paid the darkness no mind at all.

'How'd you know the way?' I asked her after a while, hoping my voice might chase away any beasts lurking around us.

'My uncle took me on a tour once.'

'And you remember it all?'

'Yes,' she said simply. 'What is your name?'

'You . . . want to know my name?'

She glanced sidelong at me, the lamplight toying with her features, making their sharp edges flicker. 'Why would I not?'

I shrugged. 'Dunno. People don't normally. Not people like you.'

'What do they call you, then?'

'Slave . . . Sometimes other names. Names Mama says I can't repeat.'

'Does that bother you?'

Nobody had ever asked me that before. 'Slave' was one of the first words I had ever learnt, alongside 'master'. It was as familiar to me as my own name.

'I'm Melantho,' I answered instead. 'And you're Princess Penelope.'

'Just Penelope will do.'

'Penelope,' I repeated with a nod.

'Melantho,' she mirrored.

We grinned at one another.

'So, how'd you do it? Keep winning that game you and your papa were playing?'

'Because my father always expects me to lose,' she said. 'Being underestimated is a woman's greatest power. That's what my mother says . . . *Used* to say.'

'She doesn't say it no more?'

'No.'

'Why not?'

'Because she's dead.' These words held no emotion, as smooth and flat as a pebble in Penelope's mouth.

I had no idea what to say to that.

'It's the way of things,' she continued, eyes set on the darkness ahead. 'Death is part of life. It is as the Gods intended.'

'How old are you?'

Penelope's eyebrows lifted. 'Ten summers. Why?'

'You don't talk like you're ten.'

'How do I talk?'

'Like a grown-up. Not like the kids I know. But kids down below are thick as mud. Well, the boys are, anyway. The other day, I saw one trying to shove worms up his nose.'

A laugh burst out of Penelope then, the force of it seeming to catch her by surprise.

'Why was he doing that?' she asked.

'I dunno.' I shrugged. 'Boys are stupid.'

She laughed again and the sound reminded me of lemons, sharp and bright. I found myself leaning into it.

We came to a familiar set of stairs, and I was met with a rush of disappointment. There was still so much I wanted to ask Penelope, but the questions tripped over themselves, tangling up inside me. Penelope kept quiet too, though the echo of her laughter still clung to her face, lightening it.

When we reached the bottom of the stairs, it was like waking from a dream. The walls here were narrow, the paint faded and cracking, floors coated with dirt, air as stale as old flatbread. It seemed impossible to think that a beautiful world existed just above our heads.

Down the passageway, I could see the guards standing watch outside our sleeping quarters. They kept the men and women separated at night, with a guard positioned at either door. I had always found their presence reassuring, as if King Tyndareus wanted his slaves watched over, kept safe. But, in that moment, the sight of them made my lungs feel tight.

'It was nice to meet you,' Penelope said. 'Melantho.'

I smiled. 'Penelope.'

Conscious of the guards now watching us, I quickly bowed. Penelope then nodded to one of them and he dutifully unlocked the door.

The guard shoved me inside and I was swallowed up by a hot, sweaty darkness, one that stuck immediately to my skin, weighing me down. The familiar stench of overcrowded bodies clogged my throat and I almost gagged. I turned back to Penelope, her face like a last gulp of fresh air, one I wanted to hold on to as long as I could. Then the door slammed shut.

I picked my way through the slumbering bodies strewn across the floor, trying my best not to trip over the sprawling limbs.

'Melantho?' My mother's voice guided me forward. She was in the far corner, sitting upright with her back against the wall. It was too dark to make out her features, but her voice was alert, as if she hadn't been sleeping at all. 'Are you all right?'

'Yes, Mama.'

She reached for my hands, her fingers damp and shaking.

'Are you . . . sure? You can tell me . . . if you're not.' She sounded strange, her words stiff.

'I'm fine, Mama. I promise.'

We settled into our usual position, my mother curled around me as I tucked myself into her warm chest.

'Did he hurt you?' she whispered against the shell of my ear.

'Who?'

'The king's brother.'

I thought about the strange way Icarius had stared at me, my insides twisting.

'No, Mama.'

'You can tell me if he did.'

'He didn't.'

She held me tighter. 'Whatever happened, it wasn't your fault, Melantho. You must know that. It's important.'

I wasn't sure what she meant, so I kept quiet.

My mother began stroking my hair then, whispering apologies into my ear. I did not understand her sadness, nor did I like the feel of it in my chest, heavy as a stone. So, I pretended to be asleep as her warm tears dripped against my cheek, her confusing whispers falling into rhythm with my breathing.

I'm sorry, forgive me, I'm sorry, forgive me . . .

I blocked her out, thinking instead of Penelope. I replayed our meeting in my mind, over and over, like tracing the edges of a new trinket, committing every detail to memory before tucking it safely away, knowing I would revisit it again once the morning found me.

2

The king did not summon me again.

I had never experienced rejection before, and I hated the feel of it, the way it lingered low in my belly, caught between a sting and an ache.

Acte still visited the kitchens nightly, and each time I watched her escorting a new slave upstairs that feeling inside me intensified.

Why them? I wanted to scream. *Why not* me?

'It's for the best,' my mother told me, though these words made little sense. How could the sweaty, overcrowded kitchens be *better* than that beautiful, glimmering world above?

'Maybe you said something the king didn't like,' my brother suggested.

It was the fifth morning after my summons, and Melanthius and I were unpacking a fresh delivery of goods. Though the cart was now empty, we loitered beside it, savouring our time together before Melanthius returned to the stables where he worked.

'I didn't say nothing to him,' I murmured, scuffing my sandals against the cart.

'Maybe you did it wrong, then.'

I stared up at my brother. Even though we were the same age, Melanthius had always been taller than me, which, for some reason, made him think he could act like the eldest.

'Did *what* wrong?'

'Well . . .' He glanced away. 'You know.'

I frowned, unused to seeing him lost for words. Usually, Melanthius had too many to fit into one breath.

'Know *what*?'

He folded his arms. '*The sex*.'

'The *what*?'

'*The sex*.'

'What's that?'

'It's what the king summons us for.'

'Oh.' I paused. 'But . . . what *is* it?'

Melanthius chewed his lip. 'Well, I was hoping you'd tell me . . . The other boys laugh when I ask.' His brows drew together. 'You *sure* you didn't have it?'

I wrinkled my nose, considering the strange new word. 'I don't think so.'

'Huh.' He pushed his dark curls off his face. 'Maybe you did, you just did it wrong.'

'I did *not*.'

'How do you know?'

'Because I *didn't*.'

He smirked at my temper, always so quick to rise. 'Maybe you were *so bad* you didn't even *know* you were doing it, and that's why the king don't want you no more.'

I shoved him hard, and he stumbled backwards, slamming against the cart.

'*Hey* . . . Melantho? *Melantho!*'

I stormed away, anger and humiliation boiling beneath my skin. I knew I was not allowed to wander off alone, but there was a horrible pressure building inside me, demanding space.

The sticky summer air clung to my skin as I stomped across the rolling palace grounds. Ahead of me, I spied the workers' fields, golden and swaying, dotted with slaves toiling beneath the steadily climbing sun. I watched as they swung their sickles, figures shimmering in the fingers of heat that rippled from the ground. Beyond them, the Eurotas river glittered like a fat, twisting snake, winding its way towards the mountains.

'*Stop!*' Melanthius panted, stumbling beside me. 'What're you *doing?*'

'Walking,' I snapped without slowing my pace.

'You'll get into trouble.'

'I don't care.'

Melanthius opened his mouth to argue, when a gaggle of slave boys hurried past, sandals slapping eagerly against the pink soles of their feet. They were heading towards a long, narrow building set apart from the palace. Though I had never stepped foot inside, I knew this to be the gymnasium where our masters trained.

'What're you doing?' I called out to the boys.

'*Shh,*' one hissed.

'We're gonna watch the princesses fight,' another whispered.

'We got bets on how quick it'll take Precious Penelope to cry.'

Penelope. Her name twisted inside me.

'I'm coming too,' I said.

'Melantho.' My brother grabbed my arm. 'They'll beat us if they catch us spying.'

'Then go back to the stables, *coward.*'

Melanthius scowled, releasing me, and I followed the boys through the uniform columns standing like tall teeth at the mouth of the gymnasium. As we crept inside, I glimpsed Spartan women stretching in the shade of the colonnades. In the centre of the space there was a rectangular training ground, and there, limned in early morning light, was the most fearsome girl I had ever seen.

'Clytemnestra,' my brother murmured, crouching beside me in the dark.

'I thought you weren't coming?' I muttered.

'Well, I can't let you get into trouble alone, can I?'

I made a face at him, before turning back to watch the princess.

Clytemnestra was completely naked, her body strong and bronzed, hair falling down her back in a tangle of gold. She was a fascinating sight, but my focus was drawn to the grey-eyed girl beside her. Unlike her older cousin, Penelope had chosen to wear a thin tunic, hair plaited tightly around her head. She was saying something, though I could not make out her words.

'If you wish to spend the summer here in Sparta,' Clytemnestra replied loudly, 'then you must train like a Spartan. Or do you wish to remain weak?'

Penelope stood very still, whilst Clytemnestra paced around her. I had seen slave boys scrap before, but their fights were just bursts of childish temper. The way Clytemnestra circled Penelope felt entirely different. It felt . . . *dangerous*.

'She's gonna hurt her.' I whispered the realization as it came to me.

My chest felt oddly tight, as if someone were clutching at it.

'I've seen Clytemnestra flatten girls before,' one of the other boys snickered. 'Maybe she'll break Penelope's big nose.'

'Or knock her out cold,' another smirked.

'Come on, *Precious Penelope*,' Clytemnestra goaded as titters rippled through the crowd of women. 'I'll let you strike first.'

'Women of Acarnania are not permitted to wrestle,' Penelope said.

She began to walk away, but Clytemnestra darted forward with frightening speed, catching Penelope's wrist and twisting her arm between them.

'*Stop it*,' Penelope gasped.

'This is the only way you will grow stronger, cousin. Trust me. It's for your own good.'

'You're hurting me.'

'I'm *helping* you!'

I was moving before I even realized it, as if an invisible rope were tugging me out from the shadows.

'*Melantho!*' My brother grabbed for my hand, but I surged forward, out of his reach.

I stopped at the shallow steps fringing the training ground. Still, nobody had noticed me, too engrossed in the brewing fight. I could have fled in that moment, could have run back to the safety of the kitchens and my mother's waiting arms.

But instead, I called out, 'Princess Penelope!'

Every head snapped towards me. I hesitated, the dusty air crawling down into my lungs, choking my next words. I had never had so many people staring at me at once. But then my gaze found Penelope's, and the ground suddenly felt steadier beneath me.

'King Icarius sent me to summon you,' I said, wracking my brain for a grown-up word, one that might make my lie sound more believable. 'He . . . *requires* your company.'

Penelope's eyebrows rose, but it was Clytemnestra who said, 'Why would my uncle send a *kitchen slave* to relay such a message?'

'He had probably just finished bedding her,' a woman snorted. 'Are children not his type?'

I was unsure what she meant by that, or why everyone found her comment so amusing. Everyone except for Penelope, whose cheeks seemed to redden.

'I'm just following orders,' I said.

'If my father has summoned me, I must obey,' Penelope announced, but Clytemnestra did not let go.

'We must finish our training first, cousin.'

'King Icarius says it's urgent,' I insisted, struggling to meet Clytemnestra's glare even from a distance. 'He sounded . . . angry.'

Penelope's lips twitched. 'You cannot deny the king, cousin.'

'He is not *my* king,' Clytemnestra spat, though she released her cousin's wrist.

Without hesitating, Penelope turned on her heel and walked towards me. I smiled as she approached, but Penelope's face was blank as she continued past.

'Come,' she murmured over her shoulder. 'Do not speak until we are away from here.'

I stumbled after Penelope as she glided away from the gymnasium, her steady steps quick yet unhurried. When we were finally back in the shadow of the palace, she halted. We were standing at the rear entrance, the one the slaves used, which led through the storage rooms, tucked away out of sight. It was quiet there, save for the chattering cicadas in the nearby olive trees.

I couldn't help but stare at Penelope. I found it impossible not to. Even though her eyes were a little too far apart, and her nose pointy, she was still the prettiest girl I had ever seen.

She absently rubbed her wrist; the one Clytemnestra had grabbed.

'Does it hurt bad?' I asked.

Penelope shook her head, then turned to look at me. 'Why did you lie?'

I stiffened. 'I didn't—'

'My father is out hunting today.'

I folded my arms across my chest. 'Oh.'

Her eyes seemed darker than they had before, and I wondered if she was angry with me.

'You could have landed yourself in a lot of trouble.'

'I know,' I mumbled to the ground.

'So, why did you do it?'

'She was hurting you.'

Penelope frowned, as if my answer were confusing to her.

'But she could have hurt *you* if she discovered you were lying,' she said.

'I know.'

'So, why risk yourself for me?'

I shrugged, but Penelope continued staring, as if she were waiting for me to say more. I glanced around, trying to think of something.

'Why do they call you "Precious Penelope"?'

She sighed, lifting her face to the sky, and I feared I had said the wrong thing.

'It was Clytemnestra who started it,' she murmured. 'When I was born, I was very sick. My cousin likes to remind me of that. The Spartans aren't fond of . . . fragile things.'

'She's mean to you.'

'It's the Spartan way. Clytemnestra doesn't know any different.'

'That don't make it right.'

Penelope smiled at that. 'No, I suppose not.'

We stared at one another for a moment, and I felt a strange shyness creeping over me. Over the past five days I had been desperate to see Penelope again, imagining all the things I might tell her, all the questions I could ask. But now she was here, every thought in my head seemed to disappear.

All except one.

'Did I do something wrong? The other night?'

Penelope's smile vanished. 'What makes you ask that?'

'The king hasn't summoned me again.'

She glanced away. 'Well . . . I . . . I asked my father not to.'

'What? *Why?*'

'For the same reason you lied to Clytemnestra.'

I frowned, shaking my head. 'But your father summons other girls. Why do *they* get to go and not me?'

Penelope winced, as if I had said something hurtful. Her fingers were fumbling together, and I noticed she was picking the loose skin around her nail beds, which seemed very un-princess-like to me.

'I cannot win every battle,' she whispered, though it felt as if she were answering an entirely different question. I was about to tell her this, when someone seized my arm, yanking me backwards.

'*Melantho!* What were you *thinking*? You're such a—' My brother cut himself short, nut-brown eyes widening as he regarded Penelope standing beside me.

'Hello,' she said.

Melanthius bowed low, addressing the ground as he spoke. 'Princess, please forgive my sister's behaviour.'

'This is your older brother?' Penelope asked me with a smile. 'You look so alike.'

'He isn't *older*; we're the same age,' I grumbled, irritated by this interruption. 'And we aren't *that* alike. Melanthius' hair is way more brown than red, and his nose is bigger. And uglier.'

My brother pinched my arm. '*Melantho.*'

'*What?* It's true.'

Penelope glanced between us, looking as if she were biting back a laugh.

'Princess, I'm sorry.' Melanthius bowed again. 'I gotta take Melantho back to the kitchens. She'll be scolded if not.'

'Yes. Of course. I am sorry for keeping you, Melantho.'

'I don't mind,' I said quickly. 'I could stay a bit more.'

'No, your brother is right. I must go as well. My father needs to speak with me, after all.' Penelope's smile curled wider. 'I am told it is urgent.'

I found myself grinning as I watched the princess walk away, wishing with all my heart that I could follow.

'*What were you doing?*' Melanthius rounded on me once Penelope had disappeared.

'What? We were just . . . talking.'

'You can't *talk* with *her*.'

'Why not? She's nice.'

My brother grabbed my wrist, squeezing tight. 'No, she isn't *nice*, Melantho. She's one of *them*.'

'One of who?'

'Our *masters*.' He spat on the ground as he'd seen the older boys do.

'She's not like them—'

'They're *all* the same, Mel.'

'Says who?'

'Says *everyone*.' He began pulling me back towards the kitchens. 'You can't trust her kind. Ever. Understood?'

I said nothing as I let him tug me away.

*

The following morning, a familiar figure stalked into the kitchens.

'You. Follow,' Acte said to me, her voice as bored as her stare.

I glanced at my mother, watching her face turn sickly pale. A spoon hung in her hand, our master's cooked oats dripping thickly on to the countertop.

'No. No . . . Not so soon,' she whispered. 'You can't . . . She's got duties here. Her place is *here*.'

'Her place is wherever our masters decide it is.' Acte's claw-like fingers dug into my shoulders, making me wince. 'Come, girl. You have been summoned.'

3

Penelope's chamber was light and airy and impeccably neat.

Streams of sunlight bathed the walls and floor, illuminating a large ivory chest painted with swirling patterns. To my right was a long bench draped with blankets and pillows. To my left the room opened out on to a balcony, the famed Taygetus Mountains towering in the distance like ancient, sleeping giants.

Penelope was at the far end of the room, working at her loom. As we approached, I watched her deftly lacing a red thread through the taut strands.

'Mistress Penelope, apologies for interrupting your work, but I have brought the slave, as you requested,' Acte said in that soft voice she only used around our masters.

'Melantho,' Penelope replied without looking up from her work. 'Her name is Melantho.'

I watched Acte's face tighten, as if some invisible hand had just pinched it.

'I brought you *Melantho*, mistress.'

The princess finally turned and smiled. 'Thank you, Acte. You are dismissed.'

Acte stiffened. 'May I ask what you intend to *do* with the girl, mistress?'

'She is to be my handmaid whilst I reside here for the summer.'

My mouth fell open, surprise rippling through me.

'A handmaid?' Acte spluttered. 'But . . . she's just a kitchen girl, mistress. She's not trained for such an esteemed position.'

'Then I will train her.'

'I must warn you, this sla— *Melantho* has been known to have trouble with her *attitude*. She has not yet learnt when to hold her tongue.'

'I can hold my tongue!' I interjected.

Acte gave me a despairing look before turning back to Penelope. 'Do you see, mistress? If you wish for a handmaid, there are far better candidates I can offer. I am sure Queen Leda has one she can spare.'

Penelope returned her attention to her loom. 'I appreciate your concern, but my decision has been made.'

'Does the king know of this?' Acte pressed.

'Of course. It was his idea I take a handmaid to make my stay more comfortable.'

'Yes, but does he know you've taken a *kitchen slave*?'

Penelope turned back, her brows floating upwards. She allowed a silence to settle into the room, punctuated by the gentle clacking of the loom's hanging weights.

'I have made my decision,' she said softly. 'And you are dismissed.'

I bit down on a smirk as Acte's cheeks reddened. She stared at Penelope for a long moment, before finally forcing a rigid bow. 'Of course, mistress. I apologize for overstepping. Forgive me.'

The princess' sharp eyes followed Acte as she strode from the room. Once she had disappeared, the stiffness in Penelope's smile peeled away, revealing something far warmer.

'Hello, Melantho.' She said my name with such familiarity, as if we were the oldest of friends.

Unsure what to do with myself, I bowed. 'Mistress.'

Penelope rose and walked towards me. 'Just Penelope is fine.'

I frowned up at her. She was at least a head taller than me. 'You really want me to be your handmaid?'

'Yes.'

'Why?'

She tilted her head. 'Do I need a reason?'

I considered that a moment. 'Did you bring me here for *the sex*?'

Penelope seemed to choke on the air, a pink flush creeping up her neck. She shook her head, at a loss for words, and I understood then that I had embarrassed her.

'Because that's why our masters summon us, you know,' I continued. 'That's what my brother says, anyway.'

'I know,' she finally managed. 'Well . . . I know enough.'

'Me too,' I said quickly. 'I know enough, too.'

There was a brief, awkward silence. We both glanced around the room, avoiding one another's eye.

'Your wrist,' I blurted out.

'Pardon?'

'Your wrist. Does it still hurt?'

'Oh.' Penelope touched it absently. 'It's fine. Thank you for asking.'

I nodded, scuffing my feet against the floor. 'So, you gonna teach me to be a handmaid now, then?'

'I suppose so, yes.' Penelope nodded. 'But first, I have something for you.'

'For . . . me?'

'A gift. For yesterday.'

I blinked at her. Nobody had ever given me a gift before.

A bubble of excitement expanded inside me as Penelope walked towards the table, then returned with a large bowl in her hands, piled high with fat, glistening honeyed figs.

She offered the bowl to me, and I stared down at the figs, unsure why my eyes were suddenly so hot, and it felt like I wanted to cry and laugh and dance all at the same time.

Penelope's face fell. 'Do you not like it?' I shook my head. 'Then what's the matter?'

'W-will . . . *will you be my best friend?*' The question escaped me in a breathless jumble.

A grin spread across Penelope's face, and the sight of it made my insides feel as if I had just swallowed a burst of sunlight.

'I would like that very much, Melantho.'

4

We became inseparable after that day, tumbling headfirst into a friendship that felt forged long ago, as if it had always existed within us, waiting to be discovered.

Before long, we refused even to spend our nights apart. Penelope had a pallet made up for me beside her bed, and though I missed the warmth of my mother's embrace, I welcomed having my own space for the first time in my life. I also welcomed the opportunity to spend more time with Penelope, often forgetting to get any sleep at all in my haste to fill more hours with her company.

We wanted to know everything about one other – every thought, every memory, every feeling – letting it become ours to share.

Whenever Penelope spoke of her royal life it was like peering into a thrilling, distant world, one I was desperate to be a part of. Though, when it came to family, Penelope said noticeably little. She briefly mentioned her elder sister, who had been married off to a faraway king when Penelope was very young. She seemed to actively dislike talking about her father, though she did recount the story surrounding her birth, how she had been born sickly and her father had instructed she be thrown into the sea. I gasped when she said this, feeling dizzy with anger. It was customary, she reminded me in a matter-of-fact tone, to discard weak children at birth, especially girls. It was said Penelope had been saved by a flock of ducks who carried her to safety. Her father had been delighted by this divine sign, for it could only have been a message from the Gods. He had cherished her ever since.

'That is how the story goes, anyway,' Penelope said.

'You don't believe it?' I asked, still mesmerized at the idea that she had been *saved by the Gods*.

She flashed that secretive smile of hers and replied, 'I think my wet nurse was very cunning, and I think my father was always jealous of the rumours surrounding my uncle's children. He wanted a child beloved by the Gods, too, so he was ready to believe any story, however fanciful.'

'So, it's true about King Tyndareus' children? That only one of each pair of twins was fathered by Zeus?'

'Apparently so. It has caused endless competition between Castor and Polydeuces. The princesses, however, do not seem to mind all that much.'

'Because everyone knows Helen is Zeus' daughter,' I pointed out. 'Because she's the most beautiful.'

Penelope tilted her head at me then, her clever eyes quietly assessing.

'Must divine power only manifest in women as beauty?'

I adored it when she asked me questions like this. It felt like she was gently prodding my brain, opening doors in my head I did not even know existed.

And Penelope asked *a lot* of questions.

Nobody, in all my life, had ever shown such an interest in me as she did. Penelope had a way of listening that made you feel like the most fascinating being to have ever existed. She would sit utterly motionless, yet her mind was never still; you could see it turning behind her eyes, examining each word I offered her as if it were a special artefact, slipping it carefully between all the other pieces of information she had collected. Penelope hoarded knowledge, I came to realize, and she had an incredible ability to remember *everything*.

'Knowledge is the only currency we women can afford,' she explained once.

It was one of the first things I loved about Penelope: her hunger to know more. Perhaps, also, I loved that she made me feel like my words were worth listening to, worth remembering.

'What do you like about me?' I asked her one night when we were lying in our beds, our words painting life into the shapeless dark.

As usual, Penelope took her time considering my question.

'I have always felt as if I were looking at the world from a distance,' she said eventually. 'But it does not feel like that when I am with you.'

'I have something for you,' Penelope told me one morning.

We were lying on the cold stone floor of her chamber, our hands splayed over our stomachs. Though summer was fading away all too quickly, the days remained warm, the air choked with a lazy, clammy heat.

'What is it?' I propped myself up on my elbow, watching as Penelope got to her feet and padded across her room.

When she returned, something was draped between her hands, sky-blue swathes of fabric shimmering in the light.

'Your gown!' I sat up, grinning. 'You finished it!'

Penelope held it out to me. 'Here.'

My eyes widened. 'What?'

'It's for you.'

'For me? But . . . it took you all summer to make that.'

'I know.'

'Are . . . are you sure?'

She laughed. 'Of course I'm sure.'

'Don't you want it?'

'I made it for *you*, Melantho.' Penelope stepped closer. 'Go on. Put it on.'

I eagerly tugged off my old, ugly tunic and tossed it aside. Penelope then helped me into the gown. It was more material than I was used to, rippling down to my ankles and gathered at my shoulder with a pin Penelope fastened for me.

'There,' she said, stepping back. 'What do you think?'

'I think . . .' I hesitated, trying to find the perfect words through the strange lump in my throat. 'I think it's the best thing in the whole entire world.'

I began twirling then, letting the gown swoosh around me in a wave of brilliant blue, so soft and light and *beautiful*. Penelope's laughter twined with mine as I took her hands, spinning her with me, letting the world melt away into a dizzy blur.

'Thank you!' I cried out, again and again as we spun.

Then, abruptly, I stopped.

'What is it?' Penelope asked, hands still warm in mine.

I stared at her for a silent moment as the realization crept in, stealing the laughter from my lungs.

This was a goodbye gift.

I looked to the balcony, to the bright brush of summer sky beyond. I imagined I could see it: the threat of autumn lingering on the horizon like a dark, ugly stain, marking the end of Penelope's stay here. The end of our time together.

'I . . . I don't have anything for you,' I murmured.

Penelope shook her head. 'That doesn't matter.'

But it *did*. In that moment, it mattered more than anything, and I felt a desperate, clawing panic at the thought of Penelope having nothing of me to take with her. Nothing to remember me by.

An idea struck, brilliant and sudden. 'What's something you've never done? Here, in Sparta.'

Penelope raised an amused brow. 'Why?'

'Just tell me.'

'Well . . .' She thought for a moment. 'I've never swum in the Eurotas river before.'

I squeezed her hands tighter. 'That's what we'll do. *That's* my gift to you.'

Penelope's smile shrank. 'Melantho . . . I am not permitted to leave the palace grounds – you know this.'

'But Clytemnestra can.'

'*She* is not my father's daughter.'

'Then we'll sneak away. Nobody will know.'

I sensed her hesitation, but now this idea had seized me I refused to let it go. I wanted to give this gift to Penelope, *needed* it. For if we did something Penelope had never done before, then it would burn me into her memory for ever.

'I'll keep you safe,' I insisted. 'Promise. It'll be fun.'

'I think this is a bad idea.'

'You think too much.'

She laughed at that. 'Have you ever swum in the river before?'

'We go sometimes to wash. I know a spot; it's real nice and not far, I swear.'

I watched her turn the plan over in her mind. 'I'm not sure . . .'

'Would *Precious Penelope* go swimming?' I challenged, folding my arms. 'Or would she spend her whole summer hiding inside?'

That convinced her.

It was surprisingly easy to slip away from the palace, the heat making the guards sluggish and oblivious. Once we were beyond the palace grounds, we skipped through the fields, past the slaves forced to work beneath the punishing sun, their skin blistering, minds melting. As we passed them, I thought of our masters shut inside, being bathed and fanned and watered. For the first time in my life, I found myself questioning the fairness of it all, a single word planted in my mind like a seed, one that would take root deep in my core – *Why?*

When we reached the Eurotas, we were both panting, and I felt guilty that I had already stained my beautiful gown with sweat and dust. Carefully, I peeled it off and hung it in a nearby tree. When I turned around, Penelope was frozen, staring at the river. The currents were gentle, rambling through the thick greenery crowding at the water's edge.

'Race you!' I cried, rushing ahead.

It took me a moment to realize Penelope was not following. When I turned back, I saw she had not even moved.

'What's wrong?' I called out.

'You go in,' she insisted. 'I'll watch.'

I hurried back up the bank towards her. 'I'm not going in without you.'

'I . . . I don't think I can, Melantho.'

'Why?'

Her eyes narrowed. 'What if I *drown*?'

I snorted. '*Drown?*'

She closed her eyes, her chest rising and falling unsteadily. 'Melantho . . . I can't.'

'You can. You just *think* you can't.' When she opened her eyes, I was standing right in front of her, my hand outstretched. 'So, stop thinking.'

A laugh escaped her, small and tight. 'Stop thinking?'

I nodded, wiggling my fingers. Something sparked in her eyes then, and she threw her hand into mine. Before she could change her mind or even strip off her gown, I dragged her into the river.

We shrieked in unison, the sun-warmed water feeling deliciously crisp against our clammy skin. I dived under, my whoop of delight escaping in a flurry of bubbles. When I surfaced, Penelope was watching me, arms folded over her chest.

'You can't just stand there. You have to go fully in.' I inched towards her, grinning. 'Do you want me to help?'

'No . . . wait – *Melantho!*'

My name turned into a shriek as I shoved her backwards into the water.

'You *pushed* me!' Penelope spluttered when she emerged, drenched and frowning.

I bit back a giggle. 'Only a little.'

She stared at me, water dripping down her face, dangling on the ends of her lashes. For a moment, I feared I had truly upset her, but then I caught that glint in her eyes, the one that always shone before any game we played. She lunged for me, and we went crashing into the water together, our laughter mingling with the bubbling currents.

We spent all morning playing in the river. Afterwards, we lay belly-up on the bank, damp limbs humming with exhaustion. We stayed that way for hours, lounging on the baking sand, time stretching around us like a long, lazy yawn.

We were like rulers of our own kingdom, as bright and endless and untouchable as the sky itself.

At one point, Penelope turned to me, propping her head on her bent arm, wet hair sticking to her flushed cheeks.

'I think this is my favourite day,' she told me.

I smiled so wide it hurt. 'I think so too.'

5

'Where are *you* going?'

It was the day after our trip to the river, and I was trundling alone through the palace hallways when the voice caught me.

Turning, I found Clytemnestra standing behind me, like a goddess just descended from Olympus. I quickly bowed and the Princess of Sparta smiled, though there was no warmth to the sharp cut of her lips. An animal pelt was slung across her shoulders, the dark, bulky fur making her appear even broader.

She cocked her head to the side, toned arms folded as she observed the gown I wore; the one Penelope had made for me. I studied her, too. She was pretty despite her best efforts not to be – her blonde hair was scraped back, dirt and bruises mingling across her skin, nose sharply crooked from one too many fights. Her brows were thick, emphasizing the striking colour of her eyes – deep brown, threaded with ribbons of gold.

'I asked you a question, slave.'

Ignoring the knot in my throat, I replied, 'I'm going to get breakfast for Penelope and me.'

It was the truth, but for some reason it tasted like a lie beneath Clytemnestra's glare.

'My mother wants to see you,' she said.

'The . . . the *queen*? Why?'

Her smile widened. 'Come with me and you will find out, slave.'

Dread sat like a coiled snake in the pit of my stomach.

I tried to ignore it as I followed Clytemnestra through the halls. She strode with a cool confidence, her legs eating up the distance with ease. I had to scurry to keep up with her, afraid of how she might react if I fell behind.

The passageway eventually opened out into a lofty room. The space here was simple, the only furniture an ornate wooden chair and richly woven rug set a few feet before it. The walls were bright with colour, depicting men on horseback, spears aloft as they chased a giant grey wolf. The scene progressed across all four walls; on the furthest and final one, the wolf had been caught, a spear protruding from its chest, blood spurting in violent splashes of crimson.

I shivered beside Clytemnestra.

'Kneel,' she said flatly. I moved to lower myself on to the rug, but she grabbed my shoulder. 'Not there.'

She motioned to the stone floor, and I obeyed, the rough surface biting into my knees.

'Eyes on the ground.'

I did as I was told, fear and confusion curdling inside me.

What could the queen want from *me*?

Was I in trouble?

Where was Penelope?

Footsteps sounded a moment later; smooth and unhurried, they whispered into the room like an evening breeze. I fought the urge to look up, focusing instead on the pale stone floor, memorizing each scuff.

Be brave.

'Is this the girl?' a voice came, soft yet strong.

'Yes, Mother,' Clytemnestra replied from behind me.

'Good.' A pause. 'Fetch my niece.'

More feet sounded and I felt a droplet of sweat skate from my temple down my nose. I watched it splash on to the floor as I repeated Clytemnestra's command, falling into rhythm with my thrumming heartbeat – *Eyes on the ground. Eyes on the ground. Eyes on the ground.*

'There you are.' That voice spoke again. 'Would you like to explain to us why we are here, Penelope?'

Penelope. My gaze snapped up, colliding with hers instantly. I felt an immediate rush of relief at the sight of her, but then I noticed how pale she looked, her mouth pressed into a small, thin line.

'Penelope?' the voice prompted again, and I glanced at the woman standing before me. Leda, wife of Tyndareus and Queen of Sparta.

She was as beautiful as all the rumours claimed her to be, dark hair unbound, skin bronzed, body full and strong. Her face was plump, nymph-like features seeming out of place on a woman who carried herself like a warrior. She reminded me of the roses in the palace garden – a beauty that could make you bleed.

'I do not know, aunt,' Penelope finally replied.

'No?' Leda looked displeased. 'What if I told you it was to do with your little trip yesterday?'

Something in Penelope's face shifted, but she replied without missing a beat, 'Around the palace grounds? Oh yes, I wanted Melantho to show me the flowers. Her father is the royal gardener here.'

I was surprised by how easily the lie rolled off her tongue. She did not even hesitate.

Leda's smile was cold. 'I see . . . And what of your trip to the river?'

Penelope drew in a breath, but before she could reply, Clytemnestra cut in, 'I *saw* you, cousin.'

Penelope's eyes flickered between the queen and the princess, nostrils flaring.

'It was my idea,' she said. 'The heat was making me feel unwell, so we went to cool off. Is that such a crime?'

'You know your father does not permit you to leave the palace grounds,' Leda cautioned. Her eyes then slipped over to me, quietly assessing. 'It seems so unlike you to wander off, Penelope. I wonder what possessed you.'

'I understand you will have to inform my father, and I will accept his punishment,' Penelope replied, following Leda's gaze. 'Melantho is not at fault.'

'I quite disagree. Tell me, slave, did you lead Penelope astray? Were you plotting to escape?' Leda pressed. I glanced at Penelope, who gave a small shake of her head. 'Look at me when I am speaking to you, girl.'

'No, your majesty.' My words fell so fragile at her feet.

Leda sighed, as if I had answered incorrectly. 'You are acting as Penelope's handmaid, yes? Although I am told you are treated more as a companion than a slave. Tell me, Melantho, how do you serve my niece?'

Penelope cut in, 'Melantho is very—'

'I am asking the slave,' Leda said.

I hesitated, struggling to find my voice amidst the cloud of unease inside me. 'I . . . I'm not sure what you mean, my queen.'

'No?' Leda clicked her tongue. 'Let me try an easier question, then. What have you and Penelope been doing all summer?'

I glanced at Penelope again, unsure how to answer. 'We've . . . been talking.'

'*Talking*,' Leda repeated slowly.

'And playing games.' I saw Penelope wince at my words. Beside her, Clytemnestra snorted. 'She also made me this gown and . . . um . . .'

I trailed off and stared at the floor again, not knowing where else to look, what else to do.

'And have you *enjoyed* your summer with Penelope?' Leda asked softly. I nodded. 'Why is that? Speak up.'

'Because she's my friend.'

'Oh . . . Oh dear.' Leda tutted. 'It seems you have not done your job at all, niece. You have not trained this girl to be a handmaid; you have trained her to be a problem. As soon as the slaves start seeing us as their *equals*, they start causing mischief. Like breaking palace rules and sneaking away for a little swim.'

'She is not my friend.' Penelope's words cut through my chest like a blade.

'I should hope not,' Leda replied. 'But it seems the slave does not think as much. You have confused the poor thing. Look at her. She's about to cry.'

I blinked furiously, forcing the tears away.

'Give me more time, aunt. I can train her—'

'You have had enough time, Penelope. An entire summer you have squandered.' When Penelope opened her mouth to argue, Leda held up a hand, silencing her. 'Let me put this plainly. Every slave beneath our roof contributes to this household. Take away their duties and what are they? Just another mouth to feed, another body to clothe. Every day you spent *talking* and *playing*, this slave became a burden not an asset. That is because of *you*, Penelope. Do you understand? Do you see the waste you have created?'

'I apologize.' Penelope matched her aunt's even tone. 'I am sure my father could reimburse whatever financial value you feel has been lost—'

'Reimburse.' Leda laughed. I had no idea what the word meant, or why it was amusing to her. 'You speak so intelligently, Penelope, but your naivety gives you away. I do not want *reimbursement*, child. I wish for something far more . . . *valuable*.' She paused, a smile creeping across her face. I did not like the look of it. 'One day you will become a wife and you will be expected to run a household of your own. As such, you must learn how to handle your slaves *properly* and, most importantly, how to handle their punishment. Your mother should have taught you such things already, but perhaps she neglected these duties in her declining state. So, now it is up to me.'

'I am grateful for the opportunity to learn from your wise counsel, Aunt Leda. As you say, this was *my* failure, and mine alone. Melantho need not be here,' Penelope insisted. 'I let her believe we were friends; it is my fault she is confused—'

'I'm not *confused*,' I snapped at her, but still Penelope refused to look at me.

Leda smirked. 'Do you see what insolence you have cultivated? I agree, it is a pity the girl must suffer for your folly, but this is the way of it. Clytemnestra, the whip, please.'

Penelope's face fell, and the sight twisted something in me.

'*No*,' she breathed.

'You made this mistake; now it is your duty to correct it,' Leda said.

Clytemnestra approached Penelope, holding a long, dark rope. She then pressed the cord into Penelope's hands, and I watched it hang there like a limp, dead snake. I had seen the boys in the stable use something similar on the horses, slapping it against their rumps to make them run faster.

Penelope's hands gripped the cord. 'I cannot—'

'You must,' Leda interrupted. 'Clytemnestra, what do Spartans say of lessons?'

'A lesson cannot be learnt without pain.'

Leda smiled at her daughter, before turning back to Penelope. 'I shall be lenient because she is only young. Tell me, how old are you, girl?'

It took me a moment to realize the queen was addressing me.

'N-nine . . . my queen.'

'Nine lashes, then.' She directed this to Penelope. 'That is more than fair.'

Understanding began to creep over me, an icy, clawing shadow.

She cannot mean . . .

Penelope shook her head. 'No.'

Irritation sharpened Leda's voice. 'Let me make this simpler for you, Penelope. Either you carry out the punishment or Clytemnestra will. And I assure you, Clytemnestra will be far less gentle.'

'Punish me instead.' Penelope held out the whip. 'I am the one who deserves the lashes. Not her.'

'Is it not obvious? This *is* your punishment, Penelope. The balance must be restored. This girl must understand you are her *superior*.'

Penelope's face was tight as a fist. Her eyes finally returned to mine, and the keenness of her fear made the panic in my belly surge upwards, coating the back of my tongue. Penelope looked as if she were about to say something, but then Leda motioned with her hands. A moment later, two guards appeared, thick fingers digging into my arms, making me yelp.

'What are you doing?' Penelope demanded.

The guards dragged me forward, whilst two more carried in a large wooden table. Deep grooves marred its surface, accompanied by dark red stains. I cried out as those rough hands pushed me down, forcing my arms out in front of me so my chest was now flush against the table. The wood bit against my cheek as a strangling panic spread through my body like wildfire. I thought I heard Penelope speak, but I could not make out her words over the roaring in my ears.

My fear was a living, writhing thing trying to burst out of my skin. I was drowning in it. Choking on it. I could not breathe. I could not think, save for the single question: *Am I going to die?*

I began to thrash violently, trying to tear myself away from the table, but it was no use; the guards held me in an iron grip. I began to pant like a dog.

Footsteps sounded behind me and the next thing I felt were hands at the hem of my gown, pulling hard. I let out a cry as it ripped, cold air slipping across my bare back.

'*I'm sorry, I'm sorry.*' I gulped out useless pleas, tears streaming. 'I won't do it again. I promise. Please. Please don't.'

I felt a warmth trickling down my legs, just as Clytemnestra muttered, 'Gods above. She's pissed herself.'

That's when I began to cry for my mother.

'Please, stop this!' Penelope shouted.

'Just get on with it,' Leda instructed.

I lifted my head just enough to glance over my shoulder. Penelope was standing behind me, the whip in her hands, horror filling her eyes as she watched me sprawled out before her.

'I cannot,' she whispered thinly. 'I will not.'

I felt a flicker of relief before I saw Clytemnestra shove Penelope aside, grabbing the whip.

No . . .

A hand slammed my head down, the impact juddering through my skull.

I heard the *crack* a moment before I felt it.

Liquid fire seared my back. I had never known pain like it. It was unbearable, carving open my skin, making my entire body spasm. I screamed, my cries for my mother strangled into a howl of agony. Before I could even catch my breath, the whip came again. It felt as if it were eating my flesh.

A darkness crept in around me, but I blinked it away, terrified of sinking into it. When my eyes focused, I saw Penelope standing in front of me, held there by another guard.

'It will be over soon, Melantho,' she was telling me, though the words sounded watery in my head, like hot broth dripping from my ears.

When the third and fourth lashes came, I felt the world grow distant; the only thing keeping me tethered to it was the pain devouring my back with tongues and teeth of fire. But even that could not stop oblivion from beckoning, and I tumbled down into an endless darkness.

Consciousness found me again as I was being peeled off the table. There was blood everywhere. So much blood. I stared at it, barely able to comprehend it was my own.

'Well done,' a voice said. Clytemnestra, I think. 'You took your punishment well.'

'Take her back to the slave quarters. She is a handmaid no more. Make sure someone tends to the wounds.'

'Yes, my queen.'

A hand pushed me forward and I stumbled, my legs giving out beneath me.

'*Gently*,' Leda snapped. 'If she can't walk, just carry her.'

Large arms slipped around my waist, and I felt the floor disappear.

The guard then draped me over his shoulder, ensuring no part of him was touching my back. I hung limply, barely able to lift my gaze. Across the room, Penelope was staring at me, grey eyes wide and glassy. She was utterly motionless, save for the slight trembling of her fists where she gripped her gown.

I held her gaze for a long moment, waiting for her to speak, to reach out for me, to comfort me, to do something. *Anything.*

But Penelope just lowered her eyes as they carried me away.

6

I recovered slowly.

I can only recall glimpses of that time, wisps of memory dancing like shadows in a storm.

My mother holding my hand.

My brother crying.

The sting of a wet cloth against my back.

And the pain. Constant and paralysing.

Consciousness came and went in faint waves that lapped against my mind. Every time I felt sleep beckon, I prayed Penelope would be there waiting for me when I woke. She would make it all better. She always did. But it was only ever my mother at my bedside, her face creased with worry, tears in her eyes. She would press her fingers to my forehead, my temples, skating a familiar route over my skin.

'I'm here,' she would whisper. 'My heart, I'm here.'

I do not know exactly when the fever found me, but I knew the hideous chill rattling through my bones, shivering over my sweat-soaked skin. Reality floated, untethered, bleeding into my dreams, my nightmares. I saw Clytemnestra standing over my bed, the whip in her hands, her face cut with a cruel smile. I felt Penelope beside me, feeding me honeyed figs, her hand resting in mine. I wanted to talk to her, but the words were always liquid in my mouth.

Everything will be all right, Penelope told me again and again, until her voice began to slip into my mother's soft lilt.

'Penelope?'

'Shh, my heart, shh.' My mother's voice soothed me back to the edges of my dreams.

'The king requires an update on her condition.' Another voice came from the pulsing darkness.

The king. Tyndareus was worried about me. He wanted to make sure I was all right.

He *cared* about me.

'She needs a doctor.' My mother again.

'You know they will not send for one. Not for us.' There was a pause. 'If she's not back on her feet soon, the king warned he would need to make . . . decisions.'

'He would sell her? Like this?'

'He is considering.'

'Acte, she's in this state because of *them*.'

It was quiet for a long moment. 'I will pray to Asclepius for her.'

'She doesn't need your prayers. She needs *medicine*.'

'She will—'

'*She will die.*'

I wanted to stay and hear the rest of the conversation, but familiar cool currents tugged me away, pulling me down and down into Morpheus' distant realm.

My mother wept when I finally woke.

We were in the corner of our sleeping quarters, and it was strange seeing the room so empty, daylight spilling through the open door. I was lying on my stomach, the ground unusually soft.

'People have been very kind,' my mother said as I stared at the blankets stacked beneath me. 'We've all been worried about you.'

I tried to sit up, but a slice of pain shot down my back.

'Careful! Try not to move. You still need to rest.'

I glanced around, my eyes catching on a crumpled heap of linen beside me.

My gown.

'I didn't know what to do with it,' my mother murmured as I reached for the torn, bloodied material.

'Where is Penelope?' I whispered hoarsely.

My mother stared at me for a long moment. She looked so tired, so sad, so *old*. Tenderly, she prised the ruined gown from my fingers and slipped her hand into mine.

'The princess has gone back home,' she told me in her gentlest voice.

'Home?'

'To Acarnania, with her father.'

'Why . . . why didn't you wake me when she said goodbye?'

My mother brought my fingers to her lips and brushed a light kiss against them. 'She didn't say goodbye, my heart.'

'But she visited,' I insisted. My mother shook her head. 'I saw her here. I heard her.'

'I've been at your side every moment, Melantho.' Her voice was frayed with exhaustion. 'The princess did not visit.'

It was then that I remembered Penelope's words. Those horrible, cruel words.

She is not my friend.

The realization sank into me, slow at first, then crashing all at once.

Though not as painful as the lashes I had endured, Penelope's betrayal cut me far deeper, opening wounds my body did not recognize, did not know how to heal.

I buried my face into the blankets and wept furious, hot tears.

Penelope had gone.

She had not said goodbye.

She did not even care.

Three summers passed.

I did not see Penelope again.

I told myself that I was glad she stayed away, that I had forgotten all about her. By the time the fourth summer rolled around, I began to actually believe the lie.

I was thirteen now and supposed myself a woman, far older and wiser than the foolish girl who had thought she could befriend a princess. I was beginning to look like a woman, too, my body marked by unfamiliar swells and dips, ones that made the boys' eyes linger. I liked the way they stared, the way they jabbed each other with their elbows when I passed them. It made me feel powerful, knowing I could make their cheeks redden and mouths gape.

Still, even this newfound interest did not stave off the boredom, not now I knew how small my world truly was. Once, those confines had felt like a comfort, familiar edges that kept me tucked in safe and warm. But now, the boundaries pressed in from all around me, making the days chafe irritably.

This was what it meant to be a slave, I realized: being expected to take up as little space as possible and be grateful for that tiny scrap of existence we were offered.

'Don't you ever want *more*?' I asked my mother one day whilst we worked, dough rolling between our worn palms.

She glanced sidelong at me. 'More?'

I waved at the kitchen around us. It was early that morning, the sun still rising, and yet the air was already laced with acrid sweat. It was the stink of too many people worked too hard in too small a space. I was sick of it, and I knew I was not the only one. Complaints about the kitchens' overcrowding had been rumbling all summer.

'Than spending our lives stuck here, serving others, never able to live for ourselves.' I slapped the dough down on to the counter. 'Than making the same bread *every* morning, day after day.'

'There are people far worse off, Melantho. People like us.'

I knew that. Every slave did. It was the silent threat that hung over us, all those horror stories about slave markets and silver mines. The knowledge of how much worse our lives could become with just a single command.

'But don't you want to be *more* than what we are?' I pressed. 'More than just a *slave?*'

Sometimes, I longed to go back to those days when I believed 'slave' was just a name I shared with my family, one that gave me a sense of belonging. But that naivety was gone, stripped from me like everything else.

And I knew *she* was to blame.

Penelope had struck something inside me that summer, a thrill I had never experienced before, one that lingered, its echo making my life feel inexplicably hollow. With her, I had glimpsed another world, and now, in its looming shadow, everything felt . . . lesser. *I* felt lesser.

And I hated her for it.

I hated her for so many things.

'All I want is for you to be happy, my heart. If I have that, what more do I need?' My mother smiled, and I sighed, throwing my hands up in defeat. She never understood.

'But I'm *not* happy. I'm *bored.*'

'Boring is good. Boring is safe.'

'I would take danger and excitement over boring and safe,' I stated. Though, even just saying the words made the scars on my back twinge.

'Don't tempt the Fates, Melantho,' my mother warned.

I scoffed. 'The Gods do not listen to *us.*'

She took my hand and squeezed tight, her dark eyes suddenly intense on mine. 'They are always listening, Melantho. Always.'

7

The morning was fresh the day my world fell apart. Autumn had finally set her claws into the earth, letting the summer heat bleed out.

I was with my mother, preparing our masters' breakfast. The kitchens hummed with activity; fires spluttered to life, pots clattered, feet shuffled to and from the storeroom. Sweet cinnamon punctuated the air as one of the cooks sprinkled it over the porridge. It was a rare and expensive spice; the smell of a luxury I would never know the taste of.

The sound of footsteps caught my attention.

I glanced at my mother, a silent question lifting my brows. A second later, guards burst into the kitchens.

'*Up. Move. Now.*'

'*I said NOW!*'

'What's going on?' I gasped.

'It's all right,' my mother whispered. 'Just stay close to me. Everything will be all right.'

Before I could even wipe my dough-caked fingers, I was swept up in a swirling current of rushing feet as the guards herded us outside.

'*Move faster.*'

'*Keep quiet.*'

'*Eyes ahead.*'

I gripped my mother's hand as we spilt out into the palace grounds. Sleepy morning mist skulked across the earth, dew-dusted grass caressing our feet. Ahead of us, a thick thread of gold tied the horizon to the sky as Helios began his daily ascent. Beneath that sky, I spied men working the fields, their spindly silhouettes like smudges of paint. Some turned to watch as the guards drove us into straight, uniform rows.

To our left were three large carts. One was filled with pigs, another with bleating sheep. The third cart was empty.

Icy dread crept up my spine. I looked at my mother again, watching the fear tighten around her like a noose.

'It's all right,' she repeated. 'Everything will be all right.'

I nodded, though we both knew it was a lie.

Panic seeped into the air, spreading like a sickness, making the silence weigh heavier on our shoulders as we waited. After what felt like an eternity, a figure finally appeared, and those tendrils of dread twisted into great talons of fear.

As Queen Leda strode towards us, familiar memories seized me, vivid and terrible. My scars began to burn, as if those tongues of fire had found me again, had come to finish what they had started, to devour me whole...

My mother squeezed my hand, tugging me back. I met her gaze, the understanding in her eyes steadying me. She knew the shape of all my scars, even those hidden deep inside.

'As you know, there has been an issue of overcrowding in the royal kitchens,' Queen Leda announced. She did not lift her voice, forcing us to strain to hear. 'There is not enough space to work and sleep, or food to go around. These are not appropriate conditions.'

It should have felt reassuring, hearing this from the mouth of our queen, but the tension in the air only sharpened.

'Today, I am going to rectify this issue. Sacrifice the few to benefit the many,' Leda continued. 'I ask for your cooperation. There is no need for this to become ... *difficult*.'

I shifted closer to my mother. 'She does not mean—'

'*Quiet*,' a guard snapped.

Silence followed, stretching dangerously thin as Queen Leda made her way down the lines. She stopped to inspect each slave, turning their face, checking their teeth, sometimes asking a question or two. After every inspection, Leda would mutter something to a guard and he would escort that slave to stand in one of two places – either beside the carts, or back towards the palace.

The word 'sacrifice' turned in my mind, but I forced myself to remain calm.

The two groups began to swell as Leda progressed through the rows of slaves. Most were being directed to the group nearest the palace, whilst the cluster by the cart appeared far smaller; I had only counted eleven slaves by the time Leda neared us. Most were older women; a few were younger but thin and sickly-looking. One was pregnant, anxiously rubbing her swollen stomach.

Leda was close now and I had a sudden, eclipsing thought that she might remember me. But, as the Queen of Sparta finally turned her attention on to me, I realized her eyes were blank, devoid of any recognition. I stared up at her face, as beautiful and cold as winter sunlight. Whilst she had permanently resided in my nightmares for the past four summers, I had not even mattered enough to be remembered.

I was nobody to her. I was nothing.

She pinched my cheeks and turned my head from side to side.

'Open,' she commanded, and I let my mouth hang open so she could assess my teeth. 'Age?'

'Thirteen,' I mumbled.

Leda flicked another glance over me then said, 'Keep.'

Beside me, I felt my mother sag with relief. She squeezed my hand before letting go, and I suddenly felt horribly exposed without her palm in mine. Before I could reach for her again, a guard seized my arm and began dragging me towards the palace.

As I stumbled away, I glanced back to watch Leda perform the same routine with my mother, turning her face from side to side, checking her teeth, asking a question. My mother held her head proudly, but I could see her hands were shaking. The sight made my throat squeeze so tight I could scarcely breathe.

I was deposited with the other 'keep' slaves. When I turned back, Leda had already moved on. Relief soared through me as I watched a guard thrusting my mother towards us. But then he began steering her left, towards the carts.

No . . .

I stepped forward, only to be met by a large arm blocking my path.

'Don't even think about it,' a guard rumbled.

My entire body grew cold as I watched my mother be discarded. Her eyes found mine and she smiled bravely, mouthing the words, *It's all right*.

'Melantho?'

I turned to find a figure hovering nearby. My father. He was not a man I knew well — our separate duties had never permitted us that luxury — but still the sight of him helped steady my hammering heart.

My father was here. He would help.

'What's going on?' he asked in that delicate voice of his, quiet eyes absorbing the scene before us.

'Back up, slave,' a guard barked.

My father obediently retreated a few steps.

'Get them back to work.' Leda's voice pulled my attention away. 'And take these ones to the market. Make sure you get a good price.'

As the guards collected chains from the empty cart, I felt the world crumble beneath me . . .

No, no, no.

The women began to wail in protest as iron collars were fastened around their throats. Some attempted to wrestle the bindings away, but they were powerless against the guards who effortlessly restrained them.

My mother did not fight as they secured her metal collar.

'*No!*' The scream ripped itself from my throat. '*Get away from her! Stop!*'

'Melantho!' My father's voice chased me as I bolted forward.

Two guards lunged at me, but I pivoted around them, slipping from their grasp as I raced ahead, my feet pounding desperately against the earth.

When I reached my mother, I flung my arms around her neck, the coldness of her shackles biting against my skin. I pulled back, panic strangling logic as I tried to tear her chains apart with my bare hands.

'They can't take you,' I wept. 'You can't leave me—'

The words were cleaved from my lungs as an arm locked around my waist, hauling me backwards. I tried to hold on to my mother's hands, but the guard tugged me so hard I thought my ribs might crack. Still, I thrashed against him, foaming at the mouth like some wild, cornered creature.

'Please, my queen, she is my daughter,' I was faintly aware of someone saying.

'Control her, then,' Leda replied flatly.

I was thrust into unfamiliar arms. My father's.

'*Do something!*' I screamed at him.

His wounded eyes lifted to my mother, then turned to our queen. His throat bobbed, his breathing shallow.

'We must obey, Melantho,' he said.

'*No, no, no!*' I sobbed. 'Help her! *Please!*'

'I cannot. I'm sorry,' he murmured to the ground, looking so small and pathetic, as if his spine had been ripped out, leaving him to melt into the dirt.

I heard chains clinking as the guards began loading the women on to the cart. At the same moment, my father tightened his grip, holding me still.

'Melantho, please be calm,' he whispered in my ear. 'Please obey.'

'I hate you!' I screamed, elbowing him hard in the stomach. He doubled over, and I took the opportunity to rip myself free.

My mother was in the cart now and I scrambled up to her, sobbing breathlessly, but two firm hands landed on my shoulders, halting me . . .

My *mother's* hands.

'Melantho, you need to stop,' she told me, voice thick and trembling. 'Please, my heart. Stop this.'

'No! I won't let them take you!' I was barely able to get the words out as I choked on desperate tears.

'You must.'

I wanted to ask her *why*. I wanted to scream it.

Why must I stop?

Why did someone as cruel and horrible as Leda get to decide our fates?

Why did she have to choose *her*?

Why, why, *why*?

I shook my head furiously, still reaching for my mother. Then my father was there again, his arms clamping around my waist like shackles of flesh and bone. I kicked and screamed as he dragged me away, my throat so raw I thought I might start spitting blood.

'I will not ask you to control her again, Dolios,' Leda warned.

My father's hand covered my mouth, his voice tight and panicked in my ear. 'Please, Melantho. Please stop. I beg you.'

In that moment, I hated him. I hated him so deeply that I felt the burn of it scorch against my heart, leaving a permanent, irrevocable mark there.

Before us, the cart rumbled to life, and I finally fell still. I could see the fear in my mother's eyes now as the slaves around her wept. Still, she forced a smile.

'Be brave, my heart,' she called to me. 'It will be all right, I promise. Everything will be all right.'

Those were the last words my mother ever said to me, and they were a lie.

8

My grief had no beginning or end.

I could not grasp its edges, could not comprehend its shape.

And so, it swallowed me whole.

Still, the traitorous world carried on, and I was expected to do the same. For slaves were not permitted to mourn. There was no space for our pain.

Time lost meaning, as did everything else. I floated through my existence, the days bleeding together, seasons passing like a phantom breeze.

When I turned fourteen, I was plucked from the kitchens to serve upstairs in the palace's entertaining quarters. Apparently, I 'did not have a face for kitchen work'. Once, this would have made me feel proud. Now, I struggled to feel much at all, other than the dull rage that lingered beneath my skin, beating like a cold, withered heart.

My new duties were simple enough. I was to be a living shadow, attentive yet invisible, waiting for the lazy swish of a hand summoning me to refill a cup or plate. It was monotonous, hollow work, but at least it kept me away from the kitchens where my mother's absence lingered in every corner, memories of her embedded like jagged shards.

Mercifully, I saw little of Queen Leda, and Princess Clytemnestra had already been sent off to marry the King of Mycenae. Princess Helen was kept shut away like some precious piece of treasure, so I was left to serve the princes, Castor and Polydeuces, and the myriad noble guests constantly plaguing the palace. Men with greasy smiles and roaming hands. Often, when they pinched my backside or grabbed my breasts,

I fantasized about tossing their wine in their arrogant faces, then slapping them for good measure. But even just the thought of such insolence made the scars on my back ache viciously. So, I learnt to swallow my rage, hating them in silence whilst they ground my existence down to barked commands.

'Here, slave.'

'More, slave.'

'Quick, slave.'

'Now, slave.'

And I silently obeyed, as compliant as wet, lifeless clay, forever moulding myself to the will of others.

'You have to play into it, darling,' a serving boy told me one day.

His name was Callias, which meant 'beautiful'. Our masters would often label us like this, using simple physical descriptors devoid of individuality. Though, this name certainly suited the boy, for he was the most beautiful thing I had ever seen. Deep umber skin, earthy eyes with elegantly aquiline features.

'You do know what I mean. Don't you?' he prompted, leaning closer to me with a conspiratorial wink.

I debated ignoring him, as I did whenever any of the other slaves tried talking to me. And yet . . . something about Callias tugged at those wilted threads of curiosity. I think it was because he did not look like any slave I had ever known. It was in the way he carried himself, with an air of something I hadn't known our kind could possess – pride.

'No,' I said flatly. 'I don't.'

We were carrying our freshly filled wine jugs back to the princes' entertaining quarters. From down the hall, I could hear the laughter of their guests, the sound clawing irritably over my skin.

'I mean *this*!' Callias gestured to my face with a flourish. 'They want us to believe we're powerless, but we're not. Not you and me.'

It was mesmerizing, the way he spoke; the rich intensity of his eye contact, the fullness of his lips just inches from my own.

I shifted my wine jug, my arms already aching with the weight. 'How so?'

'Because *we* have been gifted by Aphrodite,' Callias said. At my puzzled expression, he let out a laugh. It was a husky, intimate sound. 'Don't act modest, darling. You know you're beautiful. And our masters know it, too. They *want* us, but they don't want us to *know* they want us.' He strolled indolently as he spoke, as if he were not a slave at all, but a free man enjoying an amble through his estate. 'Do you see what I'm getting at?'

'I'm not sure . . .'

He stopped in his tracks and tugged one of my curls. 'Have you not seen the way Castor looks at you?'

'Me?'

'Yes, *you*.' A dangerous smile crept across his face. 'You have power here, Melantho. If you are willing to take it.'

Power. The word made something crackle through my veins.

I glanced down the hallway. 'What . . . what kind of power?'

Callias' smile broadened. 'Smell me.'

'*What?*'

'Smell me. Go on.'

I blinked at him, wondering if he was mad. Still, I leant in and inhaled the rich, floral scent of his skin.

'What do I smell like?' he prompted.

'Expensive,' I breathed. 'Like . . . one of them.'

'Do you see? Master Castor treats me *very* well. I get the best food, the best wine, the best clothes. And you can have it all too, you know. If you just play the game.'

'What "game"?' I drew back, suspicion edging my voice.

'Oh, it's very simple. It's the oldest game there is, and we are all players, whether we like it or not. You have all the weaponry you need right here.' He reached out to caress my cheek, and a strange heat blossomed beneath his touch, making my pulse quicken. 'You could make them *beg* for it with that face, you know.'

Callias winked, then pulled away from me as he continued, 'Power will never be given to people like us. So, we must take what morsels we can for ourselves.'

Then, without warning, he spat a glimmering glob of saliva into his wine jug. I gaped at him, utterly stunned.

'Remember, the prince's attention is fleeting.' He smirked as he turned to walk away. 'Best not waste it.'

After our conversation that day, I began watching Callias.

He seemed to command every space he occupied. He did not have the domineering authority I was familiar with, but rather a quiet, sensual power that pulsed around him, luring people in. Everything was a performance, I realized. The way he moved, the way he spoke, the way his gaze slipped and lingered, the way he threw back his head and laughed at something the princes said. Each minute movement was part of the web he spun, trapping people's attention in his glistening, beautiful snare.

As I studied him, I realized I wanted it – the control. I wanted to hold that cord of desire in my hands and tug at it like a leash.

And so I began to mirror Callias, emulating the swish of his hips, the smokiness of his laugh, that brazen eye contact that made our masters lean a little closer. I would swirl around rooms like a warm summer breeze, lingering and sweet, learning to mask the emptiness that rattled through me.

The change was immediate. Instead of barking commands, my masters would purr. Instead of summoning me with a click, they would gesture with a smile. They still saw me as property, of course. I was not stupid enough to think otherwise. But now, I was something to be coveted, and when our masters let me sit on their laps and try their wine and food, I would stare at the other, neglected slaves and feel a guilty, dizzying rush of *power*.

One night, Prince Castor cornered me in the hallway, his breath hot in my ear as he commanded, 'My chamber. Now.'

I felt a spark of triumph, but once Castor and I were alone in his quarters, the feeling quickly withered in my stomach. Suddenly, all my flirtation felt foolish. Dangerous, even.

Though Castor's chamber was enormous, the clutter made it feel stifling. Weapons, dirty clothes, broken sandals, empty wine jugs lay strewn around the space. The prince seemed unfazed by his own filth as he picked his way across the littered floor to lean against the foot of the bed, his arms braced along the frame.

He stared at me with hungry eyes. It reminded me of the way Icarius had stared at me that night, so many moons ago. Though I was less oblivious to the root of Castor's hunger now, I still did not fully understand what lurked beyond it. I had never dared venture that far.

I forced myself to hold Castor's gaze. He was handsome, admittedly. Golden curls, bronzed skin, a strong, masculine jaw. But his beauty reminded me of the myth of Narcissus, the kind that reeked of self-adoration.

'Take off your tunic,' he commanded.

Fear curled in my stomach. But then I thought of the women's sleeping quarters, of that lonely patch of floor where I lay awake each night, and the endless, echoing grief that awaited me there.

I knew, in that moment, I would do anything to avoid it.

Swallowing, I grabbed the hem of my tunic and pulled it over my head. My hands were shaking – with adrenaline or fear, I was not sure. I prayed Castor did not notice.

The cool night air kissed my bare skin, and I watched the prince's eyes trace down my body, slow and starved. Nervous anticipation hummed inside me, and I welcomed the feeling. It had been so long since I had felt anything other than anger or grief.

Castor ran his tongue over his teeth.

'Has my brother had you yet?' I didn't know what to say to that, but Castor seemed to take my silence as answer enough. 'They say Polydeuces fucks like he boxes. All power, no skill.'

He pulled off his own tunic then, throwing it in a tangled heap alongside the rest of his discarded clothes. Like most Spartans, the princes exercised naked, and so I was hardly unfamiliar with Castor's body. Yet something felt different about seeing him like this, in private, with my own clothes forgotten at my feet.

'Come here,' he instructed.

I swallowed the dry lump in my throat and stepped forward. Castor grabbed my shoulders, pulling me closer. His hands roamed freely across my body, and my muscles tensed in the wake of his touch.

He moved behind me then, and I felt his fingers skimming my scars in silent question.

'I knew you were a rebellious one,' he chuckled. 'I could see it in your eyes.'

Then, his hand flattened against my back, pushing me down on to the bed. A memory seized me, one that always lurked at the edges of my mind, pacing just beyond my thoughts. My breathing grew shallow as I felt the rough table beneath me, the guards slamming my head down, holding my wrists, the crack of the whip slicing open my flesh, Penelope watching me with wide eyes . . .

No, no, no.

I forced the memories away, biting my lip hard enough to ground myself back in the moment. I focused on my surroundings – the soft fur against my skin, the feel of Castor's large hands on my bare hips, the smell of stale wine in the hazy air.

I could not see what Castor was doing behind me, but I heard the rough whisper of skin against skin, and then the sound of him spitting. I had the sudden realization that I did not want to be there . . . I did not want to be there at all . . .

I wanted to get away.

I wanted my mother.

Without warning, Castor kicked my legs apart, spreading me out before him. I winced, biting down harder on my lip.

Be brave, my mother whispered to me as I felt Castor's warm thighs press against my own. A moment later, a sharp pain jolted deep in my core, carving through me. I stifled a yelp, tears stinging my eyes. The fur pelts brushed against my face like a soothing caress as Castor thrust into me, once . . . twice . . .

On the third drive, a strangled whimper erupted from his throat.

It was the most pathetic sound I had ever heard.

'*Fuck*,' he gasped.

I felt him slide out of me and I remained motionless on the bed, unsure what was happening.

Was it over?

Slowly, I sat up and turned to face him. As I moved, a warm, unpleasant wetness pooled between my thighs. I tried to ignore it.

'That . . . doesn't normally happen,' Castor muttered.

He scratched the back of his neck, trying to feign nonchalance, but I could see the irritation etched between his eyes, bracketing his thinned lips.

'You can leave,' he said. He did not meet my gaze.

I rose on shaky legs, relief-tinged confusion washing through me. Before I could move further, Castor's hand shot out, grabbing my arm. I glanced up at him, but his eyes were set on the wall beyond my head.

It was then that I noticed his cheeks were stained a slight pink.

'Do not tell Polydeuces.' He made it sound like an order, but I could hear the thread of vulnerability woven into his voice.

It was not a command; it was a plea.

The Prince of Sparta was pleading with *me*, a slave.

Because he was embarrassed. No, not just embarrassed.

He was *ashamed*.

A laugh bubbled inside me, but I forced myself to swallow it down as I gazed up at him, savouring every inch of his shame, mapping it in my mind so I could revisit it next time one of his kind tried to make me feel worthless.

'Of course, master.' Perhaps I was drunk on that tiny sip of power, for I added boldly, 'If it pleases you, I can fetch you more wine? It is still early.'

Castor hesitated, then smiled slowly. 'Make sure you get the good kind.'

I nodded, heading to retrieve my clothes.

'And get a cup for yourself,' he added as he collapsed into his bed. 'There's no joy in drinking good wine alone.'

I bowed my head, hiding a smirk. 'Yes, master.'

9

When I was fifteen summers old, the palace caught alight with news of Helen's impending betrothal.

'Kings, princes, heroes from all over Greece are coming here, to grace *these halls*. Are you not excited?' Callias asked me as we ambled towards the princes' entertaining quarters.

I yawned, my head hazy. After Castor had *indulged* in our company the previous night, the prince had fallen asleep, leaving Callias and me to polish off his leftover wine, as we usually did. I had developed a deep appreciation for Spartan wine, and the way it blunted those sharp, ugly edges inside me.

'The arrival of the suitors just means more work for the rest of us,' I grumbled. 'More mouths to feed, more spoilt royals to serve, more messes to clean up—'

'More beds to warm.' Callias nudged me with his elbow. 'When else will you get the opportunity to lie with a legend?'

I rolled my eyes. 'Is that all you think about?'

Callias winked, but his coy act did not fool me as easily as it once had. I knew he battled his own monsters; ones he occasionally spoke of, after one too many cups of wine. His father had been a gambler, he had told me one night, and when he lost everything, he had been forced to sell the only thing he had left to his name – his children.

Callias did a good job of pretending he did not care, and he played the role of the flirtatious, light-hearted boy well. But I knew armour when I saw it.

'I hear Ajax the Great is one of the potential suitors. Do you think he lives up to that title in *all* respects?' Callias continued with a performative grin.

'It sounds like he's overcompensating to me,' I muttered.

He laughed at that, one of his rare, genuine laughs – bright and inviting.

We paused as we neared the doorway to the princes' entertaining quarters. Sharing a smile, we spat into our wine jugs and clinked them together. This small act of rebellion had become a tradition of ours, one I had grown very fond of.

'Just think of all the wine we can spoil when the suitors arrive tomorrow,' he whispered as we entered the room.

I stifled a laugh, but the amusement died on my lips as soon as I looked up.

As soon as I saw *her*.

A ghost ripped straight from the shadows of my past.

Penelope.

The world seemed to slow in her presence, the seconds congealing together, sticking to my body, making my movements slow and awkward as I soaked her in . . .

She had always been slender, but it seemed the rest of her body had finally caught up with those long, elegant limbs of hers. Her face, too, had changed, those angular features seeming sharper, cut with an austere edge. Sunlight spilt across her high cheekbones as she assessed the board game set between her and Polydeuces. Though her features had altered, her expression remained achingly familiar – that quiet focus which seemed to consume every inch of her.

Callias brushed my arm, and I realized that I had stopped moving, stopped breathing, stopped *thinking*. It was as if my whole existence had been swallowed by Penelope's presence.

He nudged me again. '*Melantho?*'

Penelope's head snapped up, as if her own name had been called.

Her eyes were like twin blades carving through me. I had forgotten how intense her gaze was. It never felt like Penelope was looking *at* you, but rather *into* you, delving into the very darkest depths of your mind.

It took me a moment to remember I hated her.

She is not my friend.

I ripped my gaze away and forced myself to approach Castor. The prince was lounging across a bench, looking like some beautiful, vain statue brought to life. When he saw me nearing, he cast a slow, appreciative glance over my body.

'We should place bets on which suitor we believe shall be the lucky bastard,' he said, turning back to Polydeuces. 'Who do you think, brother?'

'Ajax the Great would be the obvious bet,' Polydeuces said as he mused over his next move. 'They are calling him *Aristos Achaion.*'

'The best of the Greeks.' Castor scoffed at the title. 'They say that about everyone.'

'Who do you think, then, brother?'

'My bet is on Menestheus,' he said as I refilled his cup. I felt his hand slip beneath my tunic, skating along my bare thighs. 'He is King of Athens now, after all.'

'Only because *we* placed him there,' Polydeuces drawled. 'Who do you think, cousin?'

'I do not presume to know the plans of King Tyndareus,' Penelope said quietly.

It hurt, hearing her voice. The familiarity of it dragged me back to another time, another life, to a version of myself I did not recognize any more, one crystallized in bittersweet naivety. A girl who still believed the world was a gift for her to cherish, not a burden forced upon her shoulders. A girl who thought 'slave' meant 'family'. A girl who believed she could be anything she wanted to be, even best friends with a princess.

A girl who still had a mother.

'Oh, come on,' Castor cajoled. 'You're meant to be the *smart* one in the family. So, prove it.'

Penelope gave a resigned sigh. 'Whoever he chooses, Tyndareus should make it seem as if it were Helen's decision. Menelaus of Mycenae is the most obvious candidate, a man who Helen would likely choose and is also a beneficial match for Tyndareus.'

Polydeuces gave a loud snort as he moved his counters across the board.

'And why would Helen get to *choose* her husband?' Castor scoffed.

Penelope turned to him, her gaze flat. 'Your father has invited suitors from all over Greece for the chance to win the hand of "the most beautiful woman in the world", daughter of Zeus himself, yes? These are kings, princes, famed heroes, men who are used to one thing – victory. But only *one* can be victorious here. How do you think the rest will take defeat when Helen's husband is chosen?'

Castor and Polydeuces shared a look.

'How does this relate to Helen choosing her own husband?' Polydeuces pressed, before motioning to the board between them. 'It's your turn.'

'It would be the wisest course of action,' Penelope replied, moving her counters without even looking at where she placed them. 'If Tyndareus chooses a suitor, those not chosen will feel slighted by his rejection. But if *Helen* chooses, or appears to be the one choosing, then Tyndareus can blame infatuation, or Eros' arrow of desire, or any number of innocuous motives that are far harder to raise arms against.'

Her voice was like rainfall – steady and soothing, yet with a drumming intensity to it. It was the kind of sound that made you want to close your eyes and tilt back your head, letting it seep into your skin, your bones . . .

I shivered, pushing the thought away.

'And how do *you* know Helen would pick Menelaus?' Polydeuces asked.

Penelope looked at him as if the answer were obvious. 'Because he is the brother of Clytemnestra's husband, and you know Helen follows her sister in all things.'

A smile slashed across Castor's face. 'I know what Penelope is getting at. She wants Helen to change the rules so *she* can choose her own husband, too. Is that it, cousin? After all, that is why you're here, isn't it? To pick through Helen's leftovers.'

I jolted, my jug nearly slipping from my hands. Across the room, Callias threw me a questioning glance.

'Tyndareus is to arrange my betrothal, as my father has agreed with him,' Penelope said plainly. She moved the counters again and Polydeuces' brow furrowed.

'By Zeus, if we start letting women choose their husbands, who will decide next? The *slaves*?' Castor laughed. It was an ugly sound. 'Good thing we have one right here. Why don't we ask her? Go on, girl, tell us what *you* think.' He motioned to me with his cup, causing the liquid to slosh over the edge and spill on to my sandals. 'Who do *you* think Penelope here should marry?'

'It would not be my place to say, master.'

Castor rose, throwing a heavy arm around my shoulders. 'Come now, there must be *some* thoughts in that pretty head of yours. Share them with us!'

I could feel Penelope's eyes on me now. Embarrassment prickled beneath my skin, like hot needles piercing every inch of my body.

'Look at my cousin and have a long, hard think. I said *look at her.*' Castor grabbed my face, forcing it towards Penelope. Her eyes slipped into mine and they somehow felt both intimately familiar and wholly distant.

Memories gulped inside me, making my pulse quicken. But I forced myself to push past them and to look, *really look*, at the princess before me – the clean, perfumed skin, those elegant, expensively dyed robes, her glittering jewellery and beautifully styled hair. As a child I had admired these details. Now, I hated them. I hated everything Penelope was, and how it served as a constant, taunting reminder of all I was not and could never be.

'Her heart is galloping,' Castor said, his palm planted over my chest. 'You're making her nervous, cousin.'

Penelope stared at Castor blankly. 'If you're done toying with the slave, may I return to my game? It's your turn, Polydeuces.'

The slave.

'Oh, don't be so dismissive.' Castor tutted. 'Melantho here is one of my favourites.'

'Your favourite toy changes every season, brother,' Polydeuces sniggered.

'I suppose,' Castor said, letting go of me. 'But you have to admit she's nice to look at.'

Penelope's eyes flickered to mine again, her expression indecipherable. She held my gaze for the briefest of moments, before turning back to Polydeuces.

'I said it's *your turn.*'

'Easy now, cousin.' Polydeuces chuckled, holding his hands up in mock surrender. 'What's with that tone?'

'She's probably on her bleeding, brother,' Castor announced from where he had flopped back on to his bench. 'Women are always ill-tempered when they bleed.'

Polydeuces nodded in agreement as he began moving his counters. With his free hand, he motioned to his cup. I obeyed, trying to steady the anger still churning inside me as I bent to pour his wine. Absently, my eyes flicked over the board. It was plain to see Penelope had won the game; one simple move and victory would be hers. But, when it was her turn, Penelope retreated.

'Seems you haven't been practising enough these past summers,' Polydeuces said as he proudly made the winning move Penelope had opened for him. 'I have beaten you, at long last.'

'Well done.' Penelope did not even bother reviewing the board as she rose to her feet. 'If it pleases you, I wish to retire to my room now. I am not feeling well.'

'Definitely bleeding,' Castor said smugly to his brother. 'I told you.'

The princes shared a smirk as Penelope strode towards the door. As I watched her go, a small, foolish part of me waited for her to look back.

She did not.

10

Helen's suitors arrived the following day.

Callias and I were stationed in the entertaining hall, the largest room of the palace, reserved for Sparta's major functions. Giant pillars carried lofty ceilings, like Atlas bearing the skies. Along the walls, vivid frescos depicted famous scenes from mythology, still smelling of fresh paint from the retouches Tyndareus had recently commissioned.

Beneath our feet, intricate mosaics adorned the floor. I knew every fleck of stone had been scrubbed clean by exhausted slaves, just like every other inch of the palace. Painstaking hours of endless work, so that entitled men could scuff their sandals, spill their wine and congratulate one another on their own greatness.

I felt a muscle in my jaw tic as I swallowed my frustration, watching more men funnel into the room, glowing like young gods who believed the world was theirs and theirs alone.

A dais was positioned at the far end of the space, framed by the courtyard the room spilt into. Here, Tyndareus sat upon his throne, flanked by his sons. Every new arrival approached the king first, making their formal introduction and offering generous favours. These gifts became more extravagant as the day wore on – weapons, pottery, clothing, jewellery, gold, livestock . . . One suitor even brought slaves, ten beautiful girls with flaxen hair.

Tyndareus seemed delighted at first, but as time passed, and his treasuries swelled to near bursting, the king grew withdrawn, as if a great cloud had descended over him.

I observed from the sidelines as the men interacted with one another. They were like birds in mating season, puffed up and proud, circling slowly as they offered empty platitudes, all the while quietly assessing their competition. Though the atmosphere was celebratory, there was an undeniable thread of tension woven beneath, like a bowstring pulling dangerously tauter with every new arrival.

Each time someone entered, I found my eyes darting to the doorway to see if it was *her*. But Penelope did not come. She was, no doubt, in the women's quarters with Helen. Two beautiful prizes kept safely locked away.

What did I care where she was, anyway? I had nothing to say to Penelope. And, once she was married and shipped off to some distant palace, I would never have to see her again.

My thoughts were disrupted as the largest man I had ever seen cut across the room. He looked like a weapon given life, melded from fire and iron and rage. I watched his hulking shoulders rise and fall in rhythm with his confident strides. Rather than weaving around the crowds, the giant sliced directly through them, forcing men to move out of his thundering path. Every inch of his body was corded with thick, sculpted muscle.

The various pools of conversation dried up in the man's wake, the room growing so quiet I could hear his announcement clearly.

'I am Ajax, Prince of Salamis, son of Telamon. I come as your humble guest, King Tyndareus, seeking the hand of your famed daughter, Helen of Sparta.' His voice reminded me of thunder over mountains, a thick rumble caught between craggy peaks.

I spared a glance at Callias, who was gaping at Ajax with unbridled awe.

'He's even bigger than in the stories,' he murmured beside me.

'*Ajax the Great.*' I scoffed at the name. 'I do not see what is so *great* about him.'

'Are we looking at the same man? He looks like a literal god.'

'Yes, he looks as if he could crush my head like a grape. How fantastic,'

I muttered. 'And people would give Ajax's toenail more respect than they would ever show either of us.'

Callias sniggered at that. I had not meant it as a joke.

Chatter started up again as Ajax moved away from the dais. Already, more suitors were arriving, taking their place before the king.

'Do you think there are more than Tyndareus expected?' Callias asked quietly.

'Far more. Do you see his face? He looks worried.'

'Worried? He'll be the richest man in Greece by the time Helen is wed. Do you *see* all the gifts they are bringing him?'

'Men only give gifts when they expect something in return. And every man in this room wants the same thing, but only one will get it,' I murmured, recalling Penelope's words from the day before. I hated how her voice clung to my mind so easily. 'I doubt most of the men in this room have ever been denied anything in their entire lives.'

Callias' face tightened as he regarded the room with a newfound wariness. 'They are guests; the laws of *Xenia* demand they treat their host with respect.'

'And what if they feel they have been slighted by their host? Will they believe those laws still apply? There's enough entitlement in here to rival the halls of Olympus.'

Callias considered this, teeth pressing into his soft lower lip. 'Do you think Tyndareus has a plan to keep the peace?'

I flickered my eyes to the king, watching his face slowly darken.

'I hope so.'

After an elaborate display of sacrifices to the Gods, the feasting began.

I felt like Sisyphus trapped in the Underworld. But, instead of repeatedly pushing a rock up that cursed hill, my torture was continually replenishing wine cups that never seemed to remain full. My feet were aching and blistered after hours spent flitting up and down the long tables, trying to dodge the groping hands that became bolder with every pass.

As I leant over to refill Castor's cup, the tall suitor beside him shamelessly reached out to squeeze my breasts. I waited for Castor to chastise the man, for the prince was usually territorial with his 'favourites', but he was far more preoccupied with the flaxen-haired slave sitting in his lap, one of the ten gifted by a suitor. His shiny new toy.

Swallowing my irritation, I moved on to the next empty cup, the next pair of brazen hands and wine-glazed eyes. One suitor improvised a phallus with a leg of chicken and tried to make me eat it off his crotch, whilst the others erupted into riotous laughter.

Were these really Greece's greatest heroes, chosen by the Gods? If so, I questioned the Olympians' taste, for all I could see was a horde of sweaty, drunken pigs making fools of themselves. The only talent these 'heroes' had was glutting themselves on the fruits of others' labour.

It would have been laughable if it had not been so depressing.

I was grateful when the wine finally ran out, allowing me a brief escape. I took a detour through the courtyard on the way to the storerooms, savouring the fresh air and enviable stillness.

The courtyard was vast, situated at the very heart of the palace and kept impeccably tidy by the tireless work of my father and the other gardeners. I paused, gazing at the flowerbeds. Something ugly twisted inside me, knowing my father's hands had tended to these buds, helped them flourish. I stamped on a rose, grinding the petals to dust beneath my heel.

My gaze then lifted to watch the last rays of sunlight stretching overhead, like clawed fingers refusing to let go of the day, leaving deep purple and rose bruises across the sky. I wondered, as I often did, if my mother was looking up at the sky too. Was she watching this same sunset? Was she thinking of me as she did? I closed my eyes, imagining I could hear her on the whispering breeze, that voice I was so terrified of one day forgetting.

Be brave, my heart.

'Slave.' The word cleaved through my thoughts like a rusted blade.

I turned to find a suitor standing over me.

He was not the tallest, nor the largest man, but there was a brutality to his appearance that demanded reverence, a rawness that made my stomach clench. He was like a natural element hacked from the earth, untamed by the wealth and luxury his status afforded him.

I bowed stiffly. 'May I help you, sir?'

'I tire of the celebrations. Take me to my chamber.'

'I . . . do not know where your chamber is, sir.'

His thick brows knitted together, hanging over his eyes like twin thunderclouds.

'You do not know the King of Mycenae?' he asked.

Agamemnon. I knew of him, of course. Not just because he was the king Clytemnestra had been sent off to marry, but because *everyone* knew of the House of Atreus, rumoured to be cursed by the Gods.

'Take me to my room.'

'I do not know which room is yours,' I repeated, my voice a little more hesitant.

'Are *all* Spartan slaves blundering idiots?' I bristled beneath the question but remained silent. 'Let me make this simple for you – escort me to the grandest guest room in this palace. Is that truly so difficult, girl?'

I nodded, anger souring my stomach. 'This way, sir.'

I led Agamemnon through the passageway that led to the guest wing. As the sound of the revelry faded behind us, I became aware of his eyes on me. Gripping my empty wine jug tighter, I tried to ignore the nagging unease expanding inside my chest.

'You're dressed well, for a slave. Let me guess – you are one of the princes' personal flock,' Agamemnon mused aloud as we walked. The evening shadows seemed to be pressing in closer with every step. 'They always said Tyndareus' sons had good taste in whores.'

My jaw tightened but I let his words graze me, keeping my focus ahead. Agamemnon smacked his lips and chuckled, as if tasting my discomfort.

'This is your room, sir.' I motioned to the first door we reached.

Agamemnon kept his heavy gaze on me. His face looked as if it had been carved into rock instead of flesh.

'Show me inside.'

'I am not permitted to enter the guest chambers. Master's orders,' I lied.

'I do not care.'

I forced my lips to curl into the lazy, intimate smile I had seen Callias flash countless times before.

'I still have work to do,' I murmured huskily, brushing his arm. 'But perhaps if you settle in, I can visit you later when I am done.'

It was the kind of line that would have made Castor heat and soften, becoming easy to mould in my hands. But the King of Mycenae was not so easily manipulated. His eyes darkened, mouth twisting beneath his thick beard.

'I gave you an order, slave. *Show me inside.*'

I realized there was no swaying this swine of a man, and my exhaustion from the day prickled into indignation as I turned and shoved the door open.

'*There.* There's the inside,' I snapped, before biting out the word, '*sir.*'

Without warning, Agamemnon's hand shot out and closed around my throat as he slammed me against the wall. His palm spanned the entire length of my throat, his fingers clawing up across my face, digging into my skin. My jug fell to the ground, shattering at our feet.

'What a sharp tongue you have. Perhaps we should put it to better use.'

'I serve Tyndareus, not you,' I snarled at him.

Agamemnon struck me across the face with his free hand. The impact sang through my jaw, and I tasted blood in my mouth, yet every trace of pain was incinerated by the rage surging inside me.

In that moment, it was not just Agamemnon who hit me. It was the men who had held me down as I was whipped. The men who had dragged my mother away in chains. Icarius, who had tried to bed me as a child. Castor and his vile friends, who had enjoyed my body night after night as if it were their own.

'Defy me again, slave. Go on.'

I spat at him, my blood spraying across his cheeks.

I knew this would not be worth the consequences, but at least, for this fleeting moment, I could smile up at his outrage and pretend it was.

The curl of my lips was a step too far for Agamemnon. A meaty fist tangled into my hair, yanking me towards his chamber. I tripped as I struggled against him, tumbling to the ground. Shards of the broken wine jug bit into my knees, making me yelp. Agamemnon wrenched my head upwards.

'*Help!* Help me!' I cried to the two guards patrolling the hall.

They turned and stared at me. When they noticed Agamemnon, the men visibly stiffened, before bowing their heads and disappearing.

I watched them leave, that fragile thread of hope snapping inside me.

With his hand now on the back of my neck, Agamemnon hauled me to my feet, shoved me into the room and slammed the door shut behind us.

'This could have been civilized,' he snarled as he dragged me towards the bed. 'Why must slaves *insist* on acting like animals?'

Panic sparked in my veins, but hotter than that was the fury that coursed through me, setting my blood alight.

'Help! HELP!' I screamed again. 'HEL—'

'*No one is helping a damn slave,*' he hissed into my ear as he closed a large hand around my mouth.

I bit down. Hard. So hard my jaw spasmed with the effort.

So hard my mouth filled with blood.

Agamemnon roared, releasing me. I scrambled to get away, but his giant arm shot out, blocking my path to the door. Then, he threw me down on to the bed, his bloodied hand closing around my throat again. I thrashed against him, kicking my legs wildly, but Agamemnon remained unfazed, pinning me down with brutal efficiency.

'I had heard this was how you take your women – screaming and injured,' I hissed as he towered over me, rage and fear making my tongue reckless. 'Because nobody will fuck you willingly.'

Agamemnon only laughed at that. 'Ah. So, you *have* heard of me.'

'Yes. And you know what?' I panted. 'I find it surprising how *much* people have to say about something so *little*.'

I flicked my eyes pointedly to his crotch, finding satisfaction in the ripple of fury that fractured his cold composure. Agamemnon then tightened his grip around my throat and a horrible pressure began building inside my temples, as if my head were about to explode.

'I can see why Castor likes you,' he murmured as he calmly watched me choke. 'The bold ones are always the most satisfying to break.'

As darkness began to creep in at the edges of my vision, I saw him slip a hand beneath his robes, touching himself as he watched me suffer. He slackened his hold just enough to let me take a breath, before re-applying the pressure once again, letting me dance on the blurry fringes of consciousness.

'What's the matter, girl? Nothing more to say?'

Every vile insult I had ever thought of clogged in my throat as I glared at him, hoping my eyes would scream the hatred I could not voice. But Agamemnon only smiled and continued working himself.

Finally, he released my neck as he positioned himself over me, and I knew that now was my only chance.

In my hand, the one I had hidden beneath the sheets, I gripped a shard of the broken wine jug tighter. I could feel its jagged edges biting into my flesh as I reaffirmed my grip, ensuring the sharpest edge was exposed.

As Agamemnon pushed my tunic up to my waist, I launched myself forward, throwing all my strength into slamming the shard into his thigh, burying it deep in his flesh. Agamemnon let out a howl of agony and I twisted the fragment deeper, pain lancing through my palm.

The King of Mycenae reeled backwards, his face riven with rage. It was the kind of rage I had only heard stories about: of soldiers gripped in the throes of bloodlust, ready to slaughter entire armies.

I ignored the fear ripping through me as I scrambled over the bed and bolted towards the door. Agamemnon threw himself in front of me and I recoiled, narrowly missing his grasp.

A silence held its breath as we stared at one another. Blood streamed down Agamemnon's thigh in crimson rivulets. He reached down and ripped out the shard with a grunt, before tossing it across the room.

'You've got balls, slave, I'll give you that,' he said, voice ragged. He tried to laugh, but the sound came out strangled. 'You'll pay for this, you know. Nobody makes a king bleed.'

A thought stole through me, like an icy winter breeze . . . I was about to die.

As if sensing my fear, Agamemnon smiled and took a heavy step towards me. I could see his wrath coiling inside him, tighter and tighter, preparing to unleash itself.

'King Agamemnon, I have an urgent message.' A voice sounded from behind the door.

'*Leave*,' he barked.

'I'm told the message is urgent. It's from King Tyndareus. He wishes to discuss Helen's betrothal.'

This caught Agamemnon's attention. I remained frozen, watching his fury slowly disperse as a new focus took root. He threw me a warning glare before limping towards the door. When he opened it, two grey eyes met mine.

Penelope.

But it was not the Penelope I knew. She was wearing a plain, ragged tunic and a faded scarf around her head to hide her hair. Her face was smeared with dirt, her feet clad in worn sandals. Only her eyes were the same – those bright, clever orbs that darted around the room, calmly assessing the scene.

'King Tyndareus wants you in his throne room, sir, says it's urgent,' Penelope said in an accent that was not her own.

Agamemnon let out a rush of air through flared nostrils.

'Listen here.' He jammed a finger in Penelope's face, seemingly oblivious to her identity. 'I want this girl here punished. Do you understand me, slave?'

'This one?' Penelope nodded to me. 'I don't have control of that, sir.'

'This slave *attacked* me. Do you see?'

Penelope regarded his bloody thigh, brows twitching. 'So, you want me to tell the others you were attacked . . . by a *slave girl*?' She tilted her head. 'I know it's not my place to say, sir, but word spreads pretty fast round here.'

'What are you implying?'

'I'm an admirer of the House of Atreus, is all, and I'd hate to see the chances of your brother winning Helen dashed.' Penelope shrugged. Even her mannerisms seemed looser, more relaxed. 'But . . . what if I *didn't* see this girl in here? What if she was never here at all? Maybe I saw you get in a brawl with a drunken suitor, a brawl you bravely won. A story like that would spread quick as wildfire.'

'I would take the girl's offer,' came another voice from the hallway, smooth as marble and lit with amusement. I could not see the speaker, but I noted the way Penelope stiffened. The voice continued, 'If news spreads that the mighty King Agamemnon was bested by a tiny slave girl, well . . . maybe the fearsome House of Atreus' reputation won't be quite so fearsome any more.'

'You speak to *me* of reputation, Prince of Goats?' Agamemnon snapped.

'By all means, ignore my advice,' the voice replied. 'I and the men of Greece will delight in this story.'

I could not see Agamemnon's face; I could only read the tension in his back, his muscles stiffening then releasing in a rough exhalation.

'I've had enough of this,' he growled. 'Leave. All of you. I have far more important matters to attend to.'

Penelope beckoned me forward and I rushed to her.

'She was never here. Do you understand?' Agamemnon barked.

'Who, sir?' Penelope smiled. 'I see nobody in your room.'

The King of Mycenae grunted before slamming the door behind us.

For a moment all I could do was stare at Penelope, my mind and body utterly numb.

Penelope opened her mouth to speak, when a chuckle sounded from down the hallway. Turning, I saw a man lounging against the stone wall. He looked nothing like the other suitors. Whereas they were all tall, sculpted muscle, this man was short and stocky, with a thick, barrelled chest. His skin was bronzed, his dark hair a little unruly as if he had just wandered in from a stroll across the fields. He was not handsome, yet there was a confident shine to his features that some might have believed charming.

'Well, you've certainly made an impression.' His smile was like a cat stretching, lazy and self-assured. 'Tell me, what is your name?'

I forced my hammering heart to steady itself as I glared at him.

'Melantho . . . *sir*.'

'Melantho,' the stranger repeated, turning the syllables over in his mouth as if assessing them for cracks.

'Are you all right?' Penelope whispered to me.

I balled my wounded hand into a fist, feeling a sudden rush of embarrassment as I tucked it behind my back.

'I'm fine,' I muttered.

'Come, let me escort you ladies somewhere safer,' the man interjected, motioning down the hall.

Penelope shook her head. 'Thank you for the offer, but—'

'I insist.' He cut her off with a smile.

I glanced at Penelope, and she gave a sigh before setting herself between me and the stranger.

'Are you sure you're all right?' she murmured to me.

I forced myself to match her steady pace, praying neither of them noticed how shaky my legs were, how unsteady my steps.

'Melantho?'

'I said I'm *fine*,' I snapped, refusing to meet her gaze.

The stranger was glancing sidelong at us, smirking. 'It is good to see you again, Princess Penelope.'

'Likewise, Prince Odysseus,' she replied, dropping the accent she had used with Agamemnon.

Odysseus' smile widened. 'I must say, you've had quite the change of appearance since our meeting this morning.' He made a point of glancing over her attire. 'Is there a new fashion in Sparta I am unaware of?'

'From what I hear, Prince Odysseus, you are no stranger to a disguise,' Penelope countered.

His eyes flashed at that, like a fish slipping the net. 'Then may I ask what your purpose is?'

'I merely wished to go for a stroll, but a princess is not permitted to wander at this hour.'

'Ah yes, whereas a slave can slip by *undetected*.' He drew the word out, letting it curl into a chuckle. 'Tell me, what secret business could a princess possibly have on a night like tonight?'

'Nothing of interest, I assure you,' Penelope said.

'If a beautiful, enigmatic princess should not interest me, then what should?'

I stifled a huff. Odysseus looked old enough to be Penelope's *father*.

'I assure you, Helen is the only true beauty here,' she murmured, meek and bashful and entirely not herself.

'Beauty is subjective,' Odysseus countered, edging closer.

I had a sudden, intense desire to be *anywhere* but there. As we turned off down another passageway, I glanced around us, wondering if I could slip away without either of them noticing.

'I have been thinking about what you said this morning, about allowing Helen to choose her own suitor,' Odysseus continued. 'I intend to discuss the idea with Tyndareus.'

'That is good news,' Penelope replied.

'Do you think he would take my counsel?'

She nodded. 'But I would not give it freely. I would ask for something in return. My uncle will respect a man who knows his own value.'

Odysseus' teeth gleamed as his smile widened. 'And what, princess, do you believe I should request from him?'

'That must be your decision, Prince Odysseus,' she said carefully.

'Well, there *is* something in Tyndareus' possession that I greatly desire.'

Penelope gazed up at him from beneath lowered lashes. 'And what might that be?'

Odysseus leant closer. 'I would love nothing more than to discuss such a thing with you, but alas, it appears your slave's injury needs tending to.'

Penelope whirled to look at me, that bashful poise instantly draining from her face.

'I'm fine,' I muttered, but the words were thin, my head woozy.

'Melantho,' Penelope breathed, eyes widening as she surveyed the blood splattered on the floor, trailing behind me. 'Let me see.'

Reluctantly I held my hand out, blood welling in my palm.

'Why didn't you say anything?' she asked quietly, as Odysseus observed the wound.

'I could take you to my chamber. I have remedies there. If you would like—'

'No, thank you,' she cut across him. 'We will retire now. It was a pleasure to see you again, Prince Odysseus.'

'I assure you, the pleasure is all mine.' Odysseus bowed low. 'Until next time, Princess Penelope.'

11

I felt empty as I walked into Penelope's chamber.

The numbness was so consuming, it took me a moment to realize it was not the same one we had shared as children.

'I was moved from my usual quarters, on account of the suitors,' Penelope explained. 'I prefer this, anyway; that other chamber was unnecessarily large.'

This space was, indeed, far smaller, comprising only one room. A bed was positioned in the far corner, stacked with intricately woven blankets. Opposite was a loom, where threads hung suspended like strands of unfinished time. Upon a narrow table, a few jugs were arranged in a neat line alongside a bowl for washing. Everything was impeccably tidy, just as I remembered Penelope's chamber always had been.

Her eyes followed mine as I surveyed the space, our silence stretching thin.

I pretended not to watch as Penelope removed the scarf from around her head, slipped off her sandals and padded across the rug to the unlit hearth. A single chair was positioned beside it, draped in a dark animal hide and inlaid with silver detailing.

'Would you like to sit here?' she offered. 'I can take a look at your hand.'

'I'm fine,' I muttered.

Penelope nodded then stared into the empty hearth, as if her gaze alone could summon a fire within it. Silence settled again, sharpening the awkwardness between us. Once, there had not seemed enough time in existence to fit all the words I wanted to share with Penelope.

'You can leave if you wish,' she said. 'I am not forcing you to stay.'

Go. Leave and never look back, a voice inside my head urged. *Remember who she is. Remember what she did to you.* But my body refused to comply, as if my feet were rooted to the spot.

When I looked up, Penelope was watching me again, with those eyes of hers that always saw too much.

'Would you like to talk about it . . . what happened?' she asked quietly.

Was she referring to Agamemnon or us?

It did not matter. My answer would still be the same.

'No.'

She did not press further. It was something I had once admired about her, how Penelope never forced truths from another's lips. Instead, she would let them settle and soften, then gently prise those words out when the time was right.

But I would not let her slip beneath my defences this time.

You cannot trust her kind, my brother hissed from the past.

So why are you still standing here?

The familiar glug of liquid being poured caught my attention. A moment later, Penelope was handing me a cup.

'What are you doing?'

'Offering you wine,' she said, as if it really were that simple.

'Why?'

'Because you look like you need it.'

She waved the dark liquid towards me again and, as I reached out to take it, I realized my hands were trembling. Penelope noticed too, and I hated the way it made her face soften.

'The wine will help,' she murmured. Then, at my hesitation, she added, 'Don't worry – I did not spit in it.'

My eyes flashed to hers. 'W-what?'

A small smile brushed her lips. 'I saw you and your friend. Before the suitors' banquet.'

I said nothing, waiting for the scolding, the judgement. But none came. Instead, Penelope turned and busied herself with lighting the fire.

Unsure what else to do, I decided to drink. When I treated myself to Castor's wine it always tasted like rebellion; danger and excitement and fury all swirled together on my tongue. There was not the same thrill when it was given to me out of pity. Instead, Penelope's wine had a mild tang and seemed substantially more watered down than the stuff the men drank. Still, I gulped it down eagerly, willing it to drown all thoughts of Agamemnon.

The fire spluttered to life, causing the shadows to scatter away. Penelope watched the flames for a moment, skin bathed in their amber glow. I found my eyes tracing the slope of her neck, watching the shadows play in the hollow dip at the base of her throat. My stomach clenched like a fist, and I quickly diverted my attention to Penelope's loom.

'It's a wedding veil,' she said, following my gaze.

'For you?'

'Unfortunately.'

She moved towards it and began toying with a thread, making the hanging weights clack together. The sound summoned visions, unbidden, of lazy, sun-gilded afternoons spent watching Penelope work as we giggled and chattered.

I blinked, forcing those memories back into their graves.

'Why are you dressed as a slave?'

'Let me look at your hand and I'll tell you,' Penelope countered, the spark of a challenge warming her voice.

'I already told you, I'm fine.' In truth my palm was throbbing fiercely, as were my knees from where I had fallen on the broken jug.

Still, the thought of Penelope tending to me made my skin crawl.

'At least sit, will you?'

'Is that a question or a command?'

Penelope's face tightened, but she did not rise to my resentment. Instead, she murmured a soft, 'Please.'

I stalked across the room and collapsed into the chair. I did not know why I was acting like a sulking child. It was as if my leftover fear and anger had curdled with my exhaustion and now seeped out of me in clumps of bitter petulance.

Penelope did not seem to mind my behaviour, and I found her calmness irritating. How did she always have such a firm rein on her emotions?

'You should bathe the cut,' she said, setting a bowl of water down beside me and offering a fresh cloth. 'Your knees, too.'

I said nothing as I took the rag from her, ignoring the tremor in my fingers as I dipped it into the water. I waited until Penelope walked away before I pressed the rag against my palm, stifling a hiss of pain. The shard had cut me deep when I had twisted it into Agamemnon's leg.

Still, it had been worth it.

'Do you really think he won't tell anyone what I did?' I asked without looking at her.

'I think Agamemnon's delicate ego will keep him quiet,' she replied from across the room. 'At least until Helen's hand has been secured by his brother.'

'What about after?'

Penelope's back was turned to me as she murmured, 'I cannot say.'

A cold, clammy panic crept over me as I dabbed at the wound. A moment later, Penelope appeared at my side and began refilling my empty cup.

'Don't.' I clenched the word between my teeth.

She paused. 'Why?'

'Because that's not the way this works.'

Carefully, she set the jug down before moving to retrieve the three-legged stool from beside her loom.

'And what is "this"?' Penelope asked as she placed the stool opposite me and perched herself upon it.

'*This*.' I motioned between us with the rag, now stained with my blood. '*I* serve *you*. So, just stop . . . *twisting* it, will you?'

She pressed her lips into a thin line. 'But I don't want you to serve me.'

'Then why am I here?'

'Because you're injured.'

'I can look after myself.'

'I never said you could not.'

'I don't need your pity.'

'I'm not giving it.'

'Then stop looking at me like that.'

'Like what?'

'*Like you pity me.*' The words came out in a heated rush, sharper than I'd intended. Still, Penelope did not even flinch, just folded her hands neatly in her lap and watched me with that infuriating patience of hers.

'I do not pity you, Melantho,' she said, firmer this time.

I ignored her. She had always been too good at lying.

She is not my friend.

I began dabbing the dozens of little angry cuts mottled across my skin. My frustration made me careless, and a stab of pain lanced through my kneecaps.

'*Hades' helm,*' I swore and leant back in the chair.

'What is it?' Penelope asked, voice pinched with something almost like concern.

'I think . . . there's some shards still in there,' I replied through gritted teeth.

'May I take a look?'

I wanted to say *no, leave me alone,* but exhaustion skulked between my bones, draining the fight from my body. I dropped the rag into the bowl and turned my face to the fire.

Penelope moved towards me, picking up the rag and rinsing it in the water. She then took the bowl and knelt in front of me. My eyes drifted away from the hearth, stomach knotting at the sight of the princess on her knees before me. Her gaze flickered up to mine as if sensing my thoughts, pre-empting my refusal. But I said nothing.

Taking my silence as compliance, Penelope turned her attention back to my knees.

'There are definitely still shards in there,' she murmured. 'You must get them out . . . May I try?'

'Fine,' I grunted, downing the wine she had refilled. 'Just get it over with.'

She paused momentarily, drawing in a breath. Her fingers then traced up my right leg, closing gently around my calf. Her touch made everything go still, as if every flame in Sparta had whispered out all at once.

I swallowed the sudden dryness in my mouth as Penelope guided my leg towards her and gently set my foot in her lap. Her fingers remained laced around my calf as her other hand began to gently prise out the shards embedded in my skin. She was so incredibly gentle, touching me with a care that made a strange lump knot in my throat.

I watched her as she worked, studying the way concentration etched itself into those features of hers, every detail accentuated by the flickering light of the fire. She was still the most striking thing I had ever seen.

She glanced up then, catching my gaze before I could look away, pinning it between us, raw and open. The air in the room suddenly felt too thin, the fire too hot, my pulse too fast, the stillness between us too delicate.

'Is this all right?' she whispered.

I nodded, cheeks burning as I turned my face away. I focused on the fire once again, willing myself to cling to the hatred inside me, to keep holding that shield close.

She abandoned you.

As if sensing my darkening mood, Penelope began to talk whilst she worked. 'I wanted to see the suitors; that is why I was in disguise. I am not permitted to wander the palace as a princess. But as a slave I can slip by unnoticed. I used to do it sometimes when my father entertained guests back home.'

'Why did you want to see them?'

'I wanted to assess my options.'

'I thought you didn't get a say in that,' I said, wincing as she retrieved another shard.

'I have no choice in marriage. But when it comes to choosing a suitor, men can be far more easily swayed than one might think. The trick is letting them believe it was *their* idea.'

'Like yesterday, when you let Polydeuces win your game?'

A wisp of surprise stole across her face and I hated how much I liked the sight of it, knowing how rare it was to see.

'Yes.' She nodded, staring up at me. 'Just like that.'

'Why did you do it? Let him win?'

'Sometimes it is more advantageous to lose. Polydeuces has a terrible temper . . . and I did not wish to unleash it upon you.' She paused, as if catching herself, then added quickly, 'Or any of those serving him.'

We both glanced away at the same moment, the awkwardness palpable between us.

'This might hurt. I am sorry,' she murmured as she tugged at a larger shard.

'So, you just . . . snuck around in disguise and decided . . . on a husband?' I forced the question through gritted teeth.

'Not quite.' She kept her focus on her task as she spoke. 'I have been gathering information on all the suitors for many moons now. I had narrowed my choices down to a few candidates, but I wished to see them in person before I decided which would be the best fit.'

'And have you? Chosen?'

'Odysseus, Prince of Ithaca, is the best match.'

'That suitor in the hallway? He's a bit old, isn't he?'

'He's thirty-eight summers.'

'That's over twice your age.'

Penelope smiled thinly. 'Do you think that matters to my uncle? There are suitors here who have seen over sixty summers . . . This shard is quite deep.'

I winced, gripping the chair. 'So . . . why him?'

I did not care what her answer was, did not care who she married. This was just a distraction from the pain, a channel in which to focus my thoughts.

That was all.

'They say Odysseus is an intelligent man, and he values that trait in others. He is known to treat his people with respect, and he also speaks highly of his mother and sister . . . *There*.' She held up a bloodstained fragment. 'I think that's the last of them.'

'That can't be all.'

'I think it is. I cannot see any more remnants in there—'

'No. I mean, that cannot be the only reason you chose Odysseus.'

Penelope paused, her gaze creeping up to meet mine.

'No, you're right,' she murmured, drawing in a breath. 'Ithaca is a modest kingdom of little renown. Odysseus wishes to build it into something greater. I think it would be . . . *interesting* to be the queen of an evolving kingdom. I believe there would be more opportunities for me there.'

She admitted the last part as if it were a secret, as if her ambition were a shameful thing to be kept in the shadows.

'Doesn't that usually mean war?'

She shook her head. 'Ithaca is not a military kingdom. They cannot achieve greatness through bloodshed.'

'Then how?'

'Therein lies the challenge.' Her smile itched at old, unwanted memories.

'Tyndareus might choose Odysseus for Helen.'

'Odysseus' background is far too humble for Helen,' she said, patting my knees with the soaked rag. 'And Tyndareus will let Odysseus have me because Odysseus will strike a deal.'

I frowned. 'A deal?'

'When I met Odysseus earlier today, we discussed my uncle's

current... *predicament*. I told him my plan for avoiding conflict when Helen's suitor is chosen. Odysseus will offer this solution to my uncle and in return he will ask for something he wants. My hand.'

'How can you be sure he'll ask for *your* hand?'

Penelope stared at the rag, my blood blooming across it. 'Because tonight, catching me in disguise – it surprised him. And he is a man who is rarely surprised.'

'You intended to be caught by Odysseus tonight.' I spoke the realization as it came to me. 'You *wanted* him to see you in your disguise.'

Instead of confirming this, Penelope simply asked, 'Would you like me to bandage your knees?'

I shook my head. Then, unable to stop my bitterness seeping through, I added, 'I suppose I nearly ruined it. Your little plan.'

'You did not ruin anything, Melantho. I'm just thankful I was there.'

'Why *were* you there?'

Penelope glanced away, the fire-cast shadows seeming to grow darker across her face.

'I heard you calling to the guards for help.'

My defences reared. I could feel them clanging through me, ugly and loud.

'I didn't need you. I could've handled it.'

'Exactly.' Penelope met my anger with a smile. 'I dread to think what state Agamemnon would have been in if I hadn't intervened.'

To my surprise, I felt my mouth curl upwards, but I quickly caught the smile, pressing it firmly between my lips.

'Aren't you going to punish me... for what I did to him?'

'Punish you?' Penelope shook her head incredulously. 'Of course not. He *deserved* it. Only...'

'Only what?'

Mischief danced in her eyes like tiny firelights. 'Truthfully, I think you should've aimed higher.'

'I'm not sure Clytemnestra would have been very pleased with me if I had stabbed her husband in the balls.'

'On the contrary, I think you would have been doing my cousin a favour, and perhaps all of Greece.'

Penelope held my gaze, and though neither of us laughed, I could feel our amusement mingling in the air between us, warming the space.

'May I check your palm now?' she asked.

It seemed the fire and wine had softened my temper, for I found myself obliging without protest. Penelope moved closer to me, and I tried to ignore the shiver tracing my bones as she cupped my hand atop hers, drawing my palm to her face.

'I am going to bandage it.' Before giving me a chance to refuse, Penelope retrieved a clean piece of cloth and began winding it around my palm.

Once she had secured the bandage in place, I murmured a dull 'Thanks.'

I went to pull my hand away, but Penelope's fingers tightened around mine.

'He should not get away with what he did to you, Melantho,' she whispered.

I sighed. 'But he will.'

'My uncle would be furious if he knew—'

'That someone else tried to touch his property?' I huffed a bitter laugh.

'Perhaps if I spoke with him—'

'Penelope.' I tugged my hand free. 'Just . . . don't. Please. There is no point.'

She gave a shallow nod, biting down on her lip as if having to forcibly contain the words threatening to spill out.

'Make sure this doesn't get infected,' she said instead, motioning to my palm. 'You should see if they have any yarrow in the kitchens; the herb is good for healing. Or perhaps you could ask your father?'

'Perhaps,' I muttered, not willing to admit I never spoke to the man any more. *That* was not a conversation I wanted to get into tonight. Or any night, for that matter.

'You will need to keep an eye on it,' she warned.

I shrugged, her concern grating on me. 'I'll be fine.'

'It could get infected without proper care. It's a nasty wound and—'

'I've survived worse,' I shot back. 'You of all people should know.'

Penelope went deathly still, and I saw the memories rushing through her, the same ones that haunted my dreams night after night. I could *feel* them playing out in her mind – my face pressed against the table, the sound of my sobs racking my body, the sheer agony as those tongues of fire devoured my bare back . . .

I stood abruptly. 'I need to leave.'

Penelope rose with me, though her entire demeanour had changed, growing stiff and withdrawn, as if her thoughts had collapsed in on themselves.

'You do not have to,' she managed to say quietly.

But I did.

I had to get away from her, from the insufferable pity in her eyes, from the memories strangling me like Agamemnon's hand at my throat.

'I *want* to leave,' I said.

Penelope just nodded, unable to look at me. I hated knowing what version of myself she was seeing in her mind – that weeping, terrified child, covered in her own piss and blood . . . Was that what she always saw when she looked at me?

I made for the door, but as I moved past Penelope, she grabbed my wrist, stopping me in my tracks. We stood motionless, facing in opposite directions yet so close our shoulders brushed.

I stared at the wall ahead, willing my pulse to settle, forcing those memories down and down and down . . .

'Melantho.'

How I loathed the sound of my name on her lips and all the unwanted feelings it stirred within me. But I reminded myself this effect of hers was only superficial, like a breeze may stir dead, fallen leaves, making them shift and swirl but never able to bring back to life what has already perished.

And whatever existed between us was long dead.

'I should never have left,' she whispered.

But you did.

I wanted to shout these words at her, to scream and cry and let her know just what her abandonment had done to me. But something had dampened that rage inside me, like rain upon firewood, no longer able to catch light.

So instead, I stared at the wall and said nothing at all.

I heard Penelope swallow before continuing, 'I thought I was protecting you by staying away. I was so afraid of you being hurt again . . . because of me.'

I kept my focus ahead, hating the knot thickening in my throat.

'I am sorry, Melantho.'

How long had I waited to hear those words from her?

A part of me ached to accept them, to reach out across the void between us, as if in doing so I could somehow reach through time and grasp a piece of the girl I had once been, allowing myself to glimpse what it had felt like when the world was warm and safe and kind . . .

But that world had been a lie. It had never existed, it never would. Not for me, anyway.

And though Penelope's apology had once been all I longed for, I knew now it was not enough, no matter how deeply she meant it, or how much I wanted it to be. Those three words could not change what had happened, could not change what I was.

I sensed Penelope waiting for my reply, watching the thoughts battle across my face. I had never been able to mask my emotions, not like her.

'May I be excused now, mistress?' I asked flatly.

I felt Penelope go very still, as if my words had frozen inside her.

'You know you do not have to ask that, not with me.'

I tried to ignore how wounded she sounded as I continued staring at the wall. Waiting.

After a long pause Penelope finally turned away.

'You may be excused,' she whispered into the shadows.

I nodded once and walked out of the room, forcing myself not to look back.

12

Tension choked the palace like a noose, pulling tighter by the second.

The previous day's jubilant atmosphere had withered in the morning sun, leaving behind a dryness in the air, one that cracked and strained beneath the crumbling cordiality.

I stood in the entertaining hall, a jug of wine balanced in my arms, watching the suitors attempt awkward conversation. They were growing restless, the impending decision weighing heavy on their delicate egos. Only one would claim Helen's hand today. Only one would be victorious. I glanced around at the sea of proud faces, wondering how many of these men had ever tasted defeat before. I doubted the bitter aftertaste would sit well with them.

Amongst the crowd I spied Agamemnon and felt my insides grow cold. Shrinking further into the shadows, I watched as the King of Mycenae strode across the room. As he drew closer, I noticed the slight limp he was so desperately trying to hide. I held my satisfaction tight inside me.

I did not regret my actions. I was glad I had made Agamemnon bleed, made him suffer the pain he so carelessly inflicted upon my kind. That was worth any price.

I only prayed the wound would scar, so whenever he looked upon that slice of puckered, pale flesh, he might think of me – the slave he could not break.

Beside Agamemnon was a thickly built man who I assumed must be his brother, Menelaus. He had a shock of flaming hair, a more vibrant red than my own, and an easy smile that counterbalanced Agamemnon's near-constant sneer.

My gaze then drifted to the dais where Tyndareus' throne remained empty. He had not been seen all morning, and the suitors' growing impatience was as oppressive as the heat sticking to the air.

I shifted my jug on to my other hip, wishing someone would accept a cup of wine so I could empty some of its contents. But nobody was drinking today.

A bad sign.

'They are all armed,' Callias murmured to me, his face pinched with worry.

I nodded. 'At the first sign of violence, we run. All right?'

His throat bobbed. 'All right.'

At that moment, the King of Sparta strode through the crowd, nodding greetings to his gathered guests whilst pointedly ignoring the hostility itching between them. His sons followed close behind and, in their wake, the women trundled in single file. Only Leda's face was bare; the other two were hidden behind rippling veils.

I recognized Penelope instantly.

I knew the cadence of her steps, the proudness of her spine, the elegant yet assured way her body moved, like water slipping over stone. Everything about her felt familiar, and yet she had never seemed more distant to me than in that moment, gliding through a sea of ravenous eyes.

As the Spartan royals ascended the dais, I noticed a shadow stealing into the room. The other suitors seemed oblivious to this late entry, but their kind were unversed in the art of being unnoticed. Peering closer, I caught the smirking eyes of the latecomer. Instead of brushing his attention over me, as everyone else did with us slaves, the Prince of Ithaca flashed me a conspiratorial wink. Odysseus then turned his attention to the dais, his lips quirking as if he were enjoying a joke with himself.

'Guests, friends, I hope you all had a restful slumber and that you will accept my apologies for the delay. I was handling a few . . . *pressing matters* in preparation for the impending betrothal,' Tyndareus announced. He appeared lighter this morning, the cloud that had followed him yesterday seemingly dissipated.

My gaze drifted back to Penelope. I found myself flexing my bandaged hand, the remnants of last night's tension lingering inside me. Looking at her now, so regal and remote, it seemed unfathomable – that closeness we had shared. The girl on the dais was not the same one who had knelt before me, bathing my wounds and whispering her heartbroken apologies.

Did that version of her even truly exist?

My attention then caught on Penelope's index finger methodically scratching at her thumb's nail bed, tearing the loose skin. She always did that when she was nervous, and the familiar habit made something loosen inside me. She felt like *my* Penelope again.

No, *no*. Not my Penelope.

She was not *my* anything.

I tried to summon my shield of anger, focusing on the princess' elegant robes, her expensive jewellery, her proud posture, reminding myself how small it made me feel, how meaningless.

She is not like you, and she never will be.

'Before we begin with the proceedings, I must firstly request something of you all,' Tyndareus continued. His words were like stones cast into a still lake, causing pockets of conversation to ripple outwards. He held up a hand to silence his audience. 'It has become apparent that certain *tensions* have arisen in anticipation of the decision being made today. To avoid any unwanted repercussions, I have taken Prince Odysseus' wise counsel and decided that any man wishing to be considered for Helen's hand must first swear an oath. This oath shall state that every hopeful suitor will respect Helen's marriage and will do everything in their power to protect it. This vow will be watched over by golden-throned Hera, Goddess of Marriage, and cloud-gatherer Zeus, Guardian of Oaths. Any who break it will face their divine wrath.'

Murmurs ricocheted through the room, eyes cutting to where Odysseus stood a little apart from the crowd with his arms indolently folded.

'How do we know this isn't one of Odysseus' ploys to best us?' a voice piped up.

'Because I have no interest in what you seek.' I could not make out Odysseus' face amongst the sea of turned heads, but I could hear his smirk in the curl of his words.

'Then why are you here?' came the thunderous voice of Ajax.

'I have made my desires clear to the king,' Odysseus replied.

Eyes narrowed on Tyndareus, who cleared his throat with a nod. 'In return for Odysseus' counsel, I have agreed to give my niece as his bride.'

I stared at Penelope, but she remained as motionless as a statue.

A strange satisfaction swelled inside me, knowing she had played these men so perfectly, without them even realizing she was part of their game. Yet, beneath that satisfaction, something tugged, like cords threaded around my ribs, pulling tight.

Men were slapping Odysseus on the back, shaking his hand. On the dais, Penelope still had not moved an inch, though I noticed her thumb was now bleeding, a crimson crescent moon spreading along her nail bed.

'I have a final suggestion, if you will hear it, Tyndareus?' Odysseus announced.

'Very well. The floor is yours, Prince of Ithaca.'

'I believe we should make Helen choose her husband.' Odysseus smiled at the shocked reactions, forging ahead in the silence he had created. 'After all, it is Helen who we are here for. Is it not? She is the daughter of mighty Zeus; his divinity runs in her veins. If she chooses her husband freely, then every man in this room shall know the decision is a fair one and it will not plant any malcontent.'

Tyndareus made a show of considering Odysseus' words as if this were the first time he was hearing them. I wondered if anyone else bought the act.

'Very well. We shall let Helen choose her fate. As a child of Zeus, I believe she is entitled to do so.' Tyndareus nodded, clearly taking pleasure in painting himself as a fair, benevolent king. 'Are there any objections to these conditions?'

At first, there were many. Most seemed reluctant to take the oath, unwilling to indebt themselves to another man, but Odysseus soon talked the room round. The Prince of Ithaca had a way with words, like a running stream, gentle and flowing yet determined in its destination, its currents gradually weathering all obstacles in its path. He played to the men's honour, to their glory, and they devoured his rhetoric, purpose gleaming in their eyes.

After the debates were finally settled, a bull was brought in for the sacrifice. It seemed an awful waste as I watched Tyndareus slit the poor creature's throat, its lifeblood sweating on to the stone floors for the mere purpose of assuaging the men's insufferable egos.

'Odysseus, you may do the honours,' Tyndareus declared once prayers to the Gods had been offered.

The Prince of Ithaca held up his palms. 'Thank you, but there is no need, as I am no longer a prospective suitor for Helen.'

The amity that had settled grew taut as the men turned on Odysseus. His smile was slippery around his lips, his eyes sharp as he tried to think of a way out of this predicament.

Eventually, Odysseus seemed to accept there was no escape. He gave an easy laugh as he walked forward, as if this were all a joke to him. Though, even from across the room, I noticed the tightness of his jaw.

Tyndareus held out a bowl filled with the dead beast's blood, and Odysseus dipped his hands inside.

'I swear this oath to you, Tyndareus, to defend Helen's marriage, whomever she chooses here today.' His words rang heavy and solemn throughout the room.

The other men followed suit.

The oaths took the rest of the morning, and I watched the sun stalk its way towards Callias and me, until we were standing in a direct pillar of scalding light.

Finally, the time came when Helen was to make her decision.

It felt as if the palace itself were holding its breath, the walls leaning closer to listen as the veiled girl stepped forward, robes rippling around her feet.

As I watched her, I wondered what she must make of all this. All these men gathered for her, for the rumoured beauty that rivalled the Gods'. Did she enjoy the attention? Did she loathe it? I tried to recall what Penelope had told me of Helen.

She used to relish the fuss, she had said once. *Until Theseus.*

What happened?

He stole her. Took her far away. He wanted her as his bride. She was only a child. Castor and Polydeuces were the ones who brought her back . . . She was different after that. Quieter. She never speaks of what happened. Not even to Clytemnestra.

'Well, daughter? Who is it to be?' Tyndareus prompted.

When Helen spoke, her voice glowed like sunlit marble, warm and strong.

'Menelaus,' she announced clearly. 'I choose Menelaus.'

13

'You stink worse than usual.'

My brother looked up from where he had been busy shovelling manure in the dusky horse pen. His face was tired, but his eyes shone when he saw me.

'Careful, now, sister. If you keep talking so sweet, I'll have to come give you a big hug and ruin those fancy clothes of yours.' He grinned, eyeing me with a low, sarcastic whistle. 'Castor sure keeps you well, doesn't he?'

'Castor has new toys to play with now,' I muttered.

'You even *sound* fancier,' Melanthius said as he set his shovel aside. I rolled my eyes. 'It's good to see you, Mel. It's been too long.'

I pretended not to hear the dip of emotion in his voice, moving to lean against the wall of the pen. Watery grey light filtered in behind me, illuminating the muck-stained floor. I did not know how my brother endured the stench day after day.

'I got your message,' I said. 'What's so urgent?'

'How'd you get away from the palace?'

'I volunteered to bring some leftover vegetables for the horses.'

'You're back on kitchen duty?'

I smiled tightly. 'Like I said, Castor has new playthings. And the kitchens needed extra help with all the suitors.'

'So, nobody was suspicious?'

'No.' I waved a hand. 'Everyone's too preoccupied with news of Helen's betrothal, anyway. She made her decision this morning.'

'Did you tell anyone we were meeting?'

I shook my head. 'What's up with you?'

Melanthius opened his mouth to reply, but his eyes caught on my bandaged hand. His gaze then travelled down to my legs and the fresh scabs crisscrossing over my knees.

'What's that?'

'It's nothing,' I said, pushing off the wall. 'Tell me what's wrong.'

He stared at me for a long moment. I knew he was debating whether to press me on my injuries, but neither of us had ever been very good at talking about our wounds. Thankfully, he relented and grabbed my arm, pulling me further into the stables.

When he spoke again, his voice was a sharp, urgent whisper. 'What if I told you we could leave?'

'What do you mean?'

'We're planning an escape. On the day of the joint wedding, when everyone will be too drunk and distracted to know what's what. We'll get outta here, Mel. We'll finally be *free*.'

Reckless hope flared in his eyes, so bright I found myself instinctively recoiling.

'How would we ever manage that?'

'We've got it all sorted. Don't you worry. There's six of us total. Three of the stable lads, me, you and . . . Melitta.'

'Melitta?'

'She works in the kitchens.'

I vaguely knew the girl – small and pretty, with round, freckled cheeks.

'Let me guess.' I sighed. 'You're in love with her?'

'I am, Mel. I really am.'

'You said that about the last one,' I pointed out. 'And the one before that.'

'Melitta is different.' A giddy smile spread across Melanthius' face. 'She's the one. I *know* she is.'

For some reason, his happiness only made the dread curdle thicker in my gut.

'Trying to run away is madness. You could die. Or worse.'

'It's worth the risk,' he insisted. 'Melitta is worth the risk.'

I rolled my eyes. 'You'll change your mind about her. You always do.'

'No, I won't, Mel. Not this time.'

There was something in Melanthius' expression then, a wisp of fearful hope pressing between his eyes, tightening around his mouth.

'What is it you're not telling me?'

He bit down on his lip. I could not tell if he was fighting another smile or a grimace. 'Melitta is . . . well . . . she's pregnant.'

I stared at him for a moment, stunned.

'It's yours?'

'Course, it is.'

'Are you sure?'

'*Yes.*'

The thought of Melanthius as a father filled me with a rush of fierce joy, but the consequences that came with this news overshadowed the vision. He and Melitta did not have permission to have children – that much was clear. If our masters found out, they could be sold – or worse. And Melanthius was only fifteen. I knew women were expected to carry babes at this age, yet it seemed so young to me. When I looked at my brother, I still saw the little boy who had tugged at my curls and tried to eat dirt just to make me laugh.

'Congratulations,' I finally managed, reaching for him. He cocooned my hands in his warm, rough palms.

'I want our child to be born free, Mel. I want to give them a better life than we ever had. I want Melitta to have a better life.' Purpose burnt in his voice. 'She deserves it. So does our baby.'

'So do you,' I whispered.

'And you.' He squeezed my hands. 'You'll be an aunt.'

'An aunt,' I echoed. It frightened me how much I liked the sound of it.

Melanthius hesitated, glancing at the shadows. 'Do you . . . think I should tell Dolios?'

'Why bother?'

'I just think he should know.' Melanthius' lips twisted slightly. 'He'll be the baby's grandfather, after all.'

'Dolios is *no* relative of ours,' I hissed. 'He's just a man who was once allowed to bed another slave because of good behaviour. That's all.'

'Mel . . .'

'*What?*'

Melanthius' gaze filled with a sickening swirl of love and pity. 'What happened to Mama . . . it weren't his fault. You know that.'

'We're not having this conversation. Not again.' I tugged my hands free from his suffocating grasp. 'Don't tell Dolios anything. He'll only alert our masters.'

Melanthius winced, then sighed. 'Fine.'

I stared into the shadows, letting the reality of Melanthius' news settle and take root.

An aunt . . .

'I hope you know I'm going to spoil your kid rotten,' I murmured.

My brother grinned at that. 'I guessed as much.'

'I'll keep them up far too late telling them stories and feeding them treats.'

'Oh Gods, you're gonna make them a nightmare. Just like you were.'

We laughed, allowing ourselves to indulge in this vision of the future, however distant and unreachable it felt.

'So, will you?' Melanthius whispered, words prickling with an excitement I could not fully give myself over to. 'Come with us?'

I hesitated, my focus caught by the clopping of hooves outside and a distant shout from another stable boy.

'Think it over,' Melanthius insisted, placing a hand on my shoulder. 'There's still three days till the wedding. So, just . . . take your time. All right?'

I shook my head, fear and adrenaline bubbling up into a quivering smile.

'I don't need to. I know what I want.'

14

As dawn's rosy fingertips brushed the sky, we were hauled out of bed and set to work.

After three gruelling days of preparation, it was finally the *Gamos*, the day of the wedding ceremony.

I was back in the kitchens, surrounded by the familiar faces of my childhood. It was pure chaos prepping the wedding feast, bodies scrambling to and fro, tempers bubbling over like the pots on the fire, all whilst the king's attendants barked endless orders.

Just one more day of this life, and then tomorrow . . . tomorrow. Only the Fates knew what it would bring.

'Melantho?'

I jerked my head upwards, nearly slicing my finger instead of the vegetables in front of me.

'W-what?' I blinked, realizing Callias was standing beside me, his brows furrowed. 'What did you say?'

'I said: I've been put on wine prep.' He gave me a pointed look.

'Oh.' I nodded slowly. 'That's . . . good.'

It was better than good; it was exactly as our plan had intended. With Callias on wine duty, he could ensure the stock was double its usual strength – triple, even. And the drunker our masters were, the easier it would be for us to slip away unnoticed that night.

Callias slunk closer. 'Are you all right? You seem . . . tense.'

'I'm fine.'

He braced a hand on the worktop and leant into me, the turmoil of the kitchens drowning out his next words. 'Are you sure you still want to do this?'

It was a question I had turned over and over in my mind the past few nights. But each time, no matter how frightening my thoughts became, my answer remained the same.

'Yes.'

'But have you really thought this through? Have you considered everything that could go wrong?' Callias pressed, a rare shade of seriousness darkening his voice. 'Because death is hardly the worst outcome. Even if you *do* manage it, what awaits you in those mountains . . . I'm only saying this because I care for you—'

'*Stop*. Just stop it. I've made up my mind.'

'Very well,' Callias sighed, pulling away. 'You know I will still help you, in any way that I can.'

I nodded vaguely, too distracted by those icy claws of fear sinking into me, threatening to shred what little hope I clung to.

I knew Callias thought our plan foolish; he'd said as much when I first asked him to come with us. I had dismissed his doubts then, choosing to see them as cowardice. But now, they felt far more real, far harder to ignore.

Perhaps he was right. Perhaps this *was* madness . . .

'Before I forget, I have something for you. From the princess.'

My mind snapped back to Callias. 'The princess?'

'Penelope,' he clarified. 'She found me when I was leaving Castor's chamber this morning. She was looking for you. Asked me to give you this.'

I stared at the sprig in his hand. It had a long green stem, with feathered leaves, and little white flowers crowded at one end.

'Yarrow,' I murmured, taking it from him.

'She said it would help with your wound.' Callias stared at my bandaged hand, a crease pressing between his brows. 'Melantho . . . you should've told me what happened with Agamemnon.'

A bolt of anger shot through me.

'She had no right to tell you,' I snapped. 'And I don't need this.'

'It might help—'

'I don't need her help. I made that very clear. I don't need anything from *her*.'

Callias' brows rose. 'Fine. Just toss it away, then.'

'No.'

'No?'

I shouldered past Callias, crumpling the sprig in my fist.

'Melantho?' he called after me as I pushed my way through the crowded kitchen. 'Where are you going?'

'To tell her myself.'

Fury fuelled my every step.

Thankfully, the palace was swarming with busy slaves, so nobody questioned me as I stormed my way to Penelope's chamber.

'I need to see the princess,' I told the queen's handmaids hovering outside her door.

Their chatter fell silent as they eyed me suspiciously.

'Why?' one asked.

'A private matter,' I said.

'Princess Penelope isn't allowing any visitors.'

'She won't even let *us* in. Says she doesn't need our help,' another added sourly.

'Well, I *need* to see her,' I said, pushing past them.

'You can't go in there!' a third cried.

The handmaids' squawks faded as I strode inside, the door swinging firmly shut behind me. I balled the yarrow into my fist as I marched forward, fury coating my tongue with acidic words I was ready to let fly. But when I looked up, I froze.

A goddess stood in Penelope's chamber, radiant and golden.

She wore the most beautiful gown I had ever seen, a yellow so rich it looked as if it had been woven from pure sunlight. Jewels glittered at her wrist and neck, a gold diadem dripping down her forehead, glinting in the light. Her hair had been cut short, the sheer edges brushing her jaw, leaving the elegant slope of her neck bare.

'Melantho.' Penelope stared at me, my name catching on her lips.

I blinked, forcing myself to focus.

'You . . . you gave me this,' I said, holding out the sprig of yarrow. The accusation did not come out as I intended. My anger sounded blunted, its edges dulled to a thick lump in my throat.

Penelope regarded the crumpled plant in my hand, brows slightly raised. 'I did.'

'*Why?*'

'For your wound,' she replied simply. But it was *never* that simple. Not between us.

'Well, I didn't ask you for it.'

Penelope's head tilted to the side as she studied me. I hated it when she looked at me like that, as if she were stripping my thoughts bare.

'I don't *need* it,' I continued, motioning to her with a petulant wave of my hand. 'I don't need anything from *you*.'

'Very well.'

Slowly, Penelope approached me. The gold bands on her wrist tinkled as she reached out to take the yarrow. I refused to meet her gaze as I dumped it into her palm, yet I could still *smell* her, that decadent perfume clogging my nose, full of rich spices I didn't know the names of.

She retreated, her gown whispering around her feet as if secrets were trapped within its folds. She really did look like a goddess, or the closest thing to divinity I had ever seen. I longed to move closer, to smell that rich, spiced scent again . . .

'Is that all?' she asked as she set the yarrow down on the far table.

Leave, Melantho, I ordered myself. *You've done what you came to do. Now go.*

'You cut your hair,' I blurted out.

Penelope absently brushed the shorn ends. 'It is customary for brides to offer their hair to Artemis on the eve of their wedding. It marks the end of childhood.'

'Oh.'

She stared at me, lips slightly parted as if she wanted to say more. But then she turned away, silently assessing the brooches scattered on the table before her. She picked one up, turning it over in her hands before setting it down for another.

'Why are the handmaids outside?' I heard myself ask.

Penelope turned back to me with a small gold brooch in her hands and began fastening it at her shoulder.

'Are they still upset about that? I already told them I can dress myself. I am not a child.' I noted the slight tightness in her tone. 'Well, I *would* be able to, if only I could . . .'

She trailed off, fumbling with the brooch. I had watched Penelope's hands weave threads with such unearthly steadiness, never once faltering. But now, she was struggling to fasten a simple clasp.

The realization hit me abruptly – she was *nervous*.

'Stop, stop. You're going to break it.' I sighed irritably, then strode towards her. 'Give it here.'

Penelope blinked at me, then carefully placed the brooch in my uninjured palm. I could feel her eyes on my face, searching for answers to unspoken questions. I ignored her, focusing instead on securing the brooch at her shoulder, a simple task I had done a thousand times before for Castor.

So why did this feel so *different*?

When the clasp slotted into place, I finally met her gaze. The seconds passed, thick and heavy, thudding between us like a heartbeat. Then, Penelope glanced down at herself.

'This one isn't right. The other one would be better—'

'Penelope. It's fine. You look . . .' I swallowed. 'Fine.'

'I look *fine*?' There was a shade of amusement in her voice. 'Well, isn't Odysseus lucky, then.'

'Odysseus will be . . . He'll be pleased with you.'

She tried to smile, but the corners flickered and shrank like a dying flame. She began fiddling with the brooch again, her eyes distant.

'Are you all right?' I asked before I could stop myself.

'The celebrations will be wonderful; my uncle has spared no expense. I suppose that is unsurprising, though. It is not every day there is a double royal wedding.' Penelope spoke in that empty, performative voice I had heard her use countless times around others. But never with me.

I held her gaze. 'You didn't answer my question.'

She inhaled slowly, then turned back to inspect the brooches once again.

'My whole life has been building up to this moment,' she murmured. 'Ever since I can remember, I have known this was what I was destined for. To be married. To be a wife . . . And so I spent my whole life trying to be in control of it, to guide the threads of Fate as best I could.'

'And you did. Your plan worked.'

'I know.' Her back was turned to me, so I could only read the tight lines of her shoulders. 'I just thought . . . I don't know . . . I suppose I thought if I was in control of the situation, it would make me feel better when the time came.'

'But you don't?'

Penelope bowed her head for a moment, then glanced over her shoulder at me, her eyes unbearably soft.

'I didn't mean to offend you, with the yarrow,' she said. 'I thought it would help.'

The sharp change in conversation threw me, and I suddenly felt ashamed for having stormed in there over something as ridiculous as a plant. Today of all days.

But it was never about the yarrow. The truth danced dizzyingly on my lips.

'I shouldn't have disturbed you,' I said instead.

Penelope turned to face me fully and smiled that quiet, secretive smile of hers. 'I'm glad you did, all the same.'

'Why?'

She tilted her head, considering her reply. 'You always seem to calm me down. Even when we were children. You make my mind . . . quieter.'

I laughed, the abrupt sound surprising us both. A rush of embarrassment prickled over me, but when I glanced at Penelope, her eyes were gleaming with a brightness I had not seen since that summer we had shared, long ago.

Her smiled widened. 'That is amusing to you?'

'I just don't believe anyone would ever describe me as a "calming" child. I was so . . . *chaotic*.'

'I know.' She chuckled softly. 'But I suppose I found calmness in your chaos. It was why I enjoyed your company so much.'

I hated the effect her words had on me, my traitorous heart stumbling over itself.

'I always thought it was out of pity – that you spent time with me.' The thought somehow found its way on to my lips, and I instantly regretted how pitiful it sounded aloud.

Penelope's smile vanished. 'Why would you think that?'

'Because I wasn't your friend, remember?' I knew the question was petty, but a part of me felt compelled to say it, to give voice to this wound I had carried for so long, that refused ever to heal.

Penelope said nothing for a long while and, within the depths of her silence, I found myself wishing she were not so infuriatingly impossible to read. Even as a child, Penelope had expertly worn this mask of hers, keeping her emotions tucked in close to her heart. Once, I'd believed I had learnt how to slip beneath that guise and see the *real* Penelope, the one whose eyes sparked with mischief and whose cheeks flushed with excitement at a new challenge. But now, I wondered if that had been just another performance.

It was so hard to tell, sometimes, which Penelope was the *real* one. Did she even know?

'Do you remember our conversation the night we met, when I walked you back to your quarters?' she asked quietly, eyes fixed on some distant spot.

'Only a little,' I lied.

'You made me laugh. I had not laughed since the night my mother died.'

She let the weight of her confession hang between us. In the stillness, I thought of all the times she had laughed that summer. I had believed myself foolish, back then, for wondering if Penelope only laughed like that for me. But perhaps it was not such a ridiculous thought after all.

Something twisted inside me, like sun-warmed vines constricting round my heart.

'I lied that day, to my aunt.' She spoke the same way she had cleaned my wounds the night before – so carefully gentle, so desperate not to inflict any further pain. 'You were my friend, Melantho. Perhaps not a friend I deserved, but one that I cherished, all the same. I only wish I had treated you better.'

We stared at one another, the silence between us like a great, yawning precipice we teetered at the edge of. I felt myself leaning closer.

'Melantho, I must tell you something.'

'What?' I gulped out the word, suddenly breathless.

'I—'

The door burst open then, and the queen's handmaids swarmed inside like an angry cloud of bees, shattering the moment.

'Mistress, I apologize for the intrusion, but Queen Leda is *insisting*!'

'The ceremony begins imminently, mistress!'

'We must ensure you are perfect for Master Odysseus, mistress!'

I stared at Penelope's face, watching that vulnerability recede like waves from a riverbank, leaving the cool stones beneath. It was Penelope the Princess staring at me now, her mask firmly back in place.

'Very well,' she said to them, before turning back to me. 'May we speak tomorrow? Before the gift-giving ceremony.'

I nodded numbly. 'Tomorrow.'

'It must be before the gift-giving,' Penelope clarified as the handmaids bustled around her, poking and prodding. 'I shall see you then. Goodbye, Melantho.'

'Goodbye, Penelope.'

15

The celebrations began with a grand procession through the streets of Sparta.

We slaves were not permitted to join these festivities, of course. We were to prepare the feast that awaited the guests when they returned, flush-faced and full of merriment.

My afternoon was spent carrying plates up and down the long tables, doing everything in my power to avoid Agamemnon. The food smelt divine: roasted wild boar, spiced lamb, salted fish, thick stews wafting notes of garlic and leek. My stomach gnawed at me as I watched the guests delight in every mouthful. Tyndareus had clearly wanted to flaunt his wealth; there were even some dishes I had never seen before – long, snake-like fish that glistened on the plate, and strange, rubbery creatures with eight wiggling legs.

Throughout the feast, I found my eyes regularly drifting to Penelope. She sat with the women on the opposite side of the room to the men. She and Helen had remained covered, as was customary, lifting tiny morsels of food beneath their veils as they spoke in hushed tones. Meanwhile, the men were as raucous as ever, Menelaus and Odysseus reigning proudly over them – the victors of the day. It was clear they both relished the attention.

At the end of the feasting, the two brides were brought forward by Tyndareus to their waiting husbands. One at a time, the king unveiled them, whilst the guests roared their approval.

Penelope was the first, and, when that thin material rippled away, I saw a flash of fear spark across her face, making my fingers tighten around the plate I carried.

The Prince of Ithaca's grin was as radiant as the torches burning behind him. He took Penelope's hands and she managed a smile, but all I could think was how small her palms looked in his.

Then, it was Helen's turn, and the room fell still, breaths held, eyes widening.

An audible gasp swept through the crowd as we beheld the famed Princess of Sparta. She was like sunlight incarnate, shining and radiant, brightening the room with her golden presence. Helen's hair was the palest shade I had ever seen, framing two honey-brown eyes that glowed, quietly assessing her new husband. Menelaus took her hand tentatively, as if afraid she might shatter beneath his large, clumsy fingers. Helen seemed to like his awkward gentleness, and she smiled, a slow, devastatingly beautiful smile that had her audience erupting into cheers.

After the unveiling, the music began, and tables were pushed aside so people could dance. I shrank to the shadowy corners of the room, watching the guests as they laughed and twirled and drank. Their happiness felt so strange to me, sparkling and distant, like stars swirling in the night sky. Unreachable.

Despite Helen's captivating presence, my eyes followed Penelope. She was sitting to one side, chatting quietly with her new husband. But then Odysseus rose and led her into the crowd of blurring bodies. Penelope smiled as Odysseus began spinning her round the room, faster and faster until I heard her laugh echoing through all the hollow spaces inside me.

As I watched them, a thought nagged at me – what did Penelope want to tell me tomorrow?

And why did it bother me so much that I would never find out?

'Not long now,' Callias whispered as he sidled up to me. 'They're all too drunk to remember their own names.'

'Mm.' I nodded vaguely.

I felt Callias' eyes on me, then he followed my gaze to Penelope. Her face was flushed, hair a little unruly. I had never seen her so vibrant. She and Odysseus looked gloriously happy, limned by torchlight, glowing like young gods.

'Ah,' Callias murmured. 'Eros' arrow burns so brutally sweet, does it not?'

I flinched, snapping my attention away. 'What? No, it's not . . . I'm not—'

He chuckled. 'I didn't think he'd be your type.'

I frowned, following Callias' gaze back to Odysseus.

'The Prince of Ithaca isn't *bad*-looking, I suppose. He's got a nice smile on him,' he mused. 'They seem to make a decent pair.'

'He looks more like her father,' I muttered.

'Don't all grooms? I wonder if Penelope is excited for her wedding night or afraid. What do you think?'

'I don't care,' I said, turning away from the twirling couple.

'Melantho.' Callias touched my wrist, his voice sobering. 'There's still time to change your mind. You don't have to do this.'

He was wrong. I *did* have to. I had to get away from this prison. I had to know what freedom tasted like. I had to take control of my life, even if it were only to end it – at least it would be *my* choice.

And there was power in that, even in defeat.

'I've made my decision,' I said.

Without warning, Callias leant forward and kissed me. It wasn't the first time he had done such a thing, for Castor often made us share his bed together, but neither was the kiss romantic. The tenderness between Callias and I was hard to describe, not driven by desire or passion, yet something more intimate than friendship.

'Look at that – I can still make you blush,' Callias murmured with a smile, brushing my cheek. 'I'll miss you, my friend.'

'Take care of yourself,' I said thickly, taking his hand.

'No, no, darling. I make *others* take care of *me*.' He grinned fiendishly.

'Now, go. I'll make sure everyone's cups stay full. They'll be so blind drunk they'll need days to sleep it off.'

I kissed his hand, unwilling to let go. 'Thank you. For everything.'

'Go,' he urged, brushing off my emotion with a wink. 'Go taste freedom for the both of us.'

Since childhood, I had been taught to be invisible, to shrink myself down to an undetectable size.

I used to loathe it, being forced to relegate myself to the shadows, to the corners of existence. But that night, as I hurried from the palace, I relished slipping through the world unseen.

The darkening skies looked heavy and sombre as I made my way to the stables, mottled clouds stretching across them like cracked clay. Ahead, the mountains stood as silent and eternal as a tomb. Soon we would be ascending those peaks, facing whatever lurked within them. We'd all heard the stories, of the wolves and monsters that hunted there. I had once thought they were mere fiction, meant to quell any who dared to do what we were attempting. But now, I was no longer so certain.

'Melanthius?' I whispered as I entered the stables' furthest pen.

Only silence greeted me, and I felt a sickening panic bleed through my gut.

'Melanthius? *Melanthius!*'

'*Shh.* I'm here, I'm here.' My brother's outline appeared in the darkness.

I smacked his arm. 'Don't scare me like that.'

'Don't talk so loud,' he hissed back. 'You sure nobody saw you leave?'

'I'm sure. Everyone's too drunk to see much at all.'

A tall, skinny boy stepped forward then. He looked a little older than us, with shaggy blond hair falling over his eyes.

'This is Xanthias,' my brother introduced him, then motioned to the small shadow pressed at his side. 'And Melitta.'

'I thought there were going to be more of us?' I asked.

Melanthius hesitated. 'Some pulled out.'

'Cowards,' Xanthias spat.

'They won't rat on us, will they?' I asked.

'Nah, they're cowards but they ain't no rats,' Xanthias muttered. 'Come on. We need to get moving.'

Xanthias and my brother led the horses outside: two giant, dark stallions, the largest I had ever seen. As I went to follow them, a small hand landed on my arm.

'I am happy to finally meet you,' Melitta whispered. I could not place her accent, halting yet sweetly melodic. 'Melanthius talks a lot about you.'

Through the darkness, I could only just make out her face – pretty and round, with wide, bright eyes. I noted the way her hand rested protectively over her slightly swollen stomach and was surprised by the sudden rush of emotion clogging my throat.

'Come,' Melitta gently urged. 'They're waiting for us.'

We hurried outside to where my brother and Xanthias were checking over the horses.

'They're *huge*,' I murmured.

'I thought about using the old mares the king never rides,' Melanthius said. 'But he's gonna discover we're gone no matter which beasts we take. So, we might as well take the fastest mounts to get us to the mountains, then we go on foot.'

'We're leaving the horses behind?'

'They can't handle it up on the mountains,' Xanthias answered me. 'Too steep.'

'That's why we need to move fast,' Melanthius reiterated. 'Get as far away as we can before anyone notices we're gone.'

'Hopefully that won't be until late morning at the earliest.' I hid my fear behind a shaky grin. 'Callias made sure the wine was strong enough to knock out an ox.'

The last dregs of daylight drained away as we made our escape. Melitta rode with Melanthius, whilst I was with Xanthias. The stallions galloped over the dry earth, thundering hooves falling into rhythm with my racing heart. The wind screeched in my ears, ripping at my hair and clothes with invisible claws. I buried my face into Xanthias' bony back, battling the near-constant fear that I was about to fall to my death.

After a time, my legs began to ache, my arms sore from where I had been gripping Xanthias so tightly. When I felt I could last no longer, the horses finally slowed. We were at the base of the mountains now, jagged peaks etched in stark moonlight.

'We'll go as far as the horses can manage,' Melanthius told us, pushing ahead.

A new kind of terror seized me as we ascended the steep mountain path. Two or three times our horse stumbled, struggling to find purchase on the loose, rocky terrain. Eventually, the beast refused to move, obstinately ignoring Xanthias' barked commands.

'Let's leave them here,' my brother called as he dismounted. 'We'll continue on foot.'

My thighs were on fire, but adrenaline numbed the pain as we broke into a run, scrambling further up the mountain. Night had fully fallen now, Nyx's darkness devouring all detail from the world, turning our surroundings into a shapeless, heavy mass. I could just make out the trees crowding close, their spindly branches like veins sparking across the moon-dipped sky. In the distance, a wolf howled. We all pretended we had not heard it.

Xanthias led the way, though I questioned if he truly knew where he was going. Our aim was to walk until we reached the sea, then we would find a way to pay for safe passage to take us far away from this land. A few days ago, the vagueness of this plan had been masked by the thrilling glow of possibility. Now, it dawned on me how fragile it truly was.

But there was no turning back now.

We remained silent as we pushed on. The trees grew thin around us and the path ever steeper, stretching out into treacherous expanses of loose stone. My flimsy sandals were utterly useless, and I fell over twice, my feet battered and bruised.

'Wait.' My brother's voice made me jump. It was the first anyone had spoken in a long while.

I glanced back at him, sweat dripping down my temples. 'What is it?'

'Do you hear that?' he whispered. 'Listen.'

I frowned. All I could make out was the night chorus of cicadas, and my own ragged breaths. But then, I heard it. A distant rumbling, like a storm rolling in from the horizon.

'What is that?' Melitta breathed.

'Horses,' Melathius and I said at the same time.

'We gotta move. *Fast*,' Xanthias hissed.

Panic sharpened my senses as we raced through the trees, praying we could lose our hunters on the winding mountain trails. But that thunder of hooves was closer now, accompanied by another sound, one that stilled the very blood in my veins.

Barking.

They had hounds on our scent.

A wild fear pounded through me, eclipsing my mind. I could no longer feel my screaming muscles or butchered feet, or even hear my own breath sawing out of my chest. All I could focus on, all that *mattered*, was that darkness ahead, and the freedom that lay beyond it.

We just had to keep going . . .

Just keep going . . .

A yelp sounded from behind, followed by the clattering of scattered stones. Beside me, I felt Melanthius turn.

'What are you *doing*?'

My brother ignored me, dashing back towards the figure now slumped on the ground. 'Melitta? Are you all right?'

'My ankle,' she gasped.

'*Melanthius*,' I hissed as loudly as I dared.

'I'm not leaving her. Go. We'll catch up.'

'I can't leave *you*.'

'*Go, Melantho!*' he cried, the raw, desperate fear in his voice spurring me onwards.

Ahead of me, I could just make out Xanthias scrambling through the trees. I focused on following his shadow, pushing my way through the disorientating darkness.

Just keep going.

A growl ripped open the night, followed by Xanthias crying out in pain. A moment later, an arm shot out from the blackness, locking around my stomach and hauling me off my feet. I kicked and clawed at my attacker, throwing my head back so that my skull collided with his face. There was a loud *crunching* sound as I was dropped to the floor, my forehead bashing against a rock, breath fleeing my lungs.

Something warm dribbled down my face, and I opened my eyes to find the forest spinning around me. With a cry, I began dragging myself forward on my stomach, gasping for air that would not come.

Just.

Keep.

Going.

Someone grabbed my hair as a fist collided with my face, followed swiftly by another.

And then darkness swallowed me whole.

16

I woke to the taste of blood in my mouth.

My face was pressed against something hard and cold. There was a puddle beside me, of what I could not tell.

I groaned, the sound low and harsh, seeming to cleave itself from my very bones. Shackles bit into my wrists as I pushed myself upwards, my entire body screaming in protest.

Blinking, I tried to find my bearings. The room I was in was horribly dank, swept up in shadows and dust and a frightening sense of hopelessness. Behind me, I could feel the rough ridges of a wall.

'You're alive.' The darkness spoke, its small voice not at all how I imagined the Goddess Nyx would sound.

'Who's there?' I managed, the words clunky on my tongue. I sounded drunk.

'Melitta,' came the voice again, and recognition seeped through me, followed by a rush of disappointment.

She had not made it.

Had any of us?

I could hardly recall what had happened in those final moments. My mind was like a shattered mosaic, rattling with so many broken pieces I didn't know how to fit back together. I remembered the panic, the chaos, my heart hammering in my chest as if it might explode . . .

'How long was I out?' It hurt to talk; my whole face throbbed, and there was a sharp sting above my left eyebrow.

'All night,' Melitta replied. Her voice was thin. Defeated. 'I thought you were dead.'

'Not yet,' I muttered, wincing as I shifted to sit more upright. 'The others?'

'They took them to another cell.' I heard her sniffle, trying to fight back tears. 'I told Melanthius this was a foolish idea. *I told him—*'

'He did this for you, for your . . .' I trailed off.

My eyes were slowly adjusting to the dimness, and I could just make out Melitta's outline, the crumpled curve of her body.

'You know what they do to slaves who try to escape, don't you?' She was crying now, the sound seeming to make the darkness feel heavier around us.

I said nothing, waiting for the fear to seize me. The panic.

But all I felt was a horrible, echoing numbness.

Perhaps it was too much for my body to accept, the soul-crushing realization that all my hopes and dreams had just died in my hands.

Perhaps a part of me had always known I would never escape this nightmare.

'I'll tell them it was my idea. I'll say you were forced into it,' I said.

Melitta hiccupped a sob. 'What? Why would you do that?'

'Because you have something to live for.'

'And you don't?'

I had nothing to say to that.

A screeching noise carved into the room, and I flinched as a rush of light spilt across the floor, illuminating its filthiness.

'Out,' the guard barked.

In the torchlight, I could now see how *awful* Melitta looked, bloodied and broken. I glanced down at myself, realizing I was no better.

We moved gingerly, our bodies stiff and sore, as the guard escorted us to another, larger cell. Here, a firepit painted the grim stone walls in streaks of red and gold. Before the small fire knelt three figures, their heads bowed, hands bound.

Melitta burst into tears at the sight of my brother. His right eye was swollen shut, his throat dappled with bruises. Beside him, Xanthias was slumped forward, his filthy blond hair hanging limp around his face. As I stared at the third hunched figure, my stomach plummeted to my toes...

'Callias?' I gasped. My friend looked up at me, his beautiful face horribly swollen.

The guard struck the back of my legs, and I fell to my knees. He then placed a hand on Melitta's shoulder, forcing her down beside me.

'It's gonna be all right,' Melanthius murmured to Melitta. 'I won't let them hurt you. I swear it.'

The guard left without a word and in the following stillness I felt my heartbeat quicken, the previous numbness swallowed by my rising fear.

'Callias, what happened?' I whispered.

He said nothing, just kept staring at the floor with unseeing eyes.

'I'm so sorry,' I tried again.

'I told you,' he murmured, his voice frighteningly frail. 'I told you it was a foolish plan.'

'Someone ratted us out,' Melanthius said. 'I swear on the Gods, when I find out who it was—'

'What does it matter? It's done. It's over.' The cut on Xanthias' lip split as he spoke, blood streaking down his chin.

'It's not over,' I whispered. 'Not yet.'

Xanthias' gaze slid up to meet mine. There was no fear or dread in his eyes, not even pain. There was just an abject emptiness, echoing and endless. I felt it strike deep in my core.

The door heaved open, and a terrifying figure strode in, flanked by four guards.

The King of Sparta looked exhausted. Dark circles bruised beneath his eyes and the creases lining his face seemed even more pronounced than usual. He scowled, and I noticed there were still traces of last night's wine around his lips.

Anger knotted in my stomach, thick and acidic.

What a *nuisance* we were, to interrupt his revelry.

He let the silence pace around us like a circling beast. The others kept their eyes down, but I met Tyndareus' glare with one of equal fire. I would not shrink from him. What would be the point now?

Between his fingers Tyndareus twirled a long iron rod. He then wordlessly stalked towards the firepit and placed it into the flames with a slight sigh.

'Did you know, Spartans purposefully starve their sons?' he asked. He was staring into the fire as he spoke and the shadows played across his ugly face, toying with his thick web of scars. We knew better than to reply, so we waited for him to continue. 'We feed them so little that they are forced to steal to survive. If they are caught in this act, they are punished.' He twisted the rod, and I watched the triangular tip spear the heart of the flames, glowing white-hot. 'But it is not the stealing we punish them for, rather their failure to steal *successfully*. For their failure demonstrates their inability to outsmart and outmanoeuvre their opponents. It shows they underestimated them, and to underestimate your opponents is to disrespect them. This offence cannot go unpunished. Do you see what I am getting at here?' He turned to us, the fire burning crimson in his eyes. 'I could have almost admired your bravery if you had been successful in your escape. But your little plan was so ill thought out it was simply offensive. No, no, not offensive . . . *Disrespectful.*'

I felt Melitta trembling beside me as Tyndareus began pacing, his footsteps menacingly slow.

'Tell me, do you take your king for a fool? Well, surely you must do if you thought such an idiotic plan could have outwitted me. Though, I suppose I do have *one* thing to thank you for . . .' A smile slashed across his face. 'I've been meaning to test out my new hunting dogs. They are rather remarkable creatures, are they not?'

'Fuck you,' I spat.

To my surprise, the king's smile only widened.

'I take it you're volunteering to go first, then?' he asked as two guards advanced, hauling me forward.

'No, no! Not her! Take me instead! Take—' My brother was silenced by a blow to his temple.

'Do not worry, boy, you will get your chance,' Tyndareus said as he approached the firepit. 'I want you to know I take no pleasure in this. But there is a certain *trust* between master and slave, is there not? And that trust has been broken. So now, actions must be taken to protect my property, and to ensure you remember your place.'

He removed the rod from the fire, the metal singing with a sinister, searing heat. I instinctively recoiled as Tyndareus drew closer, but the guards tightened their hold around my shoulders. One of them knotted my hair in his fist, wrenching my head backwards.

'You will want to hold still for this,' the king warned.

He angled the scorching rod just above my forehead and I stared up at the triangular end, the metal glowing so hot it rippled with veins of gold.

Be brave. My mother's voice sliced through my panic, and I willed it to centre me.

I would not give Tyndareus the satisfaction of my fear. This man had already taken so much from me; I would not let him have this. So, I closed my eyes, forcing my breathing to steady itself, my mind to focus.

Think of a happier place, think of a safe place . . .

I felt the sandy bank of the Eurotas river beneath me, my skin damp and cool, belly aching with laughter . . .

I think this is my favourite day.

'*Stop!*' A cry ripped me from the vision.

My eyes snapped open to see a figure storming in, as if she had been torn straight from my mind.

'Stop this at once,' Penelope commanded. The guards gaped at her, uncertain what to do. She was a princess, after all; they could not simply seize her.

Tyndareus lowered the rod, his anger caged between the harsh lines of his face.

'*Penelope?* What do you think you're doing?'

'I should ask you the same question, uncle.'

Tyndareus scoffed at her impudence. 'These slaves were caught escaping. *I* am carrying out the necessary punishment.'

'They are not your property, not any more,' Penelope shot back. She was fearless, her eyes blazing, face set with a stern resolution I had never seen before. 'You promised these slaves to me as my wedding present. You swore an oath. Thus, they are under *my* control. It is not your right to punish them; it is *mine*.'

Tyndareus laughed, as if this were all some elaborate joke, but at the coldness of Penelope's glare, his amusement soon withered into irritation. 'The gifts have not yet been bestowed. These slaves escaped under *my* ownership, so I shall punish them as I see fit.'

'And then what? You shall present these gifts to Odysseus and me with fresh brands on their foreheads, brands that mark them as deserters? Do you not think my husband would be offended by such a gift?'

'I will not give them as gifts at all,' Tyndareus snapped, his patience a fraying thread pulled tauter with every word. 'They are not worthy.'

'They are *mine*. You swore it on the river Styx.'

'I will give you other slaves, better slaves.'

'I want these ones.'

'Them?' Tyndareus jabbed his rod towards me. '*Look* at them. They are pitiful, disobedient creatures. You are still young, Penelope, and have yet to run a household of your own. So, trust me when I say these slaves will not be worth the trouble.'

Penelope held her uncle's glare, voice quivering with a quiet determination. 'You gave me your word. These are the ones I want.'

I stared at the king and princess, fear still sharp in my veins. Tyndareus sighed, shaking his head as if Penelope were nothing more than a petulant child.

'All the attention of the wedding has gone to your head, girl,' he muttered. 'Very well. You can have the ones I promised you.'

'Unharmed.'

'Yes, yes.' Tyndareus waved her off. 'If you really wish to burden yourself, then fine. You'll be doing me a favour.'

Glancing at the others, I felt a fragile flicker of hope kindle between us.

'But I am keeping the others.' Tyndareus' words were a fist to my gut.

'I will take all of them, uncle. You said yourself they are not worth the trouble. Let me handle—'

'Do *not* command me,' the king snarled. 'You either take the two, or you take none. Decide.'

Something shifted behind Penelope's eyes, darkening them.

'Very well, uncle,' she whispered.

No, no . . .

Tyndareus motioned to his men, and they dutifully dragged Melanthius and me to Penelope's feet. My brother was crying out for Melitta, screaming her name over and over until a guard stuffed a rag down his throat, forcing him to choke on his own silence.

Penelope kept her gaze on the king.

'May I take them away and have them . . . tidied up, uncle?' she asked stiffly. 'They need to be made presentable for the gift-giving ceremony.'

'Once I am finished here. They must first witness the consequences of their actions.'

'Uncle—'

'Do *not* test me again, girl.' The words had a serrated edge to them, so sharp they shocked Penelope into silence. 'Let me make myself very clear – the *only* reason you are not being punished for your insolence is because of your help in catching these deserters.'

I stared incredulously at Penelope, but she refused to meet my gaze.

'You will watch too, niece,' Tyndareus added. 'Now you are a wife, you must learn how to handle your property. Understood?'

Penelope bowed her head. 'Yes, uncle.'

Tyndareus clicked his fingers and two guards hauled Callias forward.

'No!' I cried. 'He's innocent, I swear it! He had no part in this!'

'Do you think you are the first to try to defy me?' Tyndareus asked as he placed the rod back in the fire. 'I know this game, slave, and I know it always requires a rat on the inside. Penelope here discovered yours rather quickly. She's always been a smart one.'

I turned to Penelope. 'What does he mean?'

She said nothing.

'Princess. Help me.' Callias tried to scramble towards her on his knees, but the guards dragged him back. 'I beg of you. Let me serve you. *Please!*'

'Save him,' I cried breathlessly, but Penelope's gaze remained fixed on the wall ahead, face vacant. '*Penelope!* Take him, not me. I'm begging you. He doesn't deserve this. Please, save him—'

A guard grabbed me, his hand smothering my cries as Tyndareus removed the rod from the flames once more.

Seizing Callias by his hair, the king pressed the searing tip into his flesh.

And all I could do was watch as the sound of my friend's screams tore me apart.

17

My blood swirled in the water like crimson puffs of smoke.

I stared down into the bowl, trying to summon the energy to continue cleaning myself, to scrub those ugly remnants of my butchered hopes and dreams from my skin.

Gods forbid I should look unsightly when I was paraded before my new masters.

I wished my brother were with me. I could still hear his screams, those animalistic noises he had made whilst Tyndareus branded Melitta. I could still *smell* her burnt flesh, the stink of it clogging my nostrils, making me gag. I knew my nightmares would reek of it for evermore.

I stared at my reflection in the water, hating every inch of untouched skin that stretched between the swelling and bruises. I should have been with the others, shivering in a cell, my forehead seared with the brand that would claim my face for ever, symbolizing what I was. What I would always be.

But here I was instead, being primped and preened for my new masters.

I pressed my palms into my eyes, hard enough to hurt. I couldn't unsee it. Callias' beautiful face being mutilated by that *monster*. He had never even wanted any part in this doomed plan; he had helped us out of kindness, out of friendship . . .

I flinched when the door opened, knocking the bronze bowl to the floor. Quietly, Penelope stepped into the room, staring at the spilt water now pooling around my feet.

'I brought a change of clothes.' She sounded hesitant, her earlier defiance drained from her body. 'The gift-giving will begin shortly.'

I glared at the wall ahead of me, fisting my hands so she couldn't see them tremble. 'My brother?'

'He is in a nearby chamber. He is being . . . less compliant.'

'He will not go to Ithaca.'

'I was hoping you could speak with him. Convince him to cooperate.'

I turned with a snarl. '*Why* would I do that?'

Penelope stared at me, her gaze tripping over every bruise and cut marring my face.

She seemed to steady herself before replying, 'Melantho, you know the fate that awaits him if he remains here. You do not want that for your brother.'

'*You* do not get to decide what *I* want. Or perhaps you think you do now that you *own* me?'

'It's not like that—'

'No? "They are mine." Those were *your* words.'

She winced. 'I was only saying that to protect you. You must know that.'

'Protect me?' I laughed, the sound ugly and ragged in my throat.

'Yes, I had to—'

'I heard what Tyndareus said. He said you *helped*.'

Penelope drew in a careful breath. 'It's not what it sounds like.'

I strode towards her so I could glare directly into her entitled, lying face.

'Did you send the guards after us – yes, or no?'

She said nothing, but I could see the guilt darkening her eyes. It was all the confirmation I needed.

I snatched the fresh clothes from her hands and stormed away.

'Please, Melantho. Just let me explain,' she pressed. 'I was worried about Agamemnon. I heard him at the celebrations; he said there was a slave he was looking for. I feared it was you. I feared he wanted retribution for what happened the other night. When I noticed you were no longer in the banquet hall, I . . . I was afraid. I could not leave, so I summoned a guard to look for you. To make sure you were safe.'

'Well, they *found me*,' I sneered over my shoulder. 'What of Callias?'

'I knew he was a friend of yours, so I told the guard to ask him if he had seen you. I didn't know they would . . . I didn't . . .' She trailed off, voice fracturing. 'This wasn't what I wanted. I had no idea what you had planned. If I had, I would never have—'

'You know what I think?' I tossed the fresh tunic aside before turning back to her. 'I think you sent the guards after me to make sure your *wedding gift* hadn't wandered too far. To keep an eye on *your property*.'

'My *property*?'

'That's what I am now, aren't I?'

Penelope stared at me for a long moment, her face unreadable. The only hint of emotion she let slip was her hands clutching tightly at her gown.

'I was going to tell you today before the ceremony. I was going to explain everything. *That* was why I wanted to speak with you,' she said quietly. 'I did this to protect you. You and your family. Don't you see? In Ithaca I will be a queen. I will have the power to make sure you can live a safe life . . . Don't you want that?'

'I *wanted* to be *free*.'

'Free?' She shook her head. 'Melantho, there is no freedom for us. Not for women. We are always owned by *someone*: a master, or husband, or father. The world won't let us exist otherwise. We are always possessions to them.'

'There is no "we",' I spat, striding towards her. 'Don't you *dare* try to compare us. You know *nothing* of what I've been through.'

'I was not—'

'You're just like the rest of them. You stood there and did *nothing*. He branded them and you just *watched*—'

'I did what I had to do to save you.'

'Why do *you* get to decide which of us is *saved*?' I was shouting now, jabbing my finger into her face. 'This is all *your fault*. All of it!'

'So, your ridiculous plan was my fault too, then?' Anger stole into Penelope's voice, and I found a vicious kind of satisfaction in hearing it.

'It *wasn't* ridiculous.'

'Of course it was, Melantho. How could you have ever believed otherwise? If the guards hadn't caught you, you would have been found by wolves, or hunters, or slave traders, or Gods know what else. Did you think for a *second* about that? Did you think *at all?* Did it even cross your mind that you could have—' The words caught in Penelope's throat, and she swallowed. 'You could have died, Melantho.'

'Of course I knew that,' I seethed. 'Did it cross *your* mind that maybe I would have *preferred* that?'

Penelope went very still then, her anger flickering out immediately. She lowered her gaze.

'I just want to help you, Melantho.'

'What about what *I want*?'

My question hung between us, hardening like ice, and I watched as a rare shyness crept over Penelope. She addressed her next words to the floor.

'I suppose I thought . . . you might have wanted this. To come to Ithaca . . . with me.'

'I don't want to go anywhere with *you*.'

A bright flash of pain carved across Penelope's face, but she quickly composed herself.

'I am afraid it has already been decided,' she said, shifting back into that steady, empty tone. 'My uncle has agreed to gift you to Odysseus and me, we cannot—'

'I am not a gift.'

She sighed, the sound grating irritably over my skin. 'Melantho, I did not—'

'*I AM A PERSON!*' I screamed at her over and over, the words like a piece of my heart being ripped out of me, bloody and raw and beating. I realized I was crying, hot tears spilling down my cheeks.

'I know,' Penelope whispered. She sounded wounded, and I hated her for being hurt by *my* pain. It did not belong to her. She did not deserve it.

'No, *you don't*. You don't understand. You *never will*.' I furiously dashed my tears away. 'You will always see me like the rest of your kind do.'

'I have always seen you as my friend, Melantho.'

'Your *friend*?' I scoffed. 'Friends do not own each other, Penelope. You would know that if you had any real ones.'

She recoiled and I felt a grim sense of victory, though the feeling was hollow in my chest.

A silence settled. Penelope stared intently at the wall behind me, her face shimmering with emotions she would not dare spill. I glared at her, willing that perfect mask to crumble.

'I hate you and every one of your kind,' I said, hoping this finishing blow might finally shatter that infuriating composure.

But it did not.

Instead, Penelope nodded, as if in agreement with my words. She then straightened her shoulders, absently patting down the folds of her gown, eyes avoiding mine.

'I must go,' she said, voice scraped clean of all feeling. 'The gift-giving ceremony will commence shortly. Then we are to depart for Ithaca.'

I watched her turn and walk towards the door, her back as straight as an arrow ready to fly.

She paused at the threshold. I wanted to look away, but I found my eyes tracing her profile, the steep angle of her nose, the graceful slice of her jaw.

'I am sorry,' she whispered. 'For the others.'

Then she walked away, and I felt a suffocating wave of exhaustion crash through me. I welcomed it, letting it pull me under as I stared into the empty space Penelope had left behind.

18

I had never seen the sea before.

I had heard stories, of course, of those wine-dark waves. Many slaves had spoken of it as if it were a living, breathing thing, a beast that paced, restless and hungry, always on the edge of a vicious temper. Only Poseidon could leash the violent creature, though he rarely did. They said the god preferred to let his tides run free, to stir fear in the hearts of those who dared venture into his domain.

In my mind, I pictured the sea as some watery monster prowling the horizon, swallowing ships in its foaming maw. But when we arrived in the bustling port town, and I stared out at that expanse of blue, I saw only . . . *beauty*, the world cracked open before me, spilling out in endless azure waves, wider than I had ever imagined it to be.

In Sparta, the skyline had always been encased by towering mountains, cupping the kingdom like a giant palm. But here, I could see where the heavens brushed the tips of the Earth, bleeding into the waves. This horizon was limitless, and, for an instant, it made me feel limitless too.

I tried to grasp hold of that fleeting, weightless sensation of *possibility*.

But then the guilt found me, staining the moment with its sharp, rotten teeth. Why did I deserve to enjoy this view whilst Callias, Melitta and Xanthias were enduring *my* punishment?

What right did I have?

The question hung over me as I stretched my aching limbs. Beside me, Melanthius stared blankly at the ground. He wore the same empty expression he'd had since leaving Sparta, when we had been packed into the cramped wooden cart we now alighted from. I knew his thoughts were elsewhere, left behind at the palace along with his heart.

Odysseus' guards herded us towards the harbour. His men were notably more polite than those of Sparta. Instead of snapping their orders as if they were scolding mutts, they spoke in calm, neutral voices: '*This way. Follow me.*'

There were ten of us in total gifted by the king, and we walked alongside the chests of gold and fine trinkets that made up Penelope's dowry. Tyndareus had been generous. Clearly, he thought his niece a worthy prize.

Ahead of us, I saw Penelope arm in arm with Odysseus. She pointed at something on the horizon, and he leant close to whisper in her ear, his lips hitched into a grin as he spoke. She laughed, the sound tinkling over the breeze.

I turned away, the view no longer seeming quite as beautiful.

Ahead, giant wooden structures were gathered in the harbour, towering so high I had to crane my neck to glimpse the top of them. *Ships*. I had only ever encountered them in paintings and stories. Shielding my eyes from the sun, I struggled to comprehend the sheer size of them. They stretched long and narrow, with giant oars spilling from their sides like legs. On the decks, wooden poles stood proud, reaching so high they looked as if they were piercing the sky.

My eyes drifted to the sailors, their bronzed faces calloused by the sea breeze, lips dry and cracked. They looked like the bark of a tree, gnarled and worn, yet there was something about them I envied – the lightness to their movements, the easiness of their smiles, the glint in their eyes.

My drifting gaze collided with my father's, and I saw his shoulders tense as he traced the bruises marring my face. An unspoken awkwardness shifted between us, and he quickly glanced away.

I wished he had stayed behind in Sparta. Penelope must have thought it would be a comfort, to embark on this new life with a parent at my side. But my father's presence only served to remind me of the one I had lost. The only true parent I had ever had.

A thought struck me then, like a knife through my chest.

'She won't be able to find us,' I whispered to Melanthius. 'If Mother ever returns to Sparta. If she comes looking for us. We won't be there.'

My brother stared ahead with frighteningly empty eyes. 'She won't be coming back.'

I knew he was right; of course I did. Sold slaves never returned. But hope was a stubborn, foolish thing, and I could not shake the feeling that leaving Sparta meant leaving behind that tiny scrap I had left, the thread that had been holding together all those broken pieces, letting me cling to the possibility that I might one day see my mother again.

'We'll never see any of them again,' Melanthius whispered.

I felt the guilt weigh heavier inside me, that familiar exhaustion rising to greet it. I wanted to lie down and sleep. To disappear. To be anywhere but in my own head.

'At least we have each other,' I murmured, reaching for Melanthius.

He said nothing as he walked ahead, leaving my outstretched hand to hang limply in the air.

It was a full day's sail to Ithaca.

Though I wanted nothing more than to gaze upon those dancing tides, we were placed in the cargo hold alongside the other 'commodities', wedged into damp shadows that tilted and groaned, making the world feel untethered and my stomach roil.

Many threw up, my brother included. When I tried to help Melanthius he just stared at me with those dead eyes, bile drying on his chin. He did not bother wiping it off.

I gave up trying to comfort him after a time, and stared into the swaying darkness, the vomit-stained air burning in my nostrils. I wondered where Penelope was. Likely being pampered above deck, enjoying the fresh, salty breeze on a cushioned throne beside her husband. The thought made the anger thicken inside me as the waves carried us away.

*

My first impression of Ithaca was that it looked deeply unwelcoming.

The island was made up of giant, rugged mountains that clutched at the sea like fists, terse tufts of greenery sprouting between their thick knuckles.

Whereas Sparta was flat and green and flushed with life, it felt as if Ithaca were purposefully trying to *repel* visitors, the harsh landscape growing steep and crooked to ward off any who wished to claim her as their home. Though, it seemed few had dared to, save for the flocks of animals that trundled over the hills like passing clouds. *Prince of Goats* – that was what Agamemnon had called Odysseus.

As we disembarked from the ship, it took a moment for the ground to steady beneath me. Around us, waves lapped at the jagged, bald shoreline, dipped plum-red in the evening light. Gratefully, I drew in a lungful of fresh air, though the stench of bile still lingered in my nose.

Scanning the harbour, I noted that the men of Ithaca appeared just as weathered as their land. Though, I was surprised to see how warmly they greeted Odysseus, as if he were an old friend, clasping hands and slapping shoulders. Further up the shoreline, I glimpsed small, ramshackle houses gathered in tight clumps – was *this* the kingdom of Ithaca?

We were quickly sorted into carts, then lugged up a narrow road beaten into the hillside. The bumpy, twisting path seemed to revive everyone's nausea, and I had to keep my eyes set on the horizon to stop my stomach from emptying itself on to the overcrowded floor.

Gradually, Ithaca's palace came into view. It was a strange, rambling structure built into the side of a large hill, towering floors clambering up the cliff edge, connected by sheer stairs left exposed to the elements. It looked as if the palace had once been decorated with bright splashes of red and blue and green, though the paint had mostly been stripped away now, feasted on by salt-toothed winds, leaving cold marble beneath, white as bone.

Once we had climbed out of the carts, we were led up those steep stairs cut into the rock. Up and up we went, past the lower levels of the palace, where I assumed the slaves resided, climbing higher and higher until the steps opened out into a large courtyard, hugged on all sides by towering colonnades. This was where the largest portion of the palace had been built, sprawling over the flattened hilltop and boasting uninterrupted views of the entire island.

I took a moment to catch my breath; the stairs had been arduous on my broken body. With my hands braced on my thighs, my gaze drifted over Ithaca, the ragged, sparse hills spilling outwards in all directions, framed by glittering waves.

Melanthius appeared beside me, eyes glazed.

'What do you make of it?' I murmured.

He shrugged. 'All prisons are the same.'

19

The eyes of Ithaca were upon us.

We were kneeling in the palace courtyard whilst Odysseus welcomed us into his home. Beside me, the other Spartan slaves kept their eyes set on our new master, but I met our audience's shameless curiosity with a glare.

Odysseus stood in front of a towering oak tree as he droned on and on. It became quickly apparent that the Prince of Ithaca loved the sound of his own voice. Strangely enough, everyone else seemed to love it too; even his slaves listened animatedly as he listed off the importance of duty and respect and loyalty. It was an effort not to roll my eyes.

All I wanted was to be left alone and sleep.

Still, Odysseus blathered on.

'I am delighted to welcome you all into my home,' he said, taking the time to make eye contact with all ten of us as he spoke. 'The slaves beneath my roof are not merely workers, they are family, and I wish to welcome you as part of that family.'

When his eyes landed on mine, I felt myself hardening beneath his warmth. I did not trust it. Did not trust *him*. This whole benevolent master act felt too rehearsed, the sentiments hollow on his tongue. I glanced at the slaves beside me – was anyone buying it?

'Let us now all join in saying: *Welcome!*'

A cheer rose and the audience threw dried fruits and nuts over us, as was customary when welcoming new slaves into a household.

Once the floor was littered with offerings, we were shepherded to one side of the courtyard beside the other palace slaves. There was a tangible tension in the air as we joined them. I did not blame them for their hostile glances. You would think we would have felt a sense of camaraderie, but there was always wariness when new slaves joined a household. After all, we were only as valued as the work we offered, and so if another slave encroached upon that, it could threaten our place.

And a slave without use was always the first to be sold.

'Now, to welcome my bride, my wife. Ithaca's future queen,' Odysseus announced.

The crowd dutifully parted as a figure glided forward. My jaw clenched at the sight of her, draped in a floaty yellow gown. Her short hair had been pinned back and adorned with a gold diadem, her skin flawless and glowing.

Her beauty infuriated me.

Odysseus took Penelope's hand, praising her lavishly. I drowned out his saccharine speech. I had no stomach for it.

Penelope bowed to a man who I assumed was King Laertes, for he looked nearly identical to Odysseus, save for a few extra wrinkles and threads of grey hair. Once the king permitted her to rise, Penelope began scanning the crowd, staring at the strangers who were now her people.

Her eyes caught mine and she did not look away, not immediately. I wondered what she made of me standing before her, bruised and battered, hair matted, clothes dirty and still stinking of our journey. Her face gave nothing away, save for a slight crease between her brows – the beginnings of a frown.

Was she *repulsed* by my appearance? Did I *offend* her royal loveliness?

I did not care. In fact, I *hoped* I did. I hoped I disgusted her just as her pompousness disgusted me.

I let my glare singe from my sockets, and I could practically *feel* Penelope stiffening beneath it. Something delicate, almost vulnerable, flickered across her face before she looked away.

I raised my chin a little higher. *Good.*

'To my wife!' Odysseus finished, pouring his wine on to the floor in libation to the Gods.

The courtyard erupted, cheers filling the darkened sky as more dried fruit and nuts were tossed over Penelope, catching in her hair and gown.

'They throw the same rubbish on the bride as well?' I muttered.

'Of course. It is tradition for all new possessions,' an Ithacan slave whispered back.

'Penelope is not Odysseus' possession; she's his bride.'

The slave chuckled as if I had said something funny. 'That's the same thing, isn't it? All wives belong to their husbands.'

I frowned. To think of Penelope as a *possession*, to think of her *like me* . . .

I watched her again, the idea settling uncomfortably inside me.

'I'm Hippodamia, by the way.' The slave looked a little younger than I was, a golden ray of a girl, with bronzed skin and rich honey-brown eyes. Most notable of all was her long blonde hair shimmering around her shoulders. 'What's your name?'

Something about the slave unsettled me: how widely she smiled, how genuinely warm her eyes seemed.

'Melantho.'

'Nice to meet you, Melantho. Welcome to Ithaca.' She beamed, and I felt myself withdrawing, like shadows chased away by the morning sun. 'You come from Sparta, don't you? Is it true the women there are allowed to exercise like the men?'

'Yes,' I murmured.

'How fascinating! Mistress Anticlea told me that Spartan women are fearsome creatures. She was Odysseus' mother, the late queen. I served as her handmaid. She passed recently; Hades protect her soul. Since then, I've been put on kitchen duty. I *hate* kitchen duty. It makes my hands stink of vegetables.' She wiggled her fingers at me, as if to prove her point. 'But now the princess is here, I'll be serving as her handmaid. Isn't that exciting?'

'You'll be Penelope's handmaid?'

She nodded. 'You know her, don't you? From Sparta? What's she like? She looks lovely.'

I watched Penelope smile as Odysseus paraded her round the courtyard. She might have been sixteen, but she looked like a child beside him.

'She's not,' I said.

Hippodamia seemed to deflate at that. 'Oh.'

'What's up with your face?' another Ithacan slave asked me. A small boy with mousy hair and missing teeth. 'Looks like you got beat bad. Did ya? Get beat bad?'

'Shh. You can't ask that – it's *rude*,' Hippodamia scolded.

'You're right. I did get beaten,' I told the boy. 'And do you know whose fault it was?' I pointed at Penelope, before turning back to Hippodamia. 'You want to know what she's like? *This* is what she's like. So, good luck.'

Fear crept into the girl's pretty face, stealing away her smile.

She did not speak to me again.

After the welcoming ceremony, we were given a brisk tour.

The palace seemed as tired as I felt, and nowhere near as large or imposing as Tyndareus' home. Yet there was a certain character to the strange, rambling building.

The woman leading our tour introduced herself as Eurycleia, the household's head slave. She was a short, stout woman, with a face as cold and coarsened as Ithaca's mountains. Her light brown hair was tied back, shot through with shocks of grey. She looked like a woman whose dedication to her duty had scrubbed her clean of any humour or sense of joy.

I knew immediately we would not get along.

My feet grew heavier with every step as we traipsed through our new prison. Everywhere we went I could smell the sea, its salty scent painting the air, filling each room with the gentle murmur of hushing waves. It was the only part of the palace I liked.

Once the tour was over, Eurycleia divided the ten of us into our new duties. To my relief, I was to work in the kitchens, a role that would keep me tucked far away from the world, and Penelope.

'What do you do?' Eurycleia asked my father, her voice as clipped and precise as freshly sharpened shears.

'My name is Dolios. I am a gardener, have been all my life,' he replied.

'Good. We need one of those.' She nodded before turning to my brother, her expression souring as she studied his black eye. 'And you?'

'Stables,' he muttered.

'We have enough stable boys.'

Melanthius stared at her. 'I've worked the stables since I could walk. It's all I know.'

'My brother is the best with horses, he—'

'Did I ask you?' the old witch snapped at me. She then observed our matching bruises with a click of her tongue. 'Seems you two are the troublemakers, then.'

Our father glanced away, shame staining his face.

'We need a goatherd,' Eurycleia continued. 'If you can handle horses, you can handle goats. Yes?'

I braced, readying myself for Melanthius to argue, to fight for his place. But he simply nodded. 'Fine.'

The utter defeat in his eyes frightened me.

'You.' I stiffened under Eurycleia's hawkish glare. 'How old are you?'

'Fifteen,' I said.

She sniffed, then nodded. 'Good. Follow me. The rest of you will be shown to the sleeping quarters.'

I glanced warily at the others. 'You said I was to work in the kitchens?'

'I'm aware,' Eurycleia snipped. 'But tonight, you are needed for another purpose. Can you sing?'

'No.'

She clicked her tongue again. 'Well, you will have to try.'

Eurycleia led me to Odysseus' private chambers.

His quarters were situated at the top of the hill, near the front of the palace, and comprised of three large interconnecting chambers with a sweeping terrace jutting out over the sea. The rooms smelt musty, every visible surface coated in dust and strange items Odysseus must have collected on his travels, and there were more wax tablets than I could count, stacked in teetering piles. It wasn't like the disarray of Castor's room, born from arrogant neglect; this mess felt purposeful, in its own chaotic way.

Standing in the centre of the space were a handful of other slave girls, all around my age. I recognized Hippodamia, though she avoided my gaze.

'What are we doing here?' I asked Eurycleia.

'I hope you do not speak to your masters with such a bold tongue?' she snapped, her testiness scratching at my nerves. 'You are to wait here until the newlywed couple return from the celebrations.'

A cold tendril of panic slithered into my gut. 'What? Why?'

Eurycleia's bushy brows pinched into a scowl. 'Do Spartans have no respect for marital traditions?'

'Tonight is the first night Mistress Penelope will spend with her husband in their marital bed,' Hippodamia explained, her voice soft against Eurycleia's harsh bark. 'It is tradition for young, unmarried women to sing outside the chamber; it brings good fortune for the consummation of the marriage. Is this not the custom in Sparta?'

'Yes, but they did all that already,' I said, feeling a sudden, desperate need to get away from this room. 'On their wedding night.'

'They did not,' Eurycleia interjected. 'Master Odysseus has always intended to legitimize his union here, in Ithaca.'

'And how would you know that?' I matched Eurycleia's tone, making her eyes flare.

'Because *I* have watched him carve his marital bed with his own two hands from the very tree that grows through this palace. Master Odysseus has spent many tireless moons sculpting that bed for this very moment. That is why it is imperative we ensure everything goes smoothly tonight.'

'I think that's down to Master Odysseus' performance, not ours,' I muttered.

Eurycleia pinched my arm.

'Speak with respect,' she scolded, before turning to the other girls. 'You are to stay here until morning, understood? No one leaves.'

The doors opened then, and the air shrivelled in my lungs as I heard Penelope's laugh. It was not the laugh I knew – this one sounded more rehearsed – yet still it set my heart racing. The sound instantly died as she entered the room, her gaze striking mine. Her eyes widened slightly, her cheeks growing two shades paler. I glanced away.

'I have the girls prepared for you, Master Odysseus.' Eurycleia bowed her head as they entered.

Odysseus grinned, throwing a surprisingly affectionate arm around Eurycleia's shoulders. 'Penelope, I believe you have yet to meet Eurycleia. This woman practically raised me from when I was a babe. She is as wonderful as she is formidable. If you need anything, Eurycleia is your woman.'

Penelope inclined her head. 'It is a pleasure to meet you.'

'The pleasure is all mine, mistress. Ithaca is delighted to have you,' Eurycleia said. She then patted Odysseus' arm, her eyes shining. 'I am so proud of you, my darling boy.'

Odysseus took her hand and kissed it. 'Thank you.'

The affection between them was deeply unsettling, like that of a mother and son.

How could a slave love their master like that?

'Goodnight. May Demeter bring you her fertility, and Aphrodite her passion,' Eurycleia said with a wink before leaving. I noticed the way her words made Penelope stiffen.

'Thank you for being here.' Odysseus turned to address us. 'I am certain your lovely voices will bring us good fortune in producing a strong, healthy heir for Ithaca. What duty could be more important than that?'

I glanced at the girls, their faces shining with purpose. Did they really eat his words up so easily? I tried to keep my attention on them, but Penelope's presence was like the tide, pulling my focus towards her no matter how hard I fought.

She was watching Odysseus, her expression calm, though I could see she was picking at her nail beds behind the folds of her gown, the skin red and sore. When I lifted my gaze back to her face, she was staring me, eyes bright with fear. The sight of it silenced the anger inside me, like icy water thrown over a flame.

Odysseus' hand landed heavily on Penelope's shoulder, making her flinch.

'I have something I wish to show you,' he told her.

He flung open the doors to his bedchamber and led Penelope forward. Inside, I caught a glimpse of the bed Eurycleia had spoken of. Indeed, it had been carved from a tree growing through the heart of the chamber, its very branches making up the framework of the bed. It was an incredible feat of craftsmanship, and I saw the way Odysseus' eyes gleamed with pride as he showed Penelope, murmuring words too low for me to catch.

I craned my neck, trying to get a better look at the bed, but then I thought of all that was about to occur within its sheets . . . Torturous glimpses burnt through my mind, of flesh and skin and lips. I felt my cheeks burning, that fist clenched around my stomach twisting tighter.

Odysseus turned to us then and gave a triumphant smile, before moving to close the doors. Over his shoulder, Penelope's eyes reached for mine. She looked so small in that shadowy room. So afraid.

So alone.

It reminded me of when we'd first met, after Penelope had walked me back to the slave quarters, and I had been so desperate to hold on to that last glimpse of her. Our eyes held, just as they had done that night, as the doors between us closed, once again locking Penelope in her world, and me in mine.

But, for the first time ever, I did not wish to be in her place.

It was the longest night of my life.

I did not sing with the other girls, but nor did I leave. As much as I wanted to, something rooted me to the spot. I told myself it was because

I did not wish to face Eurycleia's wrath for abandoning my post. But truthfully, it was the fear in Penelope's eyes that kept me there. It had laced itself inside me, tying me to that wretched room, rendering me unable to leave until I saw her again, until I knew she was safe. I still hated her, of course, but that did not mean I wanted any harm to come to her.

And I knew how ugly a man's lust could become. How terrifying it could be.

I listened intently at the doors, my whole body poised, ready to storm inside should I hear any hint of a sob, or scream, or shout . . .

But no sound came, just the warbling voices of the slaves as they sang their wedding ballads, painting the darkness with their sweet, lilting melodies.

When dawn spilt, rosy and golden, across the floor, the girls began to leave.

'Melantho, it is time for us to go,' Hippodamia whispered, voice hoarse from singing.

I said nothing, continuing to glare at the closed doors ahead of me.

I heard Hippodamia sigh as she left.

I do not know how long I waited after that, but eventually those doors opened and Penelope stepped out.

I did not move, did not even breathe, my eyes burning as I scanned every inch of her. She looked tired, her hair and clothes a little dishevelled, cheeks slightly flushed. But she appeared unharmed.

'Are you well?' My voice was a strange, strangled thing.

Penelope blinked, once, twice. It was rare to see her so surprised.

'I am,' she whispered. Then she tested a step forward. 'Melantho—'

I turned on my heel and stalked out of the room.

20

Time in Ithaca passed like a sigh, stretching endlessly onwards.

In Sparta, life had had a rhythm, like a thumping war drum – fast, monotonous, relentless. But in Ithaca, the days simply spilt into one other, like unspooling threads.

The slaves in the kitchens bumbled around sleepily, taking time to chatter and laugh as they worked. Nobody ever seemed in a rush, as if they believed their time infinite. King Laertes rose late and let us get on with our work in our own time. Meanwhile, Odysseus seemed happy to tend to his own needs. I had been utterly bemused when I first saw him sauntering into the kitchens one morning, striking up a conversation with the cook as he helped prepare his own breakfast. The cook had been unfazed by his master's assistance, as if it were a regular occurrence. He even affectionately chided Odysseus, 'You are stirring the porridge too much. You must let it thicken!' The Ithacan prince had merely laughed at the cook's reproach and held up his hands in mock surrender.

I had seen Odysseus in the fields, too, working alongside the other men, their bronzed bodies glinting beneath the harsh sun. Another time, I caught him strolling in the gardens, talking with my father, his face lit with genuine interest as he questioned him on the flowers he was tending. That was the thing about Odysseus – he *loved* to ask questions, and he spoke to everyone with the same level of unbridled affability.

It must have been an act.

Surely, he was trying to lull his slaves into a false sense of security so he could catch them out. Or perhaps he was trying to impress Penelope with this facade. Why else would he show such interest in our kind?

Yet, as the days rolled ceaselessly on, Odysseus' charming act never faltered.

Still, I did not trust him. Though, I seemed to be the only person in all of Ithaca who did not. Everyone *adored* Odysseus, even the slaves. If ever I made a derisive comment about our master, they would stare at me with baffled expressions, as if I had just condemned Zeus himself.

I quickly learnt to just keep my mouth shut, doing my best to avoid all social interactions.

I avoided Penelope, too.

Thankfully, our paths rarely crossed. Only on occasion when Odysseus hosted guests, and I assisted the serving girls. Penelope often joined these dinners, though she spoke little, if at all. She would smile blandly whilst Odysseus recounted, time and time again, the story of how he had *so cleverly* won her hand, aiding Tyndareus in his dangerous predicament. He never once mentioned Penelope's involvement in the concoction of this plan, and Penelope never interjected to correct him. She just sat there silently, a shiny trophy for Odysseus to display. On the odd occasion Penelope *did* speak, the table would always fall silent, and I would glimpse Odysseus subtly squeezing her hand. Penelope usually excused herself shortly after that.

A possession, Hippodamia had called her.

I knew all too well how men hated when their possessions spoke back.

Yet, Odysseus seemed to bask in Penelope's conversation when they were alone. I often saw them strolling arm in arm through the courtyard, deep in discussion. The sight always stoked my hatred – though the feeling seemed heavier in my chest, sadder.

Perhaps I was lonely.

I only spoke to my brother, though our conversations were scarce. Much of Melanthius' time was spent away from the palace, herding the goats he tended. I knew it wasn't good for him, being alone in the mountains with only his misery for company. Each time I saw him, it was as if a little more of my brother had disappeared, devoured by that all-consuming grief. I feared the day I would not be able to recognize him at all.

A few times, I considered how we might escape, but just the thought of it had me sweating with memories of that hideous night. Besides, Ithaca was a small island; it would be near impossible to make it on to a ship without anyone being alerted. And even if we did, what then? Travel to Sparta and break into Tyndareus' palace and free Callias and Melitta? And who was to say they were still serving there? They could have been sold for all we knew.

We would not be able to save Callias and Melitta; we would only doom ourselves. But this knowledge, however true, did not ease my guilt, only soured it. Yet, I had learnt to endure such feelings. Guilt. Loss. Grief. Anger. I had felt them all so viciously in the wake of losing my mother that now they felt dulled, blunted like an overused blade that could no longer cut as deep as it once had.

Still, each night I woke fighting for breath, my ears ringing with Callias' screams, the smell of Melitta's burning flesh catching in my throat, making me retch.

As I lay my head back down, two words would shiver on my lips, the same ones I heard my mother whispering as she lulled me to sleep.

I'm sorry, I'm sorry, I'm sorry.

Soon, summer gave way to the harvest season, the days cooling as the nights grew longer.

It was around this time that Odysseus summoned me.

As Eurycleia escorted me to the prince, I felt a cold sense of vindication. I assumed his summons could only mean one thing, the same thing it always did when a prince called a young slave to their chambers. This was my proof. Proof that Odysseus was no different to any other master.

It was an oddly comforting thought.

Eurycleia paused outside his door to throw me a cursory glance, her leathery face pinched with distaste.

'Master Odysseus is a busy man,' she told me, as if I were causing some great inconvenience by having been summoned at all. 'You should not waste his time.'

'Don't worry.' I gave her a wink. 'Men never usually last long with me.'

She sucked her teeth at that, muttering something under her breath as she opened the door and ushered me inside.

Odysseus' personal quarters were as I remembered them from the night I'd arrived at the palace, an eclectic mix of gentle chaos. Outside, I could hear the waves whispering against the rocky cliffside, scrubbing the air clean with their salty freshness.

I found Odysseus sitting cross-legged on the floor, one of the hunting dogs sprawled beside him. An upturned stool was set on his lap, made of a rich, dark wood. The prince was bent over one of the three legs, a knife poised in his hand as he etched intricate markings into its surface. Concentration tied his features together, making them seem heavier, sterner. But, when he saw me approach, his face quickly lifted into one of his familiar smiles.

Odysseus had a lot of different smiles, I had come to realize. I imagined him wielding them like weapons, having mastered the art of knowing which to unsheathe at an opportune moment.

'Melantho. Thank you for coming.' I was surprised he remembered my name. 'Please, take a seat.'

He motioned to the floor beside him. Warily, I lowered myself on to the thick rug, careful to avoid the wood shavings scattered around us.

'If you could bear with me a moment, I just need to . . .' Odysseus trailed off as he returned to his carving. He handled his knife with such delicate precision I found I could not look away, mesmerized by the slice of metal against wood. Eventually, he sat back to examine his work, closing one eye, then the other. 'There. That'll do. What do you think?'

'I don't know anything about woodcarving, Master Odysseus,' I said blandly, refusing to stoke his arrogance like all the other sycophants he owned.

Odysseus only smiled in response, shifting the stool around so the next leg was now poised before him.

'My father taught me to carve and sculpt,' he said as he sank his blade into the wood. 'I thought it some kind of magic, how he could pull such beauty from a coarse lump of wood or cold slab of stone. Those are some of the earliest memories I have: watching him work. Now, I find the act rather nostalgic.'

My thoughts flickered to my childhood, like a flame being thrown into the dark, forgotten corners of my mind. I saw my mother's hands kneading dough, the methodical motion of her knuckles, fingers and palms – strong and soothing. I ached to reach out and hold those hands in mine.

Odysseus continued speaking, but I had no interest in listening to his sentimental ramblings. He always spoke too much. I believed it was because he loved to monopolize people's attention. He was like a dull jewel that could only sparkle when others shone their light upon him.

I felt a warm huff against my skin and instinctively stiffened. A cold panic seeped through my veins as Odysseus' dog rested his head in my lap. For a sickening moment, I found myself back on that dark mountain path, fleeing for my life as those baying hounds closed in all around me . . .

'Argos likes you,' Odysseus observed. 'There's no need to be afraid. He's a soft old thing.'

I forced my muscles to unclench. 'I'm not afraid.'

The prince smiled then adjusted the stool a little in his lap. As he did so, I noticed a thick scar streaking across his lower thigh, starkly pale against his bronzed skin.

'A hunting accident,' he said, following my gaze. 'Back when I was young and foolish.'

I glanced away wordlessly, wondering how long it would be before he asked me to undress. Castor never bothered with all this pointless small talk.

'Tell me, Melantho,' he continued, shifting to face me. 'How are you finding Ithaca?'

All prisons are the same. Melanthius' voice chilled my thoughts.

'It's . . . calmer here,' I admitted, staring down at Argos' shaggy head. I wished the dog would leave me alone.

'Do you miss Sparta at all?'

'No.' The word came out harsher than I intended.

Odysseus watched me for a moment. His gaze had a prying edge, as if he were trying to slither his way between my words, to the raw truth beneath.

'It would be natural if you did, you know. I would not take offence. Sparta was your home for a long time and you—'

'Sparta was never my home.'

Odysseus went very still then, his blade poised over the wood.

'You should not interrupt me, Melantho,' he said. His anger was strange; it held no sharpness, rather it was smooth and heavy, like a stone at the bottom of a lake. Steady. Fixed.

'Apologies, master.' He held my gaze, and I wondered if he saw the hatred burning inside me as I spoke those words. I hoped he did.

He smiled. 'It's all right, Melantho. Just something to remember in future. The relationship of a slave and master is all about respect.'

I suppressed the urge to roll my eyes.

'You know, it used to bring me great shame, being the Prince of Ithaca,' Odysseus continued, surprising me. 'My kingdom seemed so small and worn compared to those of my peers. So, I tried to get away from it, travelled all of Greece and beyond. But always, Ithaca called me back. Always I came home. This place – it gets into your blood. Your bones. You can't escape it. Now, it is my mission to bring Ithaca the renown she deserves.'

His words rang with the hollowness of a well-worn performance, and I wondered how many times he had made people endure this little speech. 'One day, Melantho, you will be proud to call this land your home. I assure you.'

Slaves do not have homes, I silently screamed at him, whilst my lips formed the words, 'Yes, master.'

As if sensing my rage, Argos let out a grumble before skulking away to the shady corner of the room. A quietness settled then, the only sound coming from the raspy song of Odysseus' blade against the wood. I watched his hands as he worked, so steady and sure. Thoughts came, unbidden, and I imagined those hands on Penelope. I saw them skating over her bare skin, tracing the curves of her body . . .

'So, Melantho.' I snapped my attention back to Odysseus' face, my cheeks hot. 'I suppose you are wondering why I called you here.'

I had a perfectly good idea, though admittedly carving furniture was not exactly the foreplay I was used to.

'It is not my duty to wonder what my master's desires are. I only act upon them.'

My smile mirrored the flirtatious curl of my words as I slipped into that familiar role with ease. I would be lying if I said a part of me did not enjoy it, toying with those threads of desire, tying them like invisible leashes around my master's throat. Of course, the power was fleeting and hollow. But it was power all the same, and I had missed the taste of it.

'What is it you desire, master?' I prompted, inching a little closer to him.

'As of right now, my primary desire is to keep my wife happy,' Odysseus said, rubbing a wood shaving between his thumb and forefinger. 'That is why you are here.'

I felt the smile fade from my face. 'Because of . . . your wife?'

'It seems Penelope has a mission; one she is intent on seeing through. Do you know what that mission is?' I shook my head. 'She wishes for you to be freed.'

The ground felt unsteady beneath me as Odysseus' words sang through my veins, my soul. *Freed.*

'She... she does?' I breathed.

'She is rather insistent on the subject, and, as I am sure you know, Penelope is a determined woman.' A glimmer of pride shone in his eyes. 'Of course, I value Penelope's opinion, and if she believes you deserve your freedom, then I am inclined to believe her.'

My chest swelled so much it hurt to breathe. I felt like I was dangling on a cliffside, clutching at Odysseus' words as if they were the only things keeping me from tumbling into oblivion.

'Still, I wanted to do some investigating for myself and, to be truthful, Melantho, I have been left a little confused.'

'Confused?' I echoed.

'Well, firstly, for someone my wife supposedly admires, it appears you barely interact with her. I do not think I have seen you share a single word since you arrived here. And when I enquired with my kitchen staff, they told me they could not give an accurate estimation of your character for they know so little about you. Apparently, you rarely speak, and when you do it is only to make inappropriate remarks.' I stiffened, my hands balling into fists. *Those rats.* 'Not to mention your encounter with Agamemnon, and, of course, the little mishap that occurred on my wedding night.'

He tilted his head, studying my slow realization with a smile.

'Mishap?' I feigned confusion.

'Please, Melantho, do not insult my intelligence.' He held my gaze for a slow, tense beat. 'At least you have not tried another disastrous escape since you have been here. That is a headache I truly do not need.' He said this with a chuckle, as if we were old friends sharing a joke. 'So, tell me, Melantho, why is it my wife believes you so worthy of your freedom?'

My fists clenched tighter. 'Are not all men and women deserving of such a thing?'

'No,' Odysseus answered simply. 'There are those born to rule, and those born to be ruled. It is the nature of mankind, etched into our blood.'

'Well, what if it were in *my* blood to rule?'

Silent laughter glowed in his eyes, making his lips curl wider.

'You are interesting, Melantho. I shall give you that.' He offered the insulting words as if he were offering food to a starving mutt, expecting me to wolf them down appreciatively. 'Alas, I cannot grant you your freedom until I am convinced you are worthy of it. I am sure you understand.'

Fury shot through me, and I stared at his carving blade, now discarded on the floor. For a fleeting moment I allowed myself to imagine it – grabbing the blade and jamming it into his throat, hot blood spurting out as that patronizing smile faded from his lips . . .

Is it still in your blood to rule if it coats my hands?

'I am sure you will find a way to convince me,' Odysseus continued. 'And, truthfully, I hope you do, Melantho. For Penelope's sake. She seems very set on this.'

How I hated the way his eyes twinkled when he spoke of her.

'I'm sure I can,' I murmured, angling my body even closer. 'I could think of many, *many* ways to convince you.'

I peered up at him from beneath lowered lashes. It was the kind of gaze that stroked egos and other intimate areas, the kind of gaze that was a promise and a secret and a dare all rolled into one heady glance. It was the kind of gaze that always undid Castor and his friends.

And I willed it to do the same now.

I wanted to undo the Prince of Ithaca.

I wanted to reveal the pathetic man that lingered within him.

Let's see how patronizing he is when he is begging for my body.

I dared to reach out, to trace that scar along his thigh. Odysseus stared at my fingers for a moment, and I could feel the desire flicker inside him, curious and light, his expression lost to thoughts I knew he would never share with me.

His hand closed around my fingers, halting them.

'You are a beautiful girl, Melantho,' he said, and I loathed how gentle his voice was. 'But I have no such interest in slaves.'

'Perhaps you might like to try?'

His sigh ended in a smile. 'What I would *like* is to go and see my wife. But she insists I wait until her sickness passes.'

'*Sickness?*' I snatched my hand away.

'Not to worry, Melantho. It is perfectly common, and usually passes by the afternoon. My mother was the same when she carried my sister.' Odysseus studied my reaction with a frown. 'You have not heard the news?'

'Penelope is . . . pregnant?'

'I thought all of Ithaca knew by now.'

Odysseus continued talking but his words fell away as the realization roared through me. *Penelope is pregnant.*

'I did not know,' I finally managed.

Odysseus chuckled. 'You sound a little jealous, Melantho.'

I flinched, eyes flashing to his. 'I'm not—'

'It's all right. It's only natural. I know all women long for children. Perhaps, if you demonstrate your good behaviour, I could find you a suitable companion as a reward.'

A feverish laugh crawled up my throat. How I *longed* to tell Odysseus I'd sooner take my own life than bring one into this world.

'Thank you, master,' I said instead.

He smiled, then turned to retrieve his carving blade. 'You may go now.'

Head bowed, I rose quickly to my feet.

'And Melantho? Please do find a way to prove yourself to me.' Odysseus' voice caught me as I reached the door. 'For I would loathe to disappoint my wife.'

21

News of war came the following summer.

Word spread quickly through the palace, which was hardly surprising. If there's one thing slaves have in common, it's a love of gossip. Secrets were our trade, and we were experts at unearthing them. Our eyes and ears were everywhere, after all.

'Did you hear?' one of the kitchen girls whispered as we hauled jars of olive oil up the steep palace steps. I did not know her name. I had never bothered to ask. 'Princess Helen got herself stolen by some foreign prince!'

I gave a vague nod. I had no interest in conversation. I had no interest in anything at all beyond my duties. Since my interaction with Odysseus in the autumn, I had focused on keeping my head down and working myself to the bone. I could stomach playing the dutiful, obedient slave if it gave me my freedom.

But there had been no word from the prince.

'Paris of Troy, they call him,' the girl continued eagerly. 'They're sayin' Paris stole Helen from right under Menelaus' nose! Imagine that: hosting some Trojan in your own home and he runs off with your wife! Foreigners got no respect for our customs.'

For some reason, everyone seemed more fixated on the disrespect to Menelaus than on Helen, who had been abducted by a stranger.

'Menelaus and his brother are declaring war on Troy! They've got all of Greece to join them! Can you believe that?'

A man raising arms because his ego was bruised? Of course I could believe it. But I only shrugged as we ascended yet another flight of stairs.

The kitchens were set halfway up the palace hill. I think this was intended to be helpful, keeping an equal distance between the ground floor where we received food deliveries, and the hilltop where our masters dwelt. In reality, it just turned every trip into a headache-inducing trek.

I was sweating by the time we reached the kitchens and silently cursing whoever had thought it a good idea to build a palace into a bloody hillside.

'Did you see him? The Prince of Euboea?' one of the cooks asked as he bustled over, plucking the jars from our aching arms. 'He's come to force Master Odysseus to join the war.'

'Nah, we saw nothin',' the girl beside me answered. 'But he's wastin' his time, that's for sure. That prince won't convince Odysseus to fight.'

'He doesn't have to convince him.'

A few heads turned in our direction, surprised to hear my voice. I think several of them believed I couldn't even speak Greek.

'What d'you mean?' The girl eyed me curiously.

'Odysseus swore an oath to protect Helen's marriage,' I said. 'He has to fight.'

'How do *you* know that?'

'Because I was there when he swore it.'

She gaped at me incredulously.

'Odysseus isn't a man of war,' the cook insisted. 'He won't fight.'

'Then he will be going against his oath and the Gods will punish him.'

There was a collective gasp as someone hissed at me, 'You shouldn't say such things.'

'I'm just stating facts,' I shot back. 'If Odysseus refuses to fight, then he's not only a coward but a liar. Although, I can't say I would be all that surprised. He reeks of both.'

The kitchen fell deathly silent then, everyone frozen in place, eyes fixed behind my head.

'Melantho.'

That voice. I recognized it instantly.

Turning, I found Penelope standing behind me, a bowl of herbs cradled in her hands. In the past year I had stolen a thousand glances at her, but this was the first time our eyes had met since the morning after we had arrived.

My focus dipped to her swollen stomach, and I could not conceal my surprise at how much bigger she was than when I had last seen her strolling in the courtyard. She looked ready to burst.

A tense anticipation sparked in the air as the slaves awaited their future queen's response. I knew Penelope was not one for punishment, but I also knew she would have to do *something*. She could not have me bad-mouthing her husband and getting away with it; such a thing would only reflect badly on her.

'Come to my chambers,' she finally said. 'I wish to speak with you. Alone.'

She did not wait for me to follow as she turned and walked out.

'Close the door, please.'

Wordlessly, I obeyed Penelope's command, shutting the door behind us, then leaning back against it. I had never been inside her private chambers before, and I tried to look disinterested as I glanced around the space.

Like Odysseus' quarters, Penelope's were situated at the very top of the hill the palace stood upon. But, *unlike* Odysseus', hers were tucked away, out of sight, at the far end of a meandering hallway.

Penelope's central room was enviably large, opening out on to a sweeping balcony that overlooked the glittering sea beyond. The walls were painted with dancing women, swirling around one another in garish splashes of paint. Everywhere I looked the surfaces were covered in cushions and blankets, as if Odysseus feared Penelope might shatter at any given moment. Aside from that, the room felt markedly bare. Empty.

There were two doors set on opposite sides of the space. The one nearest to me opened on to a room with a neat row of beds, the handmaids' chamber. The other door was shut, but I assumed it led to Penelope's bedchamber. The one she would sleep in on nights she did not spend with Odysseus.

I wondered how often she used it, then immediately shoved the thought away.

Penelope had remained silent during the long walk here, keeping a steady gait despite those punishingly steep steps. Now, she was pacing back and forth over a rug, her strides somehow still elegant even with her giant stomach. I noticed the woven pattern beneath her feet had worn away, faded from where she had no doubt paced there many times before. What thoughts had chased those steps?

The silence grew taut between us. We had not been alone together since the day we had left Sparta. A familiar guilt reared up inside me, but I suffocated it instantly.

'So, is this the part where you scold me?' I asked from where I lounged against her door, arms lazily folded. The picture of insolence.

'I am not going to scold you. But you should know you cannot speak of Odysseus like that beneath his own roof.' I had clearly touched a nerve and it sharpened something inside me, to know Penelope was so defensive of *him*. 'It is utterly foolish. Are you *trying* to get yourself punished?'

I rolled my eyes. 'Yes, that's exactly what I'm doing. It's just been so long since I felt the whip cutting open my flesh, I wished for the opportunity again.'

Penelope stopped and stared at me. 'Do not say such things.'

I looked away, and she continued pacing, hands massaging her lower back. Sweat dappled her temples, though the room felt pleasantly cool.

'He is not a coward,' she continued, a little breathlessly now. 'It is not cowardly to want to stay by your family and kingdom, instead of risking your life for another king's wife.'

'If I remember correctly, it's Odysseus' fault everyone is having to risk their life for Helen,' I pointed out. 'Odysseus swore an oath. An oath *he* insisted upon. He's only got himself to blame.'

Penelope paused, wincing. She tilted her head back to stare at the ceiling as if the answers lay above us.

'Odysseus also swore an oath to Ithaca when he was named Laertes' heir. Why should Tyndareus' oath be valued above that? Surely being a king, a *father*, is more noble than being dragged to foreign lands to slay innocent men?'

'What of all the other kings and fathers forced to fight? Why should Odysseus be discounted and not they?'

'Because they *want* to – they want the glory and the riches and the fame. Odysseus does not care for those things.'

'Of course he wants those things, just at an *easier* price.'

She gasped, doubling over as if my words had been a physical blow to the gut.

'Penelope . . . what's the matter?' I took a tentative step forward, my concern for her instantly deflating all traces of my temper.

'I'm in labour,' she said with surprising calmness.

'*You're what?*'

'In labour. I have been for some time now.'

'Who else knows?'

'You would be the first.'

She then moved towards the table at the centre of the room and began gathering the various herbs she had retrieved from the kitchens.

'What are you doing?'

'I have been researching pain remedies,' she said. Her hands shook as she grabbed a bunch of crocuses and began plucking out their crimson tongues. 'The doctors were all useless, of course. You would think, with the commonness of childbirth, one of them *might* have researched a method to alleviate pain for women or make the process easier. But of course, men are not interested in the troubles of women, even when those troubles service them.'

The words streamed out of her as she ground the ingredients together with a pestle, smashing them into a bowl with unfettered frustration. Sweat trickled down her forehead, travelling along her nose to where it dangled precariously.

'What can I do to help?'

She looked at me, eyes frantic yet focused. 'I think it is time to fetch Eurycleia, but please tell her not to make a fuss. I do not want to be surrounded by flapping women.'

'What of Odysseus?'

'He cannot be disturbed.' She returned to the mixture, pouring in water before she knocked back the contents in one. From the twist of her face, I could tell it tasted foul.

'He cannot be *disturbed*? For the birth of his own child?'

Another spasm tore through her, and she bowed forward.

'Please, Melantho. Don't argue with me. Not now. We don't have time.'

I held my tongue and ran to find Eurycleia.

The old maid was lecturing some young slaves in the courtyard. When I interrupted, she threw me her usual glare. But after I explained the situation, her sourness quickly evaporated.

'Where is she?' she demanded.

'In her rooms. Where is Odysseus?'

'He cannot be disturbed.'

'But—'

'Childbirth is women's business. The men will only be a nuisance.'

We found Penelope in her bedchamber, doubled over in breathless agony. A low, horrible moan slipped from her lips, sounding more animal than human.

Without hesitation, Eurycleia swept her arms around Penelope's shoulders and guided her to the bed.

'Come now, mistress, you need to lie down. There we go. Easy does it,' she cooed, before turning to where I hovered in the doorway. 'You. Leave. Fetch the princess' handmaids.'

'*No*,' Penelope gritted out. 'Stay. Please.'

Stay. The word struck a chord inside me, reverberating through my bones.

'Very well, but you better make yourself useful and stop standing there gawking like a fish,' Eurycleia huffed. Penelope's legs were bent upwards now, and the old maid was peering between them. 'The baby isn't ready to come just yet.'

Penelope let out a quiet whimper.

'What should I do?' I asked Eurycleia.

'I need to fetch a few things. I want you to keep her distracted; she needs to stay calm until it is time to push. What are you staring at me like that for? Go stand beside her. Go on. Closer! She's *giving birth*, you silly child. She isn't infectious.'

Awkwardly, I approached Penelope, hands fidgeting at my sides.

'Lost your tongue, girl?' Eurycleia snapped as she bustled towards the door.

'I . . . I'm trying to think of what to say,' I admitted.

'It doesn't matter *what*. Just *distract her*.'

Memories gulped for air, our history so knotted between us, choking me into silence.

'Talk to me about that day,' Penelope whispered. Her eyes were closed, her sweat-dappled face lined with pain.

'What day?' I whispered back.

'My favourite day.'

I felt the memory wrap around my heart and squeeze tight. For a moment, I struggled to know where to start, but then I saw another spasm of agony steal across Penelope's face, and I forced myself to say something. *Anything.*

'It . . . it was near the end of summer,' I began, shifting uneasily. Penelope's eyes were still shut and so I closed my own, the words coming a little easier in the darkness. 'I had wanted us to do something you'd never done before. Something you would remember when you left

Sparta. I decided we should go for a swim in the river. You were unsure at first, but I somehow managed to convince you . . . So, we snuck away, and when we reached the river you didn't want to go in at first. But then I took your hand, and we jumped in together.' I found myself smiling, though my throat felt tight. 'We spent all day there, swimming and laughing and lying on the bank looking up at the sun. And I remember having this feeling in my chest . . . It's hard to describe, really. But for a moment I felt . . . *infinite*. And then you turned to me and said this was your favourite day, and I remember thinking I had never heard anything more wonderful, and all I wanted was to have a thousand more days just like that.'

I opened my eyes and realized Penelope was watching me, her gaze burning like twin silver flames. She said nothing, but the silence was a living thing between us, as bright and electrifying as a bolt of Zeus' lightning ripping open the sky.

In that moment, time seemed to hold its breath, and it felt as if the whole world had faded to nothingness around us. But then another tremor of pain gripped Penelope, and reality came crashing back into brutal clarity.

'It's time,' Eurycleia said, appearing beside the bed.

I nodded, shaking away the lingering emotion.

'I'm going to need you to start pushing, mistress. Can you do that?' Eurycleia's calm voice was at odds with my racing heartbeat. 'A nice strong push for me. Yes?'

Penelope's eyes slid to mine, and I saw how afraid she was.

'You can do this,' I said.

'Will you stay?' Her words tugged at my heart, so achingly vulnerable.

I nodded and her fingers twitched, as if in silent question. After a slight hesitation, I took her hand in mine and squeezed.

'You can do this, Penelope,' I said, firmer now. The resolution in my voice seemed to seep into her, determination flaring.

'Ready now? After three,' Eurycleia instructed. 'One, two, *three* . . .'

The cry that ripped from Penelope shuddered through me, her hand gripping mine so tightly my fingers crunched. As I watched her face contort, I felt a swell of fear mingled with pride, and I willed every ounce of energy from my body to spill into hers.

Please, Eileithyia, Great Goddess of Childbirth, please watch over Penelope . . .

She collapsed backwards on to the pillows, gasping for breath.

'Excellent work, mistress,' Eurycleia praised. 'Now take a few breaths, then we must go again. Come on now. A nice deep breath.'

I squeezed Penelope's hand again as she inhaled, readying herself for the battle ahead.

22

Something was wrong.

The baby was not coming.

Penelope had been pushing for what felt like days, wringing her body of every ounce of energy it had left. Yet still, the baby had not appeared.

It felt as if time had ceased to exist, and we were trapped in this repeating nightmare of Penelope pushing and pushing and pushing, trying to rip apart her own body.

Exhaustion had its teeth around Penelope now. She was slumped against her sweat-soaked pillows, barely able to keep her eyes open as she caught her breath. Her skin was so pale it looked almost grey in the draining light.

I glanced to Eurycleia, who was instructing Penelope with that sharp, steady voice of hers. *Breathe. Take a moment. Now push.* Yet, I could see her uneasiness — it gathered in the tightness of her shoulders, the thinness of her lips.

'You're doing great,' I told Penelope, trying to curb the anxiety in my voice.

Her head lolled to the side like a child's doll.

'Something's wrong,' I told Eurycleia.

The old maid watched Penelope, face grave. She then motioned me over and I reluctantly let go of Penelope's hand, watching it fall limp against the bed. As I approached Eurycleia, I saw the blood staining the sheets around her.

'The baby is in the wrong position,' Eurycleia murmured to me.

'What? What does that mean?'

'Calm yourself, girl.'

I glanced back to Penelope, who was rousing slightly, mumbling incoherent words.

'She'll be all right, won't she?' I whispered.

Eurycleia held my gaze, her silence sickeningly loud.

'She needs to push harder if we're going to dislodge this baby,' she said.

'*Look* at her! She's exhausted.'

'She has no choice.'

I returned to Penelope's side. In that moment, she looked heartbreakingly fragile – broken and lifeless and so very young. Only seventeen summers old. I felt the overwhelming urge to take her in my arms and protect her from all this pain. But I could not. She was trapped in the midst of this, and there was nothing I could do but force her to keep going.

I took her hand again and a horrible question tugged at me – *what if she dies?*

For so long I had been trying to drive Penelope away. Now, faced with the reality of losing her, *truly* losing her for ever, I could scarcely breathe. But I pushed that thought far away, forcing my mind to focus.

'Penelope?' I leant forward and brushed her hair from her damp face. I was surprised by how easy this intimacy felt, as if I had done it a thousand times before. 'Penelope, can you hear me? I need you to start pushing again.'

'I cannot,' she murmured, voice frighteningly thin.

My hand tightened around hers. 'You can. Just a little longer. That's all.'

'I am . . . not strong enough . . .'

I knelt on the edge of the bed now, pressing my face close to hers. 'You can do this. I know you can. We need you to push so we can get this baby out. All right?'

'Cut him out,' she whispered.

I stared at her for a silent moment.

'If they cut him out, you'll die.'

She gave me a look then, her eyes heavy with defeat, as if she believed it inevitable, as if the thread of her life had already been sliced by the Fates.

'He is in the wrong position,' she said, as if that were answer enough.

Her gaze loosened and shifted away from mine, but I grabbed her face with both my hands, forcing her to look at me.

'No. *No.* Don't you do that. Don't give up. You *can* do this. You *must* do this. For your husband . . . for your baby . . . They need you.' My words were edged with a wild desperation. '*I* need you. Do you hear? I. Need. *You.* And I will *not* let you die. You brought me to this ugly island, so don't you dare leave me here alone. I forbid it. *Do you hear me?*'

'Is . . . that a . . . command?' she whispered, the faintest thread of amusement lining her voice.

Despite myself, I laughed, though it sounded more like a sob, thick and strained in my throat.

'You bet your pampered royal arse it is,' I said, a thrill singing in my veins as Penelope huffed a delicate, raw-edged chuckle.

'*Melantho,*' Eurycleia snapped. '*How dare you!*'

I ignored her as I continued, 'You are not Precious Penelope; you never were. You are stronger than you have ever allowed yourself to realize, and I *know* you can do this. So, I need you to start pushing. For your husband. For your baby. But most importantly, for yourself. Because this is not your end.'

This is not our *end.*

A fresh wave of determination sharpened Penelope's gaze as she stared at me.

'Are you ready?' I asked, and she nodded, her eyes never leaving my face. 'On three, all right? One . . . two . . . *three.*'

It was a boy.

A healthy baby boy, with a mop of thick onyx hair just like his mother's. He was wrinkled and wriggling, and I could not take my eyes off him.

There was something about him that felt vaguely magical: how fresh he was to the world, untouched by all its ugliness.

He grizzled in Penelope's arms, as if it were a great inconvenience that he had been ripped from his warm home and into this strange, new place. As I stared at him, I wondered how something so small and fragile could have almost ended someone so important.

I was lying next to Penelope on the bed, our shoulders brushing as we gazed upon this new burst of life wriggling in her arms. Our closeness felt comfortable – natural, even. Which was strange after all the distance between us.

'He's beautiful,' I whispered.

'Is it arrogant of me to agree?' Penelope asked with a smile.

She still looked exhausted, her face deathly pale, cheeks sunken, yet her tired eyes glowed as she stared at her child. I could feel the pride and relief and wonder radiating off her, mingling with my own.

'Although, I think he will have my nose. Poor child.' She tutted.

'I like your nose,' I said. Penelope only scoffed in response. 'I'm serious. I've always liked your nose.'

'Really?'

I nudged her arm, the warmth of her body pressing into mine. 'Really.' My eyes flickered to her face, and I watched the smile grow there.

I glanced away. 'Do you think Eurycleia will be gone long?'

'I hope so. She's brilliant, but, Gods, is she intense.'

I huffed a laugh. 'I think she's going to skin me alive for ordering you around so much.'

'I seem to remember you saying something about my "pampered royal arse"?'

'Me? Never. You were delirious; you must've been hallucinating.'

Out of the corner of my eye, I saw Penelope's smile stretch into a grin.

'Strange. I'm quite certain I heard it.'

'Well, whatever I *might* have said, I got results, didn't I?' I motioned to the babe in her arms.

She chuckled at that, and I felt the sound glow inside me, so warm and alive. It never felt like that with anyone else, and I had missed the feeling.

I had missed *her*.

'You're right, you know,' she murmured, voice sobering. 'I could not have done it without you, Melantho. I mean it.'

That warm feeling in my chest intensified.

'You could have,' I whispered. 'But I am glad I was here.'

I leant forward, brushing a finger along the babe's cheek, his skin so impossibly soft.

I felt Penelope's eyes on me, and it was only when I met her gaze that I realized how close our faces had become. I could feel the warmth of her breath against my lips, could feel her unbound hair caressing my cheek. There was something in the depth of our silence, as if we were trying to let the stillness speak the words we could not form.

The door burst open then, making the baby bawl. I instantly recoiled from Penelope as Odysseus strode into the room, a huge grin cracked across his face.

'Where is he? Where is my son?' he bellowed, not even sparing me a glance as I shrank against the wall. 'By Zeus, look at him! He is perfect! My love, I am so proud of you.'

I melted further into the shadows as Odysseus cupped Penelope's face and planted a kiss on her lips, claiming them for himself.

'What of your meeting with Palamedes?' Penelope pressed. 'Are you to join Agamemnon's war?'

'We will discuss when you are rested,' Odysseus said, plucking his child from her arms and shushing him back to sleep.

'But—'

'Please, my love. Let us just be together, as a family.'

Penelope's smile wavered as she nodded, and Odysseus planted another, gentler kiss upon her lips.

I slipped from the room shortly after that.

I could not stomach any more.

23

It was the dead of night when I finally returned to the slave quarters.

I was utterly spent, my body drained from battling an onslaught of emotions. There was still so much for me to process, but I forced that cacophony of thoughts to wash away in the currents of my exhaustion.

I needed to sleep, but hunger drove me to the palace kitchens. I had not eaten since breakfast, and my gnawing stomach would keep me awake if I did not satiate it. Unlike Sparta, the kitchens were not guarded at night, though I knew I would still be in trouble if I was found in there alone. So, I slipped silently across the stone floors, willing my rumbling stomach to quieten.

A heavy thud made me freeze, my eyes adjusting to the dimness to make out a familiar shadow slumped over a table.

'It's late,' I said as I approached my brother.

His head was resting on the wooden surface, and he did not bother lifting it up as he mumbled, 'Very observant, sister.'

'Where did you get that?' I motioned to the jug set beside him.

He looked up, moonlight catching in his dark, glazed eyes, making them appear even colder than usual.

'I *borrowed* it.' His words were sluggish and stumbling. 'What? Don't give me that face. I'm celebrating. *Come on*, join me, sister!'

He held out the jug and I took it gingerly. It was almost empty. I glanced around us, wondering what would happen if we were caught with stolen wine. I had not seen any slaves whipped since arriving here, but that did not mean our masters were not capable of such a thing.

I sat down on the stool beside him. 'Shouldn't you be tending the goats?'

'It's my night off.'

'Is that what you're celebrating?'

Melanthius gave a forced laugh. 'You not *heard*? The royal baby has been born! Isn't that *wonderful* news?'

'I . . . suppose,' I hedged, my fingers playing against the painted neck of the jug.

'I'm sure Odysseus is happy. Getting to meet his child for the first time, getting to hold him in his arms.' Melanthius stared at me with dead eyes. 'Wonder what that feels like.'

'Melanthius . . .'

He snatched the jug from my hands and downed the contents.

'What, Mel? Go on. What'd you have to say to me?'

My throat felt tight, my eyes hot. I hated seeing him like this. It was as if the grief had eaten him from the inside, carving out all the remnants of the brother I had once loved so dearly, leaving nothing but this cold husk of a person.

'I know this must be hard for you,' I whispered.

Melanthius bared his crimson-etched teeth into a sneer. 'Hard? Why'd it be *hard* for me?'

'Because it's not fair—'

'Not fair? No, no, no, *this*.' He slammed his hand on the tabletop. 'This is exactly how it all works.'

'*Shh*, please. Someone might hear you.'

He spoke louder, as if to spite me. 'They get to have *everything*, and we're left with *nothing*. That's how it always is. How it always *will* be.'

'We do not have nothing, Melanthius,' I said, placing my hand over his. 'We have each other.'

'And what of Callias? What's *he* got now?' His fingers tightened around mine. 'What of Melitta? What of *my child*?'

'Stop it, Melanthius. That hurts—'

'What do *they* have, sister? Do you know? Do you even *care?*' His words jabbed at old, familiar wounds.

'Of course I care,' I snapped.

'*Do you?*' he spat with enough severity to make my heartbeat quicken.

'Just because I do not wear my suffering as openly as you does not make it any less valid.'

Finally, Melanthius loosened his biting grip, and I snatched my hand away.

'I know you are hurting, but you do not have to be cruel,' I whispered.

'This whole fucking world is cruel, sister.'

'But *you* aren't, Melanthius. This isn't who you are.'

'What if you're wrong?'

I held his gaze for a long moment, until the emptiness in his eyes gave way, revealing the sadness beneath. Such desperate, depthless sadness. I felt it clutching at my heart, mingling with my own, all those taunting unanswered questions that rotted within us both. We would never know what became of our mother, or Callias, or Melitta, or the baby . . .

That was the curse of being a slave, not being deemed worthy enough to be given answers, doomed to spend our lives with the weight of the unknown. That suffocating, shapeless grief.

There was no coming to terms with it, I knew. All we could do was endure it.

With a sigh, I placed my hand over Melanthius' again. His fingers twitched at my touch. Then, a moment later, tears filled his eyes, softening them.

'The baby will've been born by now,' he murmured thickly.

The words cleaved my heart in two.

'I know.'

I squeezed his fingers, watching the moon-silvered tears spill down his cheeks as we sat for a moment, awash with our shared grief.

Melanthius then abruptly pulled away, scrubbing furiously at his eyes. They were still red and swollen as he flashed me a stiff smile. 'Looks like I've had too much to drink again, eh?'

'You're allowed to cry, Melanthius.'

He rose to his feet. 'I just need to walk it off. That's all.'

'It's the middle of the night. You should sleep.'

'*Sleep.*' He laughed emptily at the word, then strode to the door.

At the stone threshold he froze, his tall figure engulfed in darkness.

He did not turn as he whispered into the shadows, 'Do you think they're a boy or a girl?'

I stared at his back. If only I knew what to say in that moment, which words would soothe the open wound that festered in his soul.

But what could ever suffice?

'I wish I knew, brother,' I said.

He nodded slowly, and I cringed at the uselessness of my answer.

'Melanthius, wait—'

He was gone before I could say more.

24

Odysseus found me the next morning.

I had been horribly groggy as I helped prepare breakfast, my entire body protesting its lack of sleep. When I saw the Prince of Ithaca approach me in the kitchens, I wondered if I was still dreaming.

'Hello, Melantho,' he said. He wore his familiar grin, but it seemed thinner today, as if he were struggling to muster his usual warmth. 'I hope you are well?'

I gave a vague nod. 'Penelope?'

'She is doing well also, as is my son. We have decided to name him Telemachus.'

Around us, slaves began to approach and offer their congratulations. Odysseus thanked them all proudly, as if *he* had been the one to birth the babe; *his* body ripped apart, *his* life almost lost.

'Shall we walk, Melantho? I find it easier to think when I am moving.'

Nodding again, I followed Odysseus as he strode from the kitchens and down the steep palace steps.

We trudged over the fields, beyond the boundary stones marking the palace grounds, and I forced myself to keep pace with Odysseus as we ascended a sharp slope. At its crest stood an olive tree, its spindly branches thrown to the sky, like a woman frozen mid rapturous dance. Beyond the tree, the hillside fell away to the restless sea. I watched a bird swoop down towards its surface, skimming the waves before careening back up to the sky.

'I wanted to thank you, for yesterday,' Odysseus finally said, the sea breeze twining in his hair. 'Truthfully, I am regretful I could not have been there for Penelope. I was tied up in business with the Prince of Euboea, you see. I was trying to convince him that this war does not need me.'

'Did you? Convince him?' I could not help but ask.

In Sparta I would have been struck for such a bold question, but Odysseus only sighed, turning his face to the horizon.

'Alas, it seems the Fates have me in a bind,' he murmured. 'I have only longed for two things in my life. To bring fame to these shores, and to raise a son in my image. It seems the Gods have seen fit to answer both my prayers at once.' Odysseus' eyes met mine. He looked tired as he smiled. 'The Gods have a sense of humour with these things, do they not?'

I thought of the new-born babe wriggling in Penelope's arms, the son Odysseus had barely had a chance to know.

'I'm sorry,' I whispered, and was surprised to realize I meant it.

'Sorry?' He shook his head slowly. 'They say this war will be the greatest ever fought. Is that not what every man dreams of? The grandeur of epic combat. The glory. Being able to carve one's name in history.'

Something in his expression made me say, 'Perhaps some men have simpler dreams.'

He nodded, a sadness creeping into his eyes once again. 'Perhaps.'

We were silent for a long moment, watching the rising sun bleed out across the sea, creating a long, shimmering path of crimson towards the horizon. From the cynical edge of Odysseus' smile, I knew the symbolism was not lost on him.

'You remember the discussion we had last harvest?' he asked quietly.

'I do.' How could I not? It was *he* who I feared had forgotten.

Odysseus turned to me. 'Penelope recounted all that you did for her during Telemachus' birth. Eurycleia confirmed it, too.' I raised my brows, shocked that the old maid had anything nice to say of me. 'Penelope believes she would have died without you. She believes you saved her life, and the life of my son.'

'I'm not sure about that—'

Odysseus held up a hand, silencing me. 'I understand it now – what Penelope has always seen in you – and I wish to honour my wife's request. I wish to grant you your freedom, Melantho.'

It felt as though my head had detached and was floating away, the world growing small and distant beneath me. I could not speak, could barely think, barely breathe . . .

'But I cannot do so immediately.' The words pierced through my hope, and I came crashing back down to reality. 'I depart for war imminently and I do not know when I shall return. My wife will be alone here, and I know she will need a companion, someone who can support her on the difficult road ahead.' He lowered his palm on to my shoulder. 'I want that to be you.'

'Me?' I choked. 'Why?'

'Penelope is like me; her trust is not easily won. But you have earned it, and I know that is no small feat. I want to appoint you as Penelope's chief handmaid, and I want you to look after her whilst I cannot. If you do that, then I will grant you your freedom when I return from this war. You have my word.'

My mind swam, the ground feeling unsteady beneath me.

'Do we have an agreement, Melantho?'

'Yes.' I gulped down the word, tasting the dizzying edges of freedom within it.

'I want you to say it.'

I held the Prince of Ithaca's gaze. 'You have my word.'

'Good. You should know I take such a thing very seriously.' His grip tightened, just a fraction. 'You do not want to disappoint me, Melantho.'

'I will not.'

Three days later, Odysseus set sail.

All of Ithaca was summoned to watch the prince and his army depart. I sat on the harbour wall, heels scuffing against stone as the crowds churned before me, everyone eager to catch a glimpse of their beloved prince. On the water, Odysseus' fleet bobbed proudly, the owl of Athena painted in bold colours on its sides, to honour the Goddess of War and Wisdom.

The men looked uncomfortable in their armour, clunking awkwardly as they boarded their ships. Ithaca was not a military kingdom, and so Odysseus had had to scrape together every last eligible man the island had to offer to create his 'army'. It seemed an oversight, to leave the island so defenceless. But the war would be over quickly, so everyone kept saying. Agamemnon had rallied all of Greece to his cause. The Trojans would not stand a chance.

Odysseus was last to board, soaking in the adoration of his audience. It was a peculiar crowd, made up of wives and daughters and slaves and men too old or too young to voyage with him. But their love for their prince was undeniable, their cries lifting as Odysseus embraced his father. King Laertes gripped Odysseus tightly, unwilling to let go. Beside them, Penelope held Telemachus in her arms. She looked calm as ever, yet I sensed her unease. I could not pinpoint exactly what gave it away; I could just *feel* it with a cold, prickling certainty.

Odysseus planted a firm kiss on Penelope's lips and the crowd roared. He whispered something to her – a promise, perhaps? Then, the Prince of Ithaca kissed his son's head, and I saw the flash of sadness pass between man and wife as they gazed upon their child, both aware that he might never know his father.

In that moment, an eagle soared overhead and let out a mighty cry: a sign from Zeus himself. The crowd gasped and cheered as Odysseus raised his fist in triumph.

In a flurry of activity, the men set sail. I cupped my hands around my eyes, watching the ships glide towards the horizon, dozens of bows slicing their path through the sun-gilded waves, heading on their path to glory and bloodshed.

When I turned back to the harbour, I noticed Penelope was gone.

Instinct drove me as I hurried back to the palace, urgent feet carrying me up the many, many stairs, down the long, winding halls and finally to Penelope's door. But, when I lifted my hand to knock, I found myself hesitating.

Would Penelope even *want* to see me? We had not spoken since Telemachus' birth and there was still so much uncertainty between us, so much left unsaid . . .

I realized, then, that the door was slightly ajar. Inching it open, I saw Penelope standing on her balcony with her back to me. From there, she had a perfect view of the glittering sea. Odysseus' ships were dark smudges in the distance now, like a splatter of paint on the horizon. In the cot beside the hearth, Telemachus snoozed quietly.

She did not turn as I approached, but she always seemed to sense my presence, as I did hers.

I came and stood beside her, and, as we silently watched Odysseus sail away, it struck me how truly alone Penelope was. Taken from her family, her home, and now abandoned by her husband in a land she barely knew.

Who did she have left?

I tried to think of something to say, something comforting, or perhaps even a joke to ease the tension clenched around her body. But then I thought of all the times grief had visited me, and how its hideous face was not one that could be chased away with something as useless as words. So, I chose to remain quiet, hoping Penelope might find some comfort in me sharing the weight of her silence.

'Odysseus told me of a prophecy,' she murmured after a time. 'It said if he joins the war, he will not return to this land until his son is grown.'

I tried to swallow the disappointment at how painfully far away my freedom felt in that moment.

'But the prophecy said he *will* return,' I said. 'Can you not take comfort in that?'

What would I have given to know my mother might one day come back to me? To have someone offer me that tendril of hope to cling to in my darkest moments?

I wanted to say as much, to make Penelope feel grateful for this gift I would have traded my soul for. But when she turned to look at me, I felt my jealousy wither. There was such grief in her eyes, and I felt my own reflected within it. They were different breeds of grief, of course. Hers was new and raw, cut from fear for the future, not love for the past, whilst mine was a dulled, shapeless mass that had sunk to my core and taken root. Yet, for all their differences, I still felt a connection woven through our pain, threading itself across that void between us.

'Thank you, for being here,' she whispered.

Penelope then turned and headed back inside. She picked up Telemachus, cradling him to her chest as she wandered through her chamber, draped in hazy shadows and fresh sorrow. She reminded me of a solitary ship, gliding over a midnight ocean, her destination hopelessly unknown.

'It suits you, you know,' I said, leaning against the balcony archway. 'Motherhood. You're a natural.'

Penelope smiled faintly. 'Can I tell you a secret?'

I straightened. 'Of course.'

'The thought of doing it alone terrifies me.'

Slowly, I walked towards her. 'You won't be alone.'

She glanced over at me, a ray of hope dancing in her eyes, like sunlight piercing through a storm.

'I'll be here,' I continued. 'If . . . if you would like that, I mean. If you would *want* me as your handmaid . . . I would understand if you wouldn't—'

Her smile was soft, almost sad. 'Is that what *you* want, Melantho?'

I felt Odysseus' heavy hand on my shoulder as he dangled my freedom before me.

'Yes.'

She swallowed. 'Even . . . after everything?'

The question left a space for other, unspoken ones to arise, flanked by wounded memories. The lashes on my back . . . Callias' screams . . .

Melitta's sobs . . . and my own spiteful words ringing in my ears: *This is all your fault.*

I hate you.

If only I had hated Penelope. It would have been far easier. Hate was a simple emotion – ugly and clean. I knew the shape of it well. But I could no longer fit her into that mould, nor could I fasten blame to her as easily as I once had.

No, I didn't hate her. I didn't know *what* I felt for her. She was the princess who had abandoned me after I had been lashed within an inch of my life. The princess who had set guards upon me, stealing my chance of freedom, and who had watched silently as my friends were maimed. The same princess whose family had sold my mother like an animal.

And yet . . . she was also the girl who was my first true friend. The girl who had saved me from Agamemnon's wrath and Tyndareus' punishment. The girl who had nearly shattered my heart when I'd thought I would lose her to the Underworld. The girl who had been fighting for my freedom, fighting for *me*, even when I had continually pushed her away.

There was too much between us, too many threads from the past, binding us together whilst simultaneously pulling us apart. Perhaps I would never be able to let Penelope go, but neither could I let her in, not fully.

Yet, I knew one truth for certain – Penelope was my path to freedom.

So, I nodded and said to the future Queen of Ithaca, 'Yes. Even after everything.'

25

Things were awkward between us at first.

Penelope and I were perfectly polite to one another, of course. But there was a stiffness to our interactions, a hesitancy that had us fumbling for words.

I suppose this was to be expected, after all that had come between us.

We spent every day together, learning to navigate our new dynamic as well as the uncharted waters of motherhood. It was a blur of sleepless nights and constant bawling. For a human as tiny as Telemachus, I was surprised at how much *noise* he could make. Thankfully, we were not alone on this voyage, as Penelope's two other handmaids were also there to assist.

There was Hippodamia, the girl I had met the day I arrived in Ithaca, whose presence was as bright and golden as her hair. She was all laughter and smiles, and it unnerved me – how someone like us could be filled with such easy affability.

The other handmaid was a girl called Autonoë, who I guessed to be a similar age to me. She was tall and willowy, with dusky skin and long, dark hair. Her face was delicate and ethereal, almost nymph-like, yet it had been claimed by a brutal scar, the thick, puckered skin running diagonally from eyebrow to jaw. I had tried not to stare when we were first introduced, though the sight of it made my own scars itch horribly.

Autonoë had been with us the night we'd sung outside Penelope and Odysseus' marital chamber. I remembered her voice most of all, its lovely, husky cadence. She was always singing under her breath, and, though I never admitted it, I loved listening to her.

Hippodamia and Autonoë had both served as the late queen's handmaids, and they went about their tasks with ease — fetching Penelope's meals, preparing her baths, tidying her chambers — whilst I fumbled after them, always a step behind. Strangely, Penelope did not seem to enjoy this attentiveness, adamant she could do most things herself. Often, she flat out refused our aid, leaving us to sit awkwardly aside whilst she dressed herself. She was just as steadfast about tending to Telemachus, refusing a wet nurse to feed him even when Eurycleia insisted. I wondered what could have inspired such fierceness in her. But I did not ask.

In truth, I did not say much at all.

In the shadow of Hippodamia and Autonoë's bright personalities, I felt myself retreating. I found it almost unbearable, each time they offered their quick smiles and sweet words, the feel of them sticking uncomfortably to my skin. How was it so *effortless* for them to give kindness so readily? I watched as they chattered endlessly with Penelope, giggling like sisters, growing closer with each passing day. Their warmth was a beautiful thing, but it only left me cold.

I didn't know how to be like them, how to remove this armour I had worn for so long.

But it was safer this way — to keep those boundaries clear between us. And whenever I found myself longing for that closeness with Penelope, the one we had shared the night Telemachus was born, I would force myself to remember Callias instead. To see his terrified face. To hear his blood-curdling screams. To smell his burning flesh. I would repeat those memories over and over, until the very idea of closeness made me sick to my stomach.

Until I felt myself drifting further away.

'I heard news today,' Penelope told us one night.

It was late in the evening after an especially wearing day. Telemachus had been bawling since sunrise, seemingly indifferent to everything we offered him. Now, finally, he had settled, and the four of us were nursing well-earned cups of wine by the fire.

'What news?' Hippodamia asked from where she sat beside Penelope. Autonoë was on her other side, whilst I knelt on the floor by the hearth, willing its warmth to soak into my tired limbs.

'Of the war,' Penelope replied.

This caught my attention.

News of the war trickled in slowly from the seas, morsels feasted on by hungry Ithacans eager to hear of their husbands, sons, fathers and brothers. Since Odysseus' departure, over three moon cycles ago, the atmosphere on Ithaca had been strange, as if everyone were holding their breath, suspended in time whilst they waited for the army's return. Though, I cannot say I missed them. It felt nice to have an island largely free of men, like I could breathe a little easier.

The last we had heard, Agamemnon had finally gathered all his allies, but they had been unable to sail for Troy due to unseasonably dead winds.

An act of the Gods, people had whispered. *They do not support this war.*

'The winds have finally picked up,' Penelope said, swirling her cup in her hand. 'Agamemnon's army are on their way to Troy as we speak.'

'That's good news, isn't it? The sooner they reach Troy, the sooner this war will be over,' Autonoë said in her soft voice, a faded accent rounding her vowels.

Penelope shifted in her chair. 'Agamemnon had to make a sacrifice to the Gods to be allowed passage to Troy.'

'A sacrifice to the Gods is customary,' Hippodamia replied around a sip of wine.

It seemed she had not noticed the disquiet creeping over Penelope. I remained silent, watching Penelope stare intently into the hearth.

'He was forced to sacrifice his own child,' she whispered. 'Iphigenia.'

Her words seemed to steal all the warmth from the fire, plunging the chamber into an icy stillness.

A sickness pierced my stomach. *His own child.*

'How could he do such a thing?' Hippodamia whispered, wrapping her arms around herself.

'To appease the Gods,' Penelope replied.

'Why would anyone worship a god who would demand that of them?' I muttered.

'It gives people a sense of purpose, to worship something,' Penelope mused, taking a slow sip of her wine.

The silence around us was a terrible, heavy thing. All I could think of was that faceless girl, so young and innocent. How afraid must she have been in those final moments, surrounded by a swarm of glory-hungry men? Had she looked to her father for protection? Had his betrayal been the last thing she'd seen?

After a time, Autonoë began to sing. It was a song of lamentation, one sung during funerals to honour the dead. Her beautiful voice filled the room, the heartbreaking melody seeming to pluck the threads from my past, laying my losses bare in the shadows around me. Tears were in Autonoë's eyes as she sang, and I noticed Hippodamia was crying too. I wondered what other ghosts lurked in the room, alongside my own.

When the song was over, Hippodamia and Autonoë quietly excused themselves and retired to our shared chamber in the adjoining room. I did not follow them. Instead, I stared at Penelope as she continued watching the fire, eyes glassy.

'I cannot imagine what Clytemnestra is going through,' she whispered. 'If I lost Telemachus, it would be like having my soul ripped out of me. How can a mother endure that?'

I looked away, an old pain aching through my bones. I felt Penelope's gaze snap to my face, her pity staining the air.

'I am sorry, Melantho. Forgive me. I should not have spoken so carelessly.'

'It's fine,' I murmured.

'I should have thought before I—'

'Penelope,' I cut her off gently. 'It's fine.'

We sat quietly for a moment. I considered retiring to bed, retreating behind those boundaries I had been so carefully keeping between us. But something kept me there.

'Why did you never tell me what happened to your mother?' Penelope finally asked, her voice painfully soft.

Normally, I would have snapped an unsavoury reply, letting my anger shield my wounds. But then I thought of Melanthius. I did not want to be like him, so consumed by all the ugliness inside me. So, I willed that anger to settle as I took a slow sip of wine.

'I try not to think about it,' I admitted.

I could feel Penelope watching me, waiting.

'They sold her,' I continued, in an attempt to put an end to that probing gaze. 'That's all there is to it.'

'I am sorry,' she whispered.

'I used to be envious that your mother was dead, you know. I prayed my mother was too, because at least then I would have known where she was. I would have had answers.' I stared at Penelope, waiting to see a flash of repulsion in her gaze, of anger. But there was none. 'I suppose that is rather vile . . . to have prayed for something like that.'

Penelope rested her chin on her knuckles as she considered my words.

'I think your mother would have understood why you felt like that,' she said.

I shrugged, turning to watch the fire.

'What of your father?' Penelope pressed delicately. 'I never see you two together . . .'

My lips twisted into a tight smirk. 'We both have little interest in each other's company.'

'And your brother?'

'Melanthius can be . . . hard to reach.'

Penelope was quiet a moment, turning my words over in the stillness.

'Will you tell me what she was like? Your mother,' she prompted, as if she could sense those memories inside me, pooling so close to the surface.

It had been so long since I had spoken of my mother, it was as if I had forgotten how to shape this pain into words. Yet, a part of me felt a sudden, powerful urge to talk about her, to let my mother live and breathe in this room with us, even if she could only exist through my voice.

'She was wonderful,' I whispered, throat burning. 'She was kind and funny and brave and smart and fierce.'

'She sounds like you.'

I shook my head. 'I was her biggest regret.'

I sensed Penelope shifting, moving to sit a little straighter in her chair.

'I do not think that is true, Melantho.'

But it was. I knew it was. My mother had never spoken those words aloud to me, of course, but silent truths will always find ways of being heard, and this one had whispered to me since childhood, in a language I had not understood until recently.

'I don't mean to say she did not love me,' I clarified. 'In fact, she loved me too much.'

I began tapping a finger against my cup, the *ting* of bronze the only sound in the room, like a steady, metallic heartbeat.

The heat of the fire made my eyes feel hot and itchy, and I blinked a few times before continuing, 'They make it seem like a prize, you know. When they let slaves have babies. That's how they sold it to my mother: a "reward" for her good behaviour. She fell for the lie at first. But then my brother and I were born, and I think, in that moment, she realized what she had done. She finally understood. We were not *her* children, but the king's *property*. She had not *gifted* us life but *doomed* us with it. And she always regretted that. Regretted us.'

Fat tears rolled silently down my cheeks, warmed by the firelight. I quickly dashed them away.

'I'm sorry. I should not have said anything. Forget—'

'I was never close with my mother,' Penelope said. 'Sometimes it feels like I never really knew her at all. I suppose, in a way, I didn't. My mother often took ill, so we were kept apart, and I was raised by her handmaids.

It was not her fault, though as a child I used to be so angry at her for it — for being too sick to love me.' I watched Penelope's gaze drift into memories, the ghost of that anger pressing between her brows then disappearing behind a shadow of remorse. 'When she died, I did not cry. Not a single tear. I wish I had, for then maybe I might feel less guilty for not having loved her as I should have.'

I was quiet for a long moment, absorbing the rawness of her words.

'That is why you refuse any assistance. With Telemachus.'

Penelope said nothing.

'You know, it is all right to ask for help sometimes,' I said, tilting my head to try to catch her eye. 'It won't make you any less of a mother. You don't have to do it alone.'

'I am not alone. I have you.' Her gaze slid to mine and she smiled.

I was struck by a desperate desire to keep that smile alive, and so I added with a slight smirk, 'Well, maybe *I* could do with more help.'

Penelope considered that. 'Do you truly feel that way?'

'Can you blame me? That baby is the most demanding master I've ever served. Stubborn, too. I think you've birthed a tyrant.'

Her smile curled wider, eyes sparking. 'Did you really just call my infant son a tyrant?'

'You've seen the way he screams and waves his fists around when he wants something. Tell me that isn't tyrant behaviour.'

Penelope tipped her head back and laughed, the sound like a burst of light chasing away the shadows. *Lemons* — that was what her laugh had reminded me of when I'd first heard it. So beautifully bright and sharp.

I had always loved lemons.

'I cannot believe *you* are calling my son stubborn,' she said.

'What's that supposed to mean?'

Penelope arched an eyebrow. 'Melantho, you are the most stubborn person I have ever met.'

'*I am not!*'

Penelope chuckled, shaking her head. 'It is a compliment.'

'I don't see how.'

'Well, compliments are subjective, I suppose. But I meant it as one. I have always loved your stubbornness.'

Loved. The word stirred something inside me, making my pulse quicken and my stomach coil tight. Penelope must have sensed this, for her eyes slipped away from mine quickly, as if embarrassed by the reaction she saw there. Shame crawled up my spine, and I silently cursed myself for wearing my emotions so plainly.

Shooting to my feet, I tried to sound nonchalant as I said, 'Speaking of the tyrant, I should get some sleep before his reign of terror continues tomorrow.'

Penelope only smiled faintly in response.

The door to the handmaids' chamber was situated just beyond where Penelope was sitting. As I moved to walk past her, I mumbled a quiet, 'Goodnight.'

Her hand shot out, fingers lacing around my wrist. I froze, every inch of my body becoming totally fixated on that small point of contact, on the feel of her skin against mine, as if her touch were a single flame in a starless night.

The heat in my cheeks intensified.

'Melantho.'

I tried to stare ahead, but that familiar tide pulled me to her once again, as it always did. When I looked at her, my heartbeat began to quicken, pounding so hard in my chest it felt as if my ribs had shrunk around it, squeezing too tight.

How did she always have this effect on me?

And why did nobody else?

'Perhaps your mother regretted that *this* is the world she brought you into, but I do not believe, not for a single moment, that she ever regretted *you*.'

My vision blurred as I lowered my gaze to the ground, trying not to let the tears spill again. I did not know what to reply, so I said nothing at all.

Finally, Penelope let go.

'Sleep well, Melantho.'

In the darkness of my chamber, I replayed that moment over and over in my mind, torturing myself with every minute detail as a strange, heated ache awoke in the pit of my stomach.

Eventually, sleep took me in its swift clutches, dragging me down to that dangerous realm where my thoughts reigned free.

I dreamt of bare skin kissed golden in the firelight, of slender hands gripping me tight, lips curled into a drowsy smile as they found their mark upon my body. I dreamt of long, dark hair spilling around me like liquid night, of intense grey eyes staring up into mine as those familiar lips trailed along an expanse of bare flesh, inching down and down my body . . .

When I awoke with a start, I convinced myself I did not know who that person was. It was just a faceless figure, a vision of my own design, woven from the tapestry of my dreams.

It was a stranger; it must have been.

It *had* to have been.

26

I had made a terrible mistake.

This realization settled over me as I regarded the disgust on my brother's face.

It had been Penelope's suggestion, to invite Melanthius to her quarters. She had offered a few days after we'd heard the news of Iphigenia, and a foolish, naive part of me had thought it a good idea. Melanthius and I so rarely had the opportunity to spend time together.

But now, watching him regard Penelope's quarters with such deep revulsion etched into his face, I understood the fatal error I had made.

'It's good to see you,' I said.

Melanthius remained silent, scratching an invisible mark on the table.

'Would you like some wine?' I offered, motioning to the ornate jug set beside us.

He laughed, the sound sharp and unpleasant. 'Look at you in your fancy clothes with your fancy wine. How high you've risen.'

Anger surged up my throat, coating my tongue in hot, hateful words. But I forced myself to swallow them down. I had brought my brother here to close the distance between us, not widen it.

'How have you been?' I ventured as I filled two cups, trying to steer the conversation into steadier waters.

'This what you do all day, then?' Melanthius asked coldly, ignoring the cup I set down before him. 'Sitting around *drinking* and *chatting*. A tough job you've got yourself there, sister.'

My jaw clenched. 'I was simply asking you a question.'

'Well, I didn't come here to discuss *how I am.*'

'Then why did you come at all?'

Instead of replying, Melanthius glanced around the room. 'Where is *she*?'

'Penelope is visiting King Laertes in his quarters. Hippodamia and Autonoë are out.'

'So, we're alone?'

I nodded, then stiffened as Melanthius abruptly pulled his chair closer to me. 'What are you—'

'I'm getting outta here, Mel.'

'*What?*'

'I met a sailor in town. He promised me safe passage.'

'Passage to *where*?'

'To the mainland.' He said this as if it were obvious. 'Then I'll find my way on from there to Sparta.'

'To Sparta?'

Melanthius nodded fervently. 'To Melitta. To my child.'

A knot tied in my gut. 'What have you promised the sailor?'

'Silver pieces.'

My eyes narrowed. 'Do you *have* any?'

He shrugged. 'Enough.'

'How?'

'I've got my ways.'

I did not like the sound of that, not one bit. But from the stiffness set into Melanthius' jaw, I knew he would not elaborate further.

'I want you to come with me, Mel,' he said, trapping my hands and pulling them to his chest. 'The boat leaves tomorrow night, from the old harbour. You know the one?'

I said nothing.

'Melantho.' He squeezed my hands tighter, voice softening. 'I *need* you to come with me . . . Please.'

I could not stand the feverish hope burning in his gaze. I had not seen such light in his eyes since we'd left Sparta, and a part of me ached to feed those flames, to protect them with everything I had.

But to flee Ithaca ... To return to Sparta ...

'This is madness,' I whispered, guilt aching between every word. 'You know it is.'

Melanthius let go of me instantly, anger falling across his face, eclipsing that fragile light.

'It's not madness, it's a *chance*.'

'A chance for what? To get yourself killed?' I reached for him, but he pulled further away. 'Melanthius, please—'

'I see how it is,' he whispered, voice dangerously quiet. 'So long as *you're* cared for, right, Mel? So long as *you've* got the nice room, the clean clothes, the fine wine, that's all that matters, eh? Forget the rest of us.'

My face grew hot, hands trembling into fists. 'If you think for *one second* that I have forgotten—'

'No? Then that's even *worse*. That you'd *choose* to stay here and serve the woman who had us caught and beaten, who had Melitta *taken from me*, and my chi—' The word caught in his throat, choking him.

'Penelope was only trying to protect us.'

'*Don't.*' He slammed the table with his fist, making me flinch. 'Don't you dare defend *her*.'

I hated the cold curl of fear that slithered through me. It felt so wrong to be frightened of Melanthius, when once he had been my safest harbour.

'I'm not defending her,' I said carefully, forcing myself to hold his blistering glare. 'But it's not as simple as you think—'

'No, sister. It's actually very, *very* simple.' Melanthius braced his hands on the table, leering towards me. 'Penelope is one of them, and to them *we're nothing*. We've always been nothing, and always will be.' My brother's gaze dropped, noting the flush of colour creeping up my neck, bleeding into my cheeks. 'Oh, Mel ... Don't tell me you actually believe Penelope *cares* for you? How about we count the scars on your back? Will that remind you how she *really* feels?'

'Stop it—'

'What *is* it with her?' he pressed, disgust curling around his lips. 'What hold does she have over you?'

I looked away, shame clotting inside me as that dream flooded my mind, the same one that had been plaguing me the last few nights.

'I'm done with this conversation,' I said, rising on shaky legs.

Melanthius laughed. I remembered when his laughter had been sweet and infectious, always summoning my own. The noise that escaped him now was the withered ghost of that laugh, a cruel, dead shadow chilling the room.

'O' course, run back to your Precious Penelope. Gods forbid you spend too much time with your own kind.'

'What's that supposed to mean?'

'Admit it, Mel.' He stood slowly, stepping towards me. His breath smelt rancid, of wine and grief. 'You hate your own kind. You only care for yourself.'

'That's not true—'

'Tell me, how many slaves would you step on to keep Penelope's attention? You already traded Callias and Melitta. So, how many more?' He pushed closer, forcing me to retreat a step. 'Five? Ten? A hundred?'

'That's enough. You need to *leave*.'

'Oh? You're giving *me* orders now, that it? You really have been spending too long with *their* kind, sister.'

His fury was like a shard of glass embedded into his flesh – sharp and cold and cruel, reflecting all the ugliness I recognized inside myself.

'I said *leave*.' My voice quivered from the strain of reining in my temper.

'*This* is your problem, Mel. You think yourself so above us; you always have.' He was all around me now, swallowing up every inch of space until my back was pressed against the furthest wall. 'But guess what? You're just as *worthless* as the rest of us, and no matter how much you grovel at Penelope's pampered feet, you won't *ever change that*.'

I moved to shove him away, but Melanthius caught my wrists, yanking me against his chest so he could spit his next words directly into my face.

'Listen close, sister, cause it appears you've forgotten . . . you are Penelope's *slave*. You are a *thing*, an *object*, just like the rest of us, and you'll *never* be anything more to her. You are nothing. Do you hear me? *Nothing*.'

His eyes were manic, but amidst that frenzy I saw something caught there, vulnerable and delicate, beating like the wings of a bird in a raging tempest.

'Is that what you see yourself as, Melanthius?' I asked. His lips curled into a snarl, but he remained silent. 'Because it's not true. You are *not* nothing. Not to me.'

'Don't give me your pity—'

'It's not pity. You are not—'

'I SAID *DON'T*!'

I did not see his hand until it struck, the impact singing along my cheekbone. But it was not pain that shot through me. It was rage.

Melanthius' face was suddenly bloodless, eyes wide.

'Melantho . . .' he spluttered. 'I didn't mean . . . I . . .'

'Get out.'

'Sister—'

'*GET OUT!*' I screamed, so loud it made my cheek throb.

Melanthius flinched, stumbling back a step.

Then he turned and fled.

Penelope's quarters were mercifully quiet when I returned.

I had spent the afternoon walking the hills of Ithaca, chased by my brother's vile words.

It was dark now, a stillness falling over the palace as night settled in. I was grateful for the solitude as I cut across the room to where the wine had been left out. I poured myself a drink and drained it quickly, then another.

Setting the cup down, I covered my face with my hands, feeling the heat radiate from my swollen left cheek. I pressed harder, wanting to feel the sting of Melanthius' strike once again, wanting it to *hurt*.

You only care about yourself.

'How did it go with your brother?'

I glanced over my shoulder and found Hippodamia watching me from the hearth, her brows pressed together in concern.

I said nothing, turning back to refill my wine.

'Melantho? Are you all right?'

'I'm fine.'

'Are you sure?'

'I said *I'm fine*.'

'You don't *seem* fine—'

'Well, apologies – we can't all be perfect, happy handmaids like *you* – but some of us have shit to deal with.' The words were like poison leaking from an infected wound. I couldn't have stopped them even if I had tried.

Hippodamia huffed a quiet, humourless laugh but said nothing.

I sighed, setting the wine jug down.

'I . . . It's been a long day,' I murmured, rubbing my chest with the heel of my palm, trying to dispel the guilt that had settled there. 'I want to be alone.'

I hoped Hippodamia would take the invitation to leave, but then I heard her bare feet padding over the floor and felt her draw up beside me. She picked up the jug of wine.

'Did you know I was born in a brothel in Athens?' She spoke as she filled a cup for herself. 'My mother worked there. My father . . . Well, he was only around long enough to get what he paid for. My mother died in childbirth, and I was left to grow up there alone, forced to work as soon as my body had developed enough to . . . *satisfy* the customers. I was only six when I had my first client.' She smiled at me as she brought the wine to her lips and took a sip. 'I have stories darker than Nyx herself.'

'I . . . I'm sorry. I didn't—'

She shook her head. 'No. Don't give me your sympathy. I don't need it. You know why? Because I decided long ago that my past would not define me. I decided that every day I would wake up and I would *choose* happiness. We don't have much choice in this life, Melantho, but we have choice over that. To not let them break us. *That* is my rebellion. It may seem small and insignificant to some, but it is the reason I am still here today.'

I stared at her for a long moment, mesmerized by her quiet, beautiful strength.

'How did you end up in Ithaca?' I asked.

'It turned out the brothel manager was a terrible businessman. Gambled away all his earnings. He had to sell all his whores to pay back his debts. I was carted around to a few port towns and was finally bought by King Laertes.' Hippodamia sipped her wine, watching me over the rim. I sensed she was debating her next words carefully. 'You can choose it too, you know. To be happy.'

I glanced away. 'It's not always that simple.'

'It can be. But first you must *allow* yourself to be happy.' I felt the warmth of Hippodamia's hand on my arm. It was surprisingly reassuring. 'Whoever it is you've lost, don't you think they would want you to be happy too?'

'Why are you being so nice to me?' I asked thickly.

She chuckled, her hand falling away. 'Our masters prefer it if we hate one another because we're weaker when we're divided. Friendship can be a form of rebellion too.'

We were silent a while as I let her words sink in.

'Do you . . . do you see Penelope as your friend?'

Hippodamia nodded. 'I do.'

'But she's not one of us,' I bit out. 'She's one of *them*.'

'She belongs to Odysseus, just as we do.'

'It's not the same.'

'I never said it was.'

'Penelope is a *princess*. A future *queen*.'

'And yet . . .' Hippodamia took another slow drink. 'Even when she sits upon Ithaca's throne, Penelope will still be a possession. She will still belong to a man. That is the curse all women carry. A curse that unites us.'

'So what? You think we should see Penelope as one of us, merely because she's a woman?'

Hippodamia smiled, setting her cup down gently. 'What *I* think, Melantho, is that we should see people in our own light, rather than the light the world tries to force upon us. If Penelope does not treat me as a slave, then why should I treat her as a master?'

I blinked. How did she make it sound so *simple*?

'Penelope cares a great deal for you, you know,' she added.

I felt my cheeks instinctively heat. There was a flare of delight in my chest, quickly chased by a rush of shame. I pretended to find a sudden fascination in my wine.

'I'll leave you be,' Hippodamia whispered. 'Goodnight, Melantho.'

She squeezed my arm again before leaving, and I envied how easily she wielded such warmth.

Once alone, I felt my mother's ghost creep into the stillness. I so rarely let myself think of her, but Hippodamia's words had plucked these memories from their graves, splaying them out before me.

I pictured my mother's face, how it would come alive whenever I laughed or smiled, as if my joy were the single spark that lit her own.

I pictured us in the palace kitchens, working away side by side whilst I moaned about petty, childish things. I heard my mother's reply, her voice as bright and clear as the moonlight spilling through the windows.

All I want is for you to be happy, my heart.

'But what if I don't deserve to be?' I whispered back.

I stood in my loneliness, awaiting a reply that would never come.

27

The next morning, I did not leave my bed.

Hippodamia and Autonoë let me be as I hid under the covers, quietly festering beneath the weight of my brother's words. They played over and over in my mind, like the mighty ouroboros forever eating its own tail, my thoughts turning in an endless, devouring circle.

You only care for yourself.

You hate your own kind.

You are nothing.

It was as if a sinking void had opened beneath me, my body too drained and lifeless to claw its way out.

Eventually, hunger forced me to drag myself from bed and trudge into the central room of Penelope's quarters.

'Melantho.' Her voice greeted me as soon as I entered. Though, she sounded strange, her voice clipped and formal. 'I understand you were not feeling well, and that is why you rose late. You are excused for this.'

Excused? Penelope met my frown with a pointed look, and I followed her gaze to where the King of Ithaca stood on her balcony, cradling Telemachus in his arms.

'Thank you . . . mistress,' I said, the title tasting bitter on my tongue.

Penelope gave an apologetic smile. I knew she felt uneasy around Laertes, as many of us did. The king was a peculiar man. Hippodamia said the death of his wife had completely unravelled him, and the departure of his only son seemed to have done further damage. These days, Laertes stalked through the palace like a restless, angry spirit. When he wasn't ranting wildly at the slaves, he was shouting doomed proclamations to whoever might listen. *All is lost . . . The Gods have cursed me . . . I will never again know my son's smile . . .*

I glanced around the room, looking for Hippodamia and Autonoë, but they were nowhere to be seen. No doubt they had wanted to avoid the unpleasantness of Laertes' company.

'I think he has my eyes,' Laertes said as he wandered in from the balcony.

I stifled a scoff. Telemachus quite clearly had Penelope's grey eyes. But, of course, men only wished to see their own selves reflected in the world.

'Let me see,' Penelope said, placing a hand on Laertes' shoulder to peer at her son. 'Ah, yes, so he does. The Gods have certainly blessed him.'

Laertes' mood instantly darkened at her words.

'Blessed? Telemachus is not blessed. The Gods have cursed him to never know his father.'

Penelope squeezed his shoulder. 'I have faith the Gods will return Odysseus to us. I pray for it every day.'

The king patted her hand with a condescending smile. 'You are sweet, my dear, but you are ever so naive.' He then turned to bark, 'Slave.'

He held Telemachus out to me, but Penelope intercepted, taking her son in her arms. Her smile remained perfectly in place, though it seemed tighter around her lips.

'He needs bathing. Give him to the slave,' the king ordered.

'I can do it,' Penelope said.

Laertes watched her with a disapproving frown. 'That is not your duty, Penelope. Remember our discussion.' The king stared pointedly across the room. I followed his gaze to where a large leather pouch sat on the far table. 'I hope you will think on my offer.'

Penelope nodded. 'Of course, my king.'

With that, the King of Ithaca shuffled from the room, shoulders stooped as if he held the weight of the world upon them. Once he was gone, I turned to where Penelope was setting Telemachus down in his cot.

'It's nice to see Laertes is his usual, optimistic self today, is it not?' she said dryly. 'How was Melanthius yesterday? You disappeared afterwards, so I didn't—' She cut herself short, eyes narrowing. 'What is that?'

Before I could reply she was striding towards me, gaze fixed on my cheek.

'Melantho.' Her voice was strangely quiet, strained almost. 'Who did this?'

'It's nothing.'

'Tell me it wasn't your brother.'

'I said *it's nothing*.' I turned away, hating how ugly my words sounded against the softness of her concern.

Penelope captured my chin and tilted my face back to hers. Her touch was so gentle I felt the dangerous urge to lean into it, though the feeling was accompanied by a sharp stab of guilt.

How many slaves would you step on to keep Penelope's attention?

I jerked away from her, my eyes settling on the swollen leather pouch Laertes had left on the table.

'What was Laertes' offer?' I asked.

Penelope hesitated. 'It was nothing of interest.'

'It must have been something.'

She sighed, touching a finger to her brow. 'Laertes believes I require more handmaids. Apparently, it looks *cheap* for a future queen to only have three. He was worried I did not find any of the palace slaves "suitable", and that was why I had been resistant.'

'He left you silver?'

She waved a dismissive hand. 'He said the slaver is at the market today. He wanted me to send someone to purchase more handmaids. I am going to refuse, of course.'

'What do you mean, "of course"?'

Penelope hesitated at my tone. 'Because I do not need more handmaids, and I think the slave market is barbaric. I want nothing to do with its business.'

'You already *have something to do with it*, Penelope. You *own* slaves.'

'A husband owns slaves,' she replied carefully. 'A wife owns nothing.'

We stared at one another for a tense moment, knowing this was dangerous territory for us to tread.

'How much did he give you?'

'What does it matter?'

'*What does it matter?* Are you truly asking me that?'

Penelope watched with infuriating calmness as I stalked across the room and snatched up the leather pouch.

'Do you realize what this is?' I demanded, letting the silver pieces spill across the table. '*This* is a person's life, Penelope. You have that power, *right here*, and you are asking me "what does it matter"?'

'I did not mean it like that,' she replied, her voice so maddeningly composed it only stoked my rage. Of course, *she* could be calm about this. It wasn't *her* life on the line. 'I chose the wrong wording—'

I threw the silver down in anger, the loud clatter of metal against wood silencing Penelope.

'You could save people's lives with this. Laertes has given you that power and you are going to *refuse* it?'

Penelope stared at the scattered silver. I hated how well she hid her thoughts, how she always kept me on the outside, whilst I continually bared everything for her.

We are nothing to them.

'It is not so simple,' she finally said.

Her words splintered something in my heart, and I felt my rage rush up to greet it, filling in those fissures.

'It *is* that simple; you are just refusing to see it,' I snapped as I strode for the door.

'Where are you going?'

'I need air. Do I have your permission, *mistress*?'

I watched the title land like a blow. She flinched, glancing away from me. I found no satisfaction in hurting her; if anything, it only made that pit in my stomach grow deeper.

You are nothing.

I did not wait for her reply as I stormed away.

In my hands I clutched the leather pouch, the stolen silver tinkling inside like cruel laughter, chasing me from the palace.

The market bustled with life.

Wooden stalls filled the cobbled streets, canopied by colourful stretches of fabric playing in the sea breeze. Some of the shops spilt from small, mud-brick buildings, their fronts opening out like giant gaping mouths. In the distance, I could see the Temple of Athena, modest yet proud, overlooking the hubbub below.

It felt freeing to melt into the crowds, losing myself in the vibrant current of overlapping lives. People laughed and gossiped and argued, sellers hollered over the commotion, eager to catch a buyer's attention. All around me, rich, dizzying smells filled the air. There was so much to look at I found my head snapping back and forth as I admired the stands – baked goods, fresh fish, ground spices. I lingered at one that was selling jewellery, my eyes caught by the twinkle of gold.

'The finest in Ithaca,' the seller told me with a toothy grin.

I shook my head politely as I wandered on, surprised to see most of the sellers were women. But of course they were, for the men of Ithaca had left with their prince.

The scent of freshly baked flatbread lured me towards a tucked-away shop. Inside, I saw a woman kneading dough on the countertop. Stools were set up for patrons to sit and chat whilst she prepared their food. Her strong hands worked with deft efficiency, and I saw glimpses of my mother within them as memories glowed inside me.

A hand grabbed my wrist.

I let out a yelp as I was tugged into the narrow passageway beside the baker's shop. I stumbled, panic spasming in my chest as I clutched tightly at my pouch of silver.

'Has Dionysus stolen your mind?'

I stared up at the tall, slender figure before me. Her clothes were different, tattered and worn, a drab scarf concealing most of her features, but that rainfall voice was unmistakable.

'*Penelope?*' I gaped. 'What are you *doing* here?'

'I could ask you the same thing.'

The stolen silver suddenly felt heavier in my hands.

'I'm sure you've already figured it out,' I countered, lifting my chin.

'Of course I have. But I didn't quite believe you'd be foolish enough to go through with it.'

I glared up at her. The passageway draped us in cool shadows, yet I could see the glint of her grey eyes, intent on mine. She was standing so close to me, too close. I took a step back and felt the wall press against my spine.

'You shouldn't be here.'

'I did not have much choice in the matter.' She spoke calmly, but there was an undeniable edge to her voice. 'If I had sent someone after you, how would I have explained this situation?'

I shrugged and something flared in Penelope's eyes, like a single star carving across a midnight sky.

'Do you not care about being caught?'

'It was a risk I was willing to take.'

'And what about me?'

'*You?*' I sneered. 'You wouldn't have been punished for my actions, *princess*.'

'I'm not talking about me being punished. I am talking about me being forced to witness *your* punishment.' Her voice wavered. 'I cannot go through that again, Melantho. I cannot see you be—'

She was cut off by a burst of laughter from the street. We both glanced towards the mouth of the passageway, watching the crowds filter past in a steady, bubbling stream.

'We need to go back to the palace,' she said. 'Before anyone notices we're gone.'

'I'm not going back. Not yet.'

Penelope inhaled a delicate breath, nostrils flaring. Without warning, she stepped closer to me, so close I could feel her chest brushing against mine. I pressed myself harder against the wall, willing it to swallow me up, to let me escape from the insufferable heat of her body and how it made my insides squirm.

She stared at me for a long moment, gaze burning not with anger, but something equally fierce. Something far more confusing.

I could have sworn the air between us crackled.

Whatever Penelope was going to say, she seemed to think better of it, instead turning on her heel and striding towards the mouth of the passageway.

'Where are you going?'

'If we must wait, I'm not doing it here. It smells awful,' she said over her shoulder.

Unsure what else to do, I followed her.

Penelope cut through the crowd with surprising ease, as if she had navigated these streets many times before. She walked differently here, her usual, elegant strides replaced with a casual, bouncing lope. Nobody looked twice at her. With her threadbare attire and her scarf pulled close around her face, she looked like just another slave girl running errands for their master. I glanced at the bustle of bodies around us, wondering what any of them would think if they knew their future queen stood amongst them.

We followed the hill down towards the harbour. Penelope picked her way along the edge until she found a quiet spot.

'What are you doing?' I asked as she sat down on the crumbling harbour wall.

'Waiting.'

'For what?'

She stared at the horizon as she said, 'The slaver doesn't arrive till midday. So, we must wait.' Then, she produced a small leather pouch from the belt of her tunic and handed it to me. I felt the weight of the silver inside. 'You forgot these. The ones you spilt on to the table.'

My hand tightened around the second pouch. A heaviness settled over me, and I shifted beneath its awkward weight.

'Why are you giving me this?'

'So you can buy more handmaids,' Penelope said simply.

'But you don't want any more.'

Instead of replying, she said, 'Look there.'

I followed her gaze down to the water's edge where a group of women were preparing a fishing boat, their shouts falling into chorus with the swooping gulls.

'Those women would have spent their whole lives waving off fathers and husbands as they headed out to fish,' Penelope murmured, a quiet wonder flickering in her voice. 'Now they are the ones guiding their own boat, earning their own keep. It's beautiful, isn't it?'

I sat down beside her on the wall. 'There's nothing beautiful about labour.'

'For a slave, no, you are right,' she agreed. 'But for women like that, work means independence. It means freedom. That is the gift this war has given Ithaca . . . space for the women to grow.'

We watched as the fishing boat bobbed out to sea, the women's laughter dancing over the waves. I found myself smiling at the sound, despite myself. But when I glanced back at Penelope, her expression was distant, her thoughts as limitless and unreachable as the horizon taunting us in the distance.

For a while, we said nothing. But there was something in the depth of her silence that made me finally ask, 'Why don't you want any more handmaids, Penelope?'

She let out a small sigh, hands knotting in her lap.

'That summer . . . when we were children . . .' Her eyes flickered to my back, then away again. I'd never heard her so hesitant, words brittle and stumbling. 'It . . . broke something in me . . . seeing what they did to you . . . knowing it was *my* fault . . . knowing I couldn't protect you.'

Callias' screams filled my mind, and I thought of how it had felt to watch him being branded. The guilt had devoured me whole.

Was that how Penelope had felt all this time?

I felt a shiver of shame that I had never considered it, how that day could have scarred her as deeply as it had me.

She continued, 'Afterwards, I vowed I'd never take a handmaid again. I'd never be responsible for a person's life like that . . . never let innocents be hurt because of me . . . But then, that morning after my wedding . . .' She flinched at the memory, screwing her eyes tight. 'Your friends . . . what my uncle did to them . . . because of *me*.'

I watched, stunned, as the emotions consumed her composure, leaving her so raw and vulnerable. I wondered if she might even cry; I had never seen Penelope do so before. Not a single tear. But her eyes remained dry when she opened them, her expression steadier.

'Hippodamia and Autonoë were forced upon me when I arrived here,' she said. 'I tried to refuse, but I had no choice.'

'And what about me?'

'I accepted because of your deal with Odysseus.'

'I . . . didn't know you knew about that,' I admitted quietly.

'I tried to talk him out of it,' she said with a sombre smile. 'Not of freeing you, of course. But the terms of his deal.'

'Why?'

She looked away. 'I hated the idea of you being forced to endure my company.'

I noticed that Penelope was picking at the skin around her nail beds. The old habit made her seem younger – childlike, even.

'I just don't want to hurt anyone again,' she whispered.

Her words were so painfully delicate, yet they clutched at my heart with a fierceness that stole my breath away.

I felt a sudden, overwhelming rush of *sympathy* for her, as strange as it felt to place such a thing in someone who was supposedly my master. But . . . had Penelope ever *acted* like one? She had protected me, cared for me, *fought* for me. Never once had she treated me like a slave. And yet, I had continually branded her with the title of 'mistress'.

I think we should see people in our own light.

'What happened wasn't your fault, Penelope.' The thought blossomed on my lips, a truth I had always known but been too blinded by bitterness to let myself see. 'None of it was ever your fault.'

She shook her head. 'Melantho—'

'It *wasn't* your fault.'

The firmness in my voice made her finally look at me, and her eyes were like the waves before us, churning with such devastating beauty.

'I'm sorry I made you believe it was,' I added, then, even quieter, 'I'm sorry I've been so cruel to you.'

'You were never cruel, Melantho,' she whispered. 'You were just hurting.'

We stared at one another for a long moment, the past swirling around us like warm currents. Perhaps it was being here, away from the palace, lost in the anonymous chaos of the kingdom, that made me feel as if I were *seeing* Penelope for the first time again. Not the Spartan princess, or the future Ithacan queen, but the Penelope I had met that night, so long ago. The beautiful girl wrapped in moonlight and shadows and secrets. A girl who was just trying her best in this ugly world. The girl who had kept fighting for me, no matter how many times I pushed her away.

But who had ever been fighting for *her*?

'*Come get your livestock! Pigs! Goats! Slaves!*' A voice sounded in the distance, shattering our companionable silence.

On the docks, I could see the slaver leading a procession of people behind him. Their necks were chained together, and the sound of those metal shackles clanged through my bones, making my blood turn cold.

'Melantho?' Penelope was watching me. 'Are you all right?'

My voice trembled as I asked, 'Will you come with me?'

She nodded. 'Always.'

We made our way back through the market, pushing into the swelling crowds as we followed the slaver's shouts.

The owner of the voice was a short, rotund man, his fleshy face dominated by a bulbous, sunburnt nose. He was an ugly thing, but uglier still were the words that lifted from his thin, chapped lips.

'Come, come! Take a look at the livestock! The finest you'll find in Ithaca!'

He stood beside three pens. One was being filled with pigs, the other goats, and the third was where he deposited the slaves.

They looked less than human — covered in filth, their clothes ragged, hair matted.

There were six of them altogether, two of which were women. Neither was my mother.

One was older, hair silvered and shoulders hunched with age, though she was trying to hold herself proudly. The other was the tallest woman I had ever seen. Her head was shaved, and her muscular body was covered in intricate ink markings.

A finely dressed man approached the slaver. He was old, though I had seen far older men sail with Odysseus. I wondered what ailment this one had lied about to escape the war.

'Why is she stained?' he asked, pointing at the large woman.

'It's a Thracian thing. They call 'em tattoos,' the slaver said, voice as greasy as his grin. 'You won't find a stronger slave than a Thracian slave, I can assure you. Even the women are tough.'

I stared at the Thracian, and she met my gaze. Her eyes were the colour of wet stone — dark and gleaming. There was something about her, something sharp and alive and dangerous. I half expected her to rip off those metal chains with her teeth.

The interested buyer entered the pen and grabbed one of the male slaves by the jaw, turning his face this way and that. He then barked a command, and the slave opened his mouth so he could examine the inside. The slave's eyes were eerily dead, as if he were just an animated corpse. A body without a soul.

I remembered when Leda had looked at my mother just like that, like a creature not a human. I stared at the gathered crowds as they pointed and murmured. Was this what my mother had been forced to endure? Having her humanity stripped from her as she was paraded before strangers?

My fury was so loud I could feel it thumping in my head. I wanted to cry, to scream, to claw the slaver's soulless eyes out . . .

But then a hand slipped into mine, cool and firm. Penelope's.

She was staring at me, eyes filled with a silent question: *Are you all right?*

Nodding, I curled my fingers around hers and felt a surprising burst of reassurance from her touch.

I can do this. I have to.

Letting go of Penelope's hand, I strode forward.

'Can I help you?' the slaver asked.

I stared at the man, my hatred so visceral I could *taste* it pooling on my tongue.

'How much can I get for this?'

I handed over the two pouches of silver and watched him theatrically weigh each in his hands.

'Depends. Each slave 'as their own price. But you should know, I don't sell cheap. Mine is *good-quality* stock.'

'Quality stock? What about that one?' I heard the other potential buyer snort, pointing towards the older woman. 'She's ancient.'

'I call it "experienced",' the slaver said.

'An old hag like that? She would just be a liability,' the man countered. 'You would've done yourself a favour dumping her on the journey here.'

Laughter rippled through the crowd, but the older woman kept her face blank, lifting her chin a little higher. With her bound hands, she tried to adjust her filthy tunic, holding on to whatever scrap of dignity she had left.

'The mines always take the leftovers.' The slaver shrugged before hacking up a glob of spit on to the ground.

'The mines?' I turned to him. 'She won't last a day in the mines.'

The slaver picked his teeth. 'Not my problem.'

'I'll take her.' The words escaped me as a gasp of air.

'You come back with *that* and your master will flog you silly,' the other buyer warned me.

I ignored him as I growled at the slaver, 'Do we have a deal or not?'

'O' course, my dear, o' course.' A smile slid across the slaver's face, like oil across water. He then tipped out and pocketed a portion of the silver before handing a pouch back to me, its contents considerably lighter. 'My *pleasure* doing business with you.'

I felt a dirtiness creep over my skin, sinking its way into my blood. It felt so horribly *wrong*, rewarding such a vile trade. But I knew there would be a far uglier stain upon my soul if I turned away now and left this woman to her fate.

The slaver went into the pen to unclasp the woman's chains. Once freed, he began binding a rope around her wrists.

'She doesn't need that,' I snapped.

The slaver turned to me and shrugged, before leading the old woman to my side. She looked stoic as she bowed, her olive skin blistered from sunburn. How long had she been made to stand out in pens like this one?

'What is your name?' I asked softly.

Her eyes, a lovely shade of pale green, shifted to mine. She seemed momentarily bemused by the question, as if no one had asked it for a long time.

'My name is Eurynome, mistress,' she said, voice raspy and thin, with the hint of an accent too subtle to place.

I looked down at her bare feet, cut and bruised. 'I'm afraid I walked here. Is that all right? Can you walk?'

She nodded. 'I will manage, mistress.'

A scream ripped my attention back to the pen, where the other buyer was cradling his hand, blood spurting from his fingers. Standing before him, the Thracian woman smiled, her teeth etched in crimson.

'*What did you do?*' the slaver seethed at her.

The Thracian simply smirked wider.

'You find this *funny?*'

He struck her hard across the face, but the woman barely flinched. Instead, she simply stared at the slaver, her eyes glittering with a deadly, dark promise. The slaver had enough sense to shrink back.

Behind him, the buyer was wailing, clutching his fingers to his chest.

'That beast needs to be *put down*!' he screeched. 'Do you see what it did to me? Do you *see?*'

'It was a mistake,' the slaver babbled. 'You caught her by surprise, and Thracians are easily spooked, you know—'

'A beast like that is not worthy of *any* household,' the buyer declared.

'I will handle it,' the slaver insisted.

'I demand she be put down *at once.*'

'I ain't wasting good stock. The mines will have her.'

'I'll take her!'

The buyer and slaver both spun in unison, staring at me. '*What?*'

'I said I'll take her,' I repeated, holding out my remaining silver.

'Did you see what she just did to me?' the injured man cried.

'Yes.' I smiled coldly. 'And perhaps that will teach you a lesson about sticking parts of your body into people's mouths without permission.'

A growling noise escaped the Thracian. It sounded almost like a *laugh*.

'*What* did you just say to me, *slave?*' The buyer took a menacing step closer, raising his uninjured hand to strike me.

I felt Penelope press in close at my back, putting a protective hand on my arm. But then came an eerie, jangling sound and we turned to see the Thracian shaking her chains loudly, glaring at the injured man. When he turned to look at her, she bared her bloodstained teeth in warning.

Even in chains, she was formidable.

The man's face paled as he shoved past me. 'Get out of my way. I need to see a doctor.'

The Thracian grinned as she watched him flee, before turning to wink at me.

'You don't have enough for her,' the slaver said, once the commotion had settled.

'She just bit a man's finger off in front of an audience.' I motioned to the crowd. 'Do you really think you'll sell her now?'

He shrugged. 'Plenty more ports to visit, ain't there? Ithaca is a small fish in a *very* big sea, love.'

'And how many more potential buyers will she attack?' I challenged, stepping closer. 'I bet that man wasn't the first, was he? And he won't be the last.'

'So? Not my problem if those rich idiots can't handle themselves round a Thracian.'

'No, it's not.' I shook my head. 'But it *is* your problem if that Thracian gives you a bad reputation, and word spreads fast, especially in big cities . . . Tell me, how many "rich idiots" will want to buy from a slaver with violent stock?'

The slaver glowered at me, then stared at the Thracian for a long moment, his jaw flexing. Finally, he grunted his defeat and moved to unshackle the woman.

'Bite me and I'll skin you alive,' he threatened her.

The Thracian only grinned in response, rubbing her wrists where the shackles had left open sores. The slaver then began binding her with coarse ropes.

'She doesn't need those,' I said.

The nasty little man threw me a dark look. 'Trust me, girl. This one does.'

28

'You can't have that *thing* as a handmaid!'

I massaged my temples as Eurycleia continued squawking, trying to dispel the headache that had taken root. It had been light outside when the old witch had come to Penelope's quarters to lecture us. Now it was dark, and *still* she prattled on.

Penelope listened quietly with a level of patience I could not fathom. Beside me, the Thracian smirked as she watched the drama unfold, whilst Eurynome stared at Penelope, likely still processing the fact that she was not a slave, as her disguise had implied, but rather the future queen.

'She is a danger to us all, mistress!' Eurycleia continued. 'She could very well slit our throats in our sleep!'

'Slit throat? I would not slit throat,' the Thracian said in a thick, rumbling accent. 'I would strangle. Much less messy.'

These were the first words she had spoken, and they were met with a stunned silence. I had thought she could barely understand Greek, let alone speak it. I watched the colour slowly drain from Eurycleia's face. On the opposite side of the room, Hippodamia and Autonoë looked unsure whether to be amused or afraid.

My gaze met Penelope's, and I realized she was fighting a smile.

'Do you *see*!' Eurycleia shrieked.

'She is jesting,' Penelope clarified. 'Thracians have a great sense of humour.'

'What is this "jesting"?' the tattooed woman asked, scratching her head theatrically.

Penelope gave a resigned sigh, though that smile still traced her lips.

'Mistress, I must remind you, it is *my* duty to approve the purchase of slaves.'

'I am aware, Eurycleia. But I sent Melantho to the market because I trust her judgement above all else.' I found my heart lifting at Penelope's words, even though I knew they were just a ruse to cover up my insolence.

'Melantho's judgement was to pick a savage and an old woman,' Eurycleia sneered. 'I cannot condone this, mistress. We must return these slaves at once and find you better stock. Leave it with me and I can—'

'*Eurycleia.*' I rose from my stool by the fire, unable to hold my tongue any longer in fear I might bite it clean off. 'Penelope has made her decision. Do you wish to defy the Princess? No? Then I suggest you leave. It is late and we are all tired.'

Eurycleia looked as if I had just slapped her across the face, her cheeks pink with outrage. 'Do you *hear* the way she speaks to me, mistress?'

Penelope nodded. 'Yes, I can hear Melantho perfectly fine.'

Eurycleia opened her mouth, then closed it again, flicking her gaze between Penelope and me. Pure rage burnt behind those beady eyes, and I took a deep, vicious pleasure in seeing it.

'The king will hear of this,' was all she said, turning sharply on her heel, chin pointed high.

'Such big anger for such small woman,' the Thracian commented as Eurycleia stormed out of the door. Autonoë hiccupped a laugh, covering her mouth quickly.

'So, you *do* speak Greek,' I said, folding my arms.

The Thracian grinned at me. 'A little.'

'Will you tell us your name now?' Penelope asked.

'Your people call me Thratta.'

The name meant 'woman from Thrace'. It was a lazy and common label given to slaves of her kind.

'And what's your *real* name? Your Thracian name?' I asked.

The dark gleam in her eyes shuttered at that, and I wondered how long it had been since she was asked such a question.

'That name is mine,' she said flatly.

'Very well.' Penelope motioned to the hearth. 'Thratta, Eurynome, will you take a seat?'

Eurynome looked visibly flustered by the idea. 'Oh, no, I shouldn't—'

'Please, I insist.'

The woman's eyes shone as she quietly obeyed, setting herself down gingerly in the chair beside me. She sat rigidly, and I could tell she was afraid of sullying it with her dirty clothes. Beside her, Thratta flopped down heavily, the chair seeming to groan beneath the weight of her.

Hippodamia padded over and offered them both cups of wine. Eurynome accepted gratefully, whilst Thratta declined.

'Greek wine is piss,' she huffed.

I stifled a laugh as Penelope turned to Eurynome. 'So, you said you hail from Corinth?'

'Yes, my lady. I served my master there for many, many summers,' Eurynome said.

'What happened?' Penelope asked, shaking her head as Hippodamia offered her a cup.

'He died, taken by a sudden illness.' I did not miss the dip of emotion in Eurynome's voice. 'He left me to his son in his will, wanted to make sure I was cared for, but . . .' She paused, her thin fingers lacing together in her lap. 'His son no longer saw a place for me in the household.'

'I am sorry to hear that,' Penelope said, her eyes lit with genuine sympathy. 'Forgive me for prying, Eurynome, but is that a Maeonian accent I hear?'

'Oh . . .' Her cheeks grew flushed. 'I apologize, mistress, I hadn't realized it was still so obvious . . .'

'You have nothing to apologize for,' Penelope insisted. 'There were many slaves in my father's household who hailed from Maeonia. I hear it is a beautiful place.'

'It is. The most beautiful,' Eurynome said softly, eyes heavy. 'Though I have not been there since I was a girl. Since I was . . .'

She trailed off, seeming to remember herself. Yet we all knew the tale she was about to tell; it was one so many slaves shared – a child snatched from their homeland, shipped to foreign lands by greedy slavers, then sold off to the highest bidder.

At that moment, Telemachus began squealing in Autonoë's arms. She brought him to Penelope, who shushed him with soft bouncing movements. Beside me, I noted the way Eurynome's face transformed as she gazed at mother and son.

'A baby,' she whispered. 'A true gift from the Gods.'

Penelope smiled at that. 'Would you like to hold him?'

Eurynome stared down at her dirty hands and ruined clothes, then shook her head. But Penelope rose anyway and offered the grizzling Telemachus with an encouraging nod. Eurynome took him with the quiet confidence of someone who had held countless babes in her arms. She rocked him gently, and Telemachus fell almost instantly asleep.

'He never settles that quickly. It seems you have a gift, Eurynome,' I said, and her eyes shone as they met mine.

Penelope then turned to the Thracian sprawled in her chair. 'And what of you, Thratta? What is your story?'

'My story is mine,' she said. There was an edge to her voice, one that warned us not to pry further.

Sensing this, Penelope nodded and retreated from the topic. 'Well, I warmly welcome you both to Ithaca and to the House of Laertes.'

'Are we really to be your handmaids, princess?' Eurynome asked.

'If you would like that?' Penelope said.

Thratta shrugged, but Eurynome's throat bobbed as she whispered, 'It would be an honour. An honour I never thought I would earn at this stage in my life. Thank you.'

Penelope's eyes slipped to mine as she replied, 'It is not I who deserves your thanks.'

'You're still awake?'

I was sitting on the rug by the hearth when I heard Penelope approach.

She had just bathed, her skin scrubbed and glowing, unbound hair still damp, hanging in soft waves around her shoulders. She wore just a simple gown, with no adornments, and her feet were bare as she padded towards me.

'I thought you had retired with the others,' I said.

'I cannot sleep,' she admitted.

'It's not because you're afraid of Thratta too, is it? Hippodamia and Autonoë said they were going to take shifts sleeping tonight.'

Penelope smiled, shaking her head. 'They are only afraid of Thracians because they have never met one.'

'So, you trust her? Thratta?'

'I do,' she said, moving to sit beside me. I noticed she had a small bowl in her hands, though my gaze was caught on those wet tendrils of hair seeping into her gown. 'Thratta told me she owed us a life debt. Such things are sacred to her people.'

For a moment we were quiet, our silence charged with the echo of all we had exposed earlier by the harbour.

'It was brave, what you did today,' Penelope murmured. 'I know it can't have been easy for you, dealing with the slaver.'

I shifted, awkward under the weight of her praise.

'I heard you talking to Thratta earlier,' I said, keen to deflect. 'How is it you can speak Thracian?'

Penelope's smile softened. 'One of my childhood handmaids was from Thrace. She taught me Thracian alongside Greek – in secret, of course. I think it was her act of rebellion, to teach me her tongue. I like to continue speaking it, to keep that rebellion alive for her.'

'I'm sure that would make her happy to know.'

Penelope tilted her head to the side, and I realized she was staring at my cheek. 'Would you let me put something on that?'

I brushed my face and winced. My brother's fury had left its mark.

'I have an ointment,' she continued, motioning to the bowl in her lap. 'It will help keep the swelling down.'

'I'm fine.'

She shifted closer to me then, and I could not help but marvel at the way the fire lit her freshly bathed skin, making it glow rich and golden. There were still droplets of water caught in her hair, sparkling like tiny, dripping jewels.

'Please?'

My mouth felt dry from her sudden closeness, so all I could manage was a tight nod.

She began probing my cheek, her touch gentle and lingering. She was sitting a little taller, so my eye-line was level with her neck, and I could do nothing but watch the shadows toying with that dip at the base of her throat. I watched her pulse thrum just above it. Had the beat quickened when she touched me?

She dipped her fingers into the bowl and gently rubbed the silky contents on to my cheek. She was so close now, too close, seizing all my senses.

'Are you all right?'

'Yes,' I replied a little too defensively. 'Why?'

'You look . . . uncomfortable.' She pulled away. 'Am I hurting you?'

'No, no, I'm fine.'

'If you want me to stop—'

'No. I like you touching me,' I blurted out. 'I don't mean . . . it's not that I *like it* . . . I just . . . I don't . . . I don't *mind* it.'

Hot shame rushed into my cheeks as Penelope watched me fumble for words, her mouth twitching upwards. She leant in again and continued applying the ointment, though I could still see that hint of a smile out of the corner of my eye.

'I just meant to say I'm fine,' I muttered. 'Don't worry about me.'

'I always worry about you, Melantho.'

I turned to look at her, but she caught my face with her free hand.

'Hold still.'

I obliged, trying to ignore how aware I was of her hand cupping my jaw. I swallowed, knowing she would be able to feel the motion beneath her fingertips. In the hazy corners of my mind, I sensed those dreams flickering to life, the ones I had been trying so desperately to ignore.

As if drawn by the heat of my thoughts, Penelope's eyes drifted to mine, and I was terrified of what truth she might find there, pinned so openly in my gaze. Still, I could not look away.

Our faces were so painfully close now, I could not tell where my blush ended and hers began. Penelope's eyes dropped to my mouth, and the air pulled taut between us, threatening to snap.

'That should do it,' she said abruptly, pulling away. 'The swelling should go down soon enough.'

I nodded, lifting my fingers to probe the place where hers had just been.

For a moment we were quiet, Penelope's eyes set on the flames, mine on the shadows.

'Will you tell me how it happened?' She asked so tenderly, yet still I felt those familiar walls rearing up, luring me into the protection of their cold, dark shelter ... 'Don't do that. Don't go to that place I cannot reach.'

Her words shook something inside me, and suddenly those imposing walls did not seem so safe any more, but rather ... *lonely*.

'Please,' she whispered, her gaze reaching tentatively for mine.

Perhaps it was because she said 'please', or perhaps a part of me wanted someone to know, wanted *her* to know. Whatever the reason, I told her. All of it, every ugly, painful thing Melanthius had said, and all the horrible truths that had rung between his words.

Penelope listened as she always did, with that preternatural stillness, her entire body focused on absorbing my every word, as if each were a sacred offering worth treasuring.

When I finally finished speaking, the fire had dulled to embers. I stared into the shadows once again, feeling horribly vulnerable beneath her silence, all those fragile parts of me exposed like gaping wounds.

'She was pregnant,' Penelope finally breathed. 'Melitta.'

I nodded, still not looking at her.

'It makes sense now. Why you hated me so.'

'I didn't hate you,' I said into the darkness. 'I only *thought* I did because . . . because it was easier to hate you than hate myself.'

Penelope was quiet for a long moment before asking, 'And what made you realize that?'

'Melanthius,' I admitted. 'The things he said about you – I knew they were wrong. I knew *he* was wrong. He's so blinded by bitterness . . . and I . . . I don't want to be like that any more. I don't want to be like *him*.'

I waited for the stab of guilt, the ache of betrayal . . . but none came.

'He's wrong about you too, you know,' Penelope murmured. 'Melantho . . . look at me.'

I shook my head, glaring into the ground and feeling a sudden, overwhelming desire for it to swallow me whole.

'Melanthius is wrong about you,' Penelope repeated, firmer now. 'You must understand that.'

'He isn't.'

'Melantho—'

'*He isn't.*' The words exploded out of me. '*That's* why I did it. That's why I took your silver – because Melanthius was right, and I couldn't *stand it*. I couldn't stand the guilt. I couldn't stand *myself*. I have so much . . . so much *ugliness* inside me.' I pressed a hand to my chest, rubbing the knot perpetually rooted there. 'I can feel it *constantly*. It eats me alive.'

I sensed Penelope moving closer, the warmth of her body somehow burning hotter than the embers beside us. She placed a finger under my chin, tilting my face to hers.

'This world is ugly, not you,' she whispered. 'You are a good person.'

I shook my head, vision blurring.

'You are, Melantho.'

'You're *wrong*,' I said thickly.

'I'm not.' Penelope spoke with such unyielding certainty.

'How can you be so sure?'

She arched a brow. 'Because I'm never wrong. Have you not realized that yet?'

To my surprise, a rough laugh spilt out of me, but it quickly rolled into a sob, one hewn from my very core. Penelope shifted closer, folding herself around me as I wept.

I had only ever let my mother hold me like this. I had always loathed the idea of being so vulnerable, so exposed. But in Penelope's arms I felt an overwhelming sense of . . . *relief*, like a great weight had been shifted from my soul, cascading out of me in a steady flow of tears.

Penelope's hand lifted to stroke my hair as my sobs slowly subsided, and I realized I could not remember the last time I had felt like this . . . felt *safe*.

'You are a gift to this world, Melantho,' Penelope whispered. 'You are a gift to me.'

I pulled back to look at her, tears threatening once again.

'I have been so afraid of hurting people, I allowed myself to forget all the ways I could help them,' she continued. 'You made me realize that today. You made me realize the difference I can make here.'

I sniffed. 'What kind of difference?'

Penelope smiled, reaching out to wipe my damp cheeks.

'For so long I have scorned the treatment of slaves, but what have I done about it? Nothing. It's time I changed that.' Her face was set with a stoic determination. 'The war has taken much from us, but it has also given us the opportunity to *empower* those left behind. To build something we can be proud of. I do not wish to squander that gift.'

I considered it: a kingdom ruled by Penelope, guided by her quiet strength, shaped by her unwavering compassion. It almost frightened me – how much I liked the idea, how it made me, for the first time in my life, feel a sense of *eagerness* for the future, rather than impending dread.

'And you?' she asked, a sudden timidity creeping over her. 'What will you do?'

I blinked, my eyes hot and swollen. 'What do you mean?'

'Will you go with your brother? He leaves tonight, does he not?'

'You'd . . . let me go?' I felt a strange rush of disappointment.

'I cannot say I believe your brother *deserves* your companionship after the way he's treated you . . . but I stood in the way of your freedom once, Melantho. I will not do it again.' She glanced away, shoulders tensing. 'It is your decision.'

I said nothing, and the silence seemed to stretch thin between us, strained by the answer I was not yet ready to give.

'It is late,' Penelope said suddenly, rising to her feet. 'I should retire.'

As I watched her walk away, a sudden desperation burst inside me.

'This will be the last time we see each other,' I blurted out. 'If I leave tonight.'

Penelope froze, spine stiffening, hands fisting in her gown. Slowly, she turned her face to the side, so I could make out the elegant cut of her profile, mouth thin beneath her long, sharp nose. She looked as if she were having to forcibly hold herself in place.

'I know,' she said quietly.

A stillness crept into the room. There was so much I wanted to say, the clamour of words tangling together, forming a thick, burning knot in my throat.

'Goodnight, Penelope,' was all I managed in the end.

Though her face remained impassive, I swore I heard Penelope's voice catch as she whispered, 'Goodnight, Melantho.'

29

I found my brother waiting at the harbour.

Though, 'harbour' was perhaps too grand a term for the tiny structure stretching tentatively into the sea, its edges crumbling from years of disuse.

I could just make out Melanthius through the darkness, sitting on a large cluster of rocks by the water's edge, face tilted up to the curved moon. All he had were the clothes on his back, and it made my heart heavy, knowing he had nothing else to take with him . . .

Except me.

Melanthius was quiet as I came to sit beside him, our tense silence eased by the sighing waves. I breathed in the salt-brushed air, watching the moon trace her silver fingers over the water like a lost lover's ghostly caress.

'You're not coming.'

It wasn't a question, but still I answered, 'No.'

I felt him shift beside me. 'Is it because of . . . what I did?'

'No,' I repeated, softer this time.

I turned to look at Melanthius, but his face was tilted away, features wholly consumed by the night.

'I don't understand.' There was none of the usual venom in his voice, just a suffocating sense of exhaustion. 'I don't understand how you could *choose* this life.'

I picked up a stone, turning it between my fingers as I weighed my next words.

'I rescued two women from the slave market today,' I said.

'How?'

'Laertes gave Penelope silver to purchase more handmaids and I—'

'So, you didn't *rescue* them. You *bought* them.' Disgust dried out Melanthius' voice. 'You *paid* a slaver.'

'I *bought* them their lives back,' I snapped. 'I *bought* them another chance.'

'That how Penelope justifies it, is it?'

'It was *my* decision. *I* chose to save them—'

'That's *not* saving them, Melantho! Not if they're still slaves.'

I clenched my jaw, tossing the stone away. It skimmed over the silvery waves with a satisfying *plink, plink, plink,* before disappearing beneath them.

'I saved them, Melanthius,' I gritted out. 'Because I know they'll be treated fairly in Penelope's care, and that's a far better fate than what awaited them—'

'They are—'

'*No.* Don't interrupt me. I don't want to hear it. You know why? Because for the *first* time in my life, I feel like I did something *right*. And it made me realize how sick I am of hating myself. I don't want to do it any more, Melanthius. I'm so *tired* of it.' I rubbed my face with my hands, willing the surge of emotions to steady itself before continuing. 'If I stay, I think I can help more people. Penelope wants to build something here, something important, and I want to be part of that. I want to be part of something I can feel *proud* of.'

Melanthius was silent for a painfully long moment, face still turned away, shoulders hunched as if he were shielding himself from a storm. I longed to reach out, to take his hand in mine. But I did not.

'So, you'd rather be *her* slave than my sister.' The words scraped out of him, barely a whisper, yet they hit me hard enough to bruise.

'It's not like that—'

'It's exactly like that. I gave you a choice: a chance of freedom at my side or a life here as a slave. And you chose *her*.'

'I chose *myself*. And when Odysseus returns from war, he has vowed to free me. I believe I can convince him to free you, too.'

Melanthius shook his head slowly. 'You're still so naive, Mel.'

'*I'm* naive?' I bristled, pushing closer, urging him to look at me. 'Tell me, then, Melanthius. Tell me your grand plan. Do you believe you will sail to the mainland and freedom will simply fall into your lap? Do you think you can stroll into Sparta and sweep Melitta away? You will have *no* possessions, *no* shelter, *no* support. You will likely die on the streets from starvation or disease or—'

'Is this why you came here? To tell me I'm a failure?'

I sighed, head falling into my hands. 'No. I just . . . I wanted to say goodbye. That's all.'

Melanthius gave an empty, brittle laugh. 'Well, you can save your farewells.'

Before I could ask what he meant, he finally turned to face me, letting the moonlight spill over his swollen features.

'*Melanthius*,' I gasped, instinctively reaching out to touch his bruised, bloodied face. He recoiled from my touch, as if I had moved to strike him. 'What *happened*?'

'That sailor I told you about.' He smiled, and the fresh gash along his lip began to weep. 'Turns out he weren't interested in taking me anywhere, only my silver. I don't even know if he *was* a sailor.'

'Melanthius—'

'No, no. It's all right, you can laugh. He certainly did. It *is* quite funny when you think about.' He began to laugh then, the sound horrid and forced, choking out of him in convulsive shudders. 'Stupid little slave, thinking he could simply sail away and be free.'

'Who was he?' I demanded. 'The man who did this to you.'

'What does it matter?'

'I could tell Penelope. She could—'

'*Penelope?*' That hideous laughter died instantly on his lips, swollen eyes narrowing. 'You . . . you told her about this, didn't you?'

I swallowed. 'It's not—'

'It makes sense now. It was *her*. *She* must've told the sailor not to help me. *She* did this—'

'That's not possible.' I fought to keep my voice level. 'I only told her tonight—'

'She could've sent word.'

'She didn't.'

'*How can you know that?* How—' Melanthius stilled, and it seemed as if his entire body were shrinking, collapsing in on itself as a realization struck him. 'Don't tell me you trust her, Melantho.'

Trusting someone had always seemed a terrifying thing to me, like leaping off a ledge and counting down the seconds until the ground would inevitably greet me.

But with Penelope, it did not feel like falling, not at all.

It felt like finally being caught.

'I do,' I whispered.

Even with all the bruising marring Melanthius' face, I could still see the betrayal strike his features, making him wince and recoil. A familiar poisonous guilt seeped through me, but I forced it away.

I refused to feel shame for this, for being able to trust when he could not.

Melanthius rose silently.

'Don't go.' I reached for him, but he was already too far away. 'Please, brother—'

'Don't call me that,' he hissed, turning into the night. '*You* are no sister of *mine*.'

The next morning, I woke to the sound of laughter filtering through the walls.

When I had returned to the handmaids' chamber the previous night, they had all been fast asleep. But now, the room was empty, their beds made.

I lingered in the doorway to Penelope's central living quarters. The handmaids were gathered around the large table, enjoying their breakfast. Thratta was telling a story with dramatic gestures whilst Hippodamia dished out food. Something Thratta said had them all in fits of laughter and I smiled as the sound washed over me like a sun-baked stream.

Eurynome spotted me first. 'Come join us, Melantho.'

For a moment, I hesitated, familiar excuses crowding on my tongue, but then my eyes drifted to Hippodamia, and her words from the other night flickered inside me.

Whoever it is you've lost, don't you think they would want you to be happy too?

Drawing in a breath, I approached and silently sat down beside Autonoë, who was fussing over a snoozing Telemachus. Hippodamia immediately moved to fill my plate whilst Thratta continued her story. As I gazed around the table, I was met with the strange sensation of . . . fullness.

'Penelope, there you are! We were wondering where you had got to,' Hippodamia called out.

'I apologize for my absence this morning. I needed to—'

Penelope froze mid-step, her gaze pouring into mine.

'Is . . . everything all right?' Hippodamia prompted.

Penelope's smile was like dawn, slow to appear at first, then flashing all at once, its beauty setting the world alight.

'Yes,' she breathed, eyes never leaving mine. 'Everything is wonderful.'

'Will you come join us?' Autonoë offered.

As she came to sit beside me, I couldn't help but share Penelope's smile, the edges stretching giddily wide.

'You're here,' she whispered.

I was surprised by the emotion cradling her lovely face. But then I remembered all the people in Penelope's life who were *not* here, who had left her behind, either willingly or not – her mother, father, sister, husband . . .

Was I the first who had stayed?

I couldn't think what to say, so instead I reached out and squeezed her hand.

When I went to pull away, Penelope laced her fingers through mine, holding tight. She smiled, softer this time, and I felt a warmth blossoming inside me, one that had nestled into my heart long, long ago, its golden roots woven through my very core.

Something hard bounced off the side of my head and fell into my lap.

'You not listen to my story,' Thratta said, throwing another olive at me. This time it hit my nose.

There was a brief pause, then Hippodamia broke into peals of laughter, the sound so shrill it had the others joining in, even Penelope. I felt my own laughter bubbling inside me, tentative at first, then bursting forth so forcefully I could scarcely catch my breath.

Within that bright, infectious sound, I heard my mother whisper, *All I want is for you to be happy, my heart.*

And I realized, for the first time since I'd lost her, that I wanted it too.

PART II

SWEETBITTER

30

Nine Years Later

The Prince of Ithaca steadied his arrow, readying himself for the kill.

Dappled morning light played across his tanned skin, the trees whispering in anticipation of his next move.

Telemachus looked so like his mother when he concentrated, that small crease forming between his brows, a quiet intensity shifting behind those grey eyes.

The fletching brushed his cheek as he drew in a slow, even breath. There was a moment of stillness, then the prince let his arrow fly, rising from his crouched position to watch it slice a path through the sleepy, shadow-dipped forest.

I heard a delicate *thunk*, and then a heavier one as the stag fell. The creature was dead before it hit the ground, Telemachus' arrow having pierced right through its eye.

Beside me, Thratta let out a loud, victorious whoop, causing a flock of birds to take flight.

'Telemachus,' I gasped, turning to him. 'That was incredible!'

The prince shrugged. 'Accurate aim is simply mathematics.'

He was so like his mother.

'Your first kill!' Thratta slapped him on the back, and the prince tried to hide his wince. 'Bendis has truly blessed you.'

'Bendis is a Thracian goddess,' Telemachus said shrewdly. 'It is Artemis who would have blessed me.'

Thratta laughed. 'Perhaps both our goddesses have, little prince.'

Telemachus grinned as he shouldered his bow. I could not help but marvel at how grown up he looked in that moment, honeyed rays catching on his young features, illuminating glimpses of the man he would one day become.

It was hard to believe he was already nine summers old.

Nine summers . . .

It is strange, how elusive time becomes when you are happy.

In Sparta, the seasons had passed slowly, lingering like the stubborn chill of winter bleeding into spring. But in Ithaca, they slipped by all too quickly, as if the laws of time had been loosened, letting the days spill out uncontrollably, too fast for me to keep hold of.

The prince must have read something in my expression, for he placed his small hand on my shoulder and said, 'Do not worry, Melantho. Your aim will improve in time.'

'Unlikely,' Thratta snorted.

I gave her a shove, though I might have had more luck knocking over a stone pillar.

In truth, Thratta was right. I was by no means a natural with the bow, but I still loved the thrill of holding the weapon in my hand, of feeling its power thrumming between my fingers.

It had been Telemachus' idea to have Thratta teach him to hunt. It was not surprising considering the boy had grown up on a healthy diet of Thratta's stories about her daring exploits with her tribe. King Laertes had been dismayed at the idea of a female slave, a *Thracian* slave, teaching a prince to hunt. But who else was there to take up the task? The majority of Ithaca's menfolk were still far away on the shores of Troy.

'Did someone take my bow?' I frowned, looking for the weapon I had placed down only moments before.

'Perhaps it ran away,' Thratta teased. 'It no longer wishes to be abused by your hands.'

I rolled my eyes as I rose to my feet, dusting off my knees.

'Come, Telemachus,' I said. 'Let us fetch your prize.'

Our trek back to the palace was long, weighed down by the heat sticking to the air. Thratta had the giant stag slung over her shoulders, yet she did not stumble or complain once as we walked. Instead, she sang in her mother tongue, her booming voice barely even breathless. I smiled as I watched her rust-red hair swishing merrily back and forth. Thratta had let it grow long and wild, though she kept it permanently tied back with a leather thong. Red hair was apparently a Thracian trait, and so Thratta had decided I must be one of them. I wasn't sure if this was true, but I liked the idea of fierce warrior blood flowing through me, of having a piece of history that tied me to something other than Sparta.

'Do you think there will be news when we return?' Telemachus asked as we trudged onwards.

'Perhaps,' I said, brushing the sweat from my brow.

Every day, Telemachus awaited word from Troy. Fortunately for him, we were rarely in short supply. Stories of the war were constantly pouring in from the seas, each grander than the last. It was becoming almost impossible to tell where fiction bled into fact.

It seemed Telemachus' father had made quite a name for himself over the last nine years of bloodshed. People spoke often of the cunning Odysseus constantly outsmarting the Trojans, wise Odysseus counselling the hot-headed Agamemnon, brilliant Odysseus beloved by Athena herself . . .

It grew tedious, after a while. But Telemachus wolfed these tales down greedily, as did the other boys of Ithaca, each new morsel feeding the legend of Odysseus that constantly loomed over the island. To many, he was like a god.

'Do you think Achilles will return to battle soon?' Telemachus pressed.

Achilles was another favourite amongst the young boys. Son of a goddess, and Prince of the Myrmidons, Achilles was claimed to be the greatest fighter this world had ever seen. Though, the last we had heard, the famed soldier had set down his sword, refusing to fight after

Agamemnon had stolen his captive bride. I didn't know the woman's name; nobody ever bothered to speak it.

'I don't know,' I admitted, though a guilty, secret part of me prayed Achilles wouldn't ever step foot on Troy's battlefield again. Everyone claimed the Greeks could not secure a victory without him. So, the longer Achilles refused to fight, the longer the war stretched on.

And the longer our life here would remain untouched.

'I do not care to speak of the war,' Thratta huffed from ahead of us. 'It bores me.'

'It *bores* you?' This idea seemed unfathomable to Telemachus.

'Don't forget, the Thracians fight for the Trojans,' I reminded him.

He nodded sagely. 'Does it make Thratta sad to know the Greeks will win?'

I hesitated. 'There is no certainty in war, Telemachus.'

'But we have Achilles, and my father! We cannot lose!'

Ahead of us, Thratta held up a fist, signalling for us to halt. I watched her scan the thick underbrush, her free hand hovering over the dagger at her belt.

'We are not alone,' she murmured.

Telemachus inched closer to me as I reached for the blade in my own belt. I was only marginally better with a dagger than a bow, despite Thratta's training. Still, it felt reassuring to have the weapon cool and sure in my palm.

'Wait here,' Thratta instructed as she pressed forward to investigate.

A sharp knot of fear constricted in my gut, even as I assured myself that I was over-reacting. Thratta had simply heard a noise – that was all . . .

But we were, after all, alone in the wilderness with Ithaca's most prized possession. More importantly than that, with *Penelope's* most prized possession.

I felt a sharp jab against my spine.

'Drop the blade,' a voice hissed. 'You too, boy.'

Telemachus whirled on his heels, eyes widening.

'Do as they say,' I told him, dropping my dagger and raising my hands.

Telemachus obeyed, mirroring my movements, though there was a strange, quizzical frown caught around his lips.

'We don't want any trouble,' I said, scouring the treeline for Thratta.

'Well, *I* want that stag of yours,' the voice replied. It was surprisingly high-pitched and . . . *girlish*.

I glanced over my shoulder and saw a small figure squaring up behind me. She was a tiny slip of a girl, who couldn't have been more than thirteen. She was covered in dirt, her dark hair roughly shorn and sticking out wildly around her head. She reminded me of the stray mutts I saw in town, scraggly and pitiful-looking, marred by an undeniable feral edge.

In her hands she held my bow, the arrow pointed directly into my back.

'Where'd the big one go?' she demanded. Despite her tiny stature, she had a glare that could have made the Gods themselves quake.

'Who are you?' Telemachus asked, more curious than afraid.

'Piss off, kid.'

'"Kid"? You're barely older than me!'

The girl rolled her eyes. 'The stag. Gimme it.'

A booming laugh came from beside us as Thratta suddenly materialized. For a giant woman, she was unnervingly light on her feet.

'You mean this?' she asked, letting the dead stag fall heavily to the ground. 'Go on, then, small one. Take it.'

The girl's eyes widened as she stared at the creature. It was easily triple her size.

'What's the matter?' Thratta grinned wolfishly. 'Changed your mind?'

The girl scowled up at us, her hatred as keen as the arrow at my back. But then I noticed something gleaming in her eyes, a frayed and frantic hollowness I knew all too well.

The girl was hungry.

No, not just hungry. She was *starving*.

As I looked her over again, I noticed how thin she was, her ribs visible beneath her tattered tunic, cheeks sunken. My attention then narrowed to her wrists and the familiar blistering there.

'How long ago did you escape the slaver?' I asked, turning slowly to face her.

The girl sneered, pulling the bow taut, the arrow now trained on my heart.

'Don't do anything foolish,' Thratta warned.

'The way I see it, you have two options here,' I said, still holding my hands up. 'You can take my dagger, cut off however much of the stag you can carry, and be on your way. But then you'll have to survive out here on your own. I'm guessing you're not from Ithaca. You came in on the slave ship, right?' The girl clenched her jaw, saying nothing. 'How long do you really think you can last? A few days at most?'

'Long enough,' she spat.

'Long enough for what? To sneak on to a ship and get away? Believe me, I've thought of every possibility for getting off this island, and all of them end up with you back in the slaver's hands.'

Her eyes hardened. 'What's the other option, then?'

'You come with us.'

The girl's brows rose at that, the bowstring slackening a fraction. Beside me, I felt Telemachus mirroring her surprise, whilst Thratta's smirk only widened.

'*What?*' the girl snapped.

'You come with us to the palace. You'll be given a bath, fresh clothes, a warm bed, food. You'll be safe there.'

'I'll be a *slave*.'

'It won't be like any kind of slavery you've known before.' Her eyes narrowed at that. 'I can't offer you freedom, but I can offer you a place where you will be cared for.'

The girl hesitated. 'How do I know you won't just turn me in?'

'You can't, not yet. Trust must be earned, right? But if you come with me, I assure you I will earn yours.'

'And what if you don't?'

I nodded to my bow in her hands. 'Then you can shoot me.'

'*Melantho!*' Telemachus yelped.

Suspicion sharpened the girl's glare. 'Why?'

'Why what?' I asked.

'Why would you help me?'

'It's what she does,' Thratta said with a chuckle. 'She likes to help little, lost creatures like you.'

The girl bristled at that. 'If I'm a *creature*, what does that make you?'

Thratta thundered a laugh. 'I like this one. She's got teeth on her.'

To my relief, the girl finally lowered the bow towards the ground. 'If I come with you, I'm keeping hold of this.'

I nodded, letting my hands drop to my side. 'I assumed as much.'

'Are you sure this is wise?' Telemachus murmured beside me. 'She's *insane*! Look at her!'

'She's desperate. There's a difference,' I whispered back.

'I want you to know that if you're lying about *anything*, I will gut you,' the girl warned. 'And I'll do it *slowly*.'

'Ah, she reminds me of me.' Thratta nodded proudly. 'Yes. I like her a lot.'

'What's your name?' I asked.

'What's it to you?'

'Well, I want to know whose name I need to shout to the Gods if you end up gutting me . . . *slowly*,' I shot back.

The girl seemed to like that answer; I could tell by the slight tilt of her lips. Though, she quickly caught the smile and crushed it beneath a scowl.

'Actoris.' She spat it like a curse.

'Well, Actoris.' I grinned as I picked up my dagger. 'Welcome to the family.'

31

The Queen of Ithaca looked bored.

I leant against the stone doorway to the council chamber, watching Penelope feign interest in the latest argument the fat old men of Ithaca had descended into, as was the usual course of any of their meetings.

For a moment, I allowed myself the simple, secret pleasure of admiring her – that beautiful, striking face that consumed so much of my mind. Too much, perhaps.

I don't know what you call them, those moments between breaths, the spaces between heartbeats, but Penelope seemed to occupy every one of mine.

'Something must be done about this matter,' Mentor was saying to nods of fervent agreement. The man, wrinkled as a prune, had been a close confidant of Odysseus', and the only person he trusted to look after Ithaca's council in his absence.

'More young men are leaving every day,' another councilman said, slamming a leathery fist on to the table. 'They believe they will find better opportunities elsewhere.'

Mentor nodded sombrely. 'It is the women's fault. They refuse to relinquish control of their businesses and households, even though their sons are of age now. They are *purposefully* driving them away.'

Good riddance, I wanted to snap. The fewer entitled noblemen, the better.

'Perhaps it will be advantageous for the young men to leave,' Penelope mused mildly. Her words were met with loud scoffs and shaking heads.

Still, she continued, 'There is much we can learn from our neighbouring kingdoms. If these men travel, they can gather a wealth of knowledge, teachings that will undoubtedly benefit Ithaca when they return. Not to mention the alliances they could secure for us.'

'And what if they *do not* return, my queen?' Mentor pressed.

Then the women can continue to grow. I saw the answer glow in Penelope's eyes, but instead she said, 'My husband believed that Ithacans will always be drawn back home, no matter how far they may wander.'

There was a grumble of reluctant agreement. Nobody could disagree with the word of legendary Odysseus, after all.

'Now, what of the graffiti in the harbour? How can we deter those scoundrels?' Mentor continued, and the men quickly dissolved into another inane disagreement.

Penelope caught my gaze in the doorway then, mouth quirking upwards. With just a twitch of her brow she managed to flash me a long-suffering look.

'Queen Penelope.' I gave a flourishing bow that had her eyes sparking with amusement. 'Forgive my intrusion, but your presence is required urgently.'

'Perhaps this is a good time to adjourn today's meeting,' Mentor said.

'An excellent idea,' Penelope agreed as she rose from her seat at the side of the room. As a woman, it was deemed 'inappropriate' for her to sit at the table with the men, but as a queen without her king, she was permitted to join these council meetings. Whatever logic there was in that dichotomy, it made little sense to me. But I had never been one for politics.

'Thank you for graciously allowing me to observe your discussion today, gentlemen.'

She always said this at the end of every meeting, when the men should really have been thanking *her*. If matters had been left to these cantankerous old farts, the kingdom would have fallen to ruin years ago, when Laertes relinquished his title as king and disappeared to his tiny cottage in the countryside. Fortunately for Ithaca, what it lacked in king and council was made up for by its new queen.

Under Penelope's rule, Ithaca had flourished. During her first year as queen, she had streamlined farming cycles to yield greater produce, resulting in more trade and wealth for the land. The councilmen liked to congratulate themselves on this feat, as they did for all of Ithaca's successes. But that was how Penelope intended it. She ruled from the shadows, wielding her power with subtlety, so as not to unsettle any egos and risk it being snatched from her. She had always been an expert at planting ideas in men's minds, nurturing them quietly until they blossomed into fully formed thoughts they believed to be their own ingenious creation. It was an art form, really, one I loved to see at work.

'Make sure you take time to rest, my queen,' Mentor said. He always spoke softly to Penelope, as if she were a timid creature he might frighten away. 'It is humid today.'

She smiled indulgently at him. 'I will, thank you.'

Though she was not permitted a seat at their table, the councilmen still rose and bowed as Penelope glided from the room.

'Gods, listening to those men makes me sympathize with Sisyphus,' she murmured as we strode side by side down the hallway. 'Every time I feel we are making progress, they fall back into some pointless argument. Tell me, is my presence *actually* required, or were you just saving me from my torment?'

'The latter,' I said.

She grinned. 'What would I do without you?'

I forced myself to ignore the slight flutter in my stomach.

'There is someone I'd like you to meet, though. I found her in the woods.'

Penelope arched a brow. 'In the *woods*?'

'She had an arrow to my back for most of our initial meeting, and I'm pretty sure she was about to stab me with a bread knife when I took her to the kitchens.'

Penelope gave me a despairing look, though her amusement shone through. 'She sounds . . . delightful.'

'I think she'd make a great handmaid.'

'Ah yes, the violent use of a bread knife is always a good indication of a competent handmaid.'

'Do I detect sarcasm, my queen?'

'Sarcasm?' Penelope placed a hand over her heart. 'How decidedly unladylike that would be.'

'Truly despicable.'

Penelope mirrored my smirk, and, though she was twenty-six now, the gleam in her eyes made her look like a child again, delightfully mischievous.

We walked along the colonnade fringing the central courtyard. Pillars stood in a uniform row at our side, sunlight reaching between them like eager, golden fingers. Out on the grass, a group of slaves were chatting animatedly as they enjoyed a spread of breads, cheese and olives – all food they had worked hard to produce and which now was theirs to enjoy.

This was the culture Penelope had cultivated within the safety of the palace, one where slaves worked for the mutual benefit of *everyone*, not the few royals perched at the top. We all pitched in, and we all reaped the rewards.

As we passed, the group on the lawn waved.

'She will be the fourth slave you've brought home this summer,' Penelope said as she raised a hand in greeting.

I bit my lip. 'I know you're worried about overcrowding . . .'

'I'm handling it.'

My brows rose. 'You are?'

'We have already begun work on building more homes. There's so much vacant land Laertes was just *sitting* on.' Penelope shook her head despairingly. 'The homes should be ready by harvest time; then we will start moving people in and freeing up space in the palace for new additions . . . What? What's that look for?'

My smile spread so wide it hurt. 'Nothing. I just . . . I think that's an excellent idea.'

'Of course it is. *All* my ideas are,' she teased as we cut left down a shadowy corridor. 'So, what is the name of our newest handmaid?'

'You'll truly take her as a handmaid?'

'If you think she's suitable, then why wouldn't I?'

'I didn't realize the Queen of Ithaca was so *easily* swayed.'

Penelope laughed. 'Only by you, Melantho.'

Her words were light and playful, yet they still caught in my chest, causing my heartbeat to stumble. My feet followed suit, tripping over a step. Penelope shot out a hand to steady me and my entire body stiffened beneath her touch. After so many summers at her side, one would have thought I'd be numb to Penelope's effect by now.

If she noticed my sudden rigidity, Penelope did not comment; instead she lifted her hand to my hair. For a tense moment, I thought she was going to cup my face, and I felt an unbearable warmth rush into my cheeks. But she merely plucked a twig from one of my curls, eyebrow raised in silent question.

'We were hunting in the woods,' I said. 'Telemachus made his first kill!'

'I cannot fathom how he is already old enough to be wielding a weapon.' Penelope sighed, twirling the twig between her fingers. 'Will you bring our new handmaid to our quarters? I would like to meet her.'

Our quarters. I always loved it when she called it that.

Before I could reply, we heard a clatter of sandals stumbling behind us. Penelope stepped away from me instantly, that queenly veneer falling like a veil across her features as Mentor came careening down the hallway.

I hadn't known the old man could move so fast.

'My queen,' he gasped, doubling over to catch his breath. 'I apologize . . . for . . . the urgency . . .'

'Is everything all right?' she asked.

'News . . . from Troy.'

Penelope stilled. 'What news?'

'Achilles has returned to battle. Prince Hector of Troy is dead.'

That night, the palace came alive with celebrations.

We crowded together in the banquet hall, the atmosphere as intoxicating as the wine flowing freely between us. Once, this room would have been reserved for Odysseus' esteemed guests, but these days it was ours to enjoy as we wished.

As I filled my cup, I let my gaze drift across the revelry. Autonoë was playing the lyre Penelope had gifted her a few summers back, her sweet voice weaving effortlessly through the crowd. I could hear Hippodamia's tinkling laugh as she recounted a story to a small crowd of besotted stable boys. They flocked to her like moths to a flame, drunk on her light. Thratta was seated with Actoris at one of the long wooden tables, playing some kind of ridiculous game that involved stabbing a blade between their splayed-out fingers, whilst Telemachus watched, utterly mesmerized. I would have despaired at the combination of wine and weapons, but my concern was bridled by the sheer delight on Actoris' face. She looked like a different person to the tiny ghost we had found in the woods that morning.

I even caught the cantankerous old Eurycleia *almost* smiling, though she would have certainly denied such an accusation. Mercifully, the old maid kept to herself these days, grumbling through the palace about Ithaca's 'loss of order'.

As I continued watching my friends, I felt their joy filling me to the brim with a delicious kind of warmth. But there was something lurking beneath it, a creeping sense of unease fuelled by the words on everyone's lips – *Hector is dead! Achilles has returned! The Greeks will win soon enough!*

And when they did, the war would be over. Odysseus would return. He would take his rightful seat upon Ithaca's throne, and what would become of our home? For nine summers we had been carefully building a haven within these walls, a place where people could feel safe, where happiness could grow and flourish. What would happen to all that when the men returned to claim what was theirs?

'What's that look for?'

I turned to find Eurynome at my side. Her eyes were hazy, her smile loose. It was nice, seeing her a little tipsy. She rarely let herself indulge like this.

'Nothing,' I lied, dousing my concerns with another mouthful of wine. 'I'm fine.'

'That swineherd keeps watching you, you know.'

'Eumaeus?'

Eurynome's smile was a mischievous thing. 'He never takes his eyes off you.'

I followed her gaze across the room to where Eumaeus was leaning against a wall, listening distractedly to one of the kitchen girls. When he caught me looking, he tipped his cup to me and smiled.

'You should go and talk to him,' Eurynome urged.

'Why?'

'Because he's *handsome*.'

She wasn't wrong. Eumaeus was, admittedly, very good-looking, his rich, dark features accentuating every striking detail – the cut of his beard highlighting the strength of his jaw, thick eyelashes and brows emphasizing the deep hue of his brown eyes. I knew a lot of the palace girls coveted his attention. The boys, too.

'So?' I shrugged.

Eurynome gave an exasperated huff. 'In all the summers I've known you, never once have you batted an eye at anyone. You're a beautiful girl, Melantho. You could have your pick of the lot.'

I rolled my eyes, turning away from Eumaeus' lingering gaze. 'Have you seen Penelope?'

'You know what she's like. She doesn't wish to *disturb* the celebrations.'

'I'm going to go look for her.'

Eurynome made a noise that was somewhere between a sigh and a chuckle. 'I'd ask you to stay, but I know I'd be wasting my breath. There's no keeping you two apart, is there?'

'I just don't think it's fair Penelope misses all the fun.'

'I'm sure she's fine, love.' Eurynome patted my arm. 'Better than fine. I'm sure she's elated. Her husband will finally be returning to her – at long last. Just think how *romantic* their reunion will be!'

'The war isn't over yet.' I hated how defensive I sounded.

'No, not yet.' Eurynome's smile widened. 'But soon, my dear. Very soon.'

32

I found Penelope in the courtyard, staring up at the moon.

She said nothing as I came and sat beside her on the stone bench. My gaze traced the large oak tree towering before us, its silver-limned branches murmuring in the midnight breeze.

'Why aren't you celebrating with the others?' Penelope asked after a time.

'I thought you could use the company . . . and the wine.'

I held a jug out to her, but she shook her head. I frowned, studying the sharply drawn line of her shoulders.

'What's the matter?'

'I'm afraid I'm finding the news . . . difficult to celebrate,' she admitted with a smile, though her eyes remained heavy. 'People seem to have forgotten that it was Patroclus' death that drove Achilles to return to battle. The Prince of the Myrmidons didn't slay Hector as an act of glory, but one of desperation. Because Hector took what mattered most to him.'

I stared up at the oak tree, watching the shadows seep into its roughened bark, distorting the ancient trunk into something nightmarish and strange.

In my mind, I turned over Penelope's words. Achilles had always seemed more myth than man to me, an unreachable ideal, like the Gods themselves. I had never thought of him as a person, as someone capable of loss and pain.

'So, you think the rumours are true, then? That Achilles and Patroclus were lovers?'

Penelope considered the question. 'From what people say, they clearly loved one another. Though I don't presume to know in what capacity.' My eyes drifted back to hers, drawn by that invisible tide. 'Love can come in many forms.'

We stared at each other for a moment, that familiar, unspoken *thing* shifting in the darkness between us. That *thing* I had felt growing inside me for the past nine summers, intensifying with every passing season, driving me slowly insane with its sweet torture.

Sometimes, I convinced myself Penelope could feel it too. It was almost too easy to believe that lie when she looked at me like this, her voice rich with emotion, eyes studded with stars.

'Let's go for a walk,' I said abruptly, severing the foolish thought.

Penelope laughed. 'A walk? It's the middle of the night, Melantho.'

I shrugged. 'So?'

Her smile warmed her eyes, chasing away the shadows I had seen skulking there.

She rose. 'A walk sounds perfect.'

I flung my arms out as I raced down the beach, sand spraying behind me.

The water rushed up in greeting, cold, frothy waves lapping around my calves. Behind me, I heard Penelope's laugh dancing on the breeze.

Turning, I watched her settle down on the sand, taking a delicate sip of wine. I trudged back up the beach, collapsing beside her.

'What do you think?' I gestured around us with a grin.

Penelope nodded approvingly. 'I can see why you like it here.'

Ithaca was full of beautiful, hidden coves and this was one of my favourites, cut like a pale crescent moon into the island and hugged on all sides by thickly crowded trees. It wasn't far from the palace, but it promised complete privacy.

'Are you going to share that?'

Penelope smirked. 'Share? *You* drank most of it on the walk here.'

I held out my hand expectantly. 'So?'

She passed me the wine jug and I took two big mouthfuls.

'You might regret it in the morning, you know.'

'Well, it's a good thing it's not the morning yet. Isn't it?' The words felt thick on my tongue, stumbling over themselves. 'You should learn to enjoy the moment, *my queen*.'

I handed the wine back to her and, instead of replying, Penelope took a long, slow drink. I grinned and wondered, distantly, why my cheeks felt like they were buzzing.

'What?' I asked as Penelope chuckled to herself. 'What's so funny?'

She shook her head. 'I just like seeing you like this. So . . .'

'Drunk?'

She laughed again. 'Happy. You look happy.'

'I am happy.'

Penelope's expression softened beneath the moonlight.

'Everyone else is happy too, I think,' I continued. 'Not because of Achilles or anything. I think they're just . . . happy.'

'They are.'

Lying down, I marvelled at how soft the sand felt beneath me. Splaying my hands, I dug my fingers into those tiny grains, feeling the lingering warmth of the day's sun baked within them.

'I met Actoris earlier,' Penelope said.

'What did you think of her?'

'She reminds me of you.'

I snorted. 'Because she's small and angry?'

'Because she's brave,' Penelope corrected, 'and has clearly been let down by this world.'

I closed my eyes, swallowing the sudden knot in my throat.

'I saw her laughing tonight,' I whispered. 'She's not even been here a day and already she's laughing. Do you know what that means?'

'What?'

'It means we've made something here. Something *good*.'

Even with mine closed, I could feel Penelope's eyes on me as she murmured, 'We have.'

'I wish everything could stay just like this. Always.'

Penelope said nothing, and the realization hit me a moment too late.

'I'm sorry.' I sat up, the world spinning slightly with the motion. 'That was insensitive of me. I didn't mean I wanted the war to—'

'I understand what you meant, Melantho,' she said quietly.

'It'll be over soon anyway, what with Hector now dead,' I hastened to add. 'That's what everyone is saying.'

Penelope gazed out across the night-soaked waves, her expression growing distant as it so often did when she was deep in thought. But there was something else lining her face tonight, something delicate and wistful.

'You must be . . . looking forward to it,' I prompted her. 'Odysseus finally returning.'

'Sacker of Cities,' she murmured.

'What?'

'"Sacker of Cities" — that is what they call him now.' She smiled, though the edges seemed stiff. 'It is rather a gruesome title, is it not?'

I could think of nothing to say to that, so instead I watched wordlessly as Penelope brought the wine to her lips again, taking a deep drink.

'Eumaeus asked me earlier tonight if he could court you,' she said suddenly.

I let out a surprised snort. 'Eumaeus?'

Penelope turned to study me. 'Why do you find that amusing?'

'I don't know . . . I just didn't expect you to say that.'

'You must have noticed the way he looks at you.'

'So?'

'So, would you want him to court you?'

'I don't know,' I hedged. 'I hadn't ever given it much thought.'

'Do you . . . like it?' Penelope murmured, gaze falling to the wine jug in her lap.

'Like what?'

'The way he looks at you.'

'Why, are you *jealous*?' I laughed as I said it. I had only meant it as a joke, something to ease the tension inside me. But Penelope did not laugh. Instead, she grew horribly quiet, her silence sucking all the air from my lungs until it felt as if I could not breathe.

'Perhaps I am,' she said.

I wondered, then, if I was more drunk than I realized. 'You . . . are?'

'You cannot be surprised that I am protective of you, Melantho.'

She lifted her gaze to mine, her eyes filled with a rich swirl of emotion. In so many ways Penelope was as familiar to me as my own self, like an extension of my body. Yet a simple look like that still raised my pulse as if she were something new and dangerous.

It was frightening, how easily she could unleash all those wild feelings inside me, feelings I had spent so many summers trying to rationalize, to force into the restrictive confines of 'friendship', even though I knew they would never fit.

I leapt to my feet. 'I'm going for a swim.'

Penelope glanced away. 'Now?'

'Why not?'

She paused, then chuckled, the sound chasing away that sudden tension.

'Try not to drown, please,' she sighed.

'I make no promises.'

I crashed into the waves fully clothed, the water so cold it made me shriek. Penelope called out something from the shore, her voice tilted with amusement, though I couldn't hear her over the water rushing around me.

Floating upon the moon-brushed waves, my body felt lighter than it ever had. Around me, it was impossible to see where the sky ended and the sea began. I smiled, breathing in the dark, those rich midnight blues, and I swore I could taste the stars themselves crackling on my tongue.

You cannot be surprised that I am protective of you . . .

I turned Penelope's words over and over until they became smooth in my mind, their thrilling edges worn down into something dull and unremarkable. She was merely protective because we were friends. That was all.

That had to be all.

After a time, I made my way back to the shore. The shock of the water seemed to have sobered me slightly, the ground feeling steadier beneath my feet.

Penelope smiled as I approached, but then she lowered her eyes, and a strange look tightened across her face. I glanced down at myself, realizing that my drenched gown was now clinging to my body, the soaked material leaving shamefully little to the imagination.

A heated shyness crept over me, words stalling in my throat.

I had been naked around the handmaids countless times, whenever we swam in the sea or changed in our quarters. Nudity never felt strange in their company, but under Penelope's gaze it felt . . . different.

Her eyes dipped over me again, slower this time. The air between us was thick enough to choke on.

Penelope then shook her head, as if remembering herself, and rose. 'Here.'

'Thank you,' I murmured, taking her offered shawl and wrapping it tightly around my shoulders.

She turned away and stiffly sat back down. I settled beside her, shivering slightly as sand clung to my damp body.

'Are you cold?' she asked.

'I'm fine.'

For a while neither of us spoke, and I noticed Penelope was avoiding looking at me, her eyes set on the darkness ahead.

'Do *you* think Achilles and Patroclus were lovers?'

Her question was abrupt enough to make me laugh. 'I don't know . . . It certainly *sounds* like they were, doesn't it?'

Penelope tilted her head upwards, staring at the sky with such intensity, as if she were committing each star to memory.

'Do you think *they* knew if they were?'

I frowned. 'What do you mean?'

'I just wonder if they were able to be honest with themselves... before it was all over. Did they ever admit their feelings, or did Patroclus die never knowing how Achilles truly felt?'

I stared at her for a long moment, trying to decipher her expression. But Penelope's face was like a labyrinth, filled with so many twists and turns to lose myself within, never truly knowing what lay at the heart.

'I hope they did,' I finally admitted, every word placed so carefully between us. 'For it would seem an awful waste otherwise, to think they would have spent nine summers side by side, loving each other but never admitting it.'

'So, you think they should have acted on their feelings?'

She turned to look at me then, and something in her gaze made me feel wildly unsteady yet somehow deeply rooted, as if her eyes were the sole anchor tying me to this world.

'Why are you asking me this, Penelope?'

'I suppose the news of the war has made me... reflective,' she admitted. 'Made me consider things that have been playing on my mind for a while.'

We stared at one another for a long moment, and within that fragile stillness I allowed myself to imagine it: the possibility that this same madness had been screaming inside Penelope all this time, fighting to be heard. My hope flared, so sweetly bitter in its terrible desperation.

'What things?' I pressed, daring to stoke those embers between us, willing them to catch light, to engulf her as they had me.

Her eyes flickered to my mouth, and I found myself leaning forward in anticipation of her answer. But, instead, she silently reached out a hand and brushed a damp curl from my face. Her touch lingered at my jaw, torturously gentle.

'*Penelope*,' I breathed.

Her fingers skated along my cheek then brushed over my mouth.

'Say that again,' she said.

'Penelope,' I whispered, and she traced the movement of my lips, feeling the shape of her name upon them. '*Penelope, Penelope, Penelope.*'

My heart hammered against my ribs, and I had the vague sensation I was back in the water, floating on those inky waves. Weightless amongst the stars.

Carefully, Penelope took my trembling hand, unfurling my fingers so she could place them upon her own lips.

Her mouth was devastatingly soft as she whispered, '*Melantho.*'

Nothing, in all my life, had ever felt as intimate as this, feeling the shape of my name on Penelope's mouth.

'Again,' I begged.

'*Melantho.*' It was not a name, it was an ache, a *need*.

We stared at one another, all those wild, unspoken feelings burning between us, threatening to set us both alight.

Without thinking, I pressed closer, my body melting into hers as I moved my hands to cup her face, my lips searching for the place where my fingers had just been. I could think of nothing but my desperation to feel her mouth upon mine, to touch her and taste her and . . .

'I . . . I'm sorry,' Penelope gasped, just as my mouth brushed her own.

The words were like a blow to the gut, knocking me back into reality. I blinked, frozen as she pulled away from me, guilt weighing in her eyes.

'We should not . . . I should not have—'

'Don't,' I said hoarsely. I couldn't bear to hear her excuses, to watch her try to remedy my embarrassment. 'Please just . . . don't.'

Penelope's throat bobbed and I could have sworn I saw a flitter of regret steal across her face, but she turned away before I could be certain.

'I'm sorry,' she repeated, quieter now.

It felt as if I had been falling, and my body had just hit the ground with sickening force.

What was I thinking?

What have I done?

'You were right. I've had too much wine. How foolish,' I said, jumping to my feet, my entire body burning with humiliation. 'I should . . . go lie down.'

Penelope simply nodded.

She could not even bear to look at me as I fled.

33

I raced up the beach, crashing through the trees.

I did not know where I was heading; all I knew was I had to get away, far away from Penelope, from my shame and that madness she had unleashed within me.

In the distance, a light flickered, guiding me forward like a beckoning hand. I chased after it, until the woods finally thinned out, giving way to rolling fields. A giant stone caught my foot, and I nearly went hurtling to my knees. A boundary marker, I realized. I was at the very edge of the palace grounds.

I pressed on and was met with a rich tang in the air and the sound of snuffling creatures settling in for the night. Ahead of me, Eumaeus' house shone through the dark, warm light spilling from its windows.

It took a few moments for my knocks to be answered.

Eumaeus' face was soft and drowsy with sleep. His tunic was skewed around his shoulders, as if he had just pulled it on, his hair flattened on one side. He scratched the back of his neck as he regarded me standing on his doorstep in the middle of the night with nothing but the moonlight as my companion.

'Melantho?' he murmured around a yawn. 'Is everything all right?'

'Can I come in?'

Something shifted behind his eyes, confusion giving way to politeness, and then he stepped aside.

'Of course.'

The space was small and sparse, the air permeated with the musky smell of the animals outside. A fire glowed invitingly in the corner, beside which was a table and stools draped in leather hides. In the corner was his pallet bed, the blankets and furs tangled together.

'I was not expecting guests,' Eumaeus murmured, watching me.

'Your home is lovely.'

'Thank you. I am blessed to have been gifted it,' he said. 'Mistress Penelope says she is building more homes here for the palace slaves. Her generosity is remarkable, is it not?'

I tensed, glancing away. 'Why did you leave the celebrations?'

A slight flush of colour crept up Eumaeus' neck, disappearing beneath his beard. 'Because I saw you had.'

I said nothing. I knew Eumaeus had questions, but hospitality was a sacred custom, even amongst us slaves, and so he could not ask them until I had been properly cared for.

'Would you like some food?'

I nodded, suddenly aware of how starving I was.

He motioned for me to take a seat, and I watched as he moved around his home. Despite his rugged appearance, there was something elegant and refined about the way Eumaeus held himself; his mannerisms seemed to have been plucked from another life, beyond that of small ramshackle huts and mud-coated pigs.

A few moments later, he set down a plate of bread and cheese beside a bowl of thick stew studded with chickpeas.

'Thank you.' I managed a smile.

I could feel Eumaeus' eyes on me as he took a seat. If I had known him better, I would have said he looked nervous. Tearing off a piece of flatbread, I soaked it in the stew and popped it into my mouth. A hum of pleasure escaped me.

'Is it . . . to your liking?' he asked. 'It would have perhaps been better if the stew was hot, but I—'

'It's delicious, Eumaeus,' I cut him off. His smile was so genuine it beckoned my own. 'Do you like to cook?'

He nodded. 'I am permitted my rations from the palace, and everything else I source for myself. Mistress Penelope sometimes brings me spices from the market...' Eumaeus paused, studying my face. His gaze then dropped to my damp clothes. 'Are you sure everything is all right, Melantho?'

I was surprised by the flicker of genuine concern in his voice.

'I'm fine.'

'You can tell me, if you're *not* fine,' he offered, his eyes painfully sincere.

'I just... needed some time away from the palace. Sometimes it all... It gets a bit much.'

Eumaeus nodded. 'I understand.'

I was certain he did not.

We lapsed into silence and Eumaeus glanced around the room, as if searching for something to say.

'I saw your brother the other day. He asked after you.'

I almost choked on my food. 'He... he did?'

'I believe he misses you.'

I pushed my plate aside, appetite withering. 'He's had nine summers to speak with me if he wished to.'

Eumaeus stared at my unfinished stew. 'Melanthius is a lost soul. I think... he could use some guidance. The guidance of a sister.'

My smile was so tight it stung. 'I am not his sister. Not any more. He's made that clear enough.'

'You know that's not true, Melantho. You will always be—'

I rose abruptly. 'I shouldn't have come.'

Eumaeus followed me as I moved towards the door.

'You don't have to leave.'

'I want to.'

'We don't have to talk about Melanthius... Wait, please.' He reached for my wrist. His grip was not firm – I could have broken away if I wished – but I let him hold me there. 'You don't have to leave... Unless, of course, you must return to the queen—'

'Penelope does not need me.'

'Then will you please wait? You're clearly upset, and I hate to think of you being alone like this—'

'Are you asking me to stay the night, Eumaeus?' I turned to face him, and he immediately released me, cheeks reddening. 'I know you asked Penelope if you could court me. So, we have permission. If that's what you're worried about.'

He seemed at a loss for words, yet his eyes blazed, questions flickering within them like the shadows playing across the walls.

'Say it, Eumaeus. Say you want me to stay.'

I could feel his desire expanding between us, charging the air with possibility. It felt good to be wanted like this, to have someone else's longing threaded between my hands, instead of being strangled by my own day after day.

Eumaeus' throat bobbed as he whispered, 'I want you to stay.'

I moved quickly, taking his face in my hands, and clumsily tugging his mouth to mine. His surprise felt like a spark against my lips, but it quickly melted into something else, something hungry and urgent.

When he began tugging at my gown, I suddenly stiffened, pulling away. Eumaeus blinked dazedly at me, lips slightly swollen from the urgency of our kisses.

'What's wrong?' he asked. 'Do you . . . want me to stop?'

Faded memories swirled, of all the times I'd wished Castor and his friends had asked me that very question.

Instead of replying, I undid my gown, letting it ripple to the floor. Eumaeus' eyes widened.

'Come here,' I instructed.

I did not have to tell him twice.

Eumaeus wrapped me in his large arms, and I sank into the heat of his body, letting my thoughts grow silent as instinct took over. I knew this game well; it was simple and familiar. It was a place I could disappear into, where I no longer had to be 'Melantho', rather just a body – limbs and skin and lips.

Within moments, Eumaeus was carrying me to his bed in the corner of the room, his own tunic discarded on the floor. He was surprisingly muscular, skin dusted with thick, dark hair. When he placed me upon the furs, he paused to stare at me, as if wishing to savour the moment.

'Aphrodite has truly blessed you,' he murmured.

I smiled. I had forgotten how intoxicating it could feel to be *wanted* by someone.

Taking Eumaeus' hand, I pulled him down on to me. This time, he kissed me slower, his lips migrating from my lips to trail down my neck, along my collarbone, venturing further still. With his free hand he pushed me down on to the bed, whilst his lips continued to explore. I craned my neck to watch the muscles of his back ripple and shift as he moved, glowing like a golden mountain range in the firelight.

At some point my head fell back and my eyes fluttered closed. I let my thoughts stray, the heat of the moment seeming to burn away the guard I usually held in place. In the confines of my mind, it was no longer Eumaeus' bare body over mine, no longer his lips on my skin, nor his roaming hands . . .

Penelope was smiling down at me, her curled mouth pressing against my fingertips, whispering my name.

Melantho, Melantho, Melantho . . .

'Melantho?'

I realized Eumaeus was staring at me, his face half dipped in shadow.

'*What?*' I asked, painfully aware of how defensive I sounded.

'Are you all right?'

Instead of replying, I pulled him to me, crashing my lips against his.

'Tell me you want me,' I demanded as I positioned myself over him.

'I want you.'

I closed my eyes, holding the words tight inside me.

'Say it again.'

'*I want you.*'

'Good.' I smiled down at him. 'Now show me.'

34

'You weren't in your bed last night.'

I had barely stepped foot in Penelope's quarters before the accusation speared me.

Stifling a groan, I turned to find Actoris grinning from where she was sitting cross-legged on the floor. Despite having been bathed and brushed, her short hair still stuck out in a tangle of wild spikes around her head.

'How do you know where my bed even is?' I shot back.

'Because *mine's* next to *yours*,' she said smugly. 'Penelope made me her "handmaid". Fanciest title I ever had.'

'And who gave you *that*?' I gestured at the dagger she twizzled between her fingers.

'Thratta did. Says I can come hunting with you next time.'

'You're too young to hunt.'

'I'm old enough for a man to pump a baby into me, but not old enough to hunt my own food?' She tapped her chin with the flat side of the blade. 'Seems dumb.'

'It's dangerous.'

'Serving drinks in a room of drunk, horny, old men is *dangerous*, and I was doing that when I was six.'

Defeated, I collapsed in my usual chair by the hearth, massaging my temples. 'Just do me a favour and keep away from me when you're holding that thing.'

Actoris made a few jabbing motions through the air, an unsettling grin split across her face.

'Good morning!' Hippodamia chirped as she swanned into the room, looking as radiant as ever. 'Oh Gods! Who gave *Actoris* a *knife?*'

'Apparently Thratta did,' I replied.

Hippodamia shook her head dramatically. 'That Thracian will be the death of us all.'

'And where were *you* last night?' A soft voice came from behind my chair as two hands landed on my shoulders.

I turned to find the large, dark eyes of Autonoë staring down at me. I dismissed her question with a noncommittal grunt.

'What's this?' Hippodamia asked with far too much eagerness for my liking.

'*Someone* disappeared during the celebrations and didn't come home,' Autonoë told her with a knowing grin. 'Care to share with us where you went, Melantho?'

'No.'

'Oh, come on, *pleeeeaseee*,' Hippodamia whined.

I noticed Actoris was observing us with quietly curious eyes.

'She doesn't have to tell you if she doesn't wish to,' Eurynome interjected as she shuffled into the room, looking a little fragile after the previous night's celebrations.

I gave her an appreciative smile, but Hippodamia cut in, 'Um, she mostly certainly *does*. It's handmaid rule number one – your secrets are *our* secrets.'

Autonoë nodded sagely, as if Hippodamia had said something very wise. 'She's right, you know. It's the rules.'

I could practically hear Eurynome rolling her eyes.

'So, go on then, tell us,' Hippodamia pressed, bracing her hands on both sides of my chair.

'She was with the pig boy.'

I felt the blood drain from my face as we all turned to stare at Actoris, who was tossing the blade between her hands as if it were a toy.

'*What?*' Hippodamia shrieked.

Autonoë grinned. 'Is this true, Melantho?'

'It's true,' Actoris said.

'How do *you* know?' Hippodamia frowned.

'She stinks of pigs . . . and sex.'

I felt my cheeks redden as Hippodamia and Autonoë burst into fits of laughter. The sound of their amusement made Actoris' own lips twitch, though she tried to fight it.

'Why are you being so loud?' Thratta grumbled as she strode into the room, clutching her head.

'Did someone else *indulge* too much last night?' Hippodamia giggled.

Thratta only grunted in response.

Hippodamia's smile widened. 'That's strange, because I distinctly remember you saying Greek wine was for "tiny infants".'

The Thracian clicked her tongue at that. 'I do not remember what I did or did not say. Now, what is this laughter? Tell me.'

'We were just discussing Melantho's *night-time activities*,' Hippodamia replied, wiggling her brows.

Gods, I hated her sometimes.

The Thracian cocked her head. 'Night-time activities? What is this "night-time activities"?'

'Fucking,' Actoris said without looking up from her blade.

'Did you give Actoris a knife?' I asked, desperate to divert the conversation.

'Yes.' Thratta shrugged, as if giving the girl a blade was not a severe safety risk to all of Ithaca. 'But this is not what I wish to speak of. I wish to speak of the fucking.'

Hippodamia snorted. 'I wish to speak of it too.'

'You should wash your mouths out, the lot of you,' Eurynome huffed.

'I think Melantho is the only one who needs to wash her mouth,' Actoris shot back. Hippodamia let out a howl of laughter, and I caught Actoris trying to hide another delighted smile.

'I should've left you in the woods,' I muttered, at which Actoris bared her teeth.

'I told you Eumaeus was handsome,' Eurynome murmured to me with a conspiratorial smile.

Thratta boomed a laugh. 'The *pig* boy?'

'He has always shown me kindness,' Autonoë interjected. 'I think Eumaeus is a fine match, Melantho.'

'I agree!' Hippodamia chirped. 'So, go on, then. Give us the *details*!'

I covered my face, feeling the hotness of my cheeks burn into my palms. 'No, thanks.'

'Oh, don't be like that,' Autonoë crooned, toying with my curls. 'Your hair is a mess; you *must've* had a good night.'

'Her hair is always mess.'

'Thanks, Thratta,' I muttered, peeking through my hands to see the Thracian woman grinning at me. 'Can we move on from this now, please?'

'Absolutely *not*!' Hippodamia seemed outraged by the suggestion. 'You have to at least tell us *how* it happened . . .'

Memories seared through my mind – Penelope's skin bathed in moonlight, the intensity of her eyes, filled with something I could not dare hope to name. The brush of her fingers on my lips. The shape of my name on hers . . .

I flinched, shaking my head. 'There's nothing to tell.'

'If she doesn't wish to tell, it means it was very bad,' Thratta deduced, scratching her chin like a wizened oracle. 'I am sorry for this, Melantho.'

I rolled my eyes. 'That's not true.'

Hippodamia grinned roguishly. 'So, it *was* good, then?'

'What was good?'

We all turned to see Penelope entering the room with Telemachus at her side.

The sight of her made my insides constrict with a nauseating intensity. Around me, the handmaids shared knowing glances, stifling a giggle. I stared at each of them in turn, hoping enough violence was laced into my glare to keep their mouths shut.

'Why does *she* have a knife?' Telemachus asked, pointing at Actoris.

She grinned. 'Jealous, princeling?'

'Mother, can I have a knife?'

Penelope sighed inwardly. 'No, Telemachus. Actoris, I appreciate you are new here, but we have a firm "no weapons" rule inside these walls.'

Actoris rolled her eyes. 'Fine. I'll go *outside*. Princeling, do you want to be my target practice?'

'All right!' Telemachus chirped, eagerly following Actoris out of the room.

'I'll supervise,' Eurynome added quickly, and Penelope flashed her an appreciative smile.

Once they had left, Autonoë, Hippodamia and Thratta began discussing the previous night's celebrations, mercifully avoiding the topic of Eumaeus. I tried to listen to their conversation, but my focus was consumed by Penelope. Though I did not dare look at her, I could still *feel* her as she moved across the room, her presence tingling over my skin like a phantom breeze.

When I could bear it no longer, I slipped away on to the balcony, keen to let the crisp morning air chill the fever inside me. I closed my eyes, steadying my breathing in time with the sleepy hush of the waves below.

'Why do I feel as if I am missing something?'

My heart stumbled at the sound of Penelope's voice.

'What?' I feigned ignorance as she came and stood at my side.

'The others are giggling about something, but they won't admit what. Thratta keeps making snorting sounds, like a pig.'

I'm going to kill her. 'It's nothing. Trust me.'

We kept our focus ahead, trying to ignore that heavy *thing* writhing between us. When I glanced down, I saw Penelope's nail beds were red and raw.

I heard her draw in a breath then, and my entire body braced in anticipation of her next words.

'Last night . . .' she began.

'I don't know what came over me,' I cut in quickly. 'I was . . . not myself. It was the wine – that was all. We can just forget it. Please.'

Penelope was quiet for a painfully long moment. Still, she would not look at me.

'I'm sorry,' I added.

'You have nothing to be sorry for.' There was a strange intensity to her voice, one that made the words tremble slightly. 'You did nothing wrong. So, do not apologize.'

'Oh, good! You told her!' Hippodamia exclaimed as she appeared beside us. 'I was just telling Melantho that Eumaeus is a fine choice. Don't you think, Penelope?'

'*Hippodamia*,' I hissed.

'What? I'm serious!' She elbowed me with a wink. 'I'm jealous – I wish I'd spent the night with a handsome swineherd, rather than listening to Thratta snoring.'

Dread hit me like a rush of icy water. I watched Penelope's face change, that horrible shift of understanding. Finally, she met my gaze, and I felt a strange stab of guilt low in my belly.

Hippodamia glanced between us, eyes widening. 'Oh! I thought . . . Oh Gods, you hadn't told her, had you?'

I smiled tightly. 'No.'

'Oh, Mel! You don't have to look so embarrassed!' she said, grabbing my arm. 'I'm sure Penelope agrees that you and Eumaeus make a great pair. Don't you, Penelope?'

'Please, just stop. Stop talking,' I said as calmly as I could.

Hippodamia winced, seeming to finally register the stifling awkwardness in the air. 'Sorry . . . I should . . . I'll just . . .'

She quickly retreated inside, leaving Penelope and me alone once again. She was staring at the horizon now, and I could sense the thoughts shifting behind her eyes. I ached to know just one, to be able to have a glimpse into that beautiful, brilliant mind of hers.

'Never share a secret with Hippodamia,' I said in an attempt to ease the tension.

'I could have told you that.' Penelope shot me an arched brow, though her tone lacked its usual playfulness.

Silence descended once more, and I longed to disappear within its depths.

'So . . . Eumaeus?'

I grimaced. 'It's nothing.'

'It does not sound that way.' There was a slight edge to her words, one I had not heard before. 'Only . . . last night you said you were not interested in him.'

'I didn't mean anything I said last night.'

Penelope nodded. 'I see.'

Guilt paced inside me, strange and heavy. But *why* should I feel guilty over this? Her heart was not mine to betray. It never would be.

'I'm pleased for you,' she suddenly said.

'You . . . are?' I asked, unsure why her words invited a brush of sadness against my heart.

'Yes. Hippodamia is right. Eumaeus is a good man. He will make a fine companion.'

'I wouldn't call him that.'

Penelope tilted her head. 'Why not?'

'I don't think I want a . . . *companion*.'

She considered my words, and I noticed she was shredding the raw skin around her nail beds. A part of me wanted to reach out and still her anxious fidgeting, but I pushed the urge away.

'I think it would be good for you . . . to have someone,' she said carefully. 'You should at least consider it.'

I shrugged, finding a sudden fascination in the ground. If only it would swallow me down into the halls of Hades, I would welcome the God of Death with open arms if it let me escape this excruciating moment.

'Melantho?'

I glanced up. 'Penelope?'

Our names, once so innocent on our lips, now had a torturous effect. I was certain Penelope felt it too; I could see the memories flaring behind her eyes.

She looked away. 'I'm happy for you, truly. You deserve to have somebody who will treat you well. Eumaeus is the right person for you.'

'Thank you,' I said, forcing myself to smile as her words hardened inside me like ice.

35

I began visiting Eumaeus regularly.

At first, I told myself it would be a brief distraction, something to keep my mind occupied, to stave off the madness Penelope had unwittingly infected me with. But then one night bled into another then another, spiralling away in a haze of soft midnight kisses and early morning whispers.

I felt guilty for using his love as a distraction, but I buried that guilt deep inside me, in the graveyard of all the other ugly pieces of myself I had learnt to live with. And, truthfully, I *did* care for Eumaeus. He was kind and sweet and allowed me to feel a sense of safety I had never known with a man.

He told me of his past, how he had once been a prince of a distant land but had run away from home as a young boy, lured by one of his father's slaves, a beautiful girl he had thought he loved. That girl had betrayed him, selling Eumaeus to pirates to pay for her own safe passage back to her homeland.

'What of your family? Do you not wish to return to them?' I asked when he recounted this story to me. 'You are a prince—'

'I *was* a prince,' he corrected sombrely. 'And I lost any right to that title the day I disowned my family for a stranger.'

'But you were just a *child*. Surely, they would understand—'

'What I did was wrong, Melantho. Slavery is my penance, and I am grateful for this opportunity to redeem myself in the eyes of the Gods.'

I wanted to tell Eumaeus the Gods were sadistic monsters if they believed slavery was a just punishment for a manipulated child, but I had a feeling that would not go down well.

'Through my servitude, I have learnt the importance of loyalty,' he continued, reaching out to cup my cheek. 'And for that, the Gods have rewarded me. With *you*.'

He would say things like that often, with such pride in his eyes. His love was so gentle, so genuine, the kind many men and women would dream of holding in their hands.

Yet still, I could not return it. Not in the way he deserved.

I believed there was something wrong with me; perhaps it had been since birth, or perhaps my heart had grown crooked after being broken so irreparably as a child.

Perhaps I simply *could not* love someone in that way . . .

But then I would hear Penelope's laugh, or see her smile, and I knew that was not the case. It was not that I *could not* love, but that I loved the wrong person far too much . . .

And it was destroying me.

The seasons turned, and the war did not end.

Though I was relieved, the feeling was marred by Telemachus' utter dejection. Every day I watched him rush to Penelope's side to ask, 'Any word?' and every day Penelope would respond with the same shake of her head.

The prince's hope was beginning to wither, like the summer leaves crushed beneath autumn's chilling fist.

When we entered the tenth summer of war, the news reached our shores.

Achilles was dead.

Achilles, the finest warrior this world had ever seen.

Achilles, the divine hero, born of a goddess.

Achilles, slain by Prince Paris of Troy, a mortal man.

The news wrapped Ithaca in a suffocating grief. Without Achilles, they believed the war was lost and were already mourning their beloved Odysseus.

Though I dreaded the thought of his return, Ithaca would be left dangerously vulnerable without Odysseus as king. With Laertes too old to rule and Telemachus too young, the throne would be ripe for the taking, with no army to defend it.

All we could do was wait, whilst Ithaca's future was woven upon foreign shores.

Wait and pray. Though the latter was of less interest to me.

It was Eumaeus who dragged me to the Temple of Athena each day, to entreat the goddess to watch over our 'noble and beloved master'. I would kneel beside him as he set offerings of food and wine before an indifferent statue. Then Eumaeus would pray, whilst my mind wandered along with my eyes, drifting around the lofty space draped in incense and unanswered pleas.

One such afternoon, my gaze wandered to a shadow I instantly recognized. Narrow and stooped, Dolios' figure was unmistakable. These days, I rarely saw him around the palace, and I was surprised by how much older he looked, familiar features lost between thick creases. Instinctively I turned away, as I always did when I saw him. But as I watched Eumaeus beg for Telemachus' father, I found my eyes creeping back to my own.

Dolios must have felt the heaviness of my gaze, for he turned and caught it. That usual awkwardness tightened between us, though neither of us looked away.

Fuelled by something I could not rightly name, I found myself walking towards him.

'Hello,' I said, the word absorbed by the temple's sombreness.

'Hello,' he murmured.

It was the first time we had spoken in years.

'Are you . . . well?'

He nodded, shoulders drawn slightly inwards, as if bracing himself. 'Yes . . . and you?'

I mirrored his nod. 'I am.'

We both glanced away, searching for something else to say. I swore I could feel the blank eyes of Athena staring down at us, judging our ineptness at basic conversation.

Dolios motioned to Eumaeus, lost in prayer behind me. 'I hear you two are . . .'

'Yes.'

'Eumaeus is a lucky man.'

I said nothing, that blade of guilt sinking deeper into my gut.

'It's good . . . to have someone,' my father continued, looking to Athena's stony face, as if the goddess had called his name.

Something in his eyes made me ask, 'Who were you praying for?'

'People lost long ago,' he said, and I was struck by how little I knew of the man standing before me. The ghosts of his past were strangers to me. All except one.

'I'm sure they appreciate it,' I managed.

'I have little to offer the Goddess of Wisdom,' he admitted, a touch sheepishly. 'But still, I pray she asks Hades to watch over their souls in the realm below. Your mother's, too.'

'What . . . what did you just say?'

There was a sudden stillness then, one that stiffened the air between us like that first spark of winter's chill. Dolios turned to me slowly, face paling.

'Your brother never told you?'

'Told me *what*?'

Dolios looked away, his face shadowed by something timeworn and aching.

'I thought you knew,' he murmured to the ground. 'I'm sorry.'

I grabbed his wrist, my voice taking on a harsher edge. 'Knew what?'

'Melantho?' Eumaeus called from behind me. 'What's wrong?'

'*Knew what?*' I was shouting now, the words ricocheting around us. Somewhere, distantly, I was aware of a priestess shushing me.

Dolios flinched. 'Y-your mother . . .'

'*What about my mother?*'

When he finally met my gaze, Dolios' eyes were glazed with guilt. 'She's dead, Melantho.'

36

'Melantho?'

I stood in the doorway to Penelope's bedchamber, legs on fire after running all the way there from Athena's temple. I hadn't stopped to think, to breathe; all I knew was that I had to see her.

Penelope was seated at her loom wearing the slightly distant expression of someone who had just been lost in thought. But now her eyes narrowed on mine, concern sharpening her features.

'Melantho, what is it?'

'My... my mother...' was all I could manage.

The tears came then, thick and fast. Penelope moved instantly, wrapping me in her arms, letting me weep against her chest. We had not touched like this since that night on the beach. Though I loathed to admit it, a distance had formed between us, and I knew it was my own foolish fault for my behaviour. I had driven her away, all because I could not control my poisonous emotions.

But now, Penelope held me tight, as if she never wanted to let go, as if the distance between us this past year had been nothing more than a bad dream. I wrapped my arms around her, realizing just how deeply I had needed this. Needed *her*.

'Tell me what happened,' Penelope murmured against my hair.

'My mother is dead.' Saying the words aloud was like a blade to my soul. 'She's *been* dead for all this *time*.'

Penelope pulled away to look at me, her hands resting at my shoulders, steadying me.

'How?' Her voice was barely a breath.

'Just after she was taken from me . . . a sickness broke out whilst the slaves were being held before being shipped away.' The words were a thick, tangled mess in my throat. 'It killed all the women, those who had been taken from the palace. One of the market sellers told my father.'

Penelope shook her head. 'How could he not tell you?'

'He told my brother, but Melanthius kept it from me. For all this *time*.' I spat the words, though my fury felt muted, suffocated beneath a wave of exhausted grief.

Gently, Penelope took my hand and guided me to her bed. I perched myself on the edge and watched as she moved to fetch some wine.

'Have you spoken to anyone else?' she asked, pressing the cup into my hand.

I shook my head. 'I came straight to you.'

She sat beside me, and when I met her gaze, there was such unbearable love in her eyes I could scarcely breathe.

'I'm sorry . . . if I disturbed you,' I whispered.

'Never be sorry for that, Melantho.'

'But with the news of Achilles . . . you must've been busy—'

'It doesn't matter.'

'But—'

'It doesn't matter,' she said firmly. Then, 'You look pale. Have you eaten?'

'No.'

She rose fluidly to her feet. 'Let me fetch you some food.'

A small, vulnerable part of me wanted to grab her hand, wanted to beg her not to leave. But I forced the urge away as I nodded. 'Thank you.'

'Rest, Melantho,' Penelope said. 'I'll return shortly.'

When she disappeared, exhaustion dragged me down until I found my head resting upon Penelope's pillow. It smelt so distinctly of *her*, and I felt myself relaxing into the familiar scent.

As I closed my eyes, I imagined I was a child again, my mother's body curled around me, her warm breaths brushing my ear, easing me into the sweet release of sleep.

I woke with a violent jolt.

'*Mama!*'

The world was dark, I was in an unfamiliar bed, and all I could see were the remnants of my dreams swirling around me – my mother being ripped from my hands, her body wasting away, left to rot in the dirt . . .

'Melantho, it's all right.' A voice found me in the darkness.

'Penelope?' I gasped.

She was beside me now, her hand on my back, rubbing in slow, soothing circles.

'It was a dream,' she told me. 'Just a dream.'

'Why am I in your bed?' I demanded.

'You fell asleep.'

'I . . . I shouldn't be here. I shouldn't—'

'Shh. Melantho, it's fine. Just breathe.'

I could just make her out through the gloom, kneeling beside me, her long, unbound hair brushing against my shoulders.

'I can't. I can't breathe.'

'You can, I promise. Just take your time.'

Gently, Penelope guided me back down to the pillow, then settled in beside me. She was stroking my curls now, her fingers like soft, soothing waves. I focused on the motion of them, until my breathing finally steadied, and the nightmare released me from its clutches.

'I'm sorry,' I murmured.

'Don't be. It was just a nightmare,' Penelope assured me. 'I get them too.'

'You do?' I could not imagine Penelope, always so calm and composed, ever being plagued by nightmares. 'What about?'

She seemed to hesitate, though I could not discern her expression in the dark.

'Things that happened long ago,' she whispered as she began to sit up. Instinctively my hand shot out to stop her. 'Where are you going?'

'Well, seeing as *someone* has commandeered my bed, I've been relegated to the chair,' she said, and I could hear the smile in her voice.

I didn't smile back. Instead, my grip tightened.

'Will you stay here, just a little longer?'

I knew I was being childish, but, in that moment, I couldn't bear the thought of not being near her. I sensed Penelope hesitating again, but then she lay back down, the tension inside me easing a little as she did so.

'Do you want to talk about it?' she asked. 'Your dream?'

I shook my head. 'No. It's all right.'

'But there is something you want to tell me, isn't there?'

How could she read me so well, even in total darkness?

'I'm afraid . . . you'll think less of me if I do,' I admitted.

'That's not possible, Melantho,' she said, ever so delicately.

I wrapped my arms around myself, trying to shape my thoughts into something coherent.

'When my father told me the truth today, the first thing I felt was . . . *relief*. Not sadness, or anger, or bitterness. But relief . . . All this time I've worried about her. Every day, every night, every *single second*, I've wondered where my mother is. If she's safe, if she's in pain, if she's starving or cold or afraid. I've worried about her getting older, about having nobody there to look after her. Over and over, I've worried. But now . . .'

I trailed off, the words lodging thickly in my throat like a sob threatening to split.

'Now you know she is at rest,' Penelope finished for me.

I nodded, biting my trembling lip. 'Does that make me a terrible person?'

'Of course not, Melantho. If given the choice, we would all choose peace over suffering for our loved ones. Even if that peace could only be found in the realm below.'

'What if she's not at peace, though?' I whispered. 'What if they didn't bury her properly and her soul is trapped down there?'

'*If* that is the case, then, when it is our time, we will find her on Hades' shores and we will ensure she crosses with us.'

'How?'

'Melantho, do you truly doubt I could outsmart some old ferryman?' Her voice glimmered like stars brightening the night sky.

I smiled and another wave of relief flooded through me, lulling me back towards the soft edges of sleep. But there was still more I wanted to say, more unspoken truths weighing on my heart.

A quietness settled between us, and I shifted closer, so that our faces were barely a whisper apart.

'Penelope?'

'Yes, Melantho?'

'I've missed you.'

She paused for only the briefest of moments before saying, 'I've missed you too.'

'I know the distance between us was my fault—'

'It wasn't your fault.'

'It was,' I insisted. 'Because I was foolish enough to try to kiss you.'

I don't know why I said it. Perhaps it was something about the anonymous dark that prised such honesty out of me, honesty I would have never been brave enough to voice under the harsh eyes of daylight.

Penelope had grown tense beside me, and I tried desperately to read the collection of shadows that made up her face, wondering if I had once again stepped too far.

'It wasn't foolish, and it wasn't your fault,' she said eventually. Her voice sounded strained.

'How could it not be?'

'Because I encouraged you.'

It was my turn to stiffen now, clutching at words that suddenly seemed so flimsy and insubstantial on my tongue.

'You . . . you did?' was all I could manage.

'Yes.'

'Why?'

The silence stretched so taut I thought the entire world might snap in two.

'Because . . . I wanted you to.'

Her words did not hit me as I thought they might. There was no sharp, shocking strike of realization, but rather something quieter, something gentler. A calmness washed over me, one that felt a lot like the comforting embrace of closure, or perhaps the tentative beginning of something. I could not be certain.

I found myself inching forward, until our mouths were dangerously close, so close I could feel the edges of her lips graze mine as I murmured, 'Really?'

'Really,' she murmured back.

We fell silent, our faces unbearably close. Neither of us dared close that distance, but neither did we pull away, and though our lips never met, it somehow felt more intimate, to let ourselves linger in this moment, suspended in that breath before a kiss.

This is enough, I told myself. *Let this be enough.*

And so that was how we stayed, as the night deepened around us, until we eventually slipped back into the realm of dreams.

37

'I have something I need to tell you.'

I was sitting beside Eumaeus in his home, fumbling over my words.

Two days ago, when I had awoken, alone, in Penelope's chamber, I had been struck with a wild torrent of questions and doubts. Yet, amidst that chaos, there was one certainty that cut through with startling clarity – I had to end things with Eumaeus.

But now, faced with his kind gaze and intolerably sweet attentiveness, I found myself floundering. I closed my eyes, forcing myself to dive into the speech I had spent the past days meticulously rehearsing.

'Eumaeus, I—'

'I have something I wish to say too,' he cut in. 'If I may go first?'

I felt my plan unravelling as Eumaeus took my hands in his. His palms were clammy, fingers trembling slightly. He was nervous.

A flicker of hope struck inside me – what if *he* wished to end things also?

'Melantho.' He drew in a breath, steadying himself. 'I wish to take you as my wife.'

I stared at him, uncomprehending. 'W-what?'

His smile was heartbreakingly tentative. 'I wish to take you as my wife. You can live here, with me. We could start a family together, if the Gods will it. I believe we could make each other very happy.'

The cold claws of guilt sank into my chest, stealing my breath.

'Slaves aren't allowed to marry,' I said quickly.

'Not without permission, no.' Eumaeus nodded. 'But Mistress Penelope has given us her blessing.'

Those claws turned to shards of ice beneath my skin. 'She *what?*'

'In the absence of Master Odysseus and Master Laertes, I asked for Mistress Penelope's permission to take you as my bride, and she gave it. Melantho... what is the matter? This is good news, is it not?'

'When did you ask her?' I demanded.

'Yesterday.'

I rose from my seat. 'What did she say? What were Penelope's *exact* words?'

Eumaeus stiffened, surprised by the sharpness in my tone. 'She said she was very happy for us. That I was the right person for you.'

His words were like a blow to the gut, the impact so tangible I almost doubled over.

'The right person,' I echoed.

Eumaeus was staring up at me with those sickeningly genuine eyes. 'So... what do you say?'

'What?'

He laughed a little self-consciously. 'To becoming my wife... What do you think?'

'I think... I... I need to speak to Penelope.'

Confusion creased between Eumaeus' brows, his hands slipping from mine. 'Can it not wait? Melantho—'

'I need to speak to her,' I repeated, staggering away from him.

'But... why? She has given her permission. What more do we need from her?'

I wrenched open the door to his home, gulping desperately at the sea air.

'I need to hear her say those words.'

I found Penelope in her bedchamber.

She was pacing on the rug, as she often did when she was chased by thoughts. Her hair was unbound, whispering around her narrow shoulders in waves of onyx. Grey morning light spilt into the room, painting the space in a sombre atmosphere.

When Penelope saw me, she seemed to stiffen. I had barely seen her since that night I had shared her bed. I had blamed this distance on her queenly duties, unable to face the alternative. But I could no longer hide from the truth.

She had been avoiding me.

'You gave him your *permission*,' I spat as I stormed inside.

Penelope's chest swelled as she drew in a long breath. 'I assume you are speaking of Eumaeus' marriage proposal.'

'Of course I am.'

'Then I suppose congratulations are in order.'

'*Don't give me that.*'

Penelope stiffened beneath my tone. 'You're upset. Tell me why.'

'No. *You* tell *me* why you gave him your permission.'

'I told Eumaeus he had my permission to ask, but it would be ultimately your decision.'

'And you said he was the "right person" for me.'

'I'm not sure if those were my exact words, but I said something to that effect. Yes.'

Her calmness only fed the rage burning inside me. 'And you really *believe* that?'

She stared at me for a long moment, and I saw something flicker behind that mask she wore too well, a glimpse of the emotions she would never spill. Not even for me.

'I think you should consider his offer,' she said evenly. 'Eumaeus is a good man, and he will—'

'That's not what I'm asking.' I pushed closer. 'Do *you* truly believe that *he* is the right person for me?'

'I think he is a good match.'

'I don't believe you.'

Her throat bobbed as she glanced away. 'Melantho, I know it has been a difficult few days for you. The news of your mother has—'

'Don't,' I snarled. 'Don't you *dare* use her as a defence.'

Penelope's eyes struck against mine, though her voice remained steady as she said, 'I thought this was what you wanted.'

'You know it's not.' I stepped closer again, so our chests were almost touching. 'And you know *why* it's not.'

Penelope's breathing hitched, a small fissure in that infuriating composure.

'I'm afraid I do not understand your meaning.'

Her words splintered inside me, and I turned on my heel, storming towards the door.

She chased me instantly. 'Melantho, wait—'

'No. I'm done.'

'Done? With what?'

'With *this*.' I spun to face her, waving my hand between us. 'With whatever this *thing* is that we keep pretending doesn't exist.'

She recoiled as if I had struck her.

'We are friends.' She said it like a plea.

'*Friends?*' I laughed, the sound twisting bitterly in my throat. 'Look me in the eyes and tell me what exists between us is simply *friendship*. Tell me you act the same with me as you do with Hippodamia or Autonoë or Thratta. Do you wish to kiss them also?'

'Melantho, please. Don't.' Her eyes were bright with something like desperation. Or was it fear?

'Go on. Tell me.'

'Melantho—'

'*Do it!*' I was shouting now, traitorous tears burning behind my eyes, threatening to spill. 'Tell me I'm crazy for ever thinking there was something more between us. I must be, right? If you have no idea what I'm talking about.'

'Melantho.' I hated the way she said my name, filled with such regret.

I glared up at her, shame and anger and confusion and love all raging inside me, coalescing into something ugly and desperate.

'Just *say it*. Tell me I'm delusional.'

Penelope's silence was a heavy, unbearable thing, and I wanted to drown within its depths.

'You are not delusional, Melantho,' she finally whispered. 'But you should marry Eumaeus.'

I blinked, vision blurring. '*Why?*'

Penelope eyes grew horribly distant, shifting away from mine, disappearing to a place I could never reach.

'Because I will never be yours, Melantho.'

Her words speared through me. The pain was so visceral I glanced down at my chest, as if I would actually see a wound opening there, spilling all that poisonous love and hope from my body.

'Melantho—' Penelope sounded pained, as if *her* heart were the one breaking.

I shook my head, retreating a step, then another.

'Wait—'

I turned and walked away.

And Penelope let me go.

38

I nursed a cup of wine by the hearth.

Around me, the handmaids were talking, their chatter like a distant buzz at the back of my skull.

I stared at the fire, though I could not feel its warmth. I could not feel much at all, my body deliciously numb.

'What's this?' I glanced up to see Hippodamia enter, hands set on her hips. 'Why does everyone look so glum? Are we *still* mourning Achilles?'

'Not me,' Actoris muttered. 'I'm bored stiff of everyone yappin' on about him.'

Hippodamia swanned over with a smile. 'Well, you'll be delighted to know I heard some *very exciting* news today.'

'What news?' Autonoë perked up.

'Melantho and Eumaeus, of course! They are getting married!' Hippodamia clapped her hands, eyes sparkling with delight.

Everyone turned to me.

'That's wonderful news, Melantho,' Eurynome said, moving closer to squeeze my arm. 'Congratulations.'

'Is this why you've been drinking like a fish since you got back?' Actoris snickered.

I smirked at her and, with deliberate slowness, drained my cup.

'Well?' Hippodamia urged. 'What do you have to say, Mel?'

'We're not marrying,' I muttered.

Confusion rippled between the women.

'But . . . Penelope told me she had given her approval,' Hippodamia said.

'She did, and I refused him.'

'What?' Hippodamia gasped. 'Why?'

I shrugged, moving to refill my cup. My limbs felt clumsy, and I chuckled as the wine slopped over the floor. Eurynome quickly steadied my hands, before taking the jug from me.

'I don't understand,' Hippodamia pressed. 'Eumaeus is such a lovely man—'

'Why don't you marry him, then? He's free for the taking now.'

Hippodamia seemed unsettled by my suggestion, glancing warily to Autonoë, who said, 'Are you . . . all right, Melantho?'

I flashed my teeth. 'Never better.'

'Marriage, *pah*.' Thratta made a point of spitting in the fire. 'Marriage is how they control us.'

'I'd slit my own throat before I got married,' Actoris muttered.

'But what if the marriage were for love?' Hippodamia asked, settling herself on the rug.

'*Love*.' Thratta glanced to Actoris, who mirrored her smirk. 'It is a myth.'

'That's not true!' Hippodamia shot back, cheeks reddening.

'Looks like Hip has *another* crush.' Actoris grinned viciously.

'I do not!' Hippodamia folded her arms, visibly flustered. 'You don't have to be in love to believe in it. Ah, Penelope! *You* will agree with me, won't you?'

Every inch of my body stiffened, as if a cord had been pulled taut inside me. The others appeared unchanged, as if Penelope's presence had not just tilted the entire axis of the room.

Over the years, I had perfected the art of watching Penelope out of the corner of my eye, stealing fleeting glances. But tonight, I did not care for subtlety. I stared at her, unashamedly, as she took her usual seat by the fire. She must have felt the weight of my gaze, but she ignored it as she asked, 'Agree with what, Hippodamia?'

'That you can marry for love.'

Penelope's smile was calm, measured. Of course it was.

'It is unusual, I'll admit. Marriage is primarily a business transaction between men. But that is not to say there cannot be mutual affection, given time.'

'Is that what happened with you and Odysseus?'

My vision was too hazy to decipher Penelope's expression.

'We did not have much time, sadly,' she said.

Hippodamia reached over to squeeze Penelope's hand. 'Of course, I'm so sorry. That was thoughtless of me to ask.'

'Are you sure that's a good idea?' Eurynome whispered to me as I refilled my wine again.

'What? I'm *celebrating* my marriage,' I whispered back with a grin. 'Or lack of one.'

'She will regret it in the morning,' Thratta muttered from my other side.

I ignored her as I drank, glaring at Penelope over the cup's rim, willing her to look at me.

'The mood has been foul since this news of Achilles,' Hippodamia announced. 'Let's have a song, Autonoë, darling! Something to cheer us up.'

'What song would you like?' Autonoë asked, brushing her fingers through her long, glossy tendrils.

'Let's have one about *love*,' I said loudly. 'What do you think, my queen?'

Finally, Penelope met my gaze, her expression infuriatingly blank as she replied, 'If that is what the others wish for.'

'What about a tale in honour of Achilles' passing? Of his great love for Patroclus?' Autonoë offered.

'Oh, yes! Perfect!' Hippodamia smiled, settling into the cushions she had piled behind her as Autonoë reached for her lyre.

'Penelope asked me a question once,' I interjected, rising to my feet. The world tipped beneath me and Thratta flung an arm out, but I managed to catch myself with a hand on the back of my chair. 'Do you think Achilles and Patroclus admitted their love to one another?'

There was a pause before Hippodamia answered, 'I certainly hope they did.'

'*Why?*' I pressed.

She watched me with cautious eyes. 'Well . . . it would be a shame, wouldn't it?'

'Exactly! What a shame it would be. *What a waste.*' The room tipped again, so I gripped the chair a little tighter. 'Ten summers. Imagine that. Imagine wasting *ten summers* loving someone so *pointlessly* . . . it's pathetic really, isn't it? *Utterly pathetic—*'

'Melantho.' Penelope rose, the steadiness of her voice slicing through mine. 'I think it best if you retire.'

'Is that an order, *mistress?*' I smirked as Penelope stiffened beneath the title. 'What happens if I disobey? Will I be punished? Will you have me *whipped* again? Did I ever tell you all about that?' I turned to the others, and their faces swayed around me like churning waves. 'When we were children, Penelope had me whipped.'

'Melantho,' she breathed. 'Please, do not.'

'I was only nine at the time, and I was so scared I pissed myself.' I laughed, the sound rough against the accompanying silence. 'Oh, come on, we can joke about it now. It's *funny*. Isn't it funny, Penelope?' She stared wordlessly at me, eyes filled with a pain I refused to acknowledge. 'The wounds became infected. I nearly died, you know. Actually, come to think of it, Penelope never knew that. She ran away. Seems she has a habit of running away from things that scare her, don't you, my queen?'

'*Melantho.*' My name was a warning now.

'Penelope.' I stared at her in challenge, dragging her name over my tongue. '*Penelope, Penelope, Penelope.*'

She glanced away, whilst the others shared perplexed glances.

'I still have the scars,' I continued, speaking to the room, though my eyes remained fixed on the Queen of Ithaca. 'I'm sure you've all seen already, though I try to hide them . . . Do you want to see them now? I'll show you.'

I began unclasping my gown, but a firm, tattooed hand locked around my wrist, halting me.

'Enough.' Thratta loomed over me.

'Get off,' I snapped.

She shook her head, her face blurring with the movement. I tried to break free, but she swept me into her arms, causing the room to tumble away like spilt wine.

'*Put me down!*' I shouted.

In Thratta's large arms, I was a child again, being restrained against a table as the Princess of Sparta readied the whip. I was a young girl held back as her mother was ripped from her life for ever. I was a woman pressed against a bed as a man had his way with her.

The starved memories consumed me, and I began to scream, thrashing wildly, that vicious panic stuffing itself into my lungs, choking every breath.

'Let go of her! Let go, Thratta!' a voice came.

I felt the grip around me slacken and the sudden softness of a bed.

Whose bed am I on?

I flung myself off, hurtling to the furthest corner of the room. But the walls started to warp around me, the world spinning out of control.

I wanted it to stop . . .

Make it stop . . .

'Melantho?' That voice again. 'Melantho? Can you hear me?'

I opened my mouth to say, 'Yes, Penelope,' but the words did not come; instead, the entire contents of my stomach emptied on to the floor. The smell burnt into my nostrils, my stomach roiling.

I'm sorry, Penelope. The words clogged in my throat as my consciousness bled away. *I'm sorry . . .*

39

I woke to Penelope's scent.

It took me a moment to realize I was in a bed. *Her* bed. What was I doing *here*? I squinted against the harsh morning light, a headache splitting open behind my eyes.

The room was empty, but there was a blanket crumpled on the chair beside the bed, as if someone had sat there for a long while. Perhaps all night.

I winced, sitting upright and tasting the acrid remnants of vomit in my mouth. The memories came in faded bursts like a flame sputtering to life.

I had been a fool; a drunken, embarrassing fool.

I groaned and buried my face in the pillows. I wanted to stay there, to rot quietly in my shame, but the pillows smelt too strongly of *her*.

I had to get away.

Once I had managed to drag myself from Penelope's bed, I slipped out of the palace, grateful it was too early for anyone to witness my escape.

I wandered over the hills of Ithaca as the world awoke, the waves below playfully mimicking my restlessness. I felt untethered, like a ship without a crew, left to the mercy of Poseidon's currents, its destination hopelessly unknown.

Normally, when I was in a mood such as this, I would have sought out Eumaeus, finding refuge in the reassuring security of his love, a place to hide from my own self.

If only I could have loved him back. It would have made everything so much simpler.

I should have gone to find the others: Hippodamia's soothing warmth, Autonoë's calming quietness, Thratta's and Actoris' distracting banter or Eurynome's motherly affection.

But I was too afraid.

What if they wanted answers? What if I told them? A deep shame had grown within these emotions I battled. Penelope was a wife, a mother. And she was a *woman*. I had never known anyone ever speak of such a thing, of feelings like this between two women. Was that because such a thing did not exist? Did it mean something was *wrong* with me?

I realized that, for the first time in a long while, I felt truly alone.

Somehow, I found my way to a familiar olive tree, one that grew just outside the palace grounds, overlooking the sea beyond. I sat down and watched the clouds roll by, fat and heavy with the promise of rain, their wispy bellies hanging low enough to brush the waves.

It was here that Odysseus and I had made our deal, so many moons ago.

As I gazed across the hazy sea, my thoughts reached for my mother. Her absence was a constant ache inside me, but today that pain was sharp and searing, refusing to be ignored. Could the spirits feel our grief down in the Underworld? Did our love haunt them, as they did us?

How I longed to be a child again, wrapped in my mother's arms, letting her steady hands guide my path, show me the way.

I can never be yours.

Of course Penelope could not be mine. How could I ever have been foolish enough to believe otherwise? How could I have deluded myself so completely? I had allowed my emotions to eat away at my rationality, driving myself slowly insane with this senseless dream.

'You and Mother are fighting.'

I glanced up to find a slight figure towering over me, gangly limbs etched in the late morning light.

'Hello, prince.' I sighed. 'Would you like to join me?'

Carefully, Telemachus set himself down on the ground, crossing his spindly legs. He had recently shot up and was still figuring out how to navigate his awkward, lolloping limbs.

'You and Mother are fighting,' he repeated.

I kept my tone level. 'What makes you say that?'

'She is upset. She is only upset when you argue.'

'How do you know she's upset?'

He gave me a flat look. 'Mother is easy to read.'

'You think so?'

'Yes. If you know how. Every person has their own tells; you just have to learn how to read them. Like understanding different languages.'

He was frighteningly smart for a boy of ten.

'What are my tells?'

'You're the *easiest* person to read, Melantho.'

'Excellent,' I sighed.

'I think it is brave. You never hide.' Telemachus' smile was so genuine it made my heart squeeze. 'So, what are you fighting about?'

He tilted his head in the exact same way his mother always did, dark curls flopping over his eyes.

'It's complicated.'

'I like complicated.'

I laughed, and the sound eased some of the weight inside my chest.

'Do you?'

He shrugged. 'Simple is boring. Complicated matters require thought, and that is far more interesting.'

'You don't talk like a kid, you know.'

He considered that. 'Perhaps that is why I prefer speaking with adults. I find children uncouth.'

I bit back a snort. 'Uncouth?'

'It means uncivilized.'

'I know what it means.'

He shot me a look, eyebrows slightly raised. 'Then why did you ask?'

'I just . . . It seemed a funny thing to say, is all.'

He shifted to regard the view, and I watched the way he turned my words over in that brilliant mind of his.

'I am not sure I see the humour in my statement.'

I laughed again. 'Your mother was the same, you know. She never spoke like a kid either.'

'I cannot imagine Mother as a child,' he admitted. 'What was she like?'

Memories flashed in my mind, of that grey-eyed girl with the secretive smile.

I found myself smiling as I said, 'She was mischievous.'

Telemachus seemed to like that answer, repeating the word under his breath.

'I heard you were very drunk last night,' he suddenly said. 'Is that true?'

I stifled a groan. 'Who told you that?'

'Actoris.'

'Of course,' I muttered, tickling grass beneath my fingertips. Telemachus watched my hands for a moment, as if he were reading some secret code within them.

He lifted his attention back to my face. 'Why?'

'Why what?'

'Why were you drunk?'

'I was . . . feeling sad.'

'And drinking wine helps that?'

'Sometimes,' I admitted.

He nodded, as if I had said something very wise.

'Perhaps I shall drink wine, too.'

I met his gaze. 'Are you . . . sad, Telemachus?'

'Sometimes.'

He began playing with the grass, as I had done a moment ago. I had the sense there was more he wanted to say, but perhaps he did not know how to.

'Because of your father?' I ventured.

He turned to look at the horizon, the answer lying plain across his face. 'Achilles is dead. People say my father will be next.'

I drew in a breath. 'I would not listen to what the people say. I would listen to your mother.'

Telemachus nodded again, fingers stilling in the grass. He looked so young then, just a boy longing for his father. It was strange to think Odysseus knew nothing of him, had no idea how smart and kind and wonderful his son was, how proud he would be of the young man he was becoming.

'Do you . . . think he thinks about me?' Telemachus whispered, glancing at me and quickly away again.

I reached for his hand and squeezed it tightly.

'Every single day.'

A smile hinted at his lips, eyes brightening, and, in that moment, I had never wanted Odysseus to return more. If only to see that smile always grace Telemachus' face.

We sat quietly for a little while longer, Telemachus' hand soft and small in mine.

'You should reconcile with Mother,' he said after a while, rising to his feet.

My smile faltered as I squinted up at him, shielding my eyes from the glare of the sun. 'You make it sound simple, Telemachus. I thought you did not like simple?'

He did not laugh at my words; instead, he spoke to me in a firm tone, as if he were the adult and I the child. 'Whatever has come between you, I cannot believe it is more important than what you share. Your love is the kind the poets would write about.'

In Greek, we have many different words for 'love'. Telemachus used the word *philia*, denoting the truest form of friendship, a soul-to-soul bond. I had once believed my love for Penelope was like this, intimate yet platonic. But over time, I had realized that was just a hopeful lie.

Eros was love built on desire and longing, named after the god who presided over such torture, and *pragma* was an everlasting romantic bond rooted in a committed relationship. Both of these words, I knew, would have suited better.

And therein lay the very problem Telemachus wished me to solve.

'Nobody writes poems about slaves,' I said.

Telemachus mulled that over, as if he had never considered it before. 'Well, maybe I will write one about you one day.'

My smile widened. 'You will be a poet *and* a king?'

'Mother says I can be anything I wish to be because I was born a man. And that is a gift I should not squander.'

'She's right, you know.'

He nodded. 'I know. Mother is always right.'

40

I waited until nightfall before returning to the palace.

Perhaps it was cowardly, but after my embarrassing display the previous night, I wanted to avoid the others as best I could. Especially Penelope.

Mercifully, our quarters were empty. I padded over to the hearth and began prodding the embers with an iron rod. Veins of gold and crimson pulsed to life, a few flames finally catching. As I fetched more logs for the fire, Telemachus' words lingered in my mind – *Whatever has come between you, I cannot believe it is more important than what you share.*

How could I have explained to him that it was exactly *what* we shared that had come between us? Or rather, what we did not and could never share . . .

'Melantho.'

I knew her voice too well for it to catch me off guard. It was as familiar to me as my own breath, my own heartbeat. Still, I stiffened at the sound of it, a thick, creeping tension closing around my muscles as I turned to her.

She was standing in the doorway to her bedchamber, grey eyes glinting in the shadows, just as they had done that first time we met.

We kept our distance, she draped in the silver of the moon, and I in the gold of the fire. Between us, the darkness stretched, a deep and dangerous unknown. Neither of us dared step into it.

'I wanted to apologize for my behaviour last night,' I said carefully.

'You do not have to apologize.' She was calm as ever, yet there was something in her eyes that unsettled me, something sharp and bright.

'I want to. I was foul to you.'

She said nothing.

'Penelope?' I prompted, desperate to know what thoughts plagued her.

'You are not marrying him,' she murmured.

I swallowed once. Twice. 'No.'

'*Why?*' The word was laced with a surprisingly stark thread of desperation, squeezing it tight.

'You know why, Penelope.'

She turned her face away, so it became wholly consumed by the shadows. The weight of her silence pressed in around me, but I forced myself to continue, 'I have given it a lot of thought, and I think I should leave the palace and serve Laertes. Eurycleia said he needs a slave to assist him at his cottage, and I feel this would be a . . . suitable opportunity for me. With your permission, of course.'

Penelope tilted her head, just enough for the moonlight to brush a silver finger along the length of her jaw, the rest of her face still obscured.

'You wish to leave?'

No, I ached to tell her. *But I must.*

I could not trust myself around Penelope, not any more. Every day I felt my control slipping, inch by inch. I knew one day it would snap, and I would do something truly foolish, and these poisonous feelings would infect everything beautiful we had built between us.

I needed time away, to clear my mind and purge my heart of this madness.

I needed time away from *her*, as much as the mere thought of it wounded me.

'I think it is best,' I whispered.

More silence. Its stillness felt sharper this time, cutting the night like glass. It was maddening not being able to see Penelope's face, not having a glimpse of what she might be thinking. I considered moving closer but being near Penelope always made me act in ways I regretted.

'What if I say "no"?'

Her question caught me off guard, my shock quickly followed by a familiar sting of anger.

'Then I would say that is unfair.'

'Unfair?' She huffed an empty laugh. 'You speak of abandonment, and you say *I* am being unfair?'

'*Abandonment?*'

'Yes.' She finally turned to me, her face limned in cold, silver rays. 'Is that not what you are proposing here? Laertes has deserted the throne, the war may be lost, Odysseus could be dead, and you wish to leave *now*?'

She strode towards me as she spoke, every step like flint against stone, threatening to spark a fire between us.

She stopped a few feet away, yet still it felt too close.

'I am trying to find a *solution*,' I said.

'And I am asking you to find another one.'

'You don't understand.'

'Then help me to.'

How could I? How could I put this madness into words? I was like Icarus, and she the sun, her radiance drawing me closer even when I knew how far I had to fall. That's what it felt like to want Penelope – a sweet, assured self-destruction.

'Why now?' she pressed. 'I do not understand why we cannot continue as we always have. For ten summers we have made this work between us—'

'And it has *drained me*.' I half choked on the words, caught between my desperation to speak my truth and my fear of having it finally heard. 'Every single day, it's drained me.'

She winced, as if I had struck her.

'Has it truly been so terrible,' she murmured, 'living beside me?'

'Penelope.' Her name was a pained sigh. 'You know I have loved every moment of the life we've made here, of being with you. But this . . . *thing* inside me, these feelings I cannot control . . . I know they are strange and wrong. I thought they would go away with time, but they just get worse . . . I cannot . . . I cannot keep doing this.'

She looked away, shaking her head. 'And what if *I* cannot lose you?'

'*Don't*. You do not get to push me away and then not let me leave. You are being selfish.'

'Selfish?' She whirled back to me. 'You think me *selfish?*'

'I do.'

She pushed closer again, swallowing up that narrow sliver of space between us. I tried to back away, tried to escape, but something in her eyes rooted me to the spot — there was a fire in them, one I had never seen before.

She was angry.

No, not just angry. She was *furious*, and I felt that fury calling to my own, feeding it, until the flames of our rage crackled, rich and wild and devastatingly dangerous.

'*All* I do is for others,' she said, that rainfall voice swelling with thunderstorms. 'For my husband. For my son. For Ithaca. You act on the heat of your emotions without a single thought of the consequence, but *I* have an entire kingdom to think of with every breath I take. And you dare to call *me* selfish?'

Her eyes sparked with that delicious fire and some reckless, dizzying part of me wanted to stoke it further, to see how high those flames could rise.

'You are like the tide,' I snapped. 'Continually drawing me in, then pushing me away. But when *I* wish for distance, you refuse to let me go. How is that *not* selfish?'

'If I were *truly* selfish, do you think I would have let you walk away from me the other day? Do you think I would have granted Eumaeus permission to marry you? Do you think I would have spent *ten years* denying myself the *only* thing I have ever truly wanted?'

Her words stilled the anger in my veins, emptying all thoughts from my head. Penelope's own rage seemed to recede as well, chased by a sudden diffidence.

'What . . . what *do* you want?'

She shook her head. 'I cannot—'

'What do you want?' I repeated, firmer this time.

'Melantho—'

'What do you want, Penelope?'

She stared at me, eyes desperate and searching.

'Penelope. *Tell me.* What do you wa—'

Her lips captured the words against mine.

The kiss obliterated my senses. I could not think, could not even breathe; all I could focus on was the devastating softness of her lips, and how I could feel them unravel everything I had been holding inside me, letting it all come crashing down into sweet, burning chaos.

Penelope pulled away abruptly, as if her mind had fallen two steps behind her actions.

'I-I am sorry,' she gasped.

We stared at one another, stunned. Then, I reached out, brushing the rosy flush that had risen in her cheeks, like daybreak dusting over the clouds.

'Melantho,' she whispered. I sensed the words crowding behind my name, the doubts and fears that would shatter this moment. 'We—'

I shook my head. 'Don't.'

Then, my fingers sank into her hair as I pulled her mouth to mine once again.

I was tentative at first, but my lips quickly grew desperate, giving shape to the madness that had been pulsing inside me for so long. And I could feel that madness inside Penelope too, calling to my own, a wild, heated battle cry that devoured my mind until all I could think about was tasting her and touching her.

My hands were knotted in her hair now, and hers were cupping my face, our bodies pressed in close, moulding so perfectly against one another.

And the world ceased to exist.

It was just *her*. She was the air, the sky, the ground, the breath in my lungs, the blood in my veins. She was my beginning and my end.

She was everything.

'You will undo me,' Penelope whispered as she pulled away to catch her breath.

She was right. I could feel it, that thick thread of her desire curled around my fingers. A single tug and I could unravel her completely, all that control she so carefully clung to.

I reached up, brushing my fingers along her mouth, memorizing the feel of it.

'Tell me to stop and I will,' I murmured.

She let out a shaky breath, and I felt it warm against my fingertips. Then she smiled, and my fingers traced that perfect curl of her lips.

'I don't want you to stop.'

I stared at her. 'Are you sure?'

Instead of replying, Penelope wrapped her hand around mine and led me to her bedchamber. She shut the door behind us, her movements so poised and controlled, even now. When she turned back to me, I moved instantly, knocking her against the door in my eagerness. She laughed, and I caught that beautiful sound in my mouth, wanting to swallow down every drop of it.

Lemons. Her laugh always reminded me of lemons.

'Do you know how often this has driven me mad?' I murmured, brushing that hollow dip at the base of her throat.

She smiled. 'Really?'

I lowered my head, kissing that spot and feeling her pulse jump beneath my lips. 'Really.'

'What other parts have driven you mad?' she whispered.

'Here.' I ran my fingers over her lips, then traced the length of her neck. 'Here.' They then ventured over her collarbones. 'And here.'

'A lot, then.' Her laugh was tight in her throat.

'You have no idea.'

'I do. Trust me, I do.'

I stared at her, still struggling to comprehend that this same torturous longing could have been echoing inside her all this time.

'How long?' I breathed.

Penelope's eyes softened. 'Always, Melantho.'

I kissed her again, slower this time, deeper. I felt her lips parting for me, the warmth of her tongue tentatively brushing against my own. I wondered, faintly, if this were another dream that morning would soon rip away from me.

'Is this real?' The question was a dizzy chuckle.

'I pray it is,' Penelope replied, though I sensed a hesitancy in her voice.

I pulled back to look at her. 'What is it?'

'I just . . .' She glanced away. 'I am not well versed in any of this.'

Of course. Penelope had only ever lain with Odysseus, and that had been ten summers ago now.

'I've never been with someone . . . like *this* before,' I admitted, hoping my inexperience might ease her own.

'With a woman, you mean?' she asked. I nodded. 'Does it feel . . . different?'

'It was always going to be different with you.'

Though, 'different' scarcely covered it, for this was *nothing* like those times before. With men, intimacy had always been a performance, a hollow role I disappeared into, where I ceased to exist. But here, with Penelope, it was *real*, all of it, and the thought was both exhilarating and terrifying.

'We can stop, if this is too much,' I added, as gently as I could. 'I don't want you to do anything you're not . . . comfortable with.'

Penelope shook her head. Then, she drew in a breath, holding it tightly in her chest. As her hands reached for the fastenings at her shoulder, I felt my anticipation slice through me like the keen edge of a blade. Carefully, Penelope undid each one, letting her gown ripple to the floor, pooling around her feet.

I stared at her, bared before me, my mind scarcely able to comprehend such perfection. I thought she had unravelled me before, but this was truly my undoing – seeing her like this, dressed in nothing but silvery moonlight.

With trembling hands, I unfastened my own gown, letting it crumple beside hers. Penelope's eyes widened slightly as her gaze dipped over me. For a while, we stood like that, not touching or speaking, just letting our eyes soak in the view they had been starved of for far too long.

My hand slipped into hers, but as I turned to lead her towards the bed, Penelope froze. Panic sparked through me – had her doubts taken hold of her? Had I gone too far?

I kept staring straight ahead, too afraid to turn and risk seeing the regret stain Penelope's eyes. Then I felt her fingers on my back, and I realized what had given her pause. My scars. Penelope had never seen them before, not up close like this. I had always been so careful to hide them from her.

She traced the length of each one in turn, fingers trembling.

'I'm so sorry,' she whispered thickly.

I was about to reply, but then I felt her mouth following where her fingers had just traced, and everything inside me went quiet. It felt almost holy, the way she kissed each scar with such reverence, and I found my eyes closing as her lips soothed those old wounds, allowing them to heal again anew.

'We were so young,' she whispered mournfully.

I glanced over my shoulder and saw her gaze had grown distant.

'We let the past take so much from us,' I murmured. 'Don't let it take this moment.'

She nodded, her eyes focusing on mine once more. Taking her hand again, I pulled her down on to the bed, shifting us so we were lying side by side, the heat of our bare bodies melting together.

I took a moment to simply look at her. She was like a work of art, all those elegant curves and angles. A statue etched with exquisite, painstaking detail.

'You are so beautiful,' she said, stealing the words from my own lips.

I kissed her in reply, feeling her heartbeat flutter against my chest, harmonizing with my own.

'Can I touch you?' I whispered and she smiled, nodding.

I started at her lips, tracing my fingers down and revisiting all those maddening places I had spoken of just before, then venturing further still. I felt her flesh pebble beneath my touch, her breath catching when I brushed particularly sensitive places – the underside of her breasts, the dip where her waist met her hips, the stretch of skin beneath her navel.

I was propped up on my elbow now, and I bowed my head so I could kiss her again. This kiss was slower, deeper. I did not want to rush this. I wanted to savour every moment for as long as I could, stretching out each sacred second. I would've traded my very soul with the God of Time, if it had meant I could make this night last a lifetime.

As my hand moved further down, I lifted my gaze to Penelope's, looking for any sign of reluctance. But there was only an intense longing in those eyes, a *need* so intoxicatingly potent I felt a little dazed at the mere sight of it.

I traced my fingers up to the apex of her thighs, feeling the heat of her desire radiating between them. A silent question filled my gaze and Penelope nodded as I carefully sank into the sweet warmth of her.

A gasp burst from her chest as her neck tipped backwards, hands gripping me tighter.

'Is this all right?' I whispered against her lips.

'*Yes.*' The word was a breathless gulp.

I pushed a little deeper and, *Gods*, she felt divine. Like touching the Heavens themselves. She let out a whimper, one that shivered through my very core, and I chased it with a kiss, wanting to taste the sound, to absorb every inch of it. Her lips became frantic, hands clutching at my body as if she were amidst a raging storm and I the sole raft keeping her afloat.

At some point, Penelope closed her eyes, and I studied her face, moving to the rhythm of her pleasure. Her body was like an exquisitely rare instrument, and I was learning all the ways to make it sing for me.

Penelope was breathing heavily now, and I sensed her cresting that wave, soaring upwards, higher and higher. Her hips arched against me, muscles coiling impossibly tight, making her entire body tremble. She let out another cry, and I whispered her name into her hot, open mouth, repeating it like a prayer.

'*Penelope, Penelope, Penelope.*'

I felt the moment it hit her, that rush of release crashing into her body, shattering it completely. The sound that escaped her was like the music of the Gods, so pure and divine it felt as though it should not be heard by mere mortal ears.

Her forehead was pressed into my neck, and she shuddered against me as the pleasure pulsed through her. Then, she melted into the pillows, and I watched her float back down to reality, savouring every detail. She had never looked more beautiful to me than in this moment – body limp, hair fanned out around her like a wild, twisted crown, skin flushed and dusted with sweat. To know I could do this, could bring her such satisfaction, filled me with unimaginable joy.

I could spend my entire life finding all the ways to make her look just like that.

Smiling, I stroked her hair. Such a simple action made wondrous by all the times I had denied myself this very urge.

'How did you do *that*?' The awe in her voice was enough to make me laugh.

'You speak as if that's the first time you've—' I stopped myself, noticing the look in her eyes. 'Oh. You mean, you've never . . .?'

Penelope shook her head, a sudden shyness creeping over her.

'Not even by yourself?'

'I was always . . . afraid of letting my desires run free like that, even in my own mind.' She was watching me intently now, limpid eyes bright with curiosity. 'Have you done that before . . . by yourself?'

I thought of all those sleepless nights I had lain awake, my mind crawling its way back to Penelope, no matter how many times I tried to distract myself.

'Yes,' I admitted, before adding with a smile, 'I never had your willpower.'

'I'm beginning to regret that willpower,' she muttered, her gaze gleaming with that mischief I so desperately adored. 'Now I know what I have been denying myself.'

I took her hand in mine, kissing her fingertips. 'I suppose we'll just have to make up for lost time.'

Penelope mirrored my grin. 'I suppose we will.'

I woke to warm sheets.

Dawn spilt through the windows, painting the morning in a drowsy, rosy hue.

I blinked, noticing the empty space beside me.

Penelope . . .

For a moment, I wondered if it had all been a dream, a beautiful, cruel dream. But then I saw her, sitting by the window. Outside, the flushed, erubescent sky softly wept, raindrops whispering like stolen secrets.

Penelope looked pensive, thoughts tightening across her face, furrowing her brow.

'Good morning,' I said, a touch hesitantly.

She turned to me, and the sight of her smile was like that first flare of sunrise, chasing away the darkness.

'Good morning,' she replied.

We stared at one another, giddily shy in the face of everything we had shared the night before. I could hardly comprehend it, and all that it meant. A part of me was afraid to, as if trying to make sense of this moment would risk shattering it completely.

'You snore when you sleep,' Penelope said, breaking the tension.

'I do not.'

'It's a sweet snore. You had the same one when we were children.'

'Then why did you never mention it back then?' I challenged, folding my arms.

'Because I was afraid you wouldn't want to sleep in my chamber if I told you.'

The admission made my heart swell.

'I still would have,' I murmured.

Her smile widened at that, but then I saw the corners of it catch on the edges of a thought. She turned to the window again, a quietness settling around her as she watched dawn continue to kiss the skies awake.

'What is it?' I asked.

She shook her head. 'It is still early; you should get more rest.'

Wrapping myself in the pelts strewn over her bed, I padded across to where she sat. Carefully, I took her hand in mine, tracing the shredded skin around her nail beds.

'What is it?' I asked, gentler this time. When she did not immediately reply, I whispered, 'Do you . . . regret it?'

'No.' She held my gaze. 'Never.'

'But you feel guilty?'

She said nothing, though I could see the answer weighing in her eyes. I brought her fingers to my lips, planting a kiss against them.

'You know what men are like at war,' I murmured into her palm. 'He will have taken concubines, captive women to warm his bed. Why does he deserve your loyalty when he would not give it in return?'

'Because the same rules do not govern husbands as they do wives.' She turned her face to the drizzling skies. 'And I am still his wife.'

'And *he* is still the husband who left you alone for ten summers,' I countered, trying to ignore the sting of her words.

'It was not his choice to go.'

'But it was his choice to stay, to continue fighting in a futile war to feed another man's ego.' My tone was harsher than I intended, so I kissed her hand again to soften my delivery. 'He does not deserve your guilt.'

'It is not guilt.'

'Then what is it?'

Her hand fell away. 'There are risks in what we are doing.'

'I know.'

'If anyone saw us—'

'Nobody saw us, Penelope.'

'You know Eurycleia patrols this palace like a hawk. What if she walked in now and saw you?'

'Eurycleia would never enter your bedchamber without permission, and besides, I am your *handmaid*. There are a hundred different reasons why I could be in here.'

She arched a brow, staring at the furs barely covering my body. 'Dressed like *that*?'

I shrugged. 'I could improvise a lie.'

Despite herself, Penelope smiled, though it vanished almost immediately. 'If anything were to happen to you—'

'It won't. We'll be careful.'

'Melantho—'

I kissed her then, soft and slow, silencing her doubts. Warmth pooled in my core as Penelope's hands gripped my hips, pulling me closer.

A knock came from Penelope's door, and we recoiled from one another instantly, as if the sound had forcibly thrown us apart.

'It is all right,' Penelope said as panic gulped inside me. 'Melantho? Listen to me. It is all right.'

Our eyes met, and I found comfort in the steadiness of her gaze.

'Who would be knocking at this time?'

'I do not know,' she admitted.

I moved to the corner of the room, hiding in the shadows as Penelope disappeared through the door, closing it quickly behind her. Muffled voices came from outside, too low to make out.

A few minutes passed before Penelope returned.

'Is everything all right?'

'An urgent council meeting has been called,' she said.

'Why?'

She shook her head. 'I assume to do with the war. Perhaps there has been more news.'

'Are you worried?'

'Not until I am given reason to be.'

As I helped her dress, I began to feel the harsh edges of reality creeping in around us.

'What is it?' she asked, studying my face.

'When we step out that door, we step back into the real world.'

Penelope took my hands in hers, squeezing gently. 'We never left it, Melantho. *This* is real, all of it.' She brushed a kiss against my lips. 'I will return soon. Wait for me?'

'Always.'

41

Penelope did not return.

As the morning wore on, I began to grow restless.

'You've been pacing like a caged beast all day,' Thratta said to me as she sharpened her knives at the table. 'What troubles you?'

'Nothing,' I lied.

She threw me a flat look. 'Is it because you were a drunken fool the other night? Worry not, friend. We are all drunken fools sometimes.'

'You were pretty funny,' Actoris chimed in from where she sat beside Thratta, gazing longingly at her weapons. 'You tried to take your clothes off at one point.'

'Thanks for reminding me,' I muttered.

'Has Penelope forgiven you for what you did in her chamber?' Actoris asked.

Fear spasmed in my chest. 'What?'

'For throwing up on her floor,' Actoris clarified. 'Don't you remember?'

'Oh. Yes . . . She's forgiven me.'

I noticed Thratta and Actoris sharing a look as I returned to my pacing.

'Do you think it's normal for a council meeting to last all day?' I asked.

Thratta shrugged. 'Those old men love to hear their own voices. They talk too much.'

'Your pacing is getting irritating,' Actoris snapped. 'What's up with you?'

Before I could think what to reply, Hippodamia appeared in the doorway, her face slightly flushed.

'What is it? What's happened?' I demanded.

'There's going to be a public address. Everyone is to gather outside the palace,' she said, motioning for us to follow.

There had not been a public address in the ten summers since the war began. Perhaps there had been more bad news from Troy and Penelope wanted to reassure everyone. It was brave of her, to face her people so openly, and I felt the dread inside me intensify.

The afternoon sun was hot on our backs as we gathered at the foot of the palace steps. It seemed all of Ithaca had come to hear Penelope's address, and I gazed out at the sea of bodies shifting uncomfortably beneath the heat. Aside from the slaves, the crowd was predominantly women, with a gaggle of young men gathered at the front beside a smattering of elderly ones.

A cheer arose as Penelope emerged from the palace. Above, the sun hung low in the sky, bathing the palace in its honeyed rays. Penelope smiled at the crowd, her people, and it felt strange to think I had kissed those lips just this morning.

'Thank you for gathering on such short notice,' she began, her voice steady and clear. The voice of a queen. 'Recently, we heard the unfortunate news of the death of Achilles, son of Peleus, Prince of the Myrmidons. I know his passing has unsettled us all, but further news has raced on winds from Troy and reached us just this morning. The news is this: *Troy has fallen*. Queen Helen of Sparta has been returned to Menelaus. The war is over. Greece is victorious.'

I suddenly felt very far away, the world around me growing dull and muted. I could not hear the answering roar of the crowd, just the vibrations shuddering through my bones and the jostle of animated bodies as people danced and embraced. It felt as if I were watching the scene from some distant, unknown place, and though I could see everyone's happiness, as vivid as the blazing sun, I could not *feel* the warmth of it.

I felt only coldness, and that interminable dread expanding inside me.

'I have yet further news: that it was your king, Odysseus himself, who secured this victory,' Penelope continued. She did not falter over her words, not once. They were as smooth and perfect as freshly carved marble. 'Through his cunning plan, Troy's impenetrable walls were breached, allowing Greece to secure a swift and devastating victory.'

More cheers erupted, led by the young men in the crowd. They began stamping their feet, splitting their king's name into short, sharp syllables they repeated over and over: *O-DYS-SE-US!*

They had spent their childhoods feasting on stories of the mighty man. To them, he was a living legend, a god in mortal form. Their idol. Their king.

And now he was finally coming home.

'Odysseus and his army will leave Troy imminently, once they have shared in her spoils.' Penelope's voice cut cleanly through the din. 'And our king will finally take his rightful place upon Ithaca's throne.'

More chants began then, lifting in the air, syllables intertwining wildly – *Penelope! Odysseus! Penelope! Odysseus!*

My mind flickered to the night before, when I had gasped Penelope's name in the heated dark, murmuring it over and over against her lips. Now, the crowd had snatched her name away, ripping its intimate beauty between their frenzied teeth.

They loved her, and a part of me hated them for it.

In that moment, swathed in the adulation of her loyal subjects, she had never felt more distant from me, as unreachable as the Gods themselves.

Across the feverish throng, Penelope's eyes found mine, and I saw the unspoken apology burning inside her.

As I held her gaze amidst the chaos, I knew that I had lost her.

Night had fallen when Penelope finally returned to her chamber.

I was standing by the window, watching the lights flickering in the distance like fallen stars, the sound of Ithaca's festivities brightening the midnight sky. Even from here, I could hear their victorious, drunken chants dancing on the breeze.

The other handmaids had gone to join the celebrations, swept up in the infectious atmosphere. It had not yet dawned on them what Odysseus' return truly meant, how much it would change our lives here.

Only Thratta did not join the revelry, choosing to retire to bed early. I did not blame her. After all, the Thracians had fought on the Trojans' side. It must have been sickening to witness the celebration of her own people's defeat.

I sensed Penelope's presence without turning.

'I am sorry,' she whispered, voice worn. She sounded exhausted. 'I wanted to tell you first. But the council forced me to make the public address; they wanted to quell the panic that had spread after Achilles' death.'

A silence settled, seeping into those cracks we knew had already begun forming between us.

'Please say something,' Penelope breathed.

I forced myself to turn and meet her gaze, my smile numb. 'This is good news. I am happy for you.'

Her surprise was lined with a shimmering thread of sadness. 'You are?'

I nodded. 'With Odysseus coming home, the throne will be safe. *You* will be safe, and Telemachus too. Nothing is more important than that.'

My words were true, though they rang with a hollow ache inside me.

Penelope's smile carried the heaviness in her eyes. 'And you will finally be granted your freedom.'

Freedom. The word no longer seemed as beautiful as it once had. Whereas before it had evoked so much possibility, so much hope, it now felt . . . lacking, as if a piece had been carved out of it. The only piece I had ever truly wanted.

'I would understand . . . if you chose to leave,' Penelope continued. 'But please know there would always be a place for you here, if you wanted it.'

Did I want that? Could I stand by and watch Penelope play the dutiful wife? Could I simply forget all that had passed between us?

No. I could never forget, and I knew that ugly, poisonous jealousy would eat me alive. To see her day after day with *him*, to know each night she shared *his* bed . . . And yet, what was the alternative – to never see Penelope again? Both paths were too painful to think of.

Were these really my only options – being tortured by Penelope's presence or the absence of it?

'Thank you,' was all I could reply.

'I will do everything I can,' she whispered, 'to protect what we have built here.'

She lifted her gaze to the sky, looking nothing like a wife rejoicing in her husband's imminent return. Rather, she looked as though she were in mourning, a stark sorrow cradling her face.

Instinctively, I reached up to cup her cheek. I could not help myself. Penelope leant into my touch, her eyes fluttering closed.

'*Melantho*.' My name was a whisper steeped in sorrow. 'He's coming home.'

'I know.'

'We cannot . . . not any more.'

'I know.' The words burnt in my throat.

She was right. Of course she was.

Punishment for a wife's adultery was severe, sometimes even deadly. What if it were worse for infidelity between women? We had been foolish enough to indulge our desires the previous night. The last ten summers had made us reckless with our freedom. But once Odysseus returned it would be a death sentence to continue anything between us. He was too clever, too sharp, and the palace would once again be infested with those loyal to him, men who would be all too eager to gain their king's favour.

It made me sick to my stomach, to think my love for Penelope could put her in danger. I would sooner have carved my own heart out than risk her safety.

My hand fell back to my side and Penelope slowly opened her eyes.

'I will always be his wife,' she whispered, voice broken and aching. 'What I feel for you cannot change that.'

This should not have hurt me, for I had always known it to be true. But the heart is a foolish thing, and I felt Penelope's words spear through mine, fracturing it into tiny, jagged pieces that cut me from the inside.

Penelope stared at me, her expression so calm. A part of me could have hated her for it. Yet I knew this was her way. This was how she survived. She would never fall apart, because she *could not* fall apart, not when so much rested on her shoulders. I had never learnt to master myself like her. My emotions were wild and untethered, and that made them all the more dangerous.

I pressed the heel of my palms into my eyes, willing the tears not to come.

'You can never be mine.' The words were an aching echo of Penelope's own from just a few days ago.

Carefully, she peeled each hand away from my face, forcing me to stare up into her piercing grey eyes. I knew they would haunt me for ever, those eyes.

'You own every part that matters,' she whispered.

I think she meant the words as a comfort, but they only encouraged more tears to spill.

How could we love each other so greatly, and the world still deny us? I wanted to scream at the hopelessness of it all.

'We wasted so much time,' I choked.

She reached out to brush away my tears. 'I know.'

I was certain some god or another was laughing at us, delighting in the tragically cruel timing of all this. Perhaps it was their doing. The Gods did always relish such suffering.

I turned to look at the night sky. Soon it would be morning, and with that first, tentative breath of a new day, I knew everything would change.

'When?'

Penelope followed my gaze as she replied, 'A few weeks, at most.'

A few weeks. The last ten summers seemed to spiral away between those three simple words. A few weeks and Odysseus would return and everything we had built here would be *his*. A few weeks and he would take Penelope in his arms, and kiss her and claim her, and she would be forced to accept his love and offer hers in return. I winced as images seared my mind, visions of her and *him* and all the things a wife was expected to do for a husband . . .

The room seemed to shrink around me, growing too small, too airless, *too much* . . .

'I will leave you to rest,' I said abruptly. 'You have had a long day.'

Penelope gripped my hands tighter, that calmness fracturing as she whispered, 'You do not have to go.'

Carefully, I pulled my hands free from hers.

'Goodnight, Penelope,' I whispered.

She went very still as I moved to leave, each step feeling heavier than the last.

'I will see you in the morning . . . won't I?'

As I turned to look at her, I felt the pieces of my heart slipping through my fingers like sand.

'Of course you will,' I lied.

42

A harsh shriek ripped through my dreams, wrenching me awake.

I sat bolt upright in bed, panting. The sound came again, this time more of a shout. Grabbing my oil lamp, I slipped from my sheets, the stone floor cool beneath my feet.

In the adjoining room of the rambling cottage, I found a familiar, pacing shadow. He had thankfully stopped screaming now and was muttering to himself, his frantic, senseless words painting the dark with streaks of madness.

'The boar . . . can you see it? Over there . . .'

I approached the shadow with cautious steps, as I had learnt was best.

'Master Laertes, you need to go back to bed. You need to rest.' I reached out a hand to stop his ceaseless pacing.

'Rest? No, no time for rest. The boar! We must stop the beast!'

'There is no boar, Master Laertes.'

'Come see, come see.' He strode towards the door, flinging it open and motioning to the darkness beyond. 'See! Do you see? It is coming. Quick. We must take up arms. Where is my sword?'

'You are safe,' I said, as gently as I could.

Laertes gripped my wrist, his touch cold and unpleasant. Then, something shifted in his face, urgency loosening into confusion.

'Who . . . who are you?' He released me, backing away. 'Where am I?'

'I am Melantho,' I told him, as I had done countless times before. 'And you are in your home in Ithaca. The one you retired to after you left the palace.'

He stared at me, eyes milky with age. It was hard to imagine this man had been a king, that he had fought beside famous heroes, that songs of his greatness were sung around campfires. Now he was barely even a whisper of that legend, just an old man whose shrivelled hands could no longer keep hold of reality.

'Melantho.' He nodded, though the recognition had not yet slotted into place behind his eyes. 'Yes . . . Melantho.'

'Shall I take you back to bed, master?'

He nodded again, and I locked my arm around his, feeling his soft, pliable skin slipping over thin bone.

Laertes' room was almost as simple as my own, just a bed and a hearth, with a large chest for his belongings. It seemed too modest for a former king.

'What else would I want? I have nothing left,' he had told me the day I arrived.

As Laertes eased himself into bed, I moved to stoke the fire back to life.

'Do you need anything else, master?' I asked once he was settled.

Laertes muttered something incoherent. Then, he reached for my hand, and the callouses on his palm rasped against my own. I knew there were far more exciting stories etched into his, tales from far-off lands I would never see.

'You are good to me,' he whispered. 'My dear Eurycleia.'

It was not the first time the old king had confused me with the woman, and I had given up correcting him.

'Thank you,' I said instead, staring at his hand in mine, my eyes tracing those protruding blue veins snaking like rivers beneath his mottled skin.

'I would like to visit my son's grave tomorrow,' he murmured.

'Master Laertes, your son is not dead,' I told him, the familiar words worn between my teeth.

'No?' He seemed to sit up a little straighter in bed. 'Then where is he? Bring me Odysseus.'

'He has not yet returned from Troy.'

The old king met my gaze, a glimmer of understanding flickering across his face. 'The war. The war . . . has ended?'

'Yes.'

'When?'

'Four summers ago.'

I rose early the next day, as I often did.

Outside Laertes' cottage, the world slumbered on, draped in pale mist. Overhead, the moon still clung stubbornly to the sky, a faded slash cut through the morning light.

Laertes' home was nestled amidst rolling fields bordered by thick woodland, a tiny pocket of solitude. It was a strange life here, serving a reclusive, half-mad master. Some days, it felt as if I were not really living at all, but rather lost between existences. Like an unburied soul trapped on the edge of the river Styx, denied entry to the realm beyond, yet no longer welcome in the land of the living.

I sometimes feared I would go as mad as Laertes. Solitude had a way of creeping into my mind and taking root in the gaps there. Yet, there was peace to be found in the stillness. The unending silences were an empty void for my thoughts to fill, forcing me to acknowledge that voice in my head I had so often ignored. For the first time in a long while, I allowed myself to think on my past – the good and the bad – and, gradually, I began to realize how tired I was of hiding from those memories.

I walked through fields, following the familiar path my feet had trodden many times before, until I began to hear those slow, sleepy sighs. The sound beckoned me forward until the trees thinned and spilt out on to a small, sandy beach. I took off my sandals and stood at the water's edge, letting the waves kiss my feet in eager greeting.

I closed my eyes and listened, though it was not the sea I heard before me. It was *her*. Those sweet, drowsy breaths as she slept beside me.

Four summers.

It was hard to describe how it felt to be without Penelope. It was like missing a piece of my body I could not name, her absence painfully ineffable yet constantly present. In the stillness of the night, I often imagined I could feel her missing me too, like a cry through the darkness that only my heart could hear. Sometimes, that was enough, just knowing that Penelope longed for me, that our distance hurt her also.

Other times, it felt like torture — to know she wanted this as desperately as I did, and still, we could never have it.

I would return to Penelope one day, I promised myself. I just had to learn first to control my feelings for her. But loving Penelope was in my blood, my bones, my soul.

How could I unlearn that?

I walked towards the rocky cliff that cupped the beach like a weathered hand. Here Laertes had erected a grave for his son, carving a statue of Odysseus straight into the rock face, rendering him with impressive detail. Laertes might have lost his grip on reality, but his artistic hand was still staggeringly skilled.

I stared at Odysseus' cold face, and felt a familiar rage stir inside me.

Four summers and he had not returned.

Four summers.

What could have kept him for so long? The war was long over, so what reason could Odysseus possibly have for not returning to his wife? His son? His throne?

He was not dead, that much was known. Sightings had been reported since Troy had fallen, rumours of Odysseus' adventures with Cyclopes and sirens and witches. I only knew such stories because heralds visited Laertes' cottage to relay news of his son. Though, it was a futile exercise. These days, the old king only listened to the voices in his head.

'You do not deserve her,' I told the stone-faced Odysseus. 'You never did.'

The statue just stared back at me with dead eyes.

*

I spent my days working in the fields surrounding Laertes' home.

The king had once been a proficient farmer, but his expertise seemed to have wandered with the rest of his mind. Often, I found him digging in the dirt, muttering to himself about something he had lost. I usually left him to it and did what I could to tidy up his mistakes, though I knew very little about tending to plants. Still, there was something soothing about working the land, getting my hands dirty and keeping my mind focused, wearing out my body so that sleep would find me quickly each night.

I was busy planting seeds when I heard the distant bleating. Squinting, I spied shifting dark forms spilling across the fields, accompanied by a familiar figure. I raised my hand in greeting and the figure waved back.

'Hello, sister,' Melanthius said once he finally reached me.

His nut-brown eyes were clearer than I had seen them in a long while.

'Wait there. I'll fetch you something.' I rose, dusting the dirt from my knees.

Melanthius nodded gratefully as I disappeared into Laertes' house. Despite it being mid-morning, the king was still fast asleep. He often slept through days at a time, and I knew better than to wake him.

I returned to my brother with a plate of bread and cheese. He took it with an appreciative nod, and we sat down together in companionable silence.

This was the one gift my isolation had given me – my brother. It had been during my first winter serving Laertes that Melanthius had stumbled upon the cottage. He had been seeking shelter from a brewing storm, completely unaware of who dwelt there. When I opened the door, we had stared at one another for a long, tense moment. We had not spoken since that terrible argument so long ago.

'Come in,' I had said.

When I offered him wine, he had shaken his head and replied, 'Water would be better.'

Though there was so much left unsaid between us, we spent most of that night in silence. He had eaten the meal I fixed for him and then gone to sleep. The next morning, he thanked me and left.

Since then, my brother had visited regularly.

'A wolf got some of the goats the other night,' he told me as he ate. 'I asked your Thracian friend to hunt it for me. She's nasty with a bow, that one.'

I nodded. 'I went hunting with her often.'

Melanthius laughed. I had forgotten how infectious the sound was. How much I had missed it.

'What's so funny?'

'I'm just picturing *you* holding a weapon. Terrifying stuff.' I nudged his arm, and he grinned before adding, 'She misses you, you know.'

A sting of guilt shivered through me. 'I know.'

'She said she'd visit again soon.'

Over the past four summers, my friends had visited as regularly as they could. They were the threads that kept me tethered to the world. Without them it would have been so easy to lose myself in this solitude Laertes had entombed himself within.

'Is there . . . any other news?' I ventured, trying to keep my voice neutral.

'Of Odysseus? Nah, not since his army was spotted on that witch's island. That's the last anyone heard, anyway.' He tore off another mouthful of bread. 'Penelope probably knows more; I heard she's been sending scouts after him. But she keeps to herself these days, shut away in the palace.'

It hurt even just hearing her name spoken aloud, but I kept my expression blank as I watched the goats idly snuffling around us.

'My guess is Odysseus is already dead, and his useless army are stuck without a leader to get them home,' Melanthius continued. 'And I bet you Penelope knows; she just isn't telling anyone.'

'Why do you think someone would do that? Keep a death a secret?'

I sensed Melanthius tensing, not quite meeting my eye. 'There's lots of reasons, I guess.'

'And what was yours?'

'What?'

'Why didn't you tell me about Mother?' I hadn't dared voice this question before, for fear of it shattering the fragile bond we had only just rebuilt. But it had hung over me for so long now, I knew I had to ask Melanthius eventually.

I watched his expression shift, shock melding into shame.

'How long have you known?' he murmured.

'Dolios told me, just before the war ended.'

He glanced away. 'I shouldn't've . . . I didn't mean to . . .'

'I just want to know *why*,' I said as gently as I could.

'You were so lost back then, Mel,' he whispered to the ground. 'I thought it'd break you completely if you knew . . . I told myself I was protecting you, that you'd never find out anyway, so what was the harm?' He gave me a grim smile. 'It was a dumb thought; I know that now. I was just young and stupid and scared of losing my sister. But I should've told you.'

'Yes, you should've.'

'I'm sorry.'

I stared at him for a long moment, thinking of all the lies I would have told to keep him from breaking.

'I don't forgive you,' I said. 'But I do understand. I might even have done the same.'

Melanthius nodded, letting out a slow sigh, one I sensed he had been holding for a long, long while.

'Can I ask *you* something?' His directness unnerved me, but still I nodded. 'Why don't you go back? To the palace? To Penelope?'

I tensed under the question, the same one that had haunted me night after night. Some days, the temptation to return to Penelope was unbearable. But in those feverish, fragile moments I would remind myself of all that was at stake.

'All of Greece has been watching Penelope,' I said carefully. 'They are afraid now, of queens ruling without a king at their side.'

'Because of what her cousin did?'

I nodded. 'They're waiting to tear Penelope down, like they did Clytemnestra.'

'Clytemnestra *killed* her husband,' Melanthius pointed out. 'She got what was coming to her.'

'She was avenging her daughter, the one Agamemnon *slaughtered*,' I countered sharply. 'He got what was coming to *him*.'

But blood was only deemed 'justice' when it coated the hands of men. Upon a woman's skin, it was labelled something far uglier, far more dangerous.

Melanthius frowned at me, shaking his head. 'I don't understand what this has to do with *you* being *here*.'

Everything, I wanted to scream.

Whilst Odysseus remained missing, Greece's eyes were set on Ithaca, watching, waiting, wondering if its queen would prove as traitorous as her cousin. If Penelope stepped a toe out of line, if she did anything to bring her loyalty into question, to make people believe Clytemnestra's traitorous blood flowed through her veins, then it wouldn't just be Penelope's queenly title in danger, but her life too.

I could never risk that happening, not for something as selfish as my own desire.

So, I would continue to keep my distance, to keep Penelope safe.

'It's better for me here,' I finally said. I could feel the sceptical edge of Melanthius' gaze as he watched me. 'What?'

'It's nothing.' He shrugged, turning his attention away to the distant treeline. 'It's just . . . I know about what you did. All those slaves you took in. All those people you helped . . . I just wonder why you would've left all that behind.'

I tensed, an old defensiveness flaring up inside me. 'Are you going to say I only care for myself again?'

I regretted the question immediately, hot shame pooling inside me as I watched Melanthius' face fall. He stared at the ground for a long moment before replying.

'I said a lot of things back then,' he whispered. 'Things that weren't true.'

We sat in silence, the memory of that day weighing heavily between us.

'I used to watch you sometimes, you know,' he continued softly as he began shredding the bread between his fingers. 'You and the other handmaids . . . I'd watch you with them and I saw how . . . how *happy* you looked. I'd never seen you look like that before. You looked at peace, I guess. It used to make me angry . . . That's an awful thing to admit, isn't it?' He flicked a glance at me, then looked away again. 'But, after a while, I began to look forward to those times I would see you, catching a glimpse of your smile or hearing your laugh. I wouldn't say it made *me* happy, but it made me feel . . . something.'

A knot formed in my throat as I stared at my brother, seeing that familiar pain shift across his face like old scars catching in the light.

'What I'm trying to say is . . . you don't seem happy like that any more,' he murmured. 'This place, this life – I don't think it's what you really want.'

'Sometimes it isn't about what we want, but what we *need*.'

Melanthius continued tearing the bread into tiny pieces, his thoughts loud in the following stillness.

'You deserve it, you know? To be happy. Sometimes I think you don't believe that . . . Maybe . . . maybe *I* made you not believe it.' His voice caught, but he swallowed and forged ahead. 'Sometimes I think you try and ruin it for yourself. Like when you turned down Eumaeus.'

'It would never have worked with Eumaeus.'

'I don't understand why. He's a good man.'

'You don't have to understand it,' I said stiffly.

Melanthius emptied the shredded remnants of his bread on to the grass, and together we watched the breeze toy playfully with the crumbs.

'You deserve to be happy too, you know?' I finally said.

Melanthius attempted a smile, though the edges wobbled. 'I'm not sure I know how any more, Mel.'

His words shivered through me, brushing over an old, faded memory.

'You first have to *allow* yourself to be happy,' I repeated Hippodamia's words from so long ago.

Melanthius nodded again, though I could sense the scepticism weighing inside him. I took his hand in mine.

'We can work on it. Together,' I suggested.

His smile steadied as he met my gaze. 'I'd like that.'

43

Zeus was angry.

I didn't know what had summoned his temper, but it split open the night with sharp threads of brilliant white, rain hammering like fists upon the earth. I had been asleep when the storm began, but the rageful thunder had shaken me from my dreams. It felt as if the cottage itself trembled in fear of the god's fury.

From within the house, I heard banging. With a groan, I reluctantly left the warmth of my bed and ventured into the adjoining room. Here, the winds howled through the open front door, rain lashing inside. The door was swinging on its hinges, and as I ran to fasten the latch, a terrible question choked me – *Where is Laertes?*

I dashed to his room, letting out a sigh when I found the old man safe and asleep in his bed. *Thank the Gods.*

As I wandered back to my room, the banging came again. At first, I assumed it was just the wind hammering against the cottage, but as I listened, I realized this sound was different, sharp and incessant on the front door.

Unease slithered through me. We never had visitors, save for my brother and friends. It was rare for anyone to venture out this far, especially in the middle of a night like this. Still, I knew the Gods would surely punish me if I left a visitor outside in this weather.

Carefully, I unlatched the door, bracing myself against the wind as I wrenched it open.

A tall, drenched figure stood before me. They were wrapped in a dark cloak, with their hood pulled low so I could not see their face. The stranger did not move, and their stillness seemed at odds with the stormy darkness swirling wildly around them.

'*What are you doing?*' I shouted, the words stolen immediately by the storm as icy rain struck my face. '*Get in!*'

I stepped aside, and the figure hesitated for a moment before entering.

After battling to shut the door again, I turned to the stranger. They stood in the centre of the room, water pooling beneath their sopping cloak.

'I suppose you want somewhere to stay tonight?' I asked, too tired to curb the irritation in my voice.

The stranger said nothing. They had their back to me, and I watched their hood tilt as they regarded the space.

'You should get out of those clothes – you're going to freeze to death, or flood the house,' I grumbled. 'My master will need to greet you. I will go and wake him.'

'Wait.'

That *voice*. It pierced me like an arrow, sharp and true, pinning me to the spot.

'What . . .' I trailed off as the figure turned, pulling back their hood to reveal their face.

Her face.

I stared at Penelope, and it felt as if time itself had taken a breath. I could not hear the storm any more, could not see the clay-bricked cottage around me, or feel the chill of the tiled floor beneath my feet. There was only *her*, and the hammering of my heart against my ribs.

There was nothing in the world I knew better than Penelope's face, and so my focus was immediately drawn to all the ways it had changed – her eyes were shadowed, and she looked thinner, her skin pale and cheekbones more pronounced, emphasizing the unfamiliar hollowness of her cheeks.

The silence thickened, punctuated only by a faint tapping noise. I realized, too slowly, that the sound was her teeth chattering.

She was freezing.

Had she *walked* here in this storm? It would have taken her all day.

Concern bridled every other emotion eddying inside me, pulling my thoughts into focus.

'You need to get warm,' I said, moving towards the hearth. 'Come here.'

Penelope obeyed, trailing behind me like a lost, shivering child. I threw more logs on the fire, before running to my room.

'You need to change out of your wet clothes,' I instructed when I returned, handing her one of my tunics. 'You can use my chamber.'

She nodded, her eyes landing heavily on mine. There was so much unsaid between us, so many questions begging to be asked, but I could not think on that now. Not until I had made sure Penelope was warm and safe.

'Go,' I urged softly.

She took the tunic from me and then disappeared into my room. I tended to the fire whilst I waited, and within those few moments when Penelope was gone, doubts seized my mind. Had I just imagined her? Was this all some cruel hallucination? Had I finally gone as mad as Laertes? But then she appeared in the doorway, and a deep sigh of relief escaped me.

Penelope padded silently over to the revived fire, reaching out her trembling hands towards it. Wordlessly, I handed her the fur pelt I retrieved from Laertes' favourite chair.

'Thank you,' she said as she wrapped it tightly around her shoulders. She was not looking at me, but rather at the flames, their amber fingers dancing in her eyes. Her hair was still wet, sticking to her cheeks in dark spirals.

'I'm sorry,' she murmured, her voice painfully small. 'I just . . . I had to see you. I'm sorry.'

'Don't be sorry.'

She glanced around us. 'Laertes . . . ?'

'In bed, asleep.' I motioned to his chamber. 'He won't bother us.'

She stared at the door to his room, and I watched as a raindrop gathered on the end of her lashes, sparkling in the firelight. She blinked it away before it could fall.

'Penelope, what's happened?'

She pulled the pelt tighter around herself. Despite her height, she looked so small wrapped within it. How I longed to reach out and hold her. My entire body ached for her touch, as if she were the air and I a drowning woman.

'Odysseus is not coming home,' she murmured.

'What do you mean?'

'They say he has settled on an island with a goddess. He wishes to stay with her, to start a new life. Apparently, she will make him immortal.'

'Are . . . are you certain?'

'I sent scouts to confirm it.'

'What of his army?'

She shook her head. 'I do not know.'

'He can't . . . He *wouldn't* abandon Ithaca like that,' I insisted, though the words felt flimsy between my teeth. What did I know of Odysseus, or what kind of man the war had turned him into? What could ten summers of bloodshed make someone capable of?

Penelope kept very still, unnaturally so, as if she were balancing a great weight and feared a single wrong move would make it all come crashing down.

'When people learn of this . . .'

She did not need to say it. It was clear what risk an empty throne posed. Once the news spread, ambitious men would come from all over to battle for Odysseus' abandoned title.

'What if Telemachus took his father's place?' I suggested.

'He is only fourteen. I would be slipping a noose around his throat if I announced him as king now.'

Has Odysseus not already done that? I thought bitterly. Telemachus was Odysseus' only heir; he would be seen as blocking another man's path to the throne whether he sat upon it or not.

'I will not let Telemachus ascend the throne until he is ready,' Penelope continued, the words hardened with resolution.

'Then who will sit upon it?'

'I do not know,' she said. 'I do not know what to do.'

'Penelope.' It felt strange to speak her name again, after all this time. 'We will find a way through this.'

She looked at me, gaze locking on to mine with sharp desperation, like a hand flinging out in a storm, begging to be saved. Then, she did the most remarkable thing.

Penelope began to cry.

Never, in all my time of knowing her, had I seen Penelope cry. I often wondered if she even knew how to. Yet now, it was as if all those unshed tears had finally broken free, a lifetime's worth of them streaming down her cheeks.

I moved instinctively, placing my hands on her shoulders, and drawing her into me. As I cradled her in my arms, it was as if my embrace undid something inside her, and those silent tears broke into desperate sobs that ripped through her entire body, until every inch of her was trembling with the force of them.

After a time, Penelope's tears began to lessen, and I could feel the weight of her exhaustion seeping through her body. That was when I led her to my room, my hand laced firmly in hers.

'Lie down. You need to rest.'

She obeyed, climbing into my bed with heavy limbs. I watched her for a moment, hovering at the side of the pallet.

'I will leave you to sleep. Tomorrow, we can talk—'

'Stay,' she whispered, voice small and frayed like a thread pulled taut.

I turned away and Penelope watched wordlessly as I pushed my wooden chest in front of the door, blocking anyone from entering. Laertes never stepped foot in my room, but even so, I could not risk it.

My bed was narrow, so we had to huddle close together to both fit. Penelope's body was still cold, the water from her hair seeping into the pillow. She smelt of storms and damp earth and everything I held dear in this world. She rested her cheek on my chest and her tears came again, softer this time.

I did not try to offer her words of comfort, to say, *Everything will be all right*, because I knew that was not what she wanted. What Penelope wanted, what she *needed*, was a place to let it out, all those emotions she never allowed herself to feel.

I would be that place for her, always.

Perhaps that was what it meant to truly love someone – not fighting to hold them together but making them feel safe enough to fall apart. And that was what I would do for Penelope. I would let her lie, broken, in my arms for as long as she needed, keeping every sacred piece of her safe until she felt ready to put them back together again.

At some point, her breathing slowed to steady, soft sighs, rolling like the waves I used to listen to when I imagined this moment.

As Penelope melted into the gentle release of sleep, I held her a little tighter, wondering how I would ever be strong enough to lose her again.

I awoke to empty arms and the sudden, crushing thought – *It was just a dream.*

But then something tickled my cheek, and I turned to find Penelope lying beside me, her hair spilling like dark, swirling waves between us.

For a while, I simply watched her, savouring how peaceful she looked as she dreamt, how much younger she seemed. She was thirty-one now, but I could still see glimpses of that young, cunning girl I had met all that time ago. I had loved her then, when she had teased me in the dark over honeyed figs and words I did not know. And I had loved her every day since, even when I had told myself I did not. Even when I had believed I hated her.

Penelope stirred, her eyes fluttering open. She blinked at the unfamiliar surroundings, momentarily confused, but then her gaze settled on mine.

'Melantho.'

My name had never been more beautiful than upon her lips.

We stared at one another, and all those years apart melted away, filling the cracks our distance had left behind. Carefully, Penelope reached out and began tracing the outline of my face. Her touch was so gentle, as if she were afraid that I might vanish should she press too hard. Her fingers skimmed across my lips, just as they had done that night on the beach, many moons ago.

'Penelope.' I whispered her name against her fingertips, and she smiled.

In the sweet stillness of dawn, it felt as if we were suspended in our own pocket of time, like the quiet heartbeat between sleeping and waking. A place where the clawing hands of reality could not reach us, where all that existed was her and me, and the warm sheets tangled around us.

We were both lying on our sides, our faces so close together I could not see where I ended and she began. I reached out to touch her cheeks, tracing their unfamiliar hollowness. Penelope's own fingers danced over my shoulders and chest.

'I missed these.'

I laughed. 'My freckles?'

She nodded, voice catching as she whispered, 'Unbearably so.'

'I'm sorry.' I did not want to speak of sad things, yet the guilt found its way on to my lips. 'I'm sorry I left . . . that I never said goodbye.'

'You did it to protect me. You have nothing to be sorry for.' She twirled one of my rust-red curls around her finger, then brushed it against her lips. 'Still, I fought the urge to visit you every day. A few times I even began the walk here. I nearly made it all the way once, before I turned back.'

'Why did you?'

'Because it would have been unfair. You wanted distance not only to protect me, but to protect your own feelings, too. I knew I could not see you when there was still a chance he would return.' She let my hair unfurl from her finger, watching it spring into a perfect ringlet. 'But then the news came and . . . I could not bear it any longer. I had to see you.'

'I'm glad you came.' I took her hand, relishing how perfectly my fingers slotted between hers, as if the spaces had been moulded just for me. 'Truly.'

'I am too.'

'Although, walking through a storm wasn't one of your *smartest* ideas . . .'

There was a glint in Penelope's eyes then, one I had so desperately missed.

'In my defence, it wasn't storming when I *left* the palace.'

'You just wanted to make a dramatic entrance, didn't you?'

She huffed a laugh. 'I am known for my dramatic tendencies.'

I kissed her hand. 'You were mad to walk.'

'I needed the time. To process everything,' she admitted, voice sobering. 'I am sorry . . . about last night. The state I was in . . .'

'Never be sorry for that, Penelope. Ever.'

Her smile was delicate and vulnerable, still raw from all the emotions she had let spill.

'Did you know your eyes have a little green in them?' she murmured. The unexpectedness of the question made me laugh.

'My eyes are brown.'

'They are. But sometimes when the sunlight catches in them, they're a little green too.' She ran a careful finger over my lashes. 'I used to dream about your eyes, about seeing that hint of green again.'

'I dreamt about you too,' I breathed. 'Constantly.'

We lapsed into silence once more as we gazed at one another. Nobody had ever looked at me the way Penelope did, as if I were the very centre of this world, the anchor that tethered her to it.

'I don't know what to do,' she finally said, echoing her words from last night, the ones that had undone her. Though, her eyes were dry and clear now, and I could see her mind turning behind them.

'You will get through this,' I said. 'You have been leading Ithaca for all this time, and you will continue to do so. You are smart and brave and benevolent and everything Ithaca could need in a ruler.'

'But I am not a man.'

'No, you are not. You are better than any man.'

She smiled faintly. 'Ithaca needs a king.'

'And they shall have one. Once Telemachus is ready, he will take his rightful place on his father's throne. You just have to hold on for a little longer. Deny all rumours of Odysseus' betrayal, continue as the loyal, faithful wife awaiting her husband's return. His legend will continue to loom over the throne and scare off any hopefuls until Telemachus is ready to ascend. It will be all right. I know it will.'

There was something in her expression then, a tightening of her features.

'What? What is it?' I asked.

'Come back with me.'

'Penelope—'

'It was Odysseus' homecoming that forced us apart. But he is not coming home. He has made his choice. So, let us make our own.'

'You are still his wife, and now that title matters more than ever. It is the only thing keeping you safe here. If someone suspects—'

'Who would suspect? If you were a man, yes. But most do not even believe *this* possible.' She brought our intertwined fingers to her lips. 'We will be careful.'

'I will always be a risk to you, because of what you mean to me. You know that.'

'Melantho, I am already at risk.'

I shook my head. It was unbearable to think of Penelope in danger.

How could Odysseus do this to her? How could he abandon his own wife to fend off the wolves whilst she tried to keep *his* throne safe for *their* son?

That selfish, traitorous, entitled worm.

If I ever saw him again, I vowed I would slit his throat.

'At least this risk will be one I choose for myself,' Penelope continued.

The desperation in her eyes was almost too painful to witness and I knew then that I would never leave her again. I had known the moment I saw her, soaking from the storm she had walked through to reach me.

I would not be like him. I would not abandon Penelope when she needed me most.

'Let us choose each other, Melantho,' she whispered. '*Please.*'

'If you want me at your side, I will be there.'

She let out a sigh of pure relief and we smiled at one another, our hope sparking so dizzyingly bright. In that moment, I allowed myself to imagine it – Penelope and me living together in the palace, happy and old, with Telemachus ruling as king. It felt more like a dream than a future, yet still I clung to the vision with a desperate kind of hope. Perhaps this, too, was what it meant to love someone – a willingness to leap into the dark, ready to fly or fall, so long as you did so by their side.

Penelope kissed me then and my body melted into the familiarity of hers, my hands tracing every inch of her, all those curves and dips that had tortured my memory over the past four summers.

'You are perfect,' I whispered.

She smiled against my lips. 'I am yours.'

44

If someone asked me for the definition of 'peace', I would say it was the seasons that followed my return to the palace, a time so golden in my mind it is as if the memories are encased in sunlight.

There was still the threat of the empty throne, of course. But even that could not darken my days. Rather, it served as a reminder to seize each moment, to wring out every droplet of happiness I could for as long as the Fates allowed me.

In some ways, things were as they always had been. In the day I worked and laughed and explored alongside the handmaids, and at night we gathered around the hearth to chatter and listen to Autonoë sing. Once, I might have taken such things for granted, but the years of solitude made me appreciate every second, sweetening even the most mundane moments.

Each night I would climb into my bed beside Actoris and Hippodamia, as I always had done. But once the drowsy darkness finally filled with snores, I would slip away, padding on silent feet to another chamber, another bed, where familiar hands would be waiting for me, reaching through midnight shadows to guide me into the safe harbour of her arms.

There are some things our bodies just know how to do, woven into us from the start, like breathing, or laughing, or dreaming. That was what it felt like to love Penelope, like dreaming – beautiful and instinctive, familiar yet extraordinary.

In the company of daylight, we kept our distance, rationing our affection into stolen glances and *accidental* brushes of skin. But the nights were ours and we spilt our love into those precious hours of darkness, relearning one another by the light of the moon, taking great care to memorize every sacred inch.

Afterwards, when we were wrung out with pleasure, we would lie tangled together and talk, our whispers filling the dark with thoughts and fears and hopes and dreams, just as we had done as children. As always, Penelope listened with such intense focus, gently probing me with question after question, until I fell asleep with answers half formed, the sweetness of their honesty melting on my tongue.

'Tell me: what's on your mind?' was Penelope's favourite question.

She asked it one night, whilst my head was resting on her chest and she toyed with my curls. I had been listening to the steady thrum of her heart, watching her belly rise and fall with her breaths, thinking what a miracle it was, that of all the thousands and millions of threads the Fates wove, they had allowed ours to intertwine.

'I spoke to my brother today,' I said.

'How is he?'

'I don't know. It can be so hard to tell with Melanthius,' I admitted. 'I saw Telemachus, too. I think the prince has finally forgiven me for leaving.'

When I had fled the palace, Telemachus had been just a boy, only ten summers old. Now, at fourteen, he had transformed into a young man, all gangly limbs and fits of dark moods.

I felt Penelope smile against my hair. 'I knew he would come round. He just needed time.'

'He told me I seemed happy. The happiest he has ever known me to be.'

'And are you?'

'I am.'

I traced the moonlight spilt across Penelope's bare stomach, savouring the soft whisper of her skin against mine. It was a wondrous thing, and it was a terrifying thing, to be so consumed by someone, to feel your existence irrevocably tied to theirs.

'Tell me what is troubling you,' she murmured.

Nobody had ever been able to read me as clearly as Penelope. I had once believed I hated this skill of hers, until I understood what a gift it was – to have someone truly *see* you. Truly know you.

I shifted so I could look up at her, noting the beautiful fullness and colour that had returned to her cheeks over the past few moon cycles. She looked like her old self again, and it made my heart sing to see it.

'I just . . . I suppose it scares me,' I admitted.

Her eyes were silvery in the dark. 'Being happy?'

I nodded. 'My happiness has never felt like my own. It has always felt borrowed, something I will inevitably have to give back . . . and I suppose a part of me is always waiting for that day to come.'

Penelope reached out to tuck a curl behind my ear, her thumb brushing my cheek. 'This happiness is yours, Melantho. You deserve it, every piece.'

'But it cannot last, can it?' I whispered into her palm. 'Things as perfect as this never last.'

Her thumb stilled against my skin. 'I do not know.'

I knew Penelope was not one to make grand, empty declarations. Yet, in that moment, I wished she could have lied, could have remedied my doubt with promises of eternal happiness, even if it would just have soothed it for a moment. But only the divine could grasp such concepts as eternity, and we were not gods. We were women forced to play in a game only men could win.

I settled my head back down against her chest, tracing idle circles over her bare skin.

'Do you think they watch us? The Gods?'

Penelope's fingers wandered down my spine as she replied, 'They are too busy with their beloved heroes. We are of no interest to them.'

'Do you think they would be angry if they saw us now?'

She huffed a warm laugh against my hair. 'The Gods are hardly paradigms of marital fidelity.'

'But do you ever wonder if they'd care that I . . . that I'm not a man? Would they think this . . . wrong?'

I felt Penelope's hand still against my back.

'Do *you* think this is wrong?'

'No.' I pressed my lips against her neck to seal the words between us. 'Never.'

Her fingers continued their lazy journey along my spine. 'That is all that matters to me.'

I shifted to look at her once again. 'But why are there no stories like this, like ours? Why do people only sing of love between men, or men with women?'

'Because *men* are the ones telling those stories, and they cannot fathom something existing without their involvement, especially not *sex*.' Penelope looked thoughtful for a moment before continuing, 'I do not believe men would view love between women as *wrong*. They simply would not think of it at all. It would be insignificant to them, because *we* are insignificant to them – unless we have a man to legitimize our worth.' There was no anger in her voice, just a worn resignation that chafed against each word. 'In Sparta, women sometimes took female lovers.'

I gaped at her. 'I never knew that.'

Penelope nodded. 'Even with all the freedom Spartan women were awarded, the men still didn't want others knowing about it.'

'Just like no one will ever know about us,' I murmured.

Penelope cupped my face. 'It is safer that way, Melantho.'

'I know that. But sometimes I just . . . I cannot *stand* it, to think you will always be known as *his*.'

Penelope's hand fell away, voice softening. 'But why should that matter?'

'Why should that *matter*?' I frowned, sitting up. 'Doesn't it *bother* you? People will sing of Odysseus for generations, and *you* will always be his dutiful Penelope, his obedient wife. That's the version of you the world will remember. You'll be immortalized as *his property*, and I . . .' My voice caught as the realization closed over me. 'I'll be no one in your story. I'll be nothing.'

I glanced away, ashamed of my jealousy, of how poisonous it could become. We spoke so rarely of Odysseus, and it felt like a betrayal of mine, to stain this sacred time between us with his name.

Penelope brought her fingers to my chin, gently tipping my face back to hers as she whispered, 'Let history have its lies, if it means we can have each other.'

I let her guide me back down to rest my head upon her chest. We stayed like that for a time, and I counted the seconds passing in the drowsy rise and fall of her stomach.

'It will be morning soon,' I whispered.

'I know.'

'I should go.'

'You should.'

Neither of us moved. Instead, we held each other a little tighter, as if, in doing so, we could chase away those first sips of daylight draining the darkened sky.

45

Three summers passed.

Three blissful summers.

It was more happiness than most experience in a lifetime, yet still, I was greedy for more.

The Fates, it seemed, had other plans.

It began one morning, during the seventh year since the fall of Troy.

Penelope was summoned to the throne room, and I accompanied her, as I usually did. As we walked the familiar halls our fingers brushed, my skin a whispered secret against hers. She smiled sidelong at me, gaze heating.

'You need to stop looking at me like that. It is very distracting.'

'*You* are very distracting, my queen,' I shot back quietly.

She laughed and I savoured the sound, already counting down the seconds to when Nyx would embrace the world and I could embrace mine.

We found a man waiting for us in the throne room, leaning against a pillar with graceful boredom. I walked beside Penelope as she entered, looking regal in her light blue gown, hair woven into a coronet around her head. The bright tinkling of her bracelets was the only sound in the lofty space.

I always found something vaguely sombre about this room and the empty throne set atop the dais, looking more like a tombstone than a sign of power.

Penelope never sat on that throne, nor did she ascend the dais. She knew not to wield her power with the same reckless pride as Clytemnestra had in Mycenae. Instead, Penelope walked directly to where the stranger lounged, inspecting his nails.

There was something about the man I immediately disliked; the arrogance oozed from him like sweat.

'You requested an audience with me?' Penelope spoke first, voice firm yet courteous.

The man pushed off the pillar, closing the distance between us with two swaggering steps. His eyes flicked from Penelope to me, a smile creeping across his lips.

He appeared younger than us, perhaps only just past twenty summers. From his expensively dyed robes and well-trimmed beard, I could tell he was someone of wealth. Not royalty, but a nobleman perhaps.

'Queen Penelope.' I hated the way he said her name, dragging it out like a lover's caress, so intimate and entitled. 'It is my deepest pleasure to finally meet you.'

He bowed low, his chestnut curls bouncing with the motion. Beside me, I could tell Penelope was as unimpressed by the stranger as I was, yet she feigned interest.

'Allow me to introduce myself,' the man continued, his words oily, slipping together too easily. 'My name is Eurymachus, son of Polybus. I hail from nearby Same. I have been hoping to meet with you for some time, my queen.'

'And to what do I owe the pleasure of your visit?'

'I wish to put myself forward as a candidate.'

Penelope's eyes cut up and down him, quietly accessing. 'A candidate?'

The man's smile widened. 'To claim your hand, of course. To take you as my wife.'

'My mistress is already a wife,' I snapped.

The man, Eurymachus, shifted his attention to me.

'What a sharp tongue you have,' he said, gaze dipping over my body appreciatively.

'Melantho speaks true,' Penelope said evenly. 'I am already married, Eurymachus. All of Greece knows this.'

Eurymachus glanced towards the throne, its emptiness suddenly seeming magnified, swallowing up the whole room.

'From what I hear, you are a widow,' he said.

'Careful how you speak to my queen.'

'Melantho.' Penelope's eyes met mine, and I read the unspoken words gleaming there: *He is not worth it.*

'I did not mean to offend.' Eurymachus inclined his head. 'I have merely heard word that Odysseus is dead. Is this not the case?'

'No body has been found. Thus, it is believed my husband is alive.'

'I see.' He tapped his chin theatrically. 'Then why, may I ask, has it taken the King of Ithaca seven summers to return to his kingdom?'

'The Fates have seen fit to delay my husband. That is what happens when you are beloved by the Gods. As you know, they like to test their favourites.'

'I'll admit, your faith in your husband is . . . *endearing*,' Eurymachus said, voice dripping with condescension. 'Though, I am somewhat surprised. I was told you were a woman of pragmatism.'

Penelope did not rise to the bait. Instead, she smiled with a smooth, hollow politeness. 'I am sorry to disappoint you, but it appears your journey here was wasted. Of course, I will offer you food and lodging for as long as you require before your journey back to Same.'

Eurymachus bowed his head again. 'Thank you. That is most gracious.'

'I will send for someone to escort you to our guest wing,' Penelope said. 'I hope you will make yourself at home.'

His eyes glinted. 'Oh, I certainly plan to.'

Eurymachus' presence was like a bad stench. I could smell it everywhere I went, the reek setting me on edge.

I watched him strolling around the palace, barking commands at the other slaves. Begrudgingly, we obeyed, praying our deference would hasten his departure.

Penelope had girls shadow him constantly, reporting on his every action. She also had Thratta tail Telemachus, much to the prince's distaste.

'I am not a child, Mother. I can fend for myself,' he complained.

'It is just until Eurymachus leaves,' Penelope assured him.

But Eurymachus did not leave.

He lingered, day after day, stretching Penelope's hospitality thin as he enjoyed her food and wine and even dared to push his luck with some of the slaves. A few entertained his attentions, though I knew this compliance did not stem from their own desire, rather an ingrained belief that they had to serve his. It made my blood boil.

'I want him gone,' I said.

'He will grow bored soon enough,' Penelope assured me. 'Once he realizes the uselessness of his endeavour.'

The second suitor arrived shortly after.

His name was Antinous, son of Eupeithes, a nobleman of Ithaca. He was comically young, only a little older than Telemachus. Yet despite his youthful appearance, there was something hollow and ancient about his eyes, as if he had lived many lives before and lost all love for this world.

'I already have a husband,' Penelope told him, just as she had with Eurymachus.

'Tell me, my queen, can a corpse be a husband?' Antinous replied as he picked his teeth.

I could tell Penelope was unsettled by his words, but she replied smoothly, 'King Odysseus is not dead.'

Antinous tilted his head to the side when she said that, his dark, lank hair spilling over his narrow face. He was an ugly, hawkish man.

'He has abandoned you, then?' he mused. 'I had heard those rumours too. I suppose a goddess' cunt is as good a reason as any to abandon a throne.'

Penelope stiffened, stunned by his vulgarity.

'May I be shown to my rooms now?' Antinous asked when he grew bored of her silence. 'I hear your hospitality is most *excellent*.'

That night, I lurked in the banquet hall, watching as Antinous and Eurymachus stuffed their faces and slurped their wine. It had been so long since the palace had been stained by the presence of noblemen. I had forgotten how suffocating their company could be.

'One could get used to a life like this,' Antinous said as he beckoned for a slave to refill his wine.

Eurymachus smacked his greasy lips as he helped himself to another plate of meat. 'One certainly could.'

They shared a look, and a heavy realization crept over me.

This was only the beginning.

46

The news spread like wildfire.

Pheme, the fleet-footed Goddess of Rumour, set Ithaca and all its surrounding islands alight.

Queen Penelope is welcoming suitors!

Queen Penelope is looking for a husband!

Before the waxing of the moon, the palace was filled with near fifty hopeful noblemen, all clamouring for the opportunity to claim Penelope's hand and, with it, Ithaca's throne. They drank and feasted and glutted themselves on Penelope's hospitality and, amongst the chaos, Eurymachus and Antinous reigned, stirring up the men's hearts and stoking their pride, declaring hollow sentiments such as: 'May the best man win!' and 'Penelope will only choose the *greatest* amongst us.'

These were men too young to join the Trojan war, forced to grow up in its mighty shadow, hearing endless tales of the heroes they had come so close to fighting alongside, the legends they had *almost* lived. It was evident how heavily it weighed upon them. I imagined they lay awake at night, taunted by visions of who they *could* have been had they been born a few summers earlier.

Men were obsessed with their legacies, finding ways to carve their name in history, and the suitors seemed to believe Penelope was their best opportunity. If they secured the throne and wife of the famed Odysseus, then at least their names would for ever be sung in the same breath as his.

'My husband is not dead,' Penelope would tell them time and time again, but nobody ever listened.

And nobody would leave.

'What if we force them out?' Thratta asked one evening as we sat around the hearth.

Even tucked away in Penelope's quarters, we could hear the raucous revelry of the suitors far below. Penelope had advised us not to wander the palace alone after dark any more. It made the shadows feel heavier, to know these quarters were no longer a place to simply relax, but now also to *hide*.

'With which men?' Penelope said, staring into the flames. Her face was tight, and I felt my hands twitch in my lap, longing to soothe those worried lines. 'The army was lost with Odysseus, and nearly every last eligible Ithacan man is in that hall awaiting my hand in marriage.'

Hippodamia shook her head, dismayed. 'How could they betray Odysseus like that? He is their king!'

'Of course they would betray him for power,' I interjected. 'They're all bitter and ego-bruised because the women of Ithaca refused to retreat into their shadow. They're desperate for control.'

'I could take those pampered pricks,' Actoris snarled, twirling her dagger.

'No, you can't.'

She scowled at me. 'At least let me pick off one or two.'

'If we harm a single hair on their heads, we break the hospitality laws of *Xenia*,' I reminded her. '*That* is the only thing keeping the suitors civilized. If that bind is severed, they will be within their rights to attack. To seize the throne by force.'

'And even if you were somehow possessed by Ares and able to slaughter all of them,' Penelope continued, 'many of those men are born of powerful families, families with strong allies who would retaliate in an instant.'

'So, what do we do?' Hippodamia asked quietly.

Penelope said nothing and I watched her mind turn, skimming through all the possibilities that lay ahead, mentally weaving the threads of fate.

'My queen, if I may speak?' Eurynome ventured from where she sat beside me. She was draped in pelts, as she suffered from chills these days, and I noted how small she looked beneath them. 'Would it be so terrible to take a new husband?'

'Yes,' I snapped, with more intensity than I intended. 'She's already married.'

My words hung hollow in the room. Everyone knew the truth of Penelope's abandonment now. She could no longer hide behind the promise of Odysseus' return; it was as flimsy as using a strip of fabric as a shield in battle.

'Say I chose Eurymachus to wed,' Penelope mused, and I swallowed my nausea at the mere thought. 'Marrying him would strengthen relationships with Same, but what of the suitors who hail from Zacynthus or Dulichium? Do you think they would accept such a rejection? Certainly not. They would fight, as all men do when their egos are bruised. Their blood would be spilt in these halls, some would die, and then a war would begin amongst our neighbouring islands, islands we rely heavily on for trade. Not to mention, we do not have the army or the provisions to withstand a war.' Penelope folded her hands neatly in her lap, letting out a small sigh. 'But let us say, for argument's sake, that by some miracle of the Gods the suitors accepted my choice of husband without retaliation. What do you suppose my new husband would do with Telemachus? He is the rightful heir to the throne. Do you think a new king would let him remain in Ithaca? Let him remain alive?'

For a time, nobody spoke. We just listened to the suitors' drunken laughter reverberating through the walls.

'If you cannot marry any of them, then what are we to do?' Autonoë whispered.

'We will do what all women are known to do,' Penelope said, taking a slow sip of her wine. 'We will gossip.'

Actoris coughed out a surprised laugh. '*Gossip?*'

'Exactly.' The corners of Penelope's mouth twitched upwards. 'We will spin tales of Odysseus' greatness, stories of his exploits over the past seven summers. We will breathe life into his legend so that even the mere possibility of Odysseus' return will frighten the suitors from these halls.'

'And if that doesn't work?' Actoris pressed.

Before Penelope could reply, the door was flung open and Eurycleia entered, trailed by Telemachus.

'Those men are vile, uncivilized animals,' Eurycleia spat as she hobbled over to the hearth, reaching her knotted fingers towards its warmth. 'They drink like animals, too. They are demanding more wine. *More!* They are already running our stock dry. What would you have us do, my queen?'

Penelope did not lift her eyes from the fire as she replied, 'Give them what they ask for.'

'But—'

'We must keep our guests satiated.'

'They insult us with their gluttony. It is a show of disrespect,' Telemachus cried, his angular frame tight with rage.

Penelope looked to her son. 'What would you have me do?'

'They are only here because they want father's title. Once that opportunity is gone, they will leave. Announce *me* as king. I will banish them all when I sit upon the throne.'

Penelope shook her head once. 'No.'

'Mother—'

'Please, if you would give us a moment,' she said to the room.

I caught her eye as the others left, my unspoken question rippling between us. Penelope gave a slight nod in answer. *Stay.*

Once we were alone, Telemachus strode towards his mother, every step full of tightly wound purpose.

'Why, Mother? Why will you not announce me as king?'

'Because you are not ready,' Penelope replied.

These words, so brutally simple, were a slap in Telemachus' face and, for a moment, he could only stare at his mother, trying to mask their sting.

'I am seventeen,' he said through clenched teeth. 'Younger men died on the fields of Troy for their kingdoms.'

'Is that what you wish? To die for Ithaca?'

'*I wish to fight for it.*' I had never heard such passion in Telemachus' voice before, and I felt a sudden swell of pride. 'I will fight for my father's throne. For my birthright. For this land that I love. I would fight for *you*.'

'With which army?' Penelope challenged. 'You have no swords sworn under your name, no men that will fight for your honour. You say you wish to fight, but there will be no *battle*, Telemachus, there would be only *slaughter*.'

Colour rushed to the prince's cheeks, and I watched as that shame quickly heated into anger.

'I am the only son of great-hearted Odysseus, Sacker of Cities. His blood runs in my veins. It is my *birthright* to sit upon Ithaca's throne.'

'Do you think these men care for such titles?' Penelope's voice remained steady. 'To them you are an obstacle, Telemachus, nothing more. They will cut you down the moment I announce you as king.'

'What if Ithaca's council supported me?'

'The councilmen – those still alive – are the fathers of the very suitors who roam these halls,' I pointed out.

'Melantho is right. The council cannot openly stand against you, as their loyalty is sworn to Odysseus. But neither will they support you.'

'Mentor will support me,' Telemachus insisted.

'Mentor is just one man,' Penelope countered. 'One *very old* man who has never lifted a sword in his life.'

A muscle in Telemachus' jaw ticked.

'What if I announce *myself* as king?'

Penelope tilted her head as she studied her son. A rage had appeared inside him, during his most recent flush of adolescence. It was his father's rage, I knew. I recognized its quiet heaviness, like a stone settled in his core.

'You would take your father's crown without his blessing?'

'My father is dead.'

Penelope arched a brow. 'You have proof of this?'

Telemachus glanced away as he muttered, 'I pray he is.'

Of course he would, for what was the alternative – a father who had abandoned his son for a better opportunity?

My heart ached for Telemachus as he stared at the floor, quietly suffocating beneath Odysseus' unyielding shadow. How must it have felt, to only have an intangible legend for a father?

I wished I could tell Telemachus how distinctly average his father truly was, how he was idolizing the wrong parent. But I knew he would never listen.

Slowly, the Queen of Ithaca rose from her chair and moved towards her son.

'I will see you *rule* Ithaca, not die for her,' she told him, taking his hands in hers. 'You will be a great king, Telemachus. But only once you are ready.'

'And when will that be?'

'I wish I knew.'

Telemachus recoiled from her words, snatching his hands away.

'What do *you* know of such things?' he bit back at her. 'You are just a *woman*.'

I rose to interject, but Telemachus was already storming away, robes billowing behind him with each furious stride.

'Let him go,' Penelope said, sinking back into her seat.

I moved to her, unable to keep the agonizing distance between us any longer. Standing behind her chair, I draped my arms around Penelope's shoulders, resting my cheek against hers.

'Was I too hard on him?'

'You did what you had to,' I murmured. 'To protect him.'

'And he hates me for it.'

'He will understand. Give him time.'

Penelope reached up to grip my arms wrapped around her, lips grazing my skin.

'I'm afraid for him,' she admitted, her voice so achingly vulnerable.

'I know.' I buried my face into her neck. 'But we will never let anything happen to Telemachus. You know that.'

In the silence, I could sense a poisonous anxiety creeping beneath Penelope's skin, taking root inside her. I wanted to say something reassuring, something that would keep those fears at bay, even make her smile, perhaps. But what words could suffice against all that she was facing?

So, instead, I simply held her tighter, hoping the warmth of my body against hers would be enough to chase the darkness away.

47

Bodies churned in a sea of drunken flesh.

It was chaos. Chaos wrapped in the stench of wine and sweat and meat.

I walked silently beside Penelope, wondering if there were any sight more vile than a room full of intoxicated, entitled men.

Once the suitors noticed Penelope's presence, they began to cheer, ogling her with hazy eyes. They did not look at her as a queen, but as a prize, a vessel for their own glory. I fought the urge to bare my teeth at them.

Only Hippodamia, Autonoë and I accompanied Penelope into the banquet hall. We had agreed that the fewer women the suitors fixed their sights on, the better. And Thratta and Actoris couldn't be trusted not to start a fight.

'Our queen!' Unsurprisingly, it was Eurymachus who spoke first. 'You honour us with your presence!'

He raised his cup, his handsome face shining with that infuriatingly fake smile of his. Beside him, as always, sat Antinous, his loyal dog. Antinous' soulless eyes seemed even emptier than usual, like two black pits carved into his ugly face.

'Thank you, Eurymachus.' Penelope refused to raise her voice, forcing the men to fall quiet so they could hear their prize speak. 'I wished to ensure you were all comfortable and being suitably cared for.'

There was a roar of approval, wine sloshing as cups clattered together.

'Your hospitality has been exceptional,' Eurymachus said. 'But I must tell you, my queen, we are all very keen to know when you plan on selecting a husband.'

'I already have a husband, as you well know, Eurymachus,' Penelope replied, her voice a veneer of calm, 'and I will not consider another until I have confirmation of his death.'

'Is it not common knowledge that Odysseus died some time ago?' Eurymachus pressed, then bowed his head. 'May Hades keep his soul.'

'It's time the queen stopped hiding behind Odysseus' rotting corpse,' Antinous said around a mouthful of fish. He smacked his greasy lips, pushing his long, limp hair off his face. 'Ithaca needs a king.'

Fists slammed down on tables in thunderous agreement, and I fought the overwhelming urge to lunge forward and slit Antinous' throat with one of the meat knives.

'Come now, Antinous, let us not speak of corpses in the lady's presence,' Eurymachus chided. 'Queen Penelope, you were telling us the purpose of your visit. Do continue.'

'I have brought you all a gift.' Penelope motioned to the man who had entered behind us. 'This is Phemius. He is a much-celebrated bard here in Ithaca. I have instructed him to entertain you with his excellent tales.'

The men cheered and a smile lifted Phemius' plump face, his eyes gleaming with the challenge of such a raucous audience.

'Thank you, Queen Penelope.' Phemius bowed then reaffirmed his grip on his lyre.

'I will leave you in Phemius' capable hands,' Penelope announced, before turning sharply on her heel and striding towards the door.

I followed her, with Hippodamia and Autonoë close behind. Penelope walked with steady, assured steps, but I could tell from the tension laced into her spine that she was fighting the urge to flee this den of wolves.

In the hallway, Penelope let out a small sigh.

'They have fewer manners than the hounds,' Hippodamia whispered.

'That Antinous is a nasty one,' Autonoë echoed.

From within the banquet hall, we heard Phemius' voice warbling over the din. He was singing of Odysseus, as Penelope had instructed him to, of his might and bravery, how his sharp mind could be bested by no man.

'I do not think a few songs will appease those men,' I muttered.

'No,' Penelope agreed. 'But there is still value in keeping the legend of Odysseus alive.'

Phemius began singing of Penelope then, of her exemplary loyalty and devotion to her true love, Odysseus. My eyes met hers and a chord of tension rippled between us, like the jarring twang of an untuned string. I wondered if she felt guilty when she heard her fidelity praised so lavishly. The impeccable Queen of Ithaca, the perfect wife. If Greece only knew the truth, how different those songs would be. I hated to think of it – how my love would demonize her, staining Penelope for evermore.

'Come,' she said, as if sensing the dark turn of my thoughts. 'It is not safe for us to linger here.'

As we turned to leave, I spied a tall figure slinking towards the banquet hall.

'Melanthius,' I breathed, watching my brother peer through the arched entryway. 'What's he *doing* here?'

'I do not know,' Penelope said from beside me.

'I have to warn him.'

Concern bloomed across her face. 'It is not safe—'

'Which is exactly *why* I must warn him,' I shot back.

'I'll go with her,' Hippodamia interjected. 'You two go on. We'll be safe together.'

Penelope's eyes found mine, and I could sense her heavy reluctance as she whispered, 'Be careful. Please.'

I nodded before breaking into a jog back to where my brother lurked in the shadows. He flinched as I touched his shoulder.

'What are you doing?'

Melanthius regarded me, then Hippodamia at my side. 'Eurymachus invited me.'

'He *what?*'

'He said I should join their feast tonight.'

'You cannot go in there.'

He puffed his chest out a little. 'Why not?'

'Because they're drunk, and they're fools.'

'You think I'm not good enough to sit with them?'

'*Melanthius.*' His name was a frustrated growl in my throat.

'I see how it is.' His voice hardened and I saw a bitterness lurking behind his eyes, cold and rotten and horribly familiar. '*You* can dine alongside Queen Penelope, but *I'm* not good enough to drink with some noblemen?'

'That's *not* what I said.' Something in his face gave me pause – the looseness of his gaze, the sneer on his lips. 'Have you been drinking again?'

Instead of replying, my brother stormed into the banquet hall, head held high. I saw Eurymachus' eyes narrow on Melanthius instantly, his smile curling dangerously wide as he leant to murmur something in Antinous' ear.

'We must go.' Hippodamia tugged my arm, but I shrugged her off.

'I'm not leaving him. Not with them.'

'We cannot go back in there—'

'Return to Penelope's quarters,' I told her. 'Don't wait for me.'

Before she could object, I strode into the hall and grabbed Melanthius. He turned sharply, an ugly, embarrassed fury carving across his face.

'Let go,' he snarled.

'Melanthius!' Eurymachus called, his voice cutting over the bard's lilting music. 'You came!'

Melanthius threw me a warning glare, before ripping his arm free from my grasp.

'I wouldn't turn down such an invite, sir,' he said as he walked towards the long tables laden with food and wine.

Eurymachus' eyes slid to mine. 'And you brought us a gift? How *generous* of you.'

I could only see my brother's back, but I noted the way his shoulders stiffened.

'Melantho was just leaving,' he said quickly.

'Leaving?' Eurymachus repeated. Beside him, Antinous' grin widened. 'But she'll miss all the fun! Come on, darling, come here.'

'She has to return to Mistress Penelope,' Melanthius insisted.

'Do not make me ask twice.' Eurymachus' voice was jovial, yet I could sense the threat edging each word.

I walked forward, brushing past Melanthius as I approached Eurymachus. The suitor's pale hazel eyes slipped over me.

'You are a stunning sight, aren't you?' he mused, inviting jeers from the men around him. 'A little old. But still beautiful. And those eyes.' He gave a laugh. 'You look like you want to slit my throat. It's incredibly alluring.'

I lowered my gaze to the knife on the table, arching a brow in silent challenge. Eurymachus laughed again. Beside me, Melanthius watched our interaction beneath a tight scowl.

'My brother is required by my queen,' I said evenly. 'He and I must depart immediately.'

'The queen requires *him*?' Eurymachus tapped his chin slowly. 'How strange. What use could a lonely queen have for a goatherd at *this* hour? Hmm ... Questions like that could spread some nasty rumours, you know. Are you sure Queen Penelope has summoned *him*?'

Panic flared inside me as I recognized the trap I had so foolishly fallen into.

'You are right,' I said hastily, hating that this swine had outmanoeuvred me so easily. 'I am mistaken.'

Eurymachus smirked. 'I thought so. But not to worry, for *we* have a use for your brother.'

Melanthius smiled, moving to take the empty place beside him.

'What do you think you are doing?' Eurymachus barked.

Melanthius halted. 'You said I could join you.'

'You think you can just take a seat beside *me*, slave?' Eurymachus sneered, inviting more laughter from the table. I watched my brother's cheeks redden. 'You need to *earn* your place, goatherd.'

'How?'

'The same way any young man must prove himself in this world.'

Melanthius glanced between the suitors questioningly, and I felt my heart thump sickeningly in my ears.

It was Antinous who spoke, his smile cut from the bleakest night.

'You must *fight*, boy.'

48

'You don't have to do this.'

Melanthius ignored me as he ripped two strips of fabric from his tunic and began winding them around his knuckles. His face was set with a grim determination; it lined his forehead, bracketed his downturned mouth, making him look so much older than our thirty-three summers.

He glanced over my head and I turned to see Eurymachus clapping another slave on the back. I recognized the man as Philoetius, the palace cowherd, though I hadn't ever shared more than a few words with him. He was shorter than Melanthius, but far stockier, with thick-set limbs.

'Melanthius?'

I searched his face, looking for the brother I had sat with outside Laertes' cottage, the one who had spoken such sweet, honest words.

'Why are you doing this?' I breathed.

'They won't respect me if I don't,' he muttered.

I reached for his arm. 'Men like that will *never* respect you.'

His eyes blazed, then hardened, shoulders straightening.

The sound of smashing wood and snapping strings pulled my focus away. Across the room, a suitor was gleefully bashing the bard's lyre against a pillar. He then thrust the mangled instrument back into Phemius' tearful face, his cruel laughter ringing louder as he watched the bard flee from the room.

When I turned back to Melanthius, he was already walking away, heading into the makeshift ring the suitors had formed using tables and their bodies.

Whoops and cheers ricocheted off the walls as Melanthius and Philoetius began circling one another. At his table, Eurymachus was collecting the bets his companions piled before him.

Fury blinded all other senses as I stormed forward, slamming a hand over the silver scattered before Eurymachus.

'Stop this,' I snarled. 'Penelope would not approve.'

Eurymachus' eyes travelled leisurely from my hand, up my arm, lingering at my breasts, before finally settling on my face.

'Speak that way to me again and I'll have you whipped,' he said mildly. 'Now, sit.'

'I do not answer to *you*.'

Eurymachus seemed unfazed as he picked up a silver piece, twirling it between his fingers.

'Obey me, slave, or I'll make this a fight to the death.'

He held my gaze with such calm, empty cruelty, born from a lifetime of entitlement. I knew he would do it. He would have my brother killed simply to prove his power over me. That was how little our lives meant to him.

Rage scorched through my veins.

'You harm one of Penelope's slaves, and you break the laws of *Xenia*,' I warned.

Eurymachus made an exaggerated point of looking at where my brother and Philoetius were still sizing one another up. Then he looked down at where he sat.

'Am *I* fighting?' he asked, placing a hand dramatically over his heart. 'No. Of course not. I would not debase myself in such a way. These slaves are fighting *each other*.'

'Because *you* are telling them to.'

'Semantics, my dear. Do you know what that word means? I know it's probably a tricky one for you.' He smiled, admiring my wrath as if it were a pretty trinket he wanted to collect. 'Let's try a simpler word, shall we? One I know you can understand – *sit*.'

I held his gaze, refusing to move.

Eurymachus regarded the meat knife before him. 'Perhaps I will have them fight with knives. What do you think, Antinous?'

'Knives. Definitely.' Antinous licked his lips.

Eurymachus raised a brow at me. 'What's it to be?'

I inhaled slowly, ignoring the crush of defeat as I moved to sit down.

'Ah, ah, ah, not there.' He patted his thighs. 'Your seat is right here, sweetheart.'

My pride tasted horribly bitter as I swallowed it down and forced myself to sit in Eurymachus' lap. He threw an arm around my waist, pulling me roughly against him. I felt his grin curl against my neck, his wine-stained breath hot in my ear.

'Good girl,' he purred. 'Now, let us enjoy the show.'

Eurymachus lifted a hand, signalling for the fight to begin. My insides hollowed out as I watched Melanthius and the cowherd advance on one another.

I did not even know if Melanthius knew *how* to fight, other than the scraps he had got into as a boy. Philoetius looked like he could have been a boxer, his fists large, arms strong.

I knew it was futile to implore the Gods for aid, yet I found myself uttering a foolish, desperate prayer anyway.

Melanthius made the first move, and I felt my stomach swoop with the motion of his fist as he flung out a wild jab. Philoetius dodged effortlessly, then swung a punch of his own, connecting with Melanthius' stomach. My brother doubled over, gasping for breath.

'Seems I bet on the right horse,' Eurymachus chuckled against my skin.

I felt sick to my core as I watched Melanthius straighten and raise his fists. Philoetius muttered something too low to hear. Whatever he said had Melanthius lunging for him, but the cowherd was quick on his feet, sidestepping my brother's attack with ease, using Melanthius' momentum against him.

I muffled a cry as Melanthius stumbled sideways, catching himself on the edge of a table. Laughter rippled around the room, and I knew the sound of it wounded my brother more than any strike ever could.

He scanned his audience, that sea of cold, ruthless amusement, and I willed him to look at me, to hear my silent plea: *Stop this. Yield.*

Instead, my brother launched himself at his opponent with a mighty roar. This time, Philoetius landed a fist on Melanthius' jaw, sending him crashing to the ground.

The suitors roared as Melanthius lay sprawled at their feet, blood gushing from his nose, pooling across the stone floor. He lay still for a long moment, burning in his humiliation. I tried to run to him, but Eurymachus' arm was a vice around my waist.

'Where do you think you're going?'

'Stop this,' I gasped. 'Please.'

He gave a low hum against my neck. 'And what will I get in return if I do?'

'What do you want?'

His fingers traced shamelessly over my thighs. 'You know what I want.'

Sickness roiled in my gut. Could I really do it? Could I give that part of myself to Eurymachus? No, I would not, *could* not . . . but neither could I continue watching my brother's body and soul being beaten down before my very eyes.

Before I could reply, Melanthius got to his feet again, swaying slightly. This time, Philoetius did not even give him the opportunity to attack. Instead, he barrelled into Melanthius, knocking him to the ground once again. The crowd's bloodthirsty cheers seemed to fuel the cowherd, and he threw himself on top of Melanthius. Pinned to the ground, my brother was helpless as Philoetius pummelled his face, fist after fist, and I felt each brutal hit as if I were striking my own heart.

'*Stop!*' I screamed, the plea engulfed by the crowd.

'Say it,' Eurymachus hissed in my ear. 'Say I can have you.'

Again and again those fists pounded into Melanthius, turning his face into a bloodied, broken pulp.

'*Say it.*'

'Yes.' I choked on the word.

'Yes, *what?*'

'You can have me.'

Eurymachus' chuckle skittered down my spine as he raised a hand.

'Enough!' he called out, his voice cutting cleanly through the clamour.

There was a ripple of annoyance from the suitors as Philoetius halted his onslaught. The cowherd then pushed himself off my brother and rose.

'You are victorious, my friend!' Eurymachus told him. 'Congratulations. You fought well.'

'Thank you, sir.' Philoetius bowed, his bloodied fists dripping on to the floor.

I swallowed back a sob of relief as I watched Melanthius stagger to his feet, using one of the long tables to heave himself upwards.

'*Brother,*' I whispered.

Across the room, his gaze found mine, and I swear, in that exact moment, I saw the flimsy remnants of my brother's spirit breaking, a red mist creeping over his eyes.

Melanthius flung himself forward, and I screamed as I watched him bury a knife into Philoetius' shoulder, narrowly missing his neck. The cowherd howled in agony, but the suitors drowned out his pain with violent cheers as Melanthius tackled him to the ground.

'*Make it stop!*' I cried.

Eurymachus gave a shrug. 'Seems they don't want to.'

'Maybe it will be a fight to the death after all.' Antinous grinned.

I could do nothing but watch as my brother grappled with his opponent until he was sitting atop him. He began beating him then, Melanthius slamming his fists into Philoetius' face just as the cowherd had done to him moments before. Each wet thud made my insides roil, bile coating the back of my throat. At first Philoetius struggled against the attack, but after a time he grew horribly limp.

Still Melanthius struck him. Over and over.

He looked nothing like the brother I knew. He was a creature crawled from Tartarus itself, his broken face swelling into something monstrous, covered in blood that was only partially his own.

'He's going to kill him,' I breathed, before turning to Eurymachus, my voice growing frantic. 'You must stop this. *He's going to kill him.*'

The realization caught in Eurymachus' face, and his smug smile faded as he signalled to someone. A moment later, five suitors were rushing forward, pulling my brother off the lifeless man. Melanthius thrashed like a frenzied beast, snapping his teeth, mouth foaming, blood dripping down his face, his hands, his neck . . .

'Well, well, well,' Eurymachus announced. 'It seems we have a new victor!'

The sound of applause seemed to settle the wildness in Melanthius. He grew still, panting hard as he took in the sea of approval crashing around him.

'Come, take your seat, slave. You've earned it!' Eurymachus called.

Tentatively, Melanthius approached the table. He smiled as he sat, his teeth shining a deathly white against all that blood. Eurymachus then passed him a cup of wine and my brother took a long, deep drink. Around him, the suitors began slapping his shoulders and ruffling his hair.

'Shall we go to my chamber now or later?' Eurymachus purred into my ear.

I said nothing, a numbness creeping over me as I watched a gaggle of slaves drag Philoetius away, his chest fluttering with shallow breaths. I looked back to my brother, at the triumph in his eyes.

'You were going to *kill* him.' My voice trembled.

Slowly, Melanthius' gaze slid to mine. 'He's alive, isn't he?'

I could do nothing but stare at him, at this stranger who sat before me, wearing the skin of my brother.

'*What is the meaning of this?*'

Penelope marched through the chaos like a king upon a battlefield.

Her eyes instantly cut to mine, the colour draining from her face as she surveyed the scene – Melanthius' swollen face, the bloodstains on the floor, Eurymachus' arm fastened around my waist.

'I require an answer to my question,' she said evenly.

The fresh silence was punctured by a few sniggers as everyone turned to Eurymachus.

'My queen, what a pleasant surprise,' he said smoothly. 'We just had a little incident. Two of your slaves got into a fight. But not to worry, we handled the situation.'

Penelope smiled tightly. 'How odd. It is most unusual for the slaves to fight under this roof. But I thank you for . . . *handling* the situation. My goatherd appears in need of medical attention. May he be excused?'

'Of course, my queen.' Eurymachus flicked a hand at Melanthius.

'But . . . you told me I could join you,' my brother murmured.

'And now I'm telling you to leave.'

Melanthius seemed to shrink two sizes beneath Eurymachus' quick dismissal. Yet still he obeyed, gathering what pride he could as he rose and stiffly bowed, before striding from the room.

'My handmaid must also return to her duties,' Penelope said.

Eurymachus brazenly gripped my hips as he replied, 'Your handmaid has promised to serve *me* tonight.'

I felt a sickening rush of guilt as a burst of surprise flared in Penelope's eyes. It was gone in a whisper, replaced by a steely calmness.

'It is not my handmaid's place to offer herself.'

'She claimed she had your permission,' Eurymachus lied. 'Or have you changed your mind? Do you really intend to take away your gift to me?'

He grinned, knowing he had backed Penelope into a corner.

The tension in the room was as thick as a noose, pulling tighter by the second. The suitors' eyes flickered between Penelope and Eurymachus, waiting excitedly to see if more blood might be spilt tonight.

'It is only a night, mistress,' I said, adopting the voice I had once used on Castor, sultry and bored. 'You can spare me for one, can you not?'

Finally, Penelope looked at me, her gaze like a bolt of lightning, singing through my bones. I saw the pain flash across her face, so dangerously close to the surface.

Eurymachus chuckled against my neck, his fingers trailing down my cheek.

'See, my queen? The slave wants to serve *me*. Don't you, love?'

He grabbed my chin, forcing me to look at him so he could plant his mouth upon my own. His lips tasted of sour wine, and I fought the urge to bite down on them, to make him bleed and yelp.

Eurymachus chuckled, then pushed my face away with a smirk. Before us, Penelope had grown frighteningly still, as if she were cut from some ancient, eternal rock – unmoving, unyielding. But beneath that stillness, I sensed her silent rage. She stared at my mouth and for a terrifying moment I thought she was going to snap, to finally let that mask she had worn so well for so long come crashing down.

But then, Penelope smiled. A slow, hard smile.

'Very well,' she said. 'You may have her.'

Relief rushed through me, but when I looked at Eurymachus, at his triumphant smile, I felt a cold dread creep over me.

I can do this, I told myself. *I can endure it.*

To protect the palace, to protect my friends, to protect *her* . . .

'However,' Penelope continued, raising a hand as if to halt my spiralling thoughts, 'I would first like to make an announcement.' She strode to the centre of the room, standing next to a gleaming pool of blood. 'I have taken Eurymachus' and Antinous' wise counsel into consideration and given the matter much thought. After imploring the Gods for their guidance, I have made my decision.' I had not realized how far I was leaning forward until I felt Eurymachus pull me back against him. 'I have chosen to accept the death of my husband.'

No, no, no.

'And I have decided to remarry.'

Surprise stole through the room, and immediately the suitors began to grin at one another, like a pack of wolves eyeing up their prey.

'As you are aware, there are a great many of you, and you are all exceptional candidates,' Penelope continued. 'So, I hope you will allow me the proper time to decide who amongst you I will choose as my betrothed.'

'That is most excellent news, Queen Penelope!' Eurymachus exclaimed.

She turned to him, silver fire dancing in her eyes as she said, 'I must inform you, Eurymachus, that something I value highly in a man is *control*, in all things.' She stared pointedly at his arm locked around my waist, inviting a few amused murmurs.

'And why should a woman have a say in where her husband sticks his cock?' Antinous sneered.

Penelope's lips cut upwards. 'She should not, of course, and you are free to indulge however you see fit, Antinous. I would not dream of denying you that freedom. I am merely stating *my* preference in a husband.' She turned her smile to Eurymachus, and I swore I saw its edges sharpening. 'I hope I have made myself clear.'

'Well, it hardly seems fair to deny your guests their fun,' Eurymachus countered. 'Do you not think, men?'

'Only if you're too weak to keep it in your pants,' one sniggered.

'I have no problem abstaining, Queen Penelope,' another piped up.

'Nor me!'

'I haven't even *looked* at your handmaids!'

More shouts joined the others, desperate, pathetic pleas, all vying for Penelope's attention.

'Enjoy your night, gentlemen,' she said sweetly, and my heart lifted with pride as she glided from the room.

'Get off.' Eurymachus shoved me away as soon as Penelope had disappeared.

I turned back to him, a cold triumph flooding through me.

'What's the matter, my lord?' I pursed my lips. 'Not in the mood any more?'

'Go back to your queen. *Now*,' he spat. 'Tell her I didn't touch you. Make sure she knows.'

I gave a slow, mocking bow. 'Of course. I am sure Mistress Penelope will be *most pleased* to hear that.'

49

As soon as I escaped the banquet hall, Penelope pulled me into the shadows and her waiting arms.

Our embrace was desperate and fleeting, a too-brief gulp of air amidst a raging storm.

'Are you hurt?' she asked, grey eyes wide as she reached for my face.

'I'm fine, I swear.' I took her trembling hands in mine. 'Penelope—'

She shook her head, silencing me, then tugged me down the hallway, away from the raucous laughter that chased our every step. She did not slow until she pulled me into a small storeroom. The space inside was dark and cool, the smell of olive oil lacing the air.

Penelope shut the door behind us then spun, seizing my face between her hands.

'What were you *thinking*?' She punctuated each word with a frantic kiss. 'Why did you go back in there? Why did you promise yourself to him?'

'My brother,' I gasped against her lips. 'I had to protect him.'

She drew back, growing horribly still. 'They made him fight.'

I nodded. 'It was the only way I could stop it.'

'His opponent?'

'Philoetius. He is alive . . . just about,' I added with a wince.

'They are monsters.'

'Monsters *you* said you would marry.'

Penelope nodded. 'Yes.'

'*Why?*'

'I had no choice.'

'No choice?' I spluttered. 'You should have just let him have me. You should have—'

'*Don't ever say that,*' she snapped. 'Don't you ever sacrifice yourself like that. Not for me. Not for anyone. Do you understand?'

'You cannot tell me not to sacrifice myself when *you* have done exactly that,' I threw back, fighting to keep my voice lowered. 'It would have been *one night*, and now you've damned your entire future!'

She kissed me again, as if she could not stop herself, her lips soft and wild against mine, stilling my rage.

'*Penelope.*' Her name was somewhere between a gasp and an ache. 'I cannot let you do this—'

'I do not plan on marrying any of them.' Her words were hot in my mouth.

'But you said—'

She drew back, eyes ablaze. 'I will not hand Ithaca over to any of those pigs. The throne belongs to *my son*, and I will see no other sit upon it.'

I had never seen her like this before, burning with such pure, naked rage. I cupped her cheek, in awe of the *power* radiating from her.

'You have a plan,' I whispered.

Penelope's smile was slow and beautifully fierce. 'Of course I do.'

'A *funeral shroud*?' Autonoë repeated, doubt edging her voice.

'Yes.' Penelope nodded. 'A funeral shroud.'

We were gathered in Penelope's quarters, settled into our usual places around the hearth. Hippodamia was draped across Autonoë's lap, surrounded by blankets and cushions, whilst Thratta lounged in the chair next to mine with Actoris seated cross-legged at our feet. Eurynome was nestled into the softest seat nearest the fire, with Penelope at her side.

'I'm lost,' Hippodamia admitted. 'How is a *funeral shroud* going to help us stop the suitors?'

'Are you going to *smother* them to death with it?' Actoris snickered.

Thratta's hand shot up. 'I volunteer to do the smothering.'

'There's going to be *no* smothering,' I said.

Thratta's face fell along with her hand.

'What about strangling?' Actoris grinned, grabbing one of the blankets and wrapping it around her throat. She made a dramatic choking sound, sticking out her tongue. 'I think that could work.'

I yanked the blanket from her. 'Now you're just being foolish.'

'Melantho is right.' Thratta nodded sagely. 'Rope would be much better for strangling.'

'We're strangling them with *rope*?' Hippodamia squeaked.

Eurynome shivered beneath her fur pelts. 'This all sounds a little too violent for me . . .'

'Not to worry. I will strangle them for you,' Thratta offered.

Eurynome smiled. 'Thank you, Thratta. That's very kind.'

'There will be *no* smothering *or* strangling,' I sighed, rubbing my temples to try to settle my brewing headache.

'But there *is* a funeral shroud?' Hippodamia ventured.

'Just listen to Penelope's plan, will you? All of you? *Please*,' I groaned.

Penelope's eyes met mine, humour dancing in them as she read my exasperation. It was nice, seeing that lightness in her gaze, given all that weighed upon us.

A rare, attentive silence enveloped the room as Penelope rose and walked towards the loom we had carried in from her bedchamber. Absently, she plucked a thread.

'As you know, I have told the suitors I will take a husband,' she said. Her expression was steady, but then it shifted, eyes growing misty, voice thick as she continued, 'But I shall inform them that Laertes, my dear father-in-law, is dying, and I *cannot possibly* think of marriage until I have completed a funeral shroud in preparation for his imminent departure for the realm below.'

Hippodamia sat bolt upright from her mound of cushions. 'Laertes is dying?'

Penelope blinked, and the emotion in her face vanished, replaced by a small, cunning smile. 'No. No more so than any other ageing mortal, at least. But the suitors need not know the details of his condition.'

'They will have no choice but to accept Penelope's request,' I said. 'It would incur the wrath of the Gods if they denied her the right to properly perform Laertes' burial rites.'

The handmaids shared a look, lips curling as understanding sparked between them.

'How much time will it give us?' Autonoë asked.

'As long as we need,' Penelope said, running her fingers over the loom. 'Each day I will make progress, and each night we will undo it. Only a little at a time, so we do not arouse suspicion.'

Actoris snorted. 'Those pigs will be too drunk to notice.'

Beside her, Thratta grumbled, 'I prefer the strangling plan.'

'I do too,' I admitted. 'But if we shed their blood, we could start another war. A war we cannot win.'

'But it is our *right*,' Thratta insisted. 'These men have dishonoured us.'

'It does not matter if it is rightful or not. If we take revenge, it will spark outrage across all of Greece,' Penelope pointed out. 'The only person who could do such a thing is Laertes or Odysseus. And we all know Laertes is far too old and has no interest in the throne.'

'So, if Odysseus were here, it would be his right to kill them?' Hippodamia asked.

Penelope nodded. 'That is why I have sent messengers far and wide to spread word of the suitors infesting the House of Odysseus. My husband might have been beguiled by the promises of a goddess, but I know Odysseus loves this land and would loathe to let his throne fall to anyone but his own blood.'

'Do you really believe that will be enough to bring Odysseus home?' Autonoë whispered. 'After all this time?'

'If he is still the man I once knew – yes,' Penelope said, returning to her chair beside Eurynome. 'In the meantime, I have instructed Telemachus to secure whatever allies he can, whilst we delay the suitors for as long as possible.' She paused then, taking her time to look each of us in the eye before continuing, 'It will be dangerous. The suitors will grow impatient eventually. There is only so much wine and food that will satiate them, and we saw last night what kind of brutality they consider entertainment . . . That is why I am going to temporarily rehome as many palace slaves as feasibly possible. I will place them with families in Ithaca until it is safe for them to return to their duties here. I would like you all to consider this option as well.'

I felt the others shifting around me, a mix of surprise and sadness staining the air.

Penelope's smile was thin as she went on, 'You are all incredibly important to me. For the past seventeen summers I have had the honour of living beside you, of building a home together. But now . . .' She swallowed, her voice catching as she admitted, 'I can no longer guarantee your safety within these walls.'

'We can handle ourselves,' Thratta interjected, her tone softened by the sadness in Penelope's eyes.

'She knows that,' I said gently. 'Hear her out.'

Thratta nodded, signalling for Penelope to continue.

'If I placed you with another family in Ithaca, you would have some protection from the suitors . . . but I also have another offer.' Penelope paused, lacing her hands in her lap before proceeding. 'As a woman, I cannot give you your freedom, however much I wish I could. But I can secure you safe passage out of Ithaca. A boat that will take you wherever you wish to go. You will not *legally* be free, but you will have your freedom – as much of it as I can grant you.'

'You're sending us away?' Hippodamia whispered, eyes shimmering.

Penelope reached out to take her hand. 'It is your choice.'

A sombre silence settled over us. Then, Actoris announced loudly, 'Fuck that.'

I choked on a surprised laugh. 'Actoris, you should consider—'

'Nope. I'm not considering anything,' she said, folding her arms decisively. 'I've been carted around on slaver ships since the day I was born. I've seen what it's like for us out there. I'm not interested in any of it, and I'm *not leaving*.'

'Then what of staying with another household in Ithaca—'

'Nope.' Actoris lifted her chin. 'Not happening.'

'She's right,' Hippodamia said, her hand tightening around Penelope's. 'We won't let those vultures drive us from *our* home.'

Home. I felt something thicken in my throat at the word.

'But I cannot protect you,' Penelope whispered.

'We protect each other,' Autonoë said, reaching for her other hand.

'I'm not sure what use my old bones will be.' Eurynome chuckled softly. 'But no foolish *boys* will drive me from these shores.'

Thratta nodded emphatically. 'I stand with you, Penelope. With all of you.'

'Think of what's she's offering, Thratta. You could return to Thrace.'

'I *will* return to Thrace.' She amended my words. 'But not this day. Thracians do not run from battle. We stand and we fight.'

'But your people—'

'My *people*,' she scoffed. 'My people sold me to foreigners to save their own hides. No. *You* are my people now, and I will fight at your side.' She paused, as if considering something. 'And as my people, I wish to give you a gift.'

Thratta rose to her feet then, and we all shifted a little closer, staring up at our friend towering before us, gilded in the firelight.

'Skaris.' Her voice hitched, eyes gleaming with pride. 'This is my name. When I came to these shores, it was all I had left, so I held it close. Now, I give it to you, in return for all you have given me.'

'Skaris,' we all said in turn, watching our friend blossom beneath the sound of her name.

'In my tongue it means "quick-footed",' Thratta – *Skaris* – told us.

'Thank you, Skaris,' Penelope said, bowing her head low.

I took Skaris' tattooed hand in mine, unsure what words could convey my love for her in that moment.

'And you, my friend?' she asked me. 'You will stay with us?'

'Always,' I said.

I met Penelope's gaze and smiled. Of course, I would not leave her. Even if our world came burning down that very night, I would simply hold her closer and dance in the flames.

'Then, it's decided!' Hippodamia clapped her hands excitedly. 'I think we should have a drink to celebrate. Don't you?'

Without waiting for a response, she whisked around the room in a flash of golden tresses, handing out cups.

'What are we drinking to?' Autonoë asked.

'To the return of Odysseus?' Eurynome offered.

'To the death of the suitors.' Actoris grinned.

'To the battle ahead,' Skaris announced.

'To *us*, of course,' Hippodamia corrected them all.

I smiled, my eyes finding Penelope's once again as I held my cup aloft. 'To us.'

50

For three summers Penelope's plan succeeded.

For three summers we were locked in an endless cycle.

Every day Penelope would work on Laertes' shroud, playing the dutiful, pious daughter-in-law, and every night we would gather round the loom and unpick her efforts by the light of the moon.

At the start, there had been a certain giddiness to our scheming. We were like the Gods themselves toying with the threads of fate, stalling the future with each unravelled pick. But, as time passed, our plan began to feel more like a curse than a blessing, every loosened thread a marker of yet another day forced to endure life in this prison we had once called home.

During the first full turn of the seasons, the suitors had been eager to impress Penelope with their good behaviour. But boredom had soon driven away their propriety, and before long they were back to their usual vulgar ways.

'Keep your arms up, like this,' Skaris instructed.

We were gathered in a disused storeroom, a hidden space we used to teach defence tactics to those who were interested. Though we knew we could not risk harming the suitors, Skaris taught us manoeuvres to help evade their drunken, obscene advances.

Recently, the number of those wishing to learn had swelled drastically, most of them young girls.

I sat on the sidelines, my gaze drifting over the crowd as they listened intently to Skaris' instructions. One girl caught my eye. I recognized her as one of the children we had rescued from the slave market. She had been scarcely five summers old when I had taken her hand and led her to the palace, promising safety beneath Penelope's roof. She was around sixteen now, and my eyes instantly narrowed to the all-too-familiar pattern of bruises blossoming around her neck and arms.

A sickness slithered into my stomach as I beckoned her over.

'Where did you get those?' I asked.

The girl glanced away, her cheeks reddening.

'You can tell me,' I said, as softly as I could. 'Which one of the suitors was it?'

Still she said nothing, her eyes fastened to the floor.

I lifted my hand to touch her shoulder, but she flinched so violently I thought she might tear herself in two.

'I'm sorry,' I whispered, lowering my hand. 'I'm so sorry.'

'May I return to the training now?' she mumbled.

I nodded, a horrible weight settling in my chest as she hurried away.

Even here, hidden away as we were, I could still hear the suitors' booming laughter ricocheting through the palace. I closed my eyes, trying to settle the acidic burn of hatred churning in my gut.

One day, I vowed silently. *One day they will pay.*

When we returned to Penelope's quarters, night had fallen.

Hippodamia and Actoris were seated at the loom, yawning as they unpicked threads. We had resorted to working in shifts now.

'How goes the training?' Hippodamia asked as we approached.

'Fine,' I said distractedly. 'Have you seen Penelope?'

Hippodamia and Actoris shared a look.

'She went straight to her chamber again. Didn't say a word,' Actoris muttered, nodding towards Penelope's closed door.

'She's been struggling,' Hippodamia murmured. 'Ever since Telemachus left.'

'I know.'

Three moon cycles before, Penelope had encouraged Telemachus to travel to Sparta. She had disguised the trip as a diplomatic venture, a strengthening of alliances and an opportunity for Telemachus to search for news of his father. In truth, she simply wanted her son as far away as possible from the suitors and their schemes.

But Telemachus' absence seemed to have only encouraged their plotting. I had often spied Eurymachus whispering in the other men's ears, those quiet murmurs far more sinister than any of their riotous revelry.

'What are you doing?' Skaris asked as I followed her to our chamber.

I frowned. 'Going to bed. What does it look like I'm doing?'

'It looks like you're going to *pretend* to sleep in your bed and then sneak out when you think we are all asleep,' Skaris threw back, a gleam of challenge in her eyes.

I stared at her. 'W-what do you mean?'

She shook her head. 'You just insult our intelligence now, my friend.'

'I . . .' Excuses withered on my tongue as I caught Hippodamia and Actoris sharing a smirk.

'Did you *really* think we didn't know?' Actoris snorted.

'Who else knows?'

'Only us,' Hippodamia said, quick to reassure me. 'You hide it well . . . We just know you better.'

I stared at them, waiting for the judgement, the disgust, the reminder of how *foolish* Penelope and I were. But all that came was the heavy, comforting weight of Skaris' hand on my shoulder.

'Go to her,' she said, nodding towards Penelope's door. 'She needs you.'

Penelope was awake when I entered her chamber.

She said nothing as I slipped into bed, her silence pressing into the darkness like a scream.

'Can't sleep again?' I whispered.

Penelope stared at the ceiling, moonlight curving into two small scythes against the whites of her eyes.

'Have you taken your brew?' I prompted.

Penelope had recently created a concoction to aid her sleep, a mixture of poppy milk and other mysterious ingredients. It had started as an occasional solution for restless nights, but these days she could not sleep without it. Her mind would not let her.

'I did,' she murmured, her voice laced with a tiredness no amount of sleep could ever cure.

'It'll help soon,' I said with a lightness I did not feel.

Penelope said nothing. With every passing season she had grown quieter, withdrawn further. The spark that had always burnt so fiercely inside her had dimmed to a mere flicker, and I lived in constant fear of the day it would go out completely.

'Tell me what you're thinking,' I whispered. 'Please.'

She inhaled, and I could feel how stiff she was, her body a knot of tight muscles I desperately longed to soothe.

'There was another girl with bruises,' she murmured. 'Just like the others.'

I closed my eyes, feeling the guilt-stained anger curdle in my veins.

'I saw her too,' I said.

'I tried to make her tell me who did it, but she would not speak a word. She seemed . . . ashamed.' Her voice caught.

'They are getting worse,' I murmured.

Penelope continued staring into nothingness, her face seeming to cradle every shadow in the room.

'If I were a man, I could have ended this years ago. I could have protected them. I could have protected *you*.'

'Penelope—'

'Instead, I am cursed to do *nothing*.' She gripped the sheets, her hands balling into fists. 'I am forced to *drown* in my own uselessness.'

'You are doing your best.'

'It is not enough, Melantho. I am not enough.'

Her voice was eerily empty, as if each word had been hollowed out. It was profoundly disturbing, like waking to find your home stripped bare, the well-known walls now barren and strange.

'Please,' I choked out. 'Don't say that, Penelope.'

'Three summers,' she murmured. 'Three summers and *nothing* has changed. They have only grown worse.'

'What if we think of a new plan? A new way to drive them out?'

She said nothing, and that unnerved me more than any words ever could. The Penelope I knew was forever eager to discuss an idea, always one step ahead of her opponents.

'Penelope?'

'Not tonight,' she whispered.

I nestled in closer and began kissing her neck, soft and slow. I wanted to distract her, to give her a release from the prison of her mind, if only for a few moments. My fingers skimmed over her body, following that beautifully familiar route from collarbone to hip.

Penelope's hand halted mine. 'Please. Don't.'

I pulled back, trying to ignore the sting of her rejection. 'I'm sorry.'

She shook her head, fingers softening around mine. 'I just . . . need to sleep.'

I nodded numbly. 'Yes. Of course. You should rest.'

Penelope turned to face away from me. For a long while, I simply watched her, my eyes tracing those slender shoulders that had carried far too much for far too long. In the stillness, I replayed her words over and over. She claimed she was drowning, and it was true – I could see it, could *feel* it. With each passing day she sank further into that ocean, and it terrified me to think of it: that Penelope might drift to a point I could no longer reach. I would follow her anywhere in this world or beyond – to the very depths of Tartarus itself. But her mind was the one place I could not venture and I was so scared of losing her within it. Even now, this tiny sliver of space between us felt cavernous, for though I could lean over and touch her, I knew I could not *reach* her.

She was drowning right there beside me, and I could not save her.

But I had to try.

I had to do *something*.

51

I found Eurymachus in the banquet hall.

Despite it being the early hours of the morning, the suitors' revelry showed no sign of waning.

Flies feasted on leftover food littered across the tables, the stench of rotting meat and fish permeating the air. Penelope rarely permitted any of the slaves to step foot in there, so the food was often left out for days on end.

The suitors were busy redistributing their silver pieces. Beneath my feet, fresh blood gleamed across the stone floor. I wondered if any of it was my brother's. Despite all my pleading, Melanthius still participated in the horrific fights the suitors orchestrated.

As usual, Eurymachus was seated at the head of the table, like a king amongst his subjects. He picked at the plate of food before him, his eyes glazed with wine and boredom. When he noticed me approaching, his gaze sharpened, lips coiling into a predatory grin.

'Well, well, well, to what do we owe *this* pleasure?' he asked loudly. 'Penelope's handmaids are usually kept locked away like pretty little trinkets.'

I shrugged. 'Perhaps I have grown bored of being treated as such.'

Eurymachus shared a glance with the men around him. 'Is that so?'

'Pretty little trinkets are not meant to be hidden away, after all. They are meant to be admired, are they not?' I purred, moving closer.

'Is that what you want? To be *admired*?' one of the other suitors asked me.

I smiled vapidly at him. 'Doesn't every woman?'

Eurymachus tossed a chicken bone to one of the hunting dogs skulking in the shadows. 'And what would your mistress make of this little visit?'

'Should I care?'

Suspicion sharpened his smile. 'Seems like quite the change of heart from Penelope's most treasured handmaid.'

'Why should I serve a queen who will not serve her kingdom?' I shot back. 'Ithaca needs a king; Penelope is standing in the way of that.'

'I will drink to that,' Eurymachus said, taking a slow gulp of wine. His eyes held mine over the rim of his cup, filled with a dark, intimate promise.

When he set the cup down, I dutifully moved to refill it. I then perched myself in his lap as I brought the replenished wine to his lips. He drank deeply, his gaze never leaving my face. When a dribble escaped down his chin, I caught it with a finger and licked the residue. Eurymachus' eyes heated, and I smiled before downing the rest of his wine myself.

'If I remember correctly, you still owe me,' Eurymachus hissed into my ear.

'Is that so?'

His hands moved to grip my waist, fingers digging greedily into my flesh. It took every ounce of self-control not to cringe at his touch. But I had worn disgust as desire for years in Sparta; it was a mask I knew well.

'You once promised yourself to me, yet you never *fulfilled* your word.' His breath was unpleasantly hot against my skin. 'Three summers I've waited.'

'Perhaps it's time we rectify that,' I mused.

'Perhaps you've waited too long. Perhaps I've no interest in *old* goods,' he sneered. 'You're what, now? Thirty summers? More?'

'Thirty-six summers. And if you do not value *experience*, then I suppose that is your loss.' I shrugged and began to rise, but Eurymachus' arm fastened around my waist, holding me against him.

'What of Penelope?'

I ignored the stab in my chest. 'What of her?'

'She didn't want us . . . *meddling* with her handmaids.'

I raised a brow. 'Who says she has to know?'

Eurymachus grinned before pushing us both to our feet. He locked his hand around my wrist, claiming me.

'Come,' he barked.

For the briefest moment, my body stiffened, muscles tightening with instinctive fear.

Be brave. My mother's voice found me.

I would. For Penelope. For Telemachus. For my friends.

I had to be.

I could not protect them with swords or strength or wealth, but this . . . *this* was a weapon I knew how to wield.

And so, I smiled and nodded. 'Lead the way.'

Unsurprisingly, Eurymachus had claimed the largest guest chamber.

I drew in a steadying breath as I walked inside. To my left was a large bed, its furs and blankets tangled in an angry heap. To my right was a table laden with dirty plates and empty wine jugs, fat flies buzzing lazily between them.

'Penelope never sends slaves to clean,' Eurymachus said as he followed my gaze. 'The bitch expects us to live in our filth.'

'She does not treat you with the respect you deserve,' I replied as Eurymachus kicked off his sandals. 'Shall I fetch you some wine?'

I took his grunt as a 'yes' and approached the table.

'If Queen Penelope were your wife, I'm sure you would teach her to behave,' I said as I chose one of the ornate jugs and began filling a cup.

'She has spent too long without the guidance of a man,' Eurymachus agreed. 'It has made her obstinate and arrogant.'

As he spoke, I slipped the small vial of Penelope's sleeping draught from my gown and tipped the contents into the cup. It would not be enough to send Eurymachus straight to sleep, but it should make him drowsy, enhancing the effects of the copious amounts of wine he had already consumed.

I turned back to him with a smile.

'Here, my lord.' Slinking forward, I placed the laced wine into his waiting hand.

Eurymachus brought the cup to his lips and my blood crackled with fear as I watched him hesitate, seeming to sniff the contents.

'Is it not to your liking?' I asked, feigning indifference.

Instead of replying, Eurymachus tipped back his head, downing the wine in two large gulps. Relief flooded through me, sharp and short-lived.

'Take your gown off.'

'Do you not wish to talk a little, my lord?' I purred. 'I am sure you have many interesting tales to tell.'

Eurymachus set his empty cup aside. 'I will not repeat myself, slave.'

My smile stiffened. I was not naive enough to believe the sleeping potion would let me avoid the inevitable. I had known the price I would have to pay the moment I had walked into the banquet hall.

For Penelope, I reminded myself.

For Telemachus, Skaris, Hippodamia, Autonoë, Actoris, Eurynome . . .

For every slave beneath this roof.

Slowly, I unclasped the fastenings at my shoulders, letting my gown fall to the floor. Eurymachus stared at me, his tongue running slowly over his wine-stained teeth. Guilt shifted inside me. It felt so wrong to offer my body up to someone else. This body that Penelope had blessed with so much care and affection. This flesh was *ours*, sanctified by our love, and now here I was baring it to another . . .

You're doing this for her.

'On the bed.'

I obeyed, forcing myself to shut out all thoughts of Penelope. I pushed her far, far away, to a place this ugliness could never reach.

I felt Eurymachus behind me then, his body hot against my spine. He grabbed the back of my neck and pushed me down on to the furs. For a moment, I just lay there, frozen. It was as if my soul were seeping out, leaving an empty vessel behind.

A part of me wanted to stay like this, dead beneath his touch, until it was all over.

No. Somewhere, in the hollow depths of me, a spark ignited. *Not like this.*

I would not lie like a vacant corpse beneath him, letting him abuse my body in whatever ways he pleased. If I were to stoop to such a low as sharing Eurymachus' bed, I would do it on *my* terms.

I was the master of his desire. His lust was *mine* to wield.

Eurymachus reached a hand up to brush my lips. I bit down on his fingers, not hard enough to draw blood, but enough to make him jolt with surprise. I took the opening, utilizing all Skaris' training to spin myself round, using Eurymachus' weight against him to knock him sideways.

He huffed a delighted laugh as I straddled him. 'I knew you had a bite to you. Such a vicious little creature.'

'I want to look upon the future King of Ithaca as I pleasure him,' I said, reaching beneath his robes.

'Future king.' Eurymachus' breathing hitched as I took him in my palm. 'I like the sound of that.'

'That is what you shall be, is it not?' I goaded as I worked him, encouraging a shivering gasp of pleasure. I could instantly feel his control unravelling as his pitiful lust took over. 'Well? *Will* you be king?'

'*Yes.*' He gulped down the word.

I stared at his face twisting with desire, longing to claw it off.

'Say it. Say you will be king,' I demanded, quickening my rhythm.

'I will be king,' he panted, his eyes rolling back in his head.

'And you will sit upon Ithaca's throne.'

'I will.'

'And you will rule this land.'

'*Yes,*' he cried out. 'Gods, yes.'

'Tell me when. Tell me when I can kneel at your feet.'

'Soon.'

My grip tightened, making his entire body spasm. 'When?'

'When—' The words caught in a groan.

'*When?*'

'*When I kill Telemachus.*'

I faltered, just a momentary break in rhythm, but it was enough to cut through Eurymachus' lustful haze. Before I could even register what was happening, his hand was in my hair, pulling my head back with sickening force.

'Did she send you?' he snarled. His free hand shot beneath the pillows, pulling out a concealed dagger. 'She sent her whore to seduce me. Is that it?'

'Penelope knows nothing of this,' I gasped, hot fire shooting over my scalp as Eurymachus' grip tightened. 'I have no loyalty to her. Not any more. I swear it.'

He pulled my face down to his, voice lethally quiet as he hissed, 'Prove it. Convince me and maybe I will let you walk out of this room alive.'

As I felt the sting of cold metal against my throat, a horrific vision flashed in my mind – Penelope finding my naked corpse in *his* bed, my useless soul floating beside her, trying desperately to explain: *It is not what it looks like . . .*

No. I refused to die like this, to have Eurymachus' face be the last I saw, to have his hands be the last to touch me.

An idea frantically clawed its way through the fog of my fear, and I knew that to survive this night my betrayal would have to cut even deeper.

'The shroud is a lie.'

Eurymachus' grip loosened, just a fraction. '*What?*'

'The funeral shroud for Laertes. Penelope has no intention of finishing it. She unpicks it each night; she forces us to help her.' I could feel my treachery scalding me from the inside, but stronger still was my determination, forcing me onwards. 'She has been tricking you. All of you.'

Eurymachus let go of my hair and I scrambled off him, retreating to the edge of the bed.

'That fucking bitch,' he snarled, sitting upright. The movement was a little woozy and I felt a flicker of fragile hope in my chest.

'Do you see? I can help you,' I pressed. 'We can work together.'

'*I'll kill her*,' Eurymachus seethed. 'I'll kill her for thinking she can *outsmart* me—'

'Why kill her when you could *own* her?' I countered. 'When you are king, she will be your subservient wife. Is that not more satisfying? To have that cunning mind bend to *your* will.'

He considered my words, head lolling slightly. He blinked, pressing a flat palm against the bed to steady himself.

'Ithaca deserves a great king. A valiant, cunning, *powerful* king.' My words were cracked and desperate, but I could see them slipping behind Eurymachus' bloodlust, igniting his ego. 'That is the king I wish to serve, and I will do anything to make it so.'

His gaze lifted to mine, eyes a little unfocused. 'Tell me why I should trust you.'

'I have just betrayed my queen by telling you the truth of the shroud. Is that not proof enough?'

He said nothing for an excruciatingly long moment. I glanced down at the blade still clasped in his hand. One mistake and he could slit my throat in seconds . . .

But I would not retreat now, not when I was so close to the truth.

'I can help you,' I assured him, my voice steadying. 'But only if you *let* me. I am no use to you if I am kept in the dark.'

Slowly, Eurymachus leant forward, angling his dagger towards my neck.

'I know what you really are, slave,' he whispered, the words thick and sluggish on his tongue. 'You are a *rat*.'

He dragged the tip of the blade over my collarbone, watching my chest rise and fall with each panicked breath.

'But I cannot tell if you are *my* rat or *hers*,' he continued with an indolent smile.

'I am *yours*,' I insisted.

He pulled away, leaning back heavily against the bedframe.

'Shall I tell you my secrets then, little rat?' He laughed drunkenly, though I knew it was not the wine that had loosened his mood so. 'Would you like that?'

'I would like to assist you,' I replied carefully.

'Hmm . . . Well, there is *something* you can do for me.' Eurymachus reached for his wine as he spoke, then, finding it empty, he launched the cup across the room. I tried not to flinch.

'I would be honoured.'

Instead of continuing, he pushed off the bed with an incoherent grumble and staggered over to the table. I watched silently as he retrieved another cup and proceeded to fill it, spilling a lot of wine in the process. He knocked back the cup, then a second, streaks of crimson dribbling down his chin.

'Tell me what I can do for you, my lord,' I prompted cautiously.

Eurymachus wiped his mouth with the back of his hand. 'In three days' time, I need you to ensure Penelope does not leave her quarters. That is all. Very simple, yes?'

'Telemachus is due to return then,' I breathed, suddenly feeling as unsteady as Eurymachus looked. 'That's it . . . That's when you're going to kill him.'

'*Me?* I would not dream of doing such a thing.' Eurymachus waved his blade between us, words stumbling together. 'But the seas can be a treacherous place, darling. Did you know there has been a recent increase in pirate attacks around these isles? Nasty business. Ithaca would be an ideal spot for an *ambush* . . . so I'm told.'

Blood roared in my ears. 'How can you be so certain they will attack?'

Eurymachus snorted. 'Because I paid the men enough to ensure they do a *thorough* job. They'll be spending the next few nights at the harbour eagerly awaiting our prince's return.'

Somehow, I managed to return his vile smile.

'A genius plan,' I said, sweat coating my palms. 'Ithaca will believe it was a tragic, unmotivated attack. Nobody will trace it back to you. Your hands will remain clean.'

He strode towards me then and grabbed my neck, pulling my face to his.

'And once Telemachus is dead,' he hissed against my mouth, 'I will take Penelope as my wife.'

'And if she refuses?'

Eurymachus' smile widened. 'Then she will join her son in the Underworld.'

52

Eurymachus demanded I stay the night.

I wish I could say he did not touch me again. I wish I could say the laced wine made him fall asleep instantly.

But the Fates are not so forgiving.

I had never been so desperate for the sun to rise. When it finally did, I slipped from Eurymachus' chamber only for the hawkish eyes of Eurycleia to pin me against the door. The old crone was like a ghost, perpetually haunting these passageways and materializing at the most ill-timed moments.

'After all she has done for you,' Eurycleia hissed, disgust rotting behind each word, '*this* is how you repay Mistress Penelope? By crawling into bed with one of *them*?'

I opened my mouth to argue, but a wave of exhaustion slammed into me, stealing the fight from my lips. Wordlessly, I turned and walked away.

'The Gods will punish you for this.' Eurycleia's haughty voice echoed down the hall.

'The Gods can get in line,' I muttered back.

I found Penelope sitting at her loom, working on Laertes' shroud.

Our quarters were quiet; everyone was out enjoying the small window of freedom they had whilst the suitors slept off their nightly indulgences. Everyone except Penelope.

For a moment, I simply watched her work – those fingers that moved like water, so swift I had trouble keeping up with them.

Sensing my presence, Penelope turned. She smiled when she saw me, a rare sight these days, and the beauty of it nearly broke me. But I forced myself to walk forward and take a seat on the spare stool beside the loom.

'You were gone when I awoke this morning,' she said.

Penelope's eyes were bruised with lack of sleep, her hair falling around her face in long, dark tendrils. I loved it when her hair was loose like this, and I almost reached out to tuck a strand behind her ear, but guilt held me back. I would not touch her when I still had the remnants of Eurymachus tainting my skin.

The seconds passed, and I wished I could hold on to this moment for a little while longer before I ripped it apart.

'There is something I must tell you.'

Penelope's hands stilled. She turned to look at me, though I could no longer meet her gaze.

'What is it?'

'I know what the suitors are plotting.' I forced myself to speak slowly, glaring down at the faded rug. 'Eurymachus has paid pirates to ambush Telemachus' ship upon his return to Ithaca. He has instructed them to kill everyone on board.'

Beside me, Penelope seemed to disappear, shrinking somewhere deep inside herself. She sat so motionless I could not even tell if she was breathing.

'Penelope?' I prompted. 'Did you hear what I said?'

'Yes,' she murmured. 'I heard you.'

She inhaled a delicate breath, then, to my surprise, returned to her work.

I dared to look at her again, watching the quiet focus etched across her face, the steadiness of her strong fingers. I could tell she was plotting her next move, leashing her panic with plans for a solution. It made my heart lift, to see her mind spark into action.

'How did you learn of this?' she asked.

'Eurymachus told me.' I watched as she absorbed my words, their unspoken meaning taking root.

'And why did Eurymachus tell *you*?'

Still, Penelope was focused on the loom, and I was grateful she could not see the shame staining my eyes as I admitted, 'Because I made him believe I was an ally.'

Her face changed then, those beautiful features hardening to keep her emotions sealed in tight.

'How did you manage that?'

'I told him the truth about the shroud.'

Finally, Penelope's hands halted, falling into a heap on her lap. Her silence was a horrible, suffocating thing, splintered only by the loom's hanging weights clacking together.

'I'm sorry.' My voice trembled. 'We knew this plan had run its course, and I had to gain his trust somehow, to make him believe I was on his side.'

She turned slowly to look at me. 'Is that all you did to gain his trust?'

I could do nothing but stare at her.

I knew the truth would hurt Penelope beyond words. But I could not bring myself to lie. Not to her.

'Melantho?' Her voice was filled with such tentative hope. The sound of it almost destroyed me. 'Is that all?'

'I . . . I did it to protect you.'

Penelope closed her eyes. '*Please*. Please tell me you didn't.'

I swallowed down a sob. 'I had to do *something*. I could not bear it any longer. I had to—'

'I told you *never* to sacrifice yourself like that.' Penelope snapped her eyes open, and I saw a fire raging within them.

'Someone had to gain their trust—'

'But why *you*?'

'Why should it *not* be me?' I shot back, louder than I intended. But that anger was swelling inside me now, fed by my pain, by *her* pain. 'What I am to you doesn't make me better than the others. I am still a slave, no matter what you feel for me.'

'*Nobody* should be forced to give themselves up like that.'

'No, they should not. But *this* is the world we live in, and this is the *only* weapon I know how to wield, and I was willing to do that for *you*. For Telemachus. For Hippodamia and Autonoë and Actoris and Skaris and Eurynome. For our *home*.'

Penelope opened her mouth to argue, but all that escaped her was a shaky breath.

'They're going to kill him,' she breathed.

'They won't,' I said, shifting closer to her. 'We know their plan now. We can stop this. We can save Telemachus. That is *why* I did this – don't you see?'

She shook her head, twin tears streaming down her cheeks. 'I did not ask for this. I would *never* have asked you for this.'

'I know. It was my choice, Penelope. I *had* to do something, and I knew I could handle this—'

'What if *I* cannot handle it?' she choked out, the words escaping her in breathless gulps. 'I cannot bear to think of it, of *him* with *you* . . . like *that*.'

'Then do not. What's done is done, Penelope. It is in the past now. We can leave it there.'

She stared at me for a long moment, her lovely, striking face hollowed out by pain.

'It meant nothing,' I whispered. 'You must know that.'

I reached out to take her hand, but she pulled away, eyes lowered.

Since the moment I had met her, all that time ago, Penelope had never once recoiled from my touch.

The pain in my chest was so visceral I thought my heart might have actually shattered.

Tears blurred my vision, but my voice was surprisingly steady as I said, 'Fine. Hate me if you must. It is a worthy trade for your safety and Telemachus' life.'

Penelope said nothing as I rose to my feet and walked towards the door.

At the threshold I glanced over my shoulder. Penelope had not moved an inch, hands folded neatly, spine stiff, bathed in sunshine so bright it seemed to mock her misery.

I turned and left her alone with my betrayal.

53

My bed felt horribly empty without the warmth of Penelope beside me.

All night I wrestled with the urge to go to her, to take her in my arms and beg for her forgiveness. A few times, my desperation almost won out, but then I remembered the way she had withdrawn from my touch. From *me*.

So, I stayed away.

Now, it was somehow morning again, though I was certain I had not slept. Sunlight burnt behind my closed lids, forcing me to pull my sheets over my head, burying myself deeper into the cocoon I had made. Around me, I heard the handmaids buzzing about their usual business. Gradually our chamber quietened, and I let out a sigh of relief when I was finally left alone.

'Melantho, are you all right?' came Autonoë's voice.

I pretended to be asleep, hoping she would leave. Instead, I felt the bed dip as she sat down.

'You can talk to me, if you need to,' she said after a time.

'I'm fine. I just don't feel well,' I muttered.

'I spoke with Eurycleia.'

I peered out from my sheets, squinting against the light. 'So?'

'She told me she saw you . . . leaving Eurymachus' chamber yesterday morning.'

Hot shame pooled inside me, hardening quickly into something sharper, uglier. 'And what if I did? Have you come to judge too?'

Autonoë's eyes softened. 'Of course not, Melantho.'

'Then why are you here?'

She reached out and took my hand in hers, her palms warm and dry. 'How long have we known each other?'

I frowned at the sudden change in topic. 'A long time.'

'Twenty summers. And never once have you asked about these.' She motioned to her scarred face with her free hand.

'I . . . never thought it was my place,' I said carefully.

'You must have wondered how I got them, though.'

I gave a slight shrug. 'I just hoped whoever did that to you got what they deserved.'

Autonoë hummed, her gaze drifting to the window. When she spoke again, she suddenly seemed far away, as if she were speaking from some distant place inside herself. 'Pirates came to my village when I was very young. I don't remember much of my childhood, but I remember that day . . . *Such a pretty face* – that's what they said after they murdered my parents and put me in chains. The same exact words the brothel owner said when he bought me. *A pretty face like yours will do good business.* I hated that place, hated what they did to me, what they took from me – all because of that *pretty face.*' Absently, Autonoë's hand lifted to brush her cheek, toying with the groove of her scar. 'One night, I smashed my hand mirror, and I took that pretty face away. My master was furious, of course. What client wants to bed a disfigured child? They sold me the very next day. It was shortly after that I ended up here, in Ithaca. And nobody ever spoke of my *pretty face* ever again.'

Her words hung between us, and all I could do was grip Autonoë's hand tighter.

'I . . . I'm so sorry.'

She turned back to me and smiled. 'Don't be. I am not. I would have done it a thousand times over to get myself out of that nightmare.'

'Where was it?' I asked quietly. 'Your home.'

Her smile flickered at that, like a flame choked in darkness. 'I don't know . . . I only remember its ashes.'

'Autonoë . . .' I trailed off, wishing I knew what to say.

She let go of my hand to cup my cheek. 'Please do not look at me like that, my friend. I am not telling you this to make you sad.'

I shook my head. 'Then why?'

'Because I want you to know I *understand*.'

'Understand what?'

'That sometimes we must do the wrong thing for the right reason.' She held my gaze as she spoke, her dark eyes burning with a gentle intensity. 'But that doesn't make you a bad person. I hope you know that.'

Emotions knotted in my throat, so my words came out cracked and strangled. 'What if it makes others think we are?'

Autonoë patted my cheek as she rose.

'Those who matter will always find a way to understand.'

Try as I might, I could not find comfort in Autonoë's words.

I stayed in bed for most of the day, hiding from the world, from myself. Yet I could still smell Eurymachus' body, hear his ugly panting as his sweat-slick flesh pressed against mine . . .

I forced those visions away, burying them deep inside myself, in that graveyard where all the other unwanted pieces of my past had been laid to rest.

I had told Penelope I could handle it, and it was the truth. However much I hated what I had done, I had known I could endure bedding Eurymachus. But I had not considered the one thing I *could not* handle – hurting Penelope.

I had known she would be upset, but I had hoped she would recognize this was a necessary evil. Perhaps it was heartless of me to have ever expected her to understand. I had been too blinded by my desperation to save her to really consider how deeply my betrayal would break her.

And the way she had *recoiled* from me . . . as if I were tainted somehow. Was that how she would always see me? My throat felt tight, my eyes hot as I thought of all the times Penelope had kissed my skin, her lips marking every inch of me with such sweet devotion.

She would never touch me like that again.

What if I cannot handle it?

I clutched my sides, fingers turning to claws. I wanted to peel away this flesh Eurymachus had touched, carving every inch of me he had claimed for himself so there was nothing left but bones and blood.

But Telemachus will be safe, I reminded myself over and over. *He will return to Ithaca unharmed. Penelope will not lose him.* That was worth any price.

It had to be.

I must have fallen into a fitful sleep at some point, because when I opened my eyes there was a figure looming over my bed. I instinctively flinched away.

'It's me.'

My heartbeat settled as I rubbed the sleep from my eyes. Penelope was staring at me with an unreadable expression, draped in grey afternoon light.

'What is it?' I asked.

She motioned to the door with a tilt of her head. After a tentative moment, I pulled on my gown and followed her.

I braced myself as we walked towards her bedchamber. I did not want to argue, nor could I stand the thought of seeing that hideous pain in her eyes again. But if she wanted to speak, then I knew I owed it to her to listen.

Inside Penelope's chamber, a large metal tub had been set before the fire, sleepy steam curling off the water's surface.

Wordlessly, Penelope took my hand and guided me forward. When we were standing beside the tub, she lifted a hand to the brooch at my shoulder.

'May I?' she whispered.

I nodded, watching her intently as she unfastened my gown and let it fall to the floor.

Questions crowded on my tongue, but I said nothing as she took my hand again and gently guided me into the tub. The water was deliciously warm, smelling of sweet saffron and fresh pine. I let out a hiss of pleasure as I sank into it. Beyond the window, the sun had finally broken through the clouds, golden fingers reaching towards the water's surface, making it glow like warm honey.

Penelope watched me for a moment, then slowly unclasped her own gown.

'What if someone comes in?' I asked.

'I told Skaris to keep watch.'

She stepped in, making the water rise and slosh over the edge. It was only a small tub, but Penelope managed to slip in behind me, so I was sitting between her legs, my back resting against her chest.

Retrieving a cloth, Penelope dipped it into the water before running it over my skin, along my shoulders and arms. Her touch should have been soothing, but it seemed to make that tension inside me grow tighter.

'You cannot simply wash away what I did, you know,' I muttered.

'I am not trying to.'

We were quiet for a moment. Then, I felt her fingers trace the scars on my back.

'Did he hurt you?'

I shook my head.

She kissed the tip of one scar, and the feel of her lips loosened that knot inside me, causing the tears to finally come. A sob ripped from my chest, and Penelope wrapped her arms around me, pressing her forehead against my back.

'Do you want to tell me about it?'

I could hear the hesitancy in her voice, though she tried to hide it. We both knew those details were the last thing she wanted to hear. Yet still, Penelope waited patiently, ready to listen should I need her to.

'No,' I whispered. 'It's all right.'

She kissed my shoulder before resting her chin there, her arms tightening around me. The silence was heavy yet soft, and within its depths I could feel our love and pain mingling together, dancing in the light like the steam rising from the water.

'I'm so sorry,' she whispered.

I turned to look at her and saw the tears streaming down her cheeks.

'It's not your fault.' The words ached like a bruise. 'None of this is.'

'But I should never have—'

'Penelope. It's not your fault.' I reached out to cup her fallen face. 'Just . . . promise me one thing.'

'Anything,' she murmured into my palm.

'Promise me this won't change what is between us.'

Something fierce and beautiful flared in her eyes. 'Nothing could ever change that.'

'Truly?'

Penelope smiled faintly, her grey eyes glowing a burnished silver in the sunlight. 'You are a part of me, Melantho. Always.'

We held each other for a long while, until the water grew cold, and the sun had set. Then, Penelope guided me out of the bath and began massaging warm olive oil over my skin. She always touched me with such care, as if I were something frighteningly precious.

Once I was covered, Penelope took a small, curved instrument and began scraping the oil off, leaving my body cleansed and glistening.

'What are we going to do?' I whispered into our tender silence. 'About Eurymachus' plan. Will you send word to Telemachus' ship?'

She was kneeling before me now, still devotedly tending to my skin. 'No.'

'No?'

'You were right.' Her eyes met mine and she rose slowly. 'We have spent too long sitting by, doing nothing. I am tired of hiding. I am tired of living in fear.'

'What do you plan to do?'

Resolution glowed in her eyes, as bright as a blade speared through the heart of a flame. 'I plan to end this.'

54

The moon carved her smile into the sky, a gleaming, bone-white slash.

Her rays painted the midnight waves a stark silver, the only splash of colour in a starless night. As I stared out from the shore, I could not see where the sky ended and the sea began; it was just an endless expanse yawning before me, eerily calm.

'It's too quiet,' I murmured.

Penelope stood beside me, limned by the weak flicker of my oil lamp. If she was afraid, she did not show it.

'Are you sure this will work?' Skaris asked, her sword already in her hand.

'I suppose we will find out,' Penelope said evenly.

'That's comforting,' Actoris muttered. She was standing a little way from me, and I could scarcely make her out in the dim light. Behind her, Hippodamia and Autonoë carried a chest between them.

'Remember what I said,' Penelope murmured to us. 'Run at the first sign of danger.'

I nodded, skimming the dagger concealed in my gown for reassurance as I scanned the empty harbour before us. It was the same decrepit spot where I had met my brother years before – hardly the location for a grand royal arrival, but the secluded location promised secrecy. At least, that was what Penelope had hoped when she instructed Telemachus to use this harbour upon his return.

The silence was suffocating. Nothing stirred, as if life itself had ceased to exist in this tiny, forgotten corner of the island.

'So, do we just . . . wait for them to arrive?' Hippodamia asked, her voice loud against the stillness.

Penelope shook her head once. 'They are already here.'

As if waiting for this cue, figures began to slink forward, peeling themselves from the night like strips of darkness given life. I stiffened, instinctively inching closer to Penelope. In return, her fingers brushed mine, just the lightest grazing of skin, but it was enough to steady my racing heart.

'Well, ain't this a *surprise*,' came a voice from the blackness. It was somehow both rough and mellifluous, like swathes of delicate linen ripped across jagged rocks. 'We was expectin' a prince, not a queen.'

The glow from my oil lamp did not quite reach the stranger, so I could only make out his edges – a tall, narrow build, thick beard, and the undeniable gleam of a blade.

'You know who I am, then,' Penelope said, her voice impressively steady.

'O' course. Everyone knows of Odysseus' obedient little wife,' the voice purred. 'To what do we owe this *pleasure*?'

In the darkness beyond, figures shifted. I glanced sidelong at Skaris, noting the tension in her muscles. We were armed, but we knew this was not a fight we could win. Six of us against a crew of pirates. It was laughable, really.

'I know of the deal you have with Eurymachus,' Penelope said.

The moon caught on the man's grin, making his teeth glint. 'I cannot confirm nor deny my business, love. *Client confidentiality* – you understand, I'm sure.' His voice then dropped to a low, husky murmur. 'I admire you tryin', though. You're a brave girl. Stupid, but brave. Not always the best pair, mind.'

'You misunderstand me,' Penelope said flatly. 'I am not here to expose Eurymachus' deal. I am here to offer you a better one.'

A gravelly laugh rumbled from the man's throat. Then, he leant forward, just enough that we could see his dark eyes and the edges of a jagged scar cut along his forehead.

'I do love a woman who can surprise me.' He somehow managed to make every word sound dangerously intimate upon his tongue. 'Go on, then, love, tell me what this deal o' yours is.'

'I want you to come to my palace on the day of Apollo's festival and slaughter every suitor within its walls,' Penelope said. 'Once every man is dead, *every single one*, you may take whatever you desire. I will ensure ample payment.'

'Well, well, well,' the stranger mused, leaning back so the night swallowed him once more. 'That sounds like a lotta work to me. Why shouldn't we just take you now, seeing as you've fallen so *eagerly* into our laps? I'm sure we'd get a pretty ransom for a queen.'

I stiffened at that, but Penelope countered the threat unflinchingly. 'Nobody will pay you for my life. My husband is gone, and the suitors would be all too glad to be rid of me. I would be a waste of space aboard your ship.'

'Well, you could always serve as *entertainment* for the lads. They do enjoy their playthings.'

Chuckles rippled around us, making my stomach roil.

'I am offering you the opportunity to plunder a palace, and you would prefer a *plaything*?' Penelope tutted. 'How unambitious of you.'

'You better watch that tongue, love. Remember, *you're* the one that's out here all alone. You really believe your girls can protect you?' He snorted softly. 'It's almost insultin', really.'

'And you really believe I came here alone? *I'm* insulted you think me so foolish.' Penelope lifted her face to the sky. 'Perhaps you are unfamiliar with Ithaca's landscape, but the mountain ranges are perfect vantage points for archers.'

It was a bluff, of course, but one the stranger seemed to buy, perhaps because the truth was too ridiculous to seem plausible. After all, who would believe a queen would willingly meet with pirates in the dead of night with only her handmaids at her side?

The stranger shifted. 'Eurymachus is payin' us *handsomely*, you know.'

'I will pay more.'

'How can we be sure?'

Penelope signalled, and Hippodamia and Autonoë shuffled forward then set down the chest they carried. Opening the lid, the gold inside glimmered beneath the light of my lamp.

'For three summers I have housed over one hundred men in my palace, all vying for my affections. They leave me gifts regularly – gold, jewels, trinkets. Desperation can make men so very generous.' Penelope motioned to the chest. 'This is just a taste. The rest awaits you in my palace, ready to be claimed. *If* you accept my terms.'

The shadows pressed in closer, lured by the treasure.

'And what are these "terms"?'

Penelope smiled. 'I have three. Firstly, you will call off the attack on my son. Secondly, you are to slay only the suitors within the palace; no other soul on this island is to be harmed. And lastly, you are never to speak a word of this. If anyone asks you about the attack, you are to tell them Eurymachus did not honour his payment, so you took what was rightfully yours.'

The man chuckled at that, the sound scraping against the darkness. 'How devious you are. You might even have some pirate blood in you.'

Penelope lifted her chin a little higher. 'Do we have a deal?'

My heartbeat quickened. One command. That was all it would take. One command and we could be captured, slaughtered, or worse . . .

Skaris shifted beside me, reaffirming her grip on her sword. Actoris mirrored the movement, looking surprisingly ferocious despite her tiny stature.

The silence held, the seconds passing sickeningly slowly.

Then, a large, scarred hand shot out from the darkness.

'You have yourself a deal,' he said.

The Queen of Ithaca did not smile as she took the pirate's hand and shook.

55

The Prince of Ithaca returned the following day.

There was a small group awaiting his return, consisting of Penelope, the handmaids, Eurycleia and, mercifully, no pirates.

As Telemachus disembarked from his ship, something about him seemed notably different. Though his features had not changed at all, he somehow appeared older. It was in the way he carried himself – there was a sureness to his steps I had never seen before. Clearly, his time in Sparta had served him well.

Penelope was subdued as she embraced her son, keeping her emotions locked in tight. The handmaids did not show such restraint. They descended upon Telemachus in a flurry of excited exclamations, with Skaris picking the prince up and swinging him round. Only Actoris and I held back, smirking as Telemachus tried to disentangle himself from Hippodamia's tearful kisses. Once he was free from her clutches, the prince turned to me.

'Hello, Melantho,' he said as I hugged him.

'I missed you,' I whispered, holding him tight.

He smiled, then turned to Actoris. I couldn't help but notice the slight lifting of colour in her cheeks as he approached. When she had first arrived here, Actoris had been the taller one, but now Telemachus towered over her tiny stature, his handsome face sharpened by a recent flush of manhood.

'You look older,' she said to him by way of greeting.

Telemachus nodded. 'I feel older.'

She cut her gaze up and down him, and Telemachus braced himself for one of Actoris' usual insults. But instead, she simply said, 'It suits you.'

Now it was Telemachus' turn to blush, though he tried his best to hide it. I glanced at Penelope, and, despite all that faced us, we shared a smile.

'I found the slaves you were looking for,' Telemachus said.

I was walking with him to his chambers, following the shadowy back passages only ever used by us slaves. It was still too early for the suitors to be awake, but we did not wish to take any risks. The longer Telemachus' return was kept secret, the longer he was safe.

The prince's words made me freeze. After all that had come to pass, I had forgotten what I had asked of Telemachus when he left for Sparta – to see what news he could find of my old companions.

'Melitta?' I whispered. 'Is she well?'

Telemachus came to a halt beside me and nodded. 'She serves in the kitchens. The man, Callias, was there too. He seemed quiet, but well, from what I could tell.'

My heart squeezed for my old friend.

'And Melitta's child?'

'A girl. Her name is Alcippe. She serves as Helen's handmaid. Helen seems to care for her handmaids very well.'

Alcippe. I held the name close, like a rare, secret treasure.

Telemachus then added a shade quieter, 'She looks a lot like you. Alcippe.'

I smiled, eyes prickling. 'She does?'

He nodded. 'Curly hair, fierce eyes. Looks like you wouldn't want to get on her bad side.'

A laugh spilt out of me, but I quickly muffled the sound, scanning the narrow hallway. 'We should keep moving.'

'I didn't get a chance to speak to her, though,' Telemachus admitted as we fell into step again. 'I'm sorry for that.'

'No, no.' I shook my head, then squeezed his hand. 'This is wonderful news. Thank you.'

'May I ask you something?' Telemachus tilted his face as he studied mine. 'My mother seems . . . distant. Do you know why that might be?'

'No.' The lie tasted bitter on my tongue.

Penelope had made it clear we were not to breathe a word of our plan to Telemachus, for she knew he would never approve of it. All his life, Telemachus had been fed stories of glory and honour; he would want no part in such an ignoble victory. It was best for Telemachus to believe the pirate attack to be an act of divine justice.

Doubts creased his brow as he looked to the shadows. 'I fear perhaps I have . . . disappointed her.'

I stopped walking. 'Telemachus, you could never disappoint her.'

'I returned from Sparta empty-handed.' He winced, his voice dropping to a low murmur. 'If Menelaus had given me men, I could've ousted the suitors the moment I stepped foot upon these shores.'

'That reflects badly on Menelaus, not you. He forced all of Greece to fight for *his* wife, but he would not lift a finger to aid the family of his greatest comrade.'

Telemachus nodded, though he seemed unconvinced. He then adjusted his robes and turned briskly, as if eager to escape this conversation.

'Telemachus?' My voice caught him mid-stride. 'If you were in Menelaus' place, what would you have done?'

'I would have offered my help,' he said without hesitating.

I smiled. 'And *that* is why you'll be a far greater king than he.'

A sudden rush of emotion shimmered behind Telemachus' grey eyes, seeming to catch him by surprise. He looked away, clearly embarrassed, yet smiling all the same.

'Thank you, Melantho,' he whispered.

56

'What did you *do?*'

Eurymachus cornered me in the banquet hall, as I had known he would.

'I do not know of what you speak.' I felt the wall bite into my back as he pressed closer, hands flexing into fists. It was not even noon, and his eyes were already hazy with wine.

'Telemachus returned yesterday,' he said, each word forced out through his clenched teeth. '*Alive.*'

I widened my eyes. 'Are you certain?'

'Of course I'm fucking certain. I *saw him.*' He braced his hands on either side of my head. 'So, I'll ask you again. *What did you do?*'

'Me? You think this is *my doing?*'

'That isn't an answer.'

I let out a strangled laugh. 'You believe *I* went to the pirates myself? Convinced them not to kill Telemachus? And what, exactly, do you think I had to bargain with? To persuade them to listen to a woman? A slave?'

Doubt punctured Eurymachus' rage, his body seeming to deflate as he stepped back. Over his shoulder, I saw suitors slowly filtering into the banquet hall, having finally dragged themselves out of their wine-addled slumber, ready for another day of indulgence.

Little did they know that it would be their last.

I suppressed a smile as I turned back to Eurymachus. 'You have a palace full of men who all want what *you* want, yet you point the finger at *me?*'

'Keep your voice *down*,' Eurymachus snarled.

I held his glare for a silent beat, then turned to walk away.

'Where are you going?' He caught my arm. 'You said you had news for me.'

'Why should I share anything with you when you clearly do not trust me?'

'Perhaps I . . . hastened to conclusions,' he muttered, releasing me. I was certain this was the closest Eurymachus had ever come to admitting he was wrong. 'It's difficult to know who to trust in this madhouse.'

I lowered my voice to a husky whisper. 'Did I not prove my loyalty the other night?'

He gave a dismissive grunt. 'Tell me your news.'

I masked a wince as I folded my arms. Eurymachus had grabbed me hard enough to bruise.

'Penelope will choose a husband,' I said. 'Tomorrow, during Apollo's festival. She wants to ensure every suitor is present to hear her decision.'

Eurymachus' eyes widened. 'I have done it. I have finally worn her down.'

'After you uncovered her little ploy with the shroud, she has no other option. She has admitted defeat. You have won.'

Eurymachus did not soften under my flattery.

'I heard the slaves talking; they said Penelope has dismissed them for tomorrow. Why?'

My heartbeat quickened. *If he suspects something . . .*

'Penelope always does so during the festival of Apollo,' I said neutrally. 'It is tradition.'

'These slaves are disgustingly spoilt,' he spat. 'Who will Penelope choose? Do you know?'

'No. But I know my mistress is drawn to wealth, though she would deny it. She will likely choose whoever has been most *generous* in securing her favour. Ctesippus, I believe, has given the most gifts so far, but there is still time to remedy that before tomorrow . . .'

'We have given that bitch enough. Her treasuries are overflowing.'

I raised a brow. 'And *whose* treasuries shall they become once Penelope chooses a husband?'

A slow smile crawled across Eurymachus' face. 'Perhaps more gifts are in order, then.'

'Perhaps.'

Without warning, he reached out to brush a curl from my face. His touch invited unwanted memories to claw their way up my throat, visions of his bare flesh against mine, his hands in my hair, his hot breath in my face . . .

'I must go,' I said abruptly. 'Penelope is expecting me.'

Eurymachus blocked my path, eyes darkening.

'Penelope *must* choose me tomorrow,' he hissed. 'No one else can sit upon that throne. Do you understand?'

'I understand.'

'Good.' He stepped aside. 'Once I am king, you shall be amply rewarded for your . . . *support*.'

As Eurymachus sauntered away, I caught sight of a hunched shadow scuttling out of the hall.

Eurycleia.

How much of our conversation had she heard?

I went to follow her, but my attention was caught by an outburst of cheers. The suitors were gathered in a familiar ring with two men in the centre. One was an old man I did not recognize, and the other was my brother.

I stormed towards the crowd as Melanthius began circling his opponent, drowning in mocking jeers. There was a coldness in his expression, an abject emptiness that made my chest tighten. His opponent appeared far older than him; his greying hair was thick and unruly, tangling into his beard like a foaming sea. His skin had clearly been punished by the sun, which had turned it cracked and wrinkled. Given the state of his clothes and the smell that clung to him, he must have been a beggar. How the suitors loved to prey on desperate individuals.

I did not want to watch my brother fight again, yet I found I could not look away. A small, ugly part of me was relieved that Melanthius' opponent appeared old and weak. At least the match would be over quickly.

My brother threw out a jab, his movements more controlled than the last time I had seen him brawl. I flinched, anticipating the impact on the poor man's face. But the hit never landed. One second Melanthius' fist was sailing towards his opponent, and the next moment my brother was on the floor. The beggar had felled him with one swift manoeuvre, grabbing his fist and using his momentum against him, to bring my brother crashing down. The old man landed a punch straight to Melanthius' nose, then again to his jaw, before pulling my brother into a headlock. After a brief struggle, Melanthius tapped his opponent's arm, and he released him instantly.

The beggar offered his hand to Melanthius, but my brother shoved past him and stalked out of the hall, chased by the suitors' mocking laughter. The old man watched him go, his expression unreadable beneath all that wild hair.

'What filth have you let into our palace?' Antinous bellowed as he entered the hall.

'Some wretch the pig man dragged into our halls,' Eurymachus replied, appearing at my side.

Antinous waved a hand. 'I can smell the stench of him from here. Someone send that dog away.'

'I was victorious in your competition,' the beggar said, his voice low and coarse, like knotted rope, though his accent was surprisingly refined.

'All you are is another mouth snapping at our table,' Antinous sneered, taking his usual seat. 'Be gone, mutt.'

The beggar took a step forward. 'You sit in another man's home, enjoying *his* food and *his* comforts, yet you would not share a crumb of your banquet with the likes of me?'

'Are you deaf, old man?' Antinous mocked. 'I said: *be gone.*'

The man's weathered face darkened, though his eyes flashed bright. 'The Gods do not look kindly upon such vile greed. They will punish you for it.'

Antinous rose. 'Is that a *threat*?'

'It is a fact.'

With a snarl, Antinous grabbed his stool and launched it across the room towards the beggar. But the old man moved with that same, regimented swiftness he had used to dispatch my brother. He caught the stool smoothly in his gnarled hands, plucking it from the air as if he were picking an apple from a tree.

A shocked stillness fell across the room. Then, with mockingly slow strides, the beggar approached Antinous and set the stool down beside him.

'You seem to have misplaced your seat,' he said, holding the suitor's gaze unflinchingly.

Without waiting for Antinous to reply, the stranger then turned and stalked from the hall, leaving a bemused silence in his wake.

Melanthius' face was a mess.

He was in the courtyard, leaning back against a pillar as he probed his bloodied nose. Both eyes were already starting to darken with bruising, his bottom lip fat and swollen. Older bruises also marred his skin, and fresh scars I had never seen before. He did not flinch under my scrutiny, but lifted his chin a little higher, as if he were proud of his ruined face.

'You look like shit,' I told him.

He huffed a humourless laugh. 'That what you came here to tell me?'

As I stared at him, I realized we were standing in the exact same way, mirroring each other so effortlessly: both leaning against adjacent pillars, arms folded, one ankle crossed over the other. I shifted uncomfortably, dropping my arms to my side.

'Why do you still do it – the fights?'

'They give me a cut of the winnings,' Melanthius said, prodding his swollen lip. 'Slaves work themselves to death and get nothing for it. The suitors might like me getting bruised up a bit, but at least they pay me.'

'How much do you get?'

He shrugged. 'Enough.'

'Where do you keep it? Your winnings?'

Melanthius looked away then, folding his arms tighter across his chest. 'Eurymachus keeps it safe for me.'

Of course he does.

'Don't,' he snapped.

'I didn't say anything.'

His glare clashed against my own. 'I can see it all over your face. Your judgement. You reek of it. Is that why you're here? To look down on me from your mighty high ground?'

I shook my head, forcing my temper to settle. 'I'm here because I want to make you an offer.'

His swollen eyes narrowed. 'What *offer*?'

'To go back to Sparta,' I said carefully. 'Penelope will send you as a gift to her cousin, Helen. You can return to the palace.'

Melanthius scoffed. 'So, you want to trade me from one prison to another? Is that it?'

'If you return to Sparta, you will be able to see Melitta again,' I pressed. 'To meet your child.'

His gaze hardened. 'You can't know that. She could be dead or sold for all you know.'

'That is why I never made you this offer before,' I admitted. 'I did not want to send you to Sparta unless I was *certain* there was something there for you.'

'Then why make it now?' I could tell Melanthius was trying to mask the nervous anticipation in his voice, flattening it to a dull, dead note.

I stepped towards him, my movements placatingly slow.

'Telemachus just returned from Sparta. Before he left, I asked him to look for Melitta and for your child.' My brother glanced away with a wince, as if he could not bear to hear my words. I pressed on anyway. 'He found them, Melanthius. Melitta still works at the palace, and so does your daughter.'

His eyes widened, though the rest of him seemed to shrink, as if this realization had him collapsing in on himself, unable to bear the weight of it.

'A daughter,' he breathed, something small and fragile flickering in his voice.

I nodded, throat burning as I said, 'Yes. You have a little girl, Melanthius, and you can go to her. You can be with your family—'

'As a slave,' he interrupted.

'As a *father*,' I corrected. 'Please, Melanthius. Consider what Penelope is offering. Consider what this could mean for you.'

He lowered his gaze, staring at the ground with such intensity I thought he might scorch a hole through the very earth between us.

'I will not meet my child as a failure,' he whispered.

'Melanthius—'

'Eurymachus will make me a free man,' he continued, firmer now. He lifted his face to mine, a cold determination setting his features. 'If I help him get the throne, he'll give me my freedom and let me take my winnings. Then I'll go to Sparta, and I'll buy my daughter's freedom. I'll return as the father she deserves, as a saviour not a *slave*.'

I shook my head, those sharp talons of desperation sinking into me. 'How can you believe a word Eurymachus says? He is—'

'*What?*' Melanthius pushed off his pillar, swallowing the space between us in one firm stride. 'Our master? Our superior? Entitled and rich? All the same things Penelope is, and still, you trust *her*. But you think me the fool for trusting Eurymachus.'

'It's different and you know it is,' I snapped, jabbing a finger into his chest.

To my surprise, Melanthius reached out and grabbed my hands, clutching them firmly between his.

'Melantho, listen to me. Please. *This is it*. Our path to freedom. To my *child*.' His voice was low and frayed, but his eyes were clearer than I had seen them in years, lit with that desperate, feverish hope he still clung to. 'If you care for me at all, then you'll help me put Eurymachus on that throne. That's the *only* way we can be free. Don't you see? Penelope is a woman. She can't ever free you. Eurymachus can.'

I winced, crushed beneath the weight of Melanthius' misguided faith.

'If Eurymachus sits upon that throne, he will *kill* Telemachus,' I whispered. 'I cannot let that happen.'

Melanthius let go of me, stepping backwards. 'You would choose *her* child over mine? Over your own flesh and blood?'

'It's not like that. Listen to me: Eurymachus is a *monster*; you cannot trust him.' I reached for his hands again, gripping them tightly. 'If you wish to return free, then wait until Telemachus is king, let him grant you your freedom once he is able—'

'Telemachus will never sit upon that throne, Melantho,' he warned darkly. 'Everyone in Ithaca knows that.'

'Then take Penelope's offer. Please, I'm begging you. Go to Sparta. Be with your family—'

'I *will* be with my family. Once Eurymachus is king, and I'm a free man.'

'Melanthius—'

'And if you are any sister of mine, you'll help me make that happen.'

We stared at one another for an agonizingly long moment. I did not know what to say. I did not know how to make him understand. All I could do was watch as that spark in his eyes faded away, like those last, pulsing embers dwindling to irrevocable ash.

'Does the queen know her slaves stand around gossiping like old fishwives?' A voice splintered the silence between us.

I flinched as Melanthius ripped his hands free from mine. Turning, I saw the strange beggar perched on a stone bench, watching us beneath a vacant frown.

'What did you just say?' my brother snarled.

'Melanthius, don't—'

He shoved past me and marched towards the man. 'You think you can speak to me like that?'

'How else should I speak to you?' the beggar asked, without bothering to rise. 'You are a slave, are you not?'

'And what're you? A stray dog begging for scraps.'

The beggar only smiled at that.

'What?' Melanthius goaded. 'Lost your tongue now, have you?'

'I simply do not see the point in talking to a breed such as yours,' the beggar said, flicking his eyes over my brother. 'A disloyal slave is like a cup without a bottom. Utterly useless to all.'

Melanthius jabbed his fist towards the man's face, but the beggar simply batted him away as if he were swatting a fly. Melanthius tried again, and this time the beggar caught his wrist, snapping it at an unnatural angle.

'Stop!' I cried, rushing forward. 'Stop, you're hurting him!'

The beggar released Melanthius with a slight shrug.

'Melanthius, wait,' I called, but my brother was already striding away, cradling his wrist to his chest, cheeks burning with outrage and humiliation.

A part of me wanted to run after him, but what use would that have been? What would I even have said? We stood on opposite sides of the battleground, bloodshed looming on the horizon. I could not reach Melanthius now.

I only prayed he might see sense, once all this was over.

'I apologize for my brother's behaviour,' I said to the beggar. Only he did not appear to be listening, his attention caught by one of the hunting dogs slumped at his feet. He was scratching the old mutt's ears with a surprising degree of fondness.

For a moment, I simply watched him, welcoming this quiet moment as I tried to block out thoughts of tomorrow, of what these halls might look like crawling with bloodthirsty killers . . .

'There you are.' Eumaeus' breathless voice caught me by surprise.

Though it had been ten summers since I had rejected his marriage offer, Eumaeus still did everything in his power to avoid me. Now, as he sidled up to the beggar, his eyes brushed over mine.

'Melantho,' he said stiffly.

'Eumaeus, who is in charge of this dog?' the beggar demanded. 'What is the reason for his poor state?'

'I am not sure. But I can find out, of course,' Eumaeus said. He then turned to me, awkwardness hardening his voice. 'Do you know why this creature is not cared for?'

I glanced between the two men. 'He is cared for just as the other dogs are. He is simply old.'

The dog then shuffled off to the shady cover of the colonnade, settling down for a nap on the cool stone floor. The beggar watched him go, the grooves in his forehead deepening.

'The hound of Odysseus left to rot! Who dares treat Argos with so little respect?'

The name struck inside me, shifting dust from long-faded memories. I saw a small blur of dark muscle pounding over the fields. That same creature resting his head in my lap with soft, trusting eyes.

Argos likes you.

'How do you know that name?' I asked.

The beggar seemed to ignore me, too distracted by his rising temper.

'Someone must be punished for this negligence,' he told Eumaeus.

'I will see to it.'

I glared at Eumaeus, wondering why he was treating this cantankerous old man with such deference. Who was *he* to demand punishment beneath this roof?

'The dog is *perfectly well*. He is merely sleeping,' I said. 'And nobody will be punished, for no wrongdoing has occurred.'

The beggar's focus cut back to me, and there was something deeply unsettling about those eyes; a strange detachment to them, as if his thoughts had been loosened, left to swirl wildly in his skull.

'Remember your place, girl,' he warned darkly.

'Excuse me?' I snapped, my own rage rising to greet his.

'Melantho, do not,' Eumaeus whispered.

'What? I am to simply let this stranger intimidate me, is that it? What is he doing here, anyway? Is Penelope's home not leeched upon enough? Must we have another mouth to suck this palace dry?'

'Do not act like you care for your queen's interest,' the beggar scoffed. 'We know where your loyalties lie, girl. You and the other tramps that parade as handmaids.'

'You know *nothing*—'

'Perhaps it is best you return to the suitors, Melantho,' Eumaeus interjected. 'We know it is their company you prefer, after all.'

He glared at me with such unbridled disgust, and I knew, *I knew*, Eurycleia must have told him what she had seen that morning, just as she had told Autonoë.

I balled my trembling hands into fists. 'Whatever you think you know, Eumaeus—'

'I do not need to hear more of your *lies*—'

'Enough! Let us not waste our breath on this one,' the beggar interjected. He then turned to walk away, muttering beneath his breath, 'The Fates will see fit to punish her in time.'

57

I was exhausted when I finally returned to our chambers, though my body felt keenly alert, the anticipation for the morning held like a blade to my throat.

I had spent the afternoon ensuring every detail of our plan was securely in place. Now, I wanted nothing more than to crawl into bed, hold Penelope to me and hide from the world until it was all over, until the suitors were gone and our home was *ours* once again.

Outside our quarters, I paused. I could hear a voice filtering through the walls, low and gravelly and distinctly *male*. With a swell of unease, I cracked open the door, peering inside to where a hunched figure sat beside the hearth.

The beggar.

What was he doing *here?* Penelope never allowed guests into our private space.

Kneeling before him was Eurycleia. The old slave was bathing his feet, an act usually reserved for the most respected of guests. I inched the door open a little wider, stunned by this curious interaction. Eurycleia was staring intently at the man's leg, her fingers trembling as she touched his skin. The beggar shifted in his seat, and I saw what had caught Eurycleia's attention – a deep scar stretching along his thigh, one that looked vaguely familiar.

A loud clatter made me flinch. Eurycleia had dropped her basin, water spilling around her knees. She cried out, but her voice was instantly choked by the beggar's right hand at her throat. He was on his feet now, thick fingers wrapped around Eurycleia's neck as he growled at her, words too low for me to catch.

'Get off her!' I shouted, surging inside.

Though I harboured no love for Eurycleia, I could not simply stand by as a man harmed a defenceless woman.

The beggar released Eurycleia instantly, turning to me. '*You* again.'

'How *dare* you touch her like that,' I spat at him. 'You need to leave. You have no place here. Get out. *Go!* Now!'

'Melantho.' Penelope's voice was like a rush of cold water, dousing my rage.

I turned to find her standing in the doorway. Her eyes darted between the three of us and there was something odd about her expression, a tightness I could not place.

'You are dismissed,' she said.

Eurycleia obeyed without protest, scarlet rings marring her throat as she hurried away. It took me a moment to realize Penelope was waiting for me to leave also.

'This man shouldn't be here,' I said, holding my ground.

'I was told you had asked to meet with me, my lady,' the beggar interjected. His voice had shifted now, taking on a softer, more hesitant edge. His expression had changed too, a strange shyness creeping over him.

Penelope nodded as she approached. 'I hear from Eumaeus you are well travelled. I had hoped you might have news of my husband, and I thought it best we meet here, so we may have some privacy away from my other . . . guests.'

'But—'

'That will be all, Melantho, thank you,' she said with a formality I was not used to.

'Penelope, this man tried to—'

'Please. Leave us.' The sting of her dismissal was soothed only by the guilt I sensed in her gaze. There was something else there too, some message she was trying to convey. 'Would you prepare my bedchamber for me? I will retire after I have spoken with my guest.'

I glanced back at the beggar, who was watching Penelope with an uncomfortable intensity, like he was a drowning man and she the glinting brush of shore on the horizon, beckoning him forward.

Then, all at once, it made sense.

Why the beggar knew Argos' name . . .

Why Eumaeus had treated him with such deference . . .

Why Eurycleia had reacted to the scar on his leg . . .

Why Penelope was looking at me now with such tension in her gaze . . .

I stared at the beggar, recognition seeping through me, accompanied by a slow rush of dread. He looked so much older than I remembered. The war had ravaged his features, though the starkest change of all was his eyes: once sharp and alert, they were now hollow and worn, with an unnervingly wild glint.

This was not the man I had seen sail away twenty summers ago. Rather, the rough, weathered shell of him, stripped of all that warmth and charm.

Penelope said something, though her voice sounded far away as I watched the beggar take his seat again by the hearth.

No, not the beggar. *Odysseus.*

The man who had left Penelope to fend for herself in an unfamiliar land with their newly born child. The man who had spent *ten years* fattening his ego in a pointless war whilst Penelope dutifully raised his son and led his kingdom. That same man who had spent another *ten years* delaying his homecoming, risking Penelope's life whilst he abandoned his throne to warm a goddess' bed.

Now, Odysseus had finally returned, and he was playing *games*, trying to hide his identity from the very woman who had held his land together. Did he truly believe Penelope would fall for such a trick?

'Melantho?' I blinked, realizing Penelope was staring at me, a stark thread of urgency in her eyes. 'Did you hear my request?'

'Do you not wish me to stay and . . . assist?' I asked, forcing my voice steady.

'Such insolence,' Odysseus muttered to himself.

'No, thank you,' Penelope said. 'I would like to speak with our guest alone.'

'Very well.' I nodded numbly. 'I shall prepare your chamber.'

Relief touched Penelope's face, though it did not soothe the worried lines creasing it. 'Thank you.'

I turned and walked away, every step feeling like a battle as I forced myself to leave Penelope alone with the beggar.

With her husband.

With the lost King of Ithaca.

It felt like a small eternity before Penelope returned to her bedchamber.

She looked dazed as she walked towards me, steps loose, eyes distant, as if she were drifting between thoughts.

'It's him, isn't it?' I whispered. I already knew the answer, I just needed to hear Penelope say it, needed her voice to solidify this madness into actuality.

She nodded.

It took every ounce of self-control not to run to her. I wanted to pull her into my arms and hold on as tightly as I could. But fear rooted me to my seat.

If Odysseus was lurking beneath this roof, nothing was safe any more.

'Where's his army? All the men of Ithaca . . .'

'I don't know,' she admitted.

Penelope came and sat beside me, her body stiff. I was desperate to know what had occurred between Odysseus and her, but I could tell Penelope's thoughts needed space to breathe. So, I waited, as patiently as I could, whilst the silence settled over us.

'His timing is truly impeccable,' she finally said.

Twenty years, and the day Odysseus decided to return was the eve before our plan came to fruition. The Fates were surely laughing at us.

'Did he reveal himself to you?' I asked, leaning forward.

She shook her head, a slight wrinkle of irritation pressing between her brows. 'No, he kept up his strange pretence. He thinks me clueless. It is a little insulting, I must admit.'

'A *little*?' I scoffed, shaking my head. 'Why is he doing this?'

'Because he is afraid. He does not know who he can trust.'

'So, this is some kind of *test*?'

'Yes. He clearly wishes to see who has remained loyal to him.' Penelope's eyes focused then, as if she were seeing me for the first time since walking into her room. 'You must be careful, Melantho. You cannot speak to him the way you did tonight.'

'He grabbed Eurycleia by the *throat*—'

'And I fear he will do far worse if provoked.'

I balled my hands into fists, refusing to acknowledge the fear twisting inside me. 'He cannot simply wander back in here and start threatening us—'

'Of course he can. He is the king.'

'He hasn't been a king for *twenty years*.'

'Melantho.' Penelope reached for me, gently uncurling my fingers so she could slot hers between them. 'I am not saying any of this is fair; it is simply the way of things.'

My eyes prickled – with tears of sadness or anger, I couldn't be sure. All I could see was the way Odysseus had looked at her, that desperate longing in his eyes. As if she were *his* salvation, *his* hope, *his* future.

'What do you think he is going to do?' I whispered.

'He's going to kill the suitors.'

I gaped at her. 'He *told* you that?'

Penelope toyed absently with my fingertips. 'He spoke in riddles, but his intentions were clear enough. Though, I do not think he has a plan of any sort . . . I cannot tell if it is arrogance or insanity that makes him think he can take on a hundred men alone.'

'But what of *our* plan? What of the pirates?'

'Our plan will go ahead. It is too late to change course now, and Odysseus will need the assistance if he truly wishes to defeat the suitors.' A strained smile pinched Penelope's mouth. 'However great the legend of Odysseus is, he is still only one man. I think perhaps he has forgotten that.'

'What if he discovers it was our doing—'

'He won't,' she said firmly, her hands tightening around mine. 'All threads tie Eurymachus to the pirates. Odysseus will believe it was a deal gone sour, as everyone else will.'

'And if he tries to take on the pirates himself?'

Penelope's gaze grew heavy, drifting towards the shadows. 'I cannot say what will happen.'

'What of Telemachus?'

'I believe he already knows of his father's return. He has spent the day with Eumaeus at his home. That is where Odysseus has been staying.'

'I think Eurycleia knows, too. She recognized him.' I hesitated. 'Should we tell the others?'

'In the morning. There is no point worrying them tonight.'

'So, what do we do now?'

Penelope drew in a slow breath. 'Nothing. There is nothing we can do but wait for tomorrow.'

Tomorrow. The word had never seemed so daunting, filled with too many unknowns. Mere hours before, I had been anxiously counting down the seconds until we would be free of the suitors and finally have our home back. But now, even if our plan *was* successful, this palace would never be ours again. It would be Odysseus'.

And so would Penelope.

'I shouldn't be here.' I pulled my hands free from hers, a cold panic chasing me to my feet. 'It's not safe, not when *he's* lurking in the palace—'

'He's not,' Penelope said, rising with me. 'He has chosen to continue to reside with Eumaeus.'

'It's still too much of a risk.' I strode across the room, shaking my head. 'I can't put you in danger like this. I won't.'

'Melantho.'

The strain in her voice halted my steps.

I turned back and we stared at one another, the reality of our situation hanging, unspoken, between us. I looked to the door, knowing I should go whilst realizing, with equal certainty, that I would never be able to leave her.

If this were to be the last night we shared, then the Gods themselves could not drive me away.

We both moved at once, our lips meeting like a crash of lightning, a sudden strike of brilliant light, ripping open the darkness around us.

We tumbled into bed, hungry and wild, our desire made desperate by the looming threat of daybreak. Our fingers fumbled gracelessly as we raced to undress one another, as if it were our first time again, not our last. And when our bare bodies met in a frantic whisper of skin, I knew I would for ever be tortured by this memory of her, naked and alive and so achingly beautiful in my arms.

Penelope had once said that belief gave people a sense of purpose in this life. I had never much cared for our gods, but within the depths of Penelope's love I had found my religion, and as we worshipped at the altar of our bodies, we became, for that briefest moment, the rulers of our own universe, as endless and inevitable as the Olympians themselves.

We became eternal.

When our pleasure had shattered and made us anew, we lay tangled together, breathless and limp, trying to ignore the edges of the world creeping in around us.

'Do you think we will succeed tomorrow?' I whispered into the slope of Penelope's neck. I could feel her pulse thrumming against my lips.

'Yes,' she whispered. 'I think we will.'

'And . . . afterwards?'

'We will be free of the suitors, and Ithaca shall have a king,' she murmured. 'You will be safe. Telemachus will be safe.'

'And you will be his wife again.'

She held me closer. 'I was always his wife, Melantho.'

'You know what I mean.'

It was selfish, I knew, to sink into my jealousy when there was so much more at stake. I forced the feeling away, trying desperately not to think of whose arms she might be in the next night. But his face still came, unbidden – those wild, vacant eyes, the harsh lines of his face as he sneered at me, those thick hands closing around Eurycleia's throat . . .

'He's different,' I whispered. 'Odysseus.'

'War changes men.'

'He doesn't seem . . . safe.'

'It is because he doesn't feel safe.'

I considered that for a moment, then shifted on to my elbow so I could face her properly.

'And how do *you* feel?'

'I am still deciding,' she admitted, fingers tracing the dusting of freckles across my collarbone. 'It is . . . a lot to process. I had resigned myself to the idea that I would never see him again.'

'Were you . . . happy to see him?'

'"Happy" is too simple a word.' Penelope smiled sombrely. 'But for all Odysseus has done, he is Telemachus' father, and a part of me will always care for him because of that.'

I lowered my gaze. 'Did you ever . . . love him?'

Penelope considered the question, as she always did. I knew she was never one to rush answers to appease my feelings. She would respond truthfully, and that was something I deeply admired about her. Though, still, it hurt to know the answer was not a simple, resounding 'no'.

'Once, I thought I could,' she admitted. 'Before the war, during that first full turn of the seasons in Ithaca. I *wanted* to love him, I tried to, and I feared there was something wrong with me when I realized I could not.'

'Why couldn't you?' I breathed.

The shadows curved as Penelope smiled. 'You know why, Melantho.'

My throat burnt with all the emotions I did not know how to voice. In the silence, I swore I could hear the seconds spiralling away from us, our future unravelling like the threads we had plucked from Laertes' shroud, ready to be sewn again anew.

'I cannot bear to think of a life without this,' I whispered, burying my face into her neck.

'This doesn't have to be the end,' she murmured against my hair. 'Odysseus will travel, and he will be preoccupied with his own affairs. Perhaps we could find a way—'

'Penelope.' I pulled away to look at her again. 'You know we cannot risk it.'

She was quiet then, and I realized she was crying, the moonlight turning her tears to bright pearls upon her cheeks. I kissed them away, willing my own not to fall.

'Tomorrow, if things do not go as we have planned, I will have a ship ready at the abandoned harbour. I want you to take the handmaids there, Melantho. The crew will take you far away from here, wherever you wish to go.'

'I won't leave without you.'

'You may not have a choice.'

I shifted so I was leaning over her now, hands pressed on either side of her head, my curls spilling around us.

'Penelope. I am not leaving you.'

Instead of replying, she kissed me. I knew better than to take her silence as defeat, but I did not want to argue with her. Not tonight.

She reached up to toy with one of my ringlets, tenderly tucking it behind my ear, and I could scarcely breathe for how heavy my heart weighed in my chest.

If I had loved her less, this moment would not have hurt so much. This pain, I knew, was the price of loving her as I did, so completely, so irrevocably, and it was a price I would have willingly paid over and over.

'It has been my greatest privilege to love you, Melantho, and to be loved by you. I want you to know that.'

I pressed my hand to her lips, shaking my head. 'Don't. Please. Don't do that.'

Don't say goodbye.

'Melantho,' she whispered against my fingertips.

Despite the tears burning in my eyes, I smiled.

'Say that again,' I breathed.

'*Melantho, Melantho, Melantho . . .*'

My lips replaced my fingers, and Penelope continued to whisper my name into my mouth, over and over, like a promise, a prayer, a vow carved from the very depths of her.

And I knew nothing, in all the world, would ever sound sweeter than this: my name on her tongue, shared between lips in the dark.

58

Jewels glittered like the eyes of beasts drowning in a sea of gold.

The Queen of Ithaca stood beside her mountain of gifts, the one we had spent hours assembling the previous day. Now, Penelope regarded her treasures with a look of distinct disinterest. Before her, the suitors marvelled at their gifts, the cold, glimmering sign of their power. Soon to be the price of their lives.

I suppressed a smile, but the corners faded as soon as I caught sight of Odysseus lingering in the corner of the banquet hall. Still, he kept up his ridiculous disguise, scanning the room with a quiet, contemplative frown. Today, he planned to take back his throne. His confidence in his own ability was something to behold. Odysseus was near sixty summers old now, his body ravaged by the battlefield. Did he truly believe he could defeat a hundred men alone? Had the war so thoroughly inflated his ego? Or perhaps it had eaten away at his sense of reality.

'Are you all right?' Hippodamia whispered beside me. Her voice quivered; she was nervous. We all were.

'I'm fine,' I lied. 'I just want this to be over with.'

'Me too,' she admitted, her gaze drifting around the room. 'Do you . . . feel sorry for them? The suitors?'

'No,' I said without hesitating. 'I don't.'

She nodded, jaw set. 'Neither do I.'

We had both tended to the slaves the suitors had beaten, the crying girls they had forced themselves upon. There could be no sympathy for men like that.

Their deaths would be a weight lifted from this world.

Penelope turned from her treasures to face her suitors for the final time. They fell silent almost instantly. It was strange to think how powerful yet powerless Penelope was in their company; they hung on her every word, yet she was unable to free herself from a single one of them.

'As you know,' she began, her voice ringing clearly through the banquet hall, 'I have struggled for many summers to choose who amongst you is worthy of being my husband. As it has proven an impossible decision for me to make alone, I have decided to leave this matter in the hands of the Fates and hold a competition.'

Curious murmurs rippled through the room. I forced myself to keep a neutral expression as Penelope set her plan in motion, though anxiety had found its way into my veins now, making my blood sing a shrill note in my ears.

'The rules will be simple,' Penelope continued. 'Perhaps a few of you may have already discerned your objective.'

She motioned to the twelve axe heads in the centre of the room. They had been removed from their handles, the blades buried in a long wooden table in a neat line of twelve, so the butt of each axe head was pointed up to the ceiling. In the centre of every one was an ornamental hole, each lined up perfectly with the others. At the end of the long line stood a wooden target.

'All you must do is fire a single arrow through these twelve axe heads into the target,' Penelope said. 'I think it seems a fitting contest given today is the festival of Apollo, and this is a game my late husband was very fond of. My only condition is that you must use Odysseus' beloved weapon, in respect of his memory.'

She held aloft a long, slender bow and, across the room, I saw Odysseus' eyes gleam. What the suitors did not know was that this bow was notoriously difficult to string, such was its design. Odysseus had once claimed only he himself could manage it.

Penelope placed the bow down as she declared, 'Whoever is victorious first shall win my hand in marriage.'

Excitement electrified the air. In the far corner I saw Telemachus whisper something to Eumaeus. Beside them, Odysseus had finally torn his focus away from his bow to stare at Penelope, a small smile gracing his lips.

'Good luck and may bright Apollo shine upon you,' Penelope said, before turning to her son. 'Now, the prince and I shall retire whilst the competition takes place.'

'I am staying, Mother,' Telemachus said instantly.

'Telemachus—'

'Someone needs to adjudicate, to ensure no foul play occurs,' he continued. 'But you must depart to your quarters. I shall fetch you when the matter is concluded.'

Penelope held her son's gaze. She had told him that morning of the contest, claiming it was just another stalling tactic, nothing but a ploy to keep the suitors distracted. Telemachus had believed her and agreed not to interfere. His compliance had seemed too easy, but Penelope knew why. He had been plotting with his father, concocting a plan he did not realize Penelope had all but placed into their laps.

All the suitors locked in one room with a weapon only Odysseus could wield . . .

Did they believe it was the Fates that had engineered this opportunity? Was that truly more believable than the idea of a woman having a hand in their machinations?

Though Penelope had been expecting Telemachus' refusal, she could not hide the flicker of pain in her eyes as she stared at her son. She had known Telemachus would want to fight by his father's side. This was the moment he had been dreaming of his entire life, and he would never forgive Penelope, never forgive *himself*, if he were deprived of it.

Penelope nodded, her trembling hands closing into fists.

'Very well,' she said. 'I shall take my leave.'

I swore I could see her heart splintering as she turned and swept from the hall. The handmaids followed in her wake, and I trailed a step behind, throwing a final glance over my shoulder. Odysseus was still prowling in the corner of the room, smirking as the suitors squabbled over his bow. Beside him, Telemachus was absently picking at the skin around his nail beds. He looked so young in that moment, lost in the shadow of his father.

Please. I sent a silent prayer to any god who might listen. *Please watch over him.*

Then I turned and left, locking the doors behind me, knowing that when I next stepped foot in that hall, the fate of Ithaca would be sealed.

We raced back to Penelope's quarters.

It would not be long before the pirates descended upon the palace. Penelope had made her instructions clear, but those men were lawless killers. None of us wanted to run the risk of crossing their path, for who knew if they would keep to their word once bloodlust gripped them? It was a risk Penelope had accepted, but that had been before she knew her son and husband would be shut inside with those murderous men.

At least the palace hallways were empty. The slaves would all be at the market now, enjoying the festival celebrations. I had made sure Melanthius and Dolios were amongst them, safe and utterly clueless as to the bloodshed about to be unleashed within these walls.

'Do you think Telemachus will be all right?' Actoris whispered, a rare note of fear sounding in her voice.

I nodded with a certainty I did not truly feel. 'The pirates were instructed to only harm the suitors.'

'And he will have Odysseus at his side,' Hippodamia said, with a touch of awe I found irritating.

'We will pray to the Gods,' Eurynome added.

'I wish I could see it,' Skaris muttered. 'I wish I could watch those vultures bleed.'

'We remain in my chamber until it is over,' Penelope instructed. She had sealed her emotions in so tight, leaving her voice glassy and cold.

I reached for her hand, her palm clammy against mine.

'He will be all right,' I murmured.

She nodded, her eyes shimmering.

'Penelope,' Autonoë called from behind us. 'Weren't all the slaves dismissed?'

We halted, turning to where Autonoë was standing on the balcony overlooking the central courtyard.

'Yes. They were,' Penelope said.

I went to stand beside Autonoë, unease swelling inside me as I caught sight of a shadow rushing between the olive trees below.

Melanthius.

A strangled gasp escaped me.

'I have to go to him,' I said, turning to Penelope.

'No.' Her expression was so blank one could have thought her callous, unfeeling. But I knew her better than that.

'If he steps foot in that hall he could die.'

'As could you.'

'Penelope—'

'He's made his choice, Melantho. You know you cannot convince him otherwise.'

She was right, and a dark part of me knew this was all futile, that my brother was already lost. But what else was I to do? How could I live with myself if I walked away now? Even if my brother was beyond saving, I still had to try.

'I need to *warn* him,' I pressed. 'I can't just let him die like this.'

'And I cannot let you go.'

'Penelope—'

'*Please.*' The word cracked along with her composure. 'Stay with me.'

'I have to help him.'

'Why must it be *you?*'

'Because he has nobody else,' I whispered.

'I will go with her,' Skaris said, her hand warm on my shoulder. 'We will be careful.'

Penelope's eyes darted between us, the corners of her lips trembling, ready to form the word 'no'. But then she inhaled a slow, steadying breath and closed her eyes. When she opened them again, her expression was sharpened by a newfound focus.

'Be as quick as you can. If you see the pirates, you run. If you see a suitor, you run. If you see Odysseus, you run. Whatever you do, do not step a *single foot* inside that hall. Do you understand me? Do not go anywhere near it.'

Skaris nodded, before turning to me. 'Come, we must move.'

I went to follow her, but Penelope caught my wrist, pulling me abruptly into her arms. The embrace was too quick, too breathless, too tangled with emotions we could not let spill.

'Come back to me,' she whispered into my ear.

Before I could reply, she had released me and was already striding away.

Eurynome offered me a grave nod, whilst Hippodamia and Autonoë squeezed my hands before turning to follow Penelope.

'Don't do anything stupid,' Actoris warned me.

I smiled. 'Keep them safe, will you?'

My small, fierce friend nodded before running to catch up with the others.

'Did you see where your brother was heading?' Skaris asked once we were alone.

I nodded grimly. 'For the weapons stash.'

59

I had never seen my brother wield a sword before.

It disturbed me, how menacing the blade looked in his hand.

He stood in the shadowy storage room, a large sack slung over his shoulder, sword held out before him.

'What are you doing?' I asked as I moved to block the doorway beside Skaris.

'Did you really think me so stupid?' he shot back.

'Melanthius—'

'I know Penelope is up to something. Why else would she dismiss all of us?'

'A dismissal *you* should've listened to,' Skaris growled.

'And I saw you all yesterday, stealing the suitors' weapons. Hiding them away in here,' Melanthius continued, gesturing around himself. 'Telemachus is gonna try to kill them, isn't he? He's more of a fool than I thought.'

'It's out of our hands now,' I said as carefully as I could. 'We must leave the bloodshed to them, brother.'

'Don't you *see*? *This* is how I'll prove myself to Eurymachus. I'll bring him the blade that'll allow him to slay the prince once and for all.'

'Melanthius—'

'Join me, Mel.' His voice had a manic edge to it. 'Together we'll prove ourselves to Eurymachus. We'll finally be *free*.'

'You know I can't do that.'

His eyes flashed, face darkening. 'Then *move*.'

'I cannot do that either, brother.'

'You'd really do this? You'd stand in the way of my freedom?'

'You will find only death in that hall,' Skaris warned. 'Do not be a fool. Listen to your sister.'

Melanthius raised his blade. 'Move.'

I shook my head, unshed tears blurring my vision. 'I won't let you go in there.'

Gently, Skaris nudged me aside as she stepped towards my brother. 'Drop the weapons.'

'*I said move!*' He was shouting now, a frantic, desperate roar. '*Do as I say!*'

My fear was so crippling I could do nothing but watch, utterly frozen, as Skaris inched further into the storage room.

'Drop the weapons,' she repeated.

'*Move, now! I mean it!*'

Still, Skaris pushed closer, hands held out placatingly. 'Drop them. It will be all right, friend. You have my word.'

Melanthius' gaze shifted to mine, and I saw the guilt pressing behind his eyes as he let the sack of weapons fall to the floor in a heavy, defeated clatter.

'I'm sorry,' he whispered. 'Forgive me.'

It happened so fast; one moment he was standing before us, the next his blade was slashing open Skaris' thigh. A furious howl of pain ripped from her throat as she fell to the ground. I dropped to my knees beside her, placing my hands over the wound as hot blood throbbed between my fingers.

'*What did you do?*' I screamed at Melanthius.

He blinked, the sword quivering in his hands.

'This is *your fault*,' he cried. 'I didn't want this. I tried to make you understand. I didn't—'

'You need to help me stop the bleeding.'

Melanthius shook his head, the strained whites of his eyes glinting in the light, shot through with veins of red.

'Melanthius!' I shouted, but he was already shoving past us, the weapons sack slung over his shoulder as he sprinted towards the banquet hall.

I called his name again, a ravaged, desperate cry, but it was no use. He was already gone.

Skaris gripped my arm. 'You must stop him.'

'I can't leave you like this.'

'This? This is nothing. A scratch.' Her laugh was frayed, sweat dripping down her temples. 'You must go.'

'Skaris—'

'You cannot let him arm them.'

'But your leg—'

She grabbed my face. '*Telemachus will die, Melantho.*'

A sickening clarity shot through me.

'I'll come back,' I promised as I rose. 'Just stay hidden, all right?'

'You waste time! Go, *now*!'

Turning away from my bleeding friend, I willed my guilt to fuel me as I broke into a sprint. I darted across the courtyard, careening down the passageway where my brother had just disappeared. My sandals clattered frantically against stone as I pushed myself *faster, faster,* my muscles screaming in protest, each breath a blade in my lungs.

Then, I heard them. The screams.

The bloodshed had begun.

I glimpsed Melanthius just ahead.

He was faster than me, but the sack of weapons had slowed his pace considerably. More cries lifted, the echo of violence ringing through the passageway, ricocheting off the walls in a hideous cacophony of screams. Somewhere, distantly in my mind, I heard Penelope's voice – *Do not step a* single foot *inside that hall.*

But Skaris was right: if the suitors were armed, it would change everything. Telemachus could die. Odysseus could die. And then what would become of us?

Melanthius was at the door to the banquet hall now. I hurled myself at him, but he shoved me aside with ruthless force.

'Walk away, Melantho.' It sounded more like a plea than a threat.

The tip of his blade was poised against my heart, so I could do nothing but watch as he heaved the latch off the doors and pushed them open.

For a moment, Melanthius and I simply gaped at the nightmarish scene before us.

Bodies were strewn across the floor, arrows protruding from their skulls and throats. In the centre of the room, Odysseus was standing on a table, his bare body drenched in blood as he fired arrow upon arrow into the horde of panicked suitors around him. Telemachus and Eumaeus fought at his side, slicing down men with the swords they must have smuggled into the hall. But, even unarmed, there were clearly too many suitors. They swarmed the three of them like a mighty, crashing wave, threatening to drown father, son and slave in their violent current.

The sound of the doors opening had caught Odysseus' attention and he now stared at my brother and me, his eyes narrowing on the sack slung over Melanthius' shoulder. He then shouted something to Telemachus, though I could not hear his command over the hideous din.

Melanthius' face was pale as he beheld Odysseus standing before him. He had thought the king long dead. But here he was, looking like some vengeful god in mortal form, enacting his brutal judgement upon the world.

'It's him,' Melanthius whispered, letting the weapons fall to the floor, blades spilling out of the sack. 'It's really him.'

The suitors had noticed us now and they surged forward, frantically reaching for the scattered swords. Once they were armed, Odysseus, Telemachus and Eumaeus would stand no chance.

They would be like lambs to the slaughter.

Across the carnage, my gaze clashed into Telemachus'. His face was filled with such panicked confusion, eyes widening as he regarded the weapons at my feet. I wanted to call out to him, *It isn't what it looks like* . . .

But what use were such excuses? I had failed to protect Telemachus, failed to stop my brother.

And now, we would all die because of it.

The Prince of Ithaca straightened his spine, readying himself to face his final moments with courage, to fight to the bitter end. He looked so like his mother in that moment – a brave, stoic leader.

But then a noise sounded from behind me, an ominous rumble of thunderous feet, followed by a torrent of masked figures pouring through the doorway, whooping with fierce delight as they shoved Melanthius and me aside.

Penelope's pirates.

They had come.

I staggered to the sidelines as the pirates collided with the now-armed suitors. The clash of metal made my very bones quake, yet my body felt shackled to the ground, paralysed by fear. Everywhere I looked, blood sprayed in violent arcs of crimson as stomachs and throats were sliced open. I sensed death's cold hand brush over me as it reached to pluck the souls of fallen men, and I knew, with a gasping lucidity, that if I did not move, I would surely join them in the realm below.

I looked to the doorway, which was now completely blocked by clashing bodies. The only way out was to run directly *into* the fighting.

Come back to me.

It was Penelope's voice that spurred my feet forward, forcing me into the fray.

The chaos swallowed me in one brutal bite. It was like jumping into a raging sea, having the currents toss me this way and that, spinning me over until the sky and Earth bled into one disorientating blur.

It was all so *loud*: the smashing swords, the roar of attackers, the cries as men fell around me. I wanted to cover my ears, wanted to scream, but all I could do was keep moving towards the doorway, towards safety.

Towards Penelope.

A suitor stumbled into me, blocking my path. He held my gaze for a beat, a brush of recognition filling his eyes before a blade emerged between them. Hot blood sprayed across my face, and I choked on a silent cry as his body crumpled, revealing a grinning pirate behind him.

'You look lost, little mouse,' the pirate chuckled.

I veered sideways, colliding with another body. The force knocked me to the ground, sending me sprawling across a suitor's lifeless corpse, his flesh still warm with the life so recently taken from him. I tried to push myself upright, but a foot landed on my back, then another on my arm, and a third narrowly missed my skull.

Frantically, I began scrambling on my hands and knees, but something caught my gown, tugging me backwards. Turning, I found myself staring into the cruel face of Antinous, an arrow protruding from his neck. He gripped my gown tighter, his mouth opening as he tried to speak, but only blood escaped his lips. His eyes were more alive than I had ever seen them, and he looked so much younger, just a boy terrified of dying alone.

I ripped free from his grasp and continued crawling forward.

An upturned table was the only shelter I could find. I threw myself behind it, gulping down fractured breaths as I watched the pirates and suitors continue their brutal dance of metal and blood. My heart was a wild, panicked beast in my chest, my body drenched in sweat, every inch humming with a sickeningly fierce adrenaline.

Come back to me.

I had to keep moving.

Rolling on to the balls of my feet, I readied myself to make another desperate dash for the door. But then I saw him, just beyond my hiding spot, skimming the fringes of the battle as he desperately searched the bodies of fallen suitors. Melanthius.

I was not the only one who had noticed him.

Eumaeus was pointing his sword in Melanthius' direction, whilst Odysseus drew back his bow, setting my brother in his sights.

'*Melanthius!*' I screamed, hurling myself at him.

We tumbled sideways as Odysseus' arrow sliced across the floor, mere inches from my brother's head.

'Run!' I shouted, tugging Melanthius to his feet.

'But the suitors—'

'They have already lost! *Look* at them!'

All the colour drained from my brother's face as he regarded the massacre around us and the man reigning over it – the bloody, vengeful King of Ithaca. Fear sank its teeth into Melanthius, and he stared at me with helpless eyes.

'He's going to kill me,' he whispered.

The bodies still on their feet were thinning out now, finally clearing our escape path. I grabbed Melanthius' hand, hauling him across the banquet hall and through the open doors.

'Who were those men?' Melanthius gasped as we sprinted down the hallway. 'Are they Odysseus' men?'

'I don't know,' I lied.

As we came to a fork in the passageway, Melanthius drew to a sudden stop.

'Take the right,' he said. 'I'll go left.'

'*What?*'

'He's going to kill me, Melantho. If you stay with me, he'll kill you too.'

Before I could argue, Melanthius' head snapped up, eyes widening.

'Eurymachus!' he cried out, rushing down the passageway to where a figure was half slumped against the wall.

Eurymachus was clutching his throat with both hands, blood spilling down his chest, dripping in a thick trail behind him. With difficulty, he turned, eyes widening as he regarded us. It was then that I saw the extent of his injury – an arrow had punctured his throat, the broken end protruding from the wound.

He tried to speak, but all that escaped him was a wet choking sound.

'What can I do? Tell me what to do.' I hated the desperation in Melanthius' voice.

Eurymachus lowered his bulging eyes to the sword in my brother's hands. Melanthius followed his gaze.

'I need this,' he said tightly. 'And you can't wield it, not like that.'

Without warning, Eurymachus slammed himself into Melanthius, knocking him against the wall with surprising force given his dire state. My brother flailed backwards, head cracking against stone, sword tumbling free from his grasp.

Eurymachus lunged for the weapon but slipped on his own blood, landing heavily on his knees.

'I was helping you!' Melanthius shouted at him, blood now spilling from a wound on his head. I heard a sob swell in his throat as he repeated, '*I was helping you.*'

Eurymachus gulped down wet, laboured breaths. He then used the last of his energy to spit blood at my brother's feet. He could only manage to gargle out a single word: '*Slave.*'

I strode towards Eurymachus, every single thought lost to the blinding wave of fury crashing over me. The pathetic man did not even have the strength to stand, and I savoured the sight of him kneeling before me, struggling for breath. Eurymachus' eyes lifted to mine, and I saw such boundless hatred rotting within them.

I planted my foot on his chest and kicked him to the ground.

'Melantho—'

I ignored my brother's gasp as I bent down and closed my hand around the arrow jutting out from Eurymachus' throat. He tried to stop me, but the fight had leaked from his body along with his lifeblood.

'Look at me,' I commanded. 'I want you to know that *this* will be the last face you see in this world. The face of a woman. The face of a slave.'

With that, I ripped the arrow free.

Hot blood spurted over me as Eurymachus spasmed on the floor, his eyes locked on to mine as he gulped for air that would not come.

As I watched him die, I felt nothing, just the residue of that blinding rage simmering in my veins.

Once his body was still, I turned to my brother. Before either of us could think what to say, footsteps sounded down the hall, and I turned to see Eumaeus sprinting towards us, determination hardening his features into something cold and unrecognizable.

'Melanthius, we must go. Now,' I hissed.

But my brother would not move. He remained slumped against the wall, such abject defeat weighing on him as he stared at Eurymachus' lifeless body.

'*Melanthius!* We have to go!'

But it was too late. Eumaeus was already beside us, blade poised at my brother's throat.

'You must face your king and answer for your crimes,' he commanded. 'Both of you.'

'Not her,' Melanthius murmured. 'Take me, but let her go. She had no part in this.'

'The king will be the judge of that,' Eumaeus snapped, forcing him to his feet. 'He will decide all our fates.'

60

The King of Ithaca was dressed in nothing but the blood of his enemies.

He paced before us, indifferent to the corpses strewn at his feet, heavy steps fuelled by an agitated energy.

I did not pity the suitors; they had deserved to die. Yet, as Eumaeus marched us towards Odysseus, it brought a chill to my bones seeing all those bodies littered throughout the banquet hall, piled in hideous mounds of twisted flesh.

'Master, I have the traitors here,' Eumaeus called out.

Odysseus raised a halting hand, turning instead to where Telemachus approached him. My heart lifted to see the prince, alive and unharmed. He was handing Odysseus a robe, his emotions sealed tightly behind a blank stare.

'What did you just say to me?' Odysseus growled as he dressed.

'I said we'll take our payment now.' I recognized the voice behind the mask, the soft roughness that toyed with every syllable. The pirate was lounging against a table, fingering one of the twelve axe heads.

'Payment?' Odysseus bit out.

'We helped with your little rat problem, didn't we?' the pirate drawled, motioning to the bodies around him.

'I did not ask for nor need your help,' Odysseus retorted, the tendons in his neck bulging. 'You cannot invade my palace and expect payment for such a crime. You are fortunate I am letting you leave here with your lives.'

I held a breath tight in my lungs, panic rising on a tide of nausea.

If they exposed Penelope now . . .

'We expect our payment, one way or another,' the pirate said, lazily wiping his bloodied blade on the body of a suitor. He then nodded to the pile of Penelope's gifts. 'That'll do nicely.'

'*That* belongs to my wife,' Odysseus said.

'I don't think she'll mind,' the pirate chuckled. 'Come on, now. Let's not make this difficult. I'm sure you don't want to die before you're reunited with your lovely little wife. She's been waiting so *very long* to see you.'

Odysseus stiffened, dignity and self-preservation waging war across his crimson-stained face. He eyed the pirates surrounding him, all still armed. These men were nothing like the pampered suitors, spoilt nobles who were better at wielding a wine cup than a blade. No, these were trained killers, men to whom death was an old friend.

And this was not a battle the King of Ithaca could win.

I felt my heart jump into my mouth, pulsing wildly against my tongue as we awaited Odysseus' reply. Slowly, the King of Ithaca turned to look at his son, his scowl fading into a sigh.

'Make it quick,' he muttered to the pirate.

'It'll be as if we were never here.'

Odysseus glowered at the man, hands flexing at his sides. 'You *were* never here. You never stepped foot in my palace; your ship never tainted Ithaca's waters. Understood?'

I could hear the smile in the pirate's voice as he echoed, 'Understood.'

Whilst he sauntered away, Odysseus turned and pointed at my brother. 'Bring him here.'

Eumaeus obediently dragged Melanthius to Odysseus' feet, forcing him down on to his knees. Odysseus surveyed my brother for a long moment, the whites of his eyes stark against all that blood.

'I remember you,' he said, the words soft with something almost like nostalgia. 'The goatherd who came from Sparta.'

My brother said nothing. Beyond him, the pirates were hauling their treasure away, indifferent to the rest of us.

Odysseus continued his pacing, but when his foot struck a corpse, he froze. He stared down at the mangled body before him with a horrified sort of fascination, and I noticed his hands had begun trembling. He balled them quickly into fists, turning away as he snapped at my brother, 'I need time to think what to do with you.'

'Just kill me like the rest of them,' Melanthius whispered to the ground.

No. I stepped forward, but Eumaeus blocked my path.

'He has brought this upon himself,' he murmured to me, almost apologetically. 'This is the will of the Gods, Melantho. You must let it be.'

'*Fuck your gods,*' I snarled.

'You wish to die like them?' Odysseus asked Melanthius, motioning to the corpses stacked around us. 'You do not *deserve* their death. They were vile creatures, yes, but they were not indebted to me. They saw an opportunity and they took it, *abused* it. For that, I took their lives. But *you*, slave – I took you into *my* home, into *my* family. I gave you shelter and food. I gave you good, honest work. I treated you with respect, and this . . . *this* is how you repay me? You conspire with my enemies beneath my *own* roof?'

'I only—'

'*I did not give you permission to speak!*' Odysseus roared, spittle flying from his lips, veins throbbing at his temples. 'This is *my* house. This is MY HOME.'

Melanthius let his head hang.

'And *you*.' Odysseus turned his blistering glare on to me. 'Did you think I had forgotten our deal? I warned you of the consequences.'

'Please.' Melanthius threw himself forward, clutching Odysseus' ankles. 'Punish me. I'm guilty. I helped the suitors. I brought them the weapons to kill your son. It's true. But my sister is innocent. She tried to stop me. I swear it on the river Styx. Do what you must with me, but please let her go. I beg you.'

'It's true, Father.' Telemachus stepped forward, voice loud yet trembling. 'Melantho is a good woman. I can attest to that. She is innocent.'

'*Innocent*,' Odysseus spat, his glare still fixed on me. 'Tell me, was it your *innocence* that had you whispering secrets to the suitors whilst you spread your legs for them? Oh yes, Eurycleia has informed me about your *liaisons*.'

I felt the rage sear through me. *That old, evil witch...*

'It's not true, Father!' Telemachus protested. 'Melantho would never ally herself with their kind. Tell him, Melantho. Tell him it isn't true.'

'It's not,' I insisted.

'So, you never shared Eurymachus' bed?' Odysseus pressed. 'You never told him of my wife's ploys?'

'Father, she would *never*.'

Odysseus turned to his son. 'Have you ever known Eurycleia to lie?'

Telemachus hesitated, meeting my gaze. 'But you wouldn't... would you...?'

'I... I didn't mean... It was...' My voice was brittle, breaking into useless shards that lodged in my throat.

Telemachus looked as if I had struck him. '*Melantho?*'

'I was protecting you,' I tried. 'Please, let me explain—'

'Do you see the lies she spins? You saw her yourself, bringing weapons to arm the suitors against us. She is as guilty as they are.'

The prince's lips trembled, then hardened into a firm line as he met his father's gaze. 'What will you do with her?'

'I will decide her fate in due course,' Odysseus said. 'But first, we must purge these halls of this bloodshed before the Gods take offence. Eumaeus, take the goatherd away and keep watch over him.'

Eumaeus bowed low. 'Yes, master.'

'Telemachus, find Eurycleia,' Odysseus ordered. 'Tell her to bring me the rest of the queen's handmaids.'

My hands were blistered and raw from scrubbing away all evidence of Odysseus' massacre.

Around me, my friends worked in fearful silence. When Eurycleia led them into the hall, I had seen the horror carve open their faces as they beheld the gruesome scene.

'Clean,' Odysseus had instructed us.

So, we cleaned.

As others came in to drag the bodies away, we got down on to our hands and knees and scrubbed at the gory mess, and scrubbed and scrubbed and scrubbed, all whilst Odysseus prowled around us.

Time lost all meaning. We could have been cleaning for hours or days, yet the blood never seemed to lessen. It was everywhere – on my clothes, my skin. I swore I could even *taste* it: that thick, metallic tang...

'What *happened*?' Hippodamia breathed beside me. 'We were so worried about you.'

I met her gaze and felt her fear spark against mine. I couldn't think what to say to her, how to explain.

My attention drifted to the others. Autonoë was choking on the stench of death, whilst Actoris stole worried glances at Skaris. Her wound had been bound but it was clearly still troubling her. Even poor Eurynome had been forced to work on her knees, her movements painfully stiff.

Autonoë tossed another bucket of water across the floor. The King of Ithaca halted mid-stride and stared at the bloodied river pooling around his feet. I swore I saw him shiver.

'Melantho?' Hippodamia brushed my arm.

'Where is Penelope?' I asked.

'Eurycleia locked her in her rooms. She said it was under the king's instruction. He wanted this mess cleared before she sees it.' Hippodamia fell silent as Odysseus stalked past. Once he was a safe distance away, she continued, 'Penelope nearly lost her mind when you did not return. If she hadn't been distracted with tending to Skaris' leg, she would've come after you.'

Come back to me. Her voice ached in my mind – a torturous plea.

'I'm sorry,' I murmured.

'Don't be.' Hippodamia reached for my hand, a hesitant smile lifting her lips. 'It's done. It's over now.'

My gaze snapped back to Odysseus, to those menacing, restless strides. 'It's not over,' I whispered. 'Not yet.'

61

Night had fallen by the time we finished.

I stood beside my friends as Odysseus surveyed the spotless room, my muscles aching fiercely. I drew in a slow breath, the stench of blood and death permanently scalded into my nostrils.

I could feel the same suffocating exhaustion weighing down the others as we awaited Odysseus' assessment of our work. We all longed to return to our quarters, to bathe and sleep and escape this nightmare. But there was still that look in Odysseus' eyes, that agitated hunger.

I knew his vengeance was not satiated, not yet.

Telemachus lurked in the corner of the room, his face ashen. He had been quiet ever since Eumaeus had dragged my brother away, as if the reality of this day had finally come crashing down upon him. He had never killed a person before, and now so many souls stained his hands.

Odysseus did not seem to notice his son's unease. Or perhaps he chose not to.

'At least your cleaning skills are still exemplary,' Odysseus said. He then walked down our line and stopped before Actoris, his thick frame towering over her. 'You. Follow.'

Panic stole my breath as I watched Actoris hesitate. She glanced to Telemachus, who gave her a subtle nod. Then, lifting her chin a little higher, she followed the King of Ithaca out of the door. Moments later, he returned, this time beckoning Skaris to follow. Odysseus continued in this way until I was the last left in the hall.

'Where is he taking us?' I asked Telemachus once we were alone. He remained pointedly silent. 'I did not betray you, Telemachus. You must know that.'

'So, Eurycleia lied about what she saw?' he asked quietly.

'You don't understand—'

'No. Clearly I do not.'

'Everything I did was to protect you, to protect your mother. I was *never* on their side; you must know that. I *pretended* to ally myself with them for information.'

The Prince of Ithaca met my gaze for a silent beat, then looked away. I wanted to storm over and shake some sense into him, but Odysseus appeared in the doorway, summoning me with a large, open hand.

Numbly, I followed the king as he led me to the courtyard, flanked by Telemachus. We walked in silence towards the large oak tree at the centre of the square. Darkness had crept over the palace now, and it took a moment for my eyes to adjust, to realize what hung from that tree.

Six nooses.

I froze, my eyes darting to the handmaids – my friends, my sisters – who were standing side by side with rope around their throats. Even in the blackness, I could make out the bruising on Actoris' and Skaris' faces. Clearly, they had put up a fight, but now the two of them stood bound and gagged, with Eumaeus beside them, his sword held in silent warning.

'Move,' Odysseus commanded me.

'You can't do this,' I choked out.

Odysseus ignored me, grabbing my arm and hauling me towards the final noose. I battled against him, but he was unnervingly strong, forcing the rope around my throat with ease.

'Father!' Telemachus shouted, following behind us. 'What are you doing? What is this?'

'*Justice.*' Odysseus snarled the word.

'These women are innocent!'

'*Innocent?* They spread their legs for our enemies. They conspired to have *you* killed. They dishonoured their queen. And you call them *innocent?*'

Telemachus froze, trembling hands clenching into fists at his sides. 'You're wrong, Father.'

Odysseus released me to turn towards his son, blade lifted. '*What did you say?*'

Telemachus held up his hands. 'Father, f-forgive me. But these women raised me. I know them. They are innocent. I swear it.'

'They have manipulated you,' Odysseus spat, lowering his sword. 'Eurycleia has told me all I need to know.'

Rage scorched my insides, but it was quickly chased by a rush of fear as Odysseus forced my hands behind my back. Beside me, I held the eyes of Autonoë, tears streaming down her scarred cheeks.

'It'll be all right,' she whispered to me.

We both knew it was a lie.

'Get the rope. Bind her hands like the others,' Odysseus ordered.

'Father—'

'Are you my son, or are you a coward? Bind her.'

Telemachus stared at Odysseus: the man he had idolized his entire life; the legend he so desperately wished to live up to; the father he had always longed to impress. Then, he turned to look at us: the women who had raised him, who were always by his side, who had loved him since he had been just a babe in his mother's arms.

The Prince of Ithaca swallowed, then picked up the rope and walked towards me. He could not meet my gaze as he began binding my wrists.

'Go and get your mother,' I breathed. 'She will stop this.'

He glanced at me, his eyes like two gaping wounds, glistening and raw.

'This is all I can do,' he murmured, before turning away.

Helplessly, I looked to where Autonoë and Hippodamia quietly wept. To Eurynome holding her head proudly despite her shivering body. To bloody and bruised Actoris furiously trying to rip herself free from her bindings. To Skaris, who seemed a little woozy with blood loss, Eumaeus' blade angled at her throat.

'You know this is wrong,' I shouted at Eumaeus.

'Do not speak to me of *wrong*,' he retorted, his voice lit with purpose, blazing like a funeral pyre. 'You betrayed our queen, our prince, our king. You betrayed *all* of Ithaca. This is the justice my master calls for, the *Gods* call for, and I shall abide by it.'

'Do you see? *That* is what it means to be a true servant of this household. Loyalty, above all else,' Odysseus declared. 'Now, the Gods shall see you answer for your crimes.'

'Penelope would not want this!' My words sounded hoarse, roughened by the noose biting at my throat.

The King of Ithaca turned slowly then stalked towards me. He stopped inches away from my face, and, beneath the pale gaze of the moon, I noticed how bruised his eyes were, the skin puffy and drooping, as if he had not slept in days. Longer, perhaps.

The blood on his face had started to dry, gathering in the deep creases bracketing his features, emphasizing every groove. He looked so old, his face beaten down to a gnarled husk of the man I had once known.

This was Ithaca's beloved king, whom they had waited two decades for. Their *salvation*.

But I saw no salvation in his eyes, only death.

'What did you say?' he asked, his voice lethally soft.

I leant as far forward as the rope would allow.

'Penelope would not want this,' I repeated.

As I held his glare, I realized there was more than just death written in those sharp eyes of his. Something else lurked there too, something dangerously delicate. He reminded me of a cornered beast – lost and frantic, perhaps even afraid.

Odysseus mirrored my movement, leaning in so close our lips were almost touching.

'And what would *you* know of what *my* wife wants?'

So many retorts danced on my tongue, begging to be flung into his bloodied face. But I bit the truth back, grinding it between my teeth.

'Ask her yourself,' I said. 'Bring her here. See what she thinks of your *justice*.'

'You have put my wife through enough. You will not trouble her a moment more.'

I turned to Telemachus, panic seeping into my voice. 'You know your mother would not want this. *Please. Do something*.'

'Do you see how their kind speak to us when they are not kept in check? There is no respect here.' Odysseus threw his arm around Telemachus, making him flinch. 'Son, it is time I show you how a true king handles his household.'

I could feel the shadow of death creeping into the courtyard then, leeching all warmth from the air. Time seemed to thicken and slow, seconds trudging past as if they were minutes, hours.

Come back to me.

Odysseus was saying something to Telemachus, and the prince bowed his head and turned to leave. But before he walked away, Telemachus' eyes flickered to mine. Over the years, I had read a million silent messages through Penelope's eyes, and I saw that same look in Telemachus' gaze now, willing me to understand.

This is all I can do. His words came back to me, and it was in that moment I realized . . . my bindings were loose. With just a little force, I would be able to free my hands.

But if I freed myself, what then? I knew I wouldn't have time to untie the others, nor could I leave them there to die. What if I somehow lured Odysseus away? If I provoked him into giving chase to me, could that allow the others a chance to escape?

This fragile burst of hope was quickly eclipsed by the sight of Telemachus dragging a naked, bound slave into the courtyard and placing him at Odysseus' feet.

My brother.

I began desperately pulling my wrists from their bindings, but panic made my hands clumsy as the King of Ithaca stared down at Melanthius.

'If you were a better man, I would give you a speech. I would speak of loyalty and honour and the price of each. But . . .' Odysseus tilted his head to the side, a slow, menacing movement. 'You are not worthy of such words.'

With that, he bent towards Melanthius, yanking back his head. My brother's eyes collided with mine and I froze.

I could not think. Could not breathe.

'Nor are you worthy of a dignified death,' Odysseus said. 'You chose to live in dishonour, and so shall you die in her humiliating embrace.'

With a grim smile, the King of Ithaca took his dagger to Melanthius' face and carved off his nose.

The world tilted beneath me, my knees crumpling, making the noose pull tighter around my throat, choking back my screams.

Then Odysseus took the blade to my brother's ears.

'Don't look,' Autonoë gasped beside me. '*Look away, Melantho.*'

But I could not.

I could do nothing but watch as Melanthius began crawling on his stomach, desperate to get away, whilst Odysseus calmly discarded his dagger for his sword. With unhurried steps, the King of Ithaca kept pace with Melanthius, then kicked him on to his side before bringing his blade down on to his bound wrists, then his ankles, striking again and again until each hand and foot was hacked clean off. Lastly, he took his blade to my brother's groin, and only then did I look away.

'Wait until he's dead, then hang the others,' Odysseus instructed, sword clattering to the ground.

'Should we not kill him now?' Telemachus asked weakly.

Odysseus' eyes were utterly empty as he turned to his son. 'No. Let him bleed. Let him suffer. Then feed the pieces to the dogs.'

A scream ripped from my throat as I finally wrenched my hands free, tugging the noose over my head. I ran to my brother, falling to my knees, desperate sobs cleaving my chest as I stared down at his mutilated body. He was still breathing, too-thin breaths, each one sounding more painful than the last. Around us, the pieces of him were strewn across the ground – his hands, his feet, and other parts I could not bear to look at.

The acidic tang of vomit crawled up my throat.

'Melanthius.' I wept, cradling him to me. 'I'm here, Melanthius.'

His eyes were glassy, his face, so like my own, now barely recognizable. He tried to say something, but no sound escaped, just a steady river of blood pooling into his mouth from the hole where his nose had been.

'It's all right. Don't speak,' I told him.

But still he tried, eventually managing a small, choked word: '*Forgive—*'

'Shh. Don't talk. Just rest, Melanthius.'

'*Forgive . . . me . . .*'

'It's all right,' I whispered, desperate for his final moment not to be one of shame or guilt. 'There is nothing to forgive.'

I glanced up to see Odysseus watching us, his expression eerily distant, hands trembling at his sides. Next to him, Telemachus looked as if he were fighting back tears. The prince met my gaze and a memory cut through the chaos of my grief.

'Your child, Melanthius. Your daughter. I never told you her name.'

My brother's breaths were growing fainter now, but I saw his eyes slightly flare with recognition.

'Your daughter,' I repeated, forcing my voice to steady itself. 'Her name is Alcippe, and she serves as the handmaid of Queen Helen. She is a beautiful girl, with curly hair like ours.'

'Alcippe,' he murmured.

'That's right. She's your daughter.' My tears splashed on to his ruined face. 'Your beautiful little girl. She *lives*, Melanthius. She *lives*.'

'*Alcippe.*' Her name escaped him in a final, sighing breath as his eyes slowly dulled, his body growing slack beneath me.

I stared at my brother, scarcely able to comprehend the sight of him, so lifeless in my arms. My brother, who had only ever wanted a better life for his child, yet the world had denied him at every turn, had punished him so cruelly.

I bowed my head, whispering two trembling words as I closed his eyes for ever. '*Be free.*'

Slowly, I looked to Odysseus, and the hatred in my glare seemed to knock him back into his body, throwing the king into motion.

'Do you think I wished for this? Do you think I wished for *any* of this?' he was shouting now as he stalked towards me, hands still shaking. 'Was I not a benevolent king? Did I not treat you with compassion? All I asked for was your loyalty. Your respect. Still, you chose to defy me.'

A wild cacophony of fury and grief ripped through me as I spat at his feet.

'You will *never* have my respect. You who abandoned your throne, your wife, your child, your home, wasting twenty years feeding your own ego. You who returned to these shores without a single one of your soldiers, men you swore to lead, to *protect*. You who calls slaughtering innocents "justice". Where is the glory in that? Where is the honour? You are no hero. *You are a disgrace. You are*—'

Odysseus lunged for me, rage devouring his features. His fingers caught my hair, wrenching my head back.

'You know *nothing* of what I have done, what I have *suffered*.'

'I pray that suffering never ends,' I snarled back. 'I pray you never know peace.'

He laughed viciously. '*Peace?* She abandoned me *long* ago.'

'I hope you rot—'

'*Enough!*' His hands were at my throat and a horrible pressure swelled inside my head, so intense I thought my skull might explode from the force of it.

I kicked and thrashed beneath him, trying to gulp down breaths that would not come. Panic shuddered through me, growing hazier with every jerk of my body. I could hear familiar voices screaming my name, but they were frighteningly faint . . . the world shrinking away . . . darkness bleeding outwards . . .

And I couldn't breathe.

I couldn't . . .

I . . .

Come back to me.

Penelope. Her name was a shimmering thread, tying me to this body, this world.

She would not let me go.

Come back to me.

I wanted to. Oh Gods, I wanted to.

I didn't want to leave her.

I didn't want to die.

But I couldn't find my way back. Everything was too murky, melting into a sea of hazy, thick shadow . . . and I was sinking . . . sinking . . .

Until I heard it. A scream.

It ripped through the darkness, through my mind, my very soul.

Her scream.

Then . . . air. Sweet, precious air filled my lungs. I gulped it down desperately, my throat feeling as if it were being carved open with blades of fire.

Slowly, the world seeped back into focus, those shadowy waves receding to the edges of my vision.

'Penelope?' a voice murmured.

Her name was no longer a thread but a bolt of pure lightning in my veins, forcing the life back into my body. I pushed myself to my knees and saw a figure standing before me, etched in silvery moonlight, hair billowing on a midnight breeze.

Penelope.

I tried to call her name, but only a hoarse gasp escaped me. Her grey eyes cradled mine, shimmering with shards of love and pain and rage.

I reached for her, and she moved towards me. But then a shadow fell between us, blocking her path.

'Penelope,' Odysseus repeated, softer now.

'What is going on here?' she demanded.

'You are not supposed to be here,' he said. 'This is no place for a woman.'

She dared a step forward, moving back into my line of vision. 'What are you doing to my handmaids?'

'You must leave.'

'I demand an explanation.'

'I will not ask you again,' Odysseus warned, a dangerous edge creeping into his voice. 'I will explain everything in time.'

A silent war was waged across Penelope's face as her gaze swept around the courtyard, from Melanthius' motionless body, to our weeping friends, to her trembling son. Finally, those grey eyes settled on me.

I'm sorry, they seemed to say. *Forgive me for this.*

'Odysseus?' Penelope suddenly gasped, turning to peer at him through the gloom. 'Is . . . is that really you?'

A peculiar timidity crept over the King of Ithaca then, seeming so out of place on his bloodied, brutal body.

'I . . . I did not wish for our reunion to be like this,' he muttered, glancing away.

Penelope's hand flew to her mouth, and, with a dramatically feminine flourish, she crumpled to the ground. But Odysseus was there to catch her, and I could do nothing but watch as that monster cradled my whole heart in his murderous hands.

'It *is* you,' Penelope whispered, reaching up to touch his face. She spoke in a voice that was not her own, soft and cloying. 'Odysseus. My Odysseus.'

'It is me,' he murmured, holding her tight. 'I am here, Penelope.'

He leant in then, perhaps to kiss her, but Penelope turned her face away.

'I feel unwell.' She pressed the back of her hand to her forehead. 'This . . . this is all too much.'

'You must go to your rooms,' Odysseus agreed. 'I will fetch Eurycleia—'

'I do not think I can walk.' She gripped him tighter. 'Will you carry me to our chamber?'

'I have matters to attend to here.'

'Let Telemachus handle them.' Penelope stared at her son. 'He knows what he must do.'

Odysseus looked reluctant. 'Penelope—'

'*Please.*' She stroked his face with such tenderness.

I wanted to scream or vomit, yet all I could do was stare dumbly at them, gulping down breaths into my ruined throat.

'Take me to our marriage bed – the one you made for us,' Penelope whispered. 'Please, husband.'

This request seemed to strike Odysseus like a blow, causing his face to crumple. He began to cry then, tears streaking clear paths down his bloodied cheeks as he lifted Penelope into his arms. He carried her so gently, with hands capable of such violence.

'I tried to return to you sooner. I am sorry, I—'

'Let us not talk of this here,' Penelope murmured.

Odysseus nodded, then looked to Telemachus. 'Hang the slaves then burn the bodies. I want nothing left of them.'

Telemachus nodded. 'Yes, Father.'

Penelope's eyes reached for mine, our hearts shattering against one another's as the King of Ithaca carried his wife away.

62

I held Melanthius in my arms as his body grew cold.

I could not cry for him. I was beyond tears now, in some weightless, liminal space where emotions hung suspended within that crushing darkness of grief.

'Eumaeus, leave us,' I heard Telemachus say.

'Master, are you quite sure?'

'*Do not question me!*' the Prince of Ithaca roared. He sounded like his father. 'I said leave! *Now!*'

There was a brief silence, then the shuffling of steps which slowly faded.

Wordlessly, the Prince of Ithaca walked forward and picked up the sword his father had discarded. I tensed as I stared at the boy I had helped to raise, the boy I loved as my own flesh and blood, the boy who was made from the person I cared for most in this world.

'Are you going to kill me now, prince?' I muttered.

Telemachus stared at the blade as if he were still deciding. Then he stormed towards Actoris and sliced her bindings.

'Help me free the others,' he commanded. 'Quickly.'

Actoris spat out the rag Odysseus had used to gag her, then turned on Telemachus, her eyes filled with such hatred they made the prince flinch.

'You would've let us *die*,' she snarled. 'You snivelling, spineless *coward*.'

'Please,' Telemachus whispered thickly. 'We don't have much time.'

Without saying another word, Actoris shoved past him and began untying Skaris.

I knew I should help; we might only have a few precious moments before Odysseus returned. But I could not bring myself to leave Melanthius alone with only the severed pieces of himself as company.

'Melantho.' A frayed voice came from beside me. A hand on my arm. Hippodamia. 'We must leave now.'

'She went with *him*,' I choked out.

'Penelope did not have a choice,' Hippodamia reminded me. 'She did it for us.'

I knew it was true. Penelope had recognized that she could not stop Odysseus with her rage; she could only pacify him as a wife to a husband. She had always known how to play him best. But that had not made it hurt any less to see Penelope embrace the man who had just butchered my brother . . .

'We must go, my friend,' Skaris said, limping heavily to my side.

I gulped down a panicked breath. 'I cannot leave him like this.'

'You must,' she told me, her voice firm yet not unkind. 'Your brother has left this place. So must you. It is what he would want.'

I shook my head, even though I knew she was right.

'Someone needs to tell our father,' I said, the words shaky and thin. 'He should know. He needs to know.'

'I will tell him,' Telemachus said, standing before us.

Hippodamia brushed my shoulder. 'Melantho . . .'

'I cannot leave her, either,' I whispered. The tears had found me now, hot and desperate. 'What if he hurts her? What if he—'

'He will not,' Telemachus insisted.

'He is a *monster*,' I snarled up at him.

'No, he's *not*.' His voice trembled, like a child verging on a tantrum. 'He is my *father*.'

'You saw what he did,' Actoris snapped.

Telemachus lowered his eyes to my brother's mutilated body, then quickly glanced away.

'Penelope has given us the gift of time,' Hippodamia urged, her cheeks glistening with tears. 'We must not waste it.'

'She prepared a ship for us,' Autonoë told Telemachus, her voice surprisingly calm. 'At the abandoned harbour. That is where we must go.'

Telemachus blinked. 'A ship? But why . . . *How* did she—'

'We don't have time to explain,' Actoris bit out.

'It is time,' Eurynome whispered to me. In that moment, her voice reminded me of my mother's, so soft with love and concern. 'It is time to let him go.'

I held Melanthius a little tighter, willing the warmth of my body to somehow force the life back into his.

I wasn't ready to lose him. I wasn't ready to say goodbye.

But my brother was long gone.

With shaky fingers, I brushed a curl from Melanthius' closed eyes, then leant down to kiss his forehead.

'Telemachus.' I glared up at the prince. 'Promise me you will bury him. Do not leave his soul to wander. You owe me that.'

The prince nodded, though he could not meet my gaze. 'I swear it on the river Styx, Melantho. He will find peace in the afterlife.'

The moon-tipped waves danced before us.

A ship was waiting at the abandoned harbour, just as Penelope had said it would be.

A sailor was sitting in a small rowing boat, eyeing us curiously. We were, after all, an unusual sight – a bedraggled collection of women with blood drying beneath our fingernails and tears staining our cheeks. But, mercifully, the man did not ask any questions. Penelope had paid the sailors generously for our passage and their discretion, using a portion of the gifts the suitors had given her.

I stared at the glittering silver path stretching towards the horizon, then lowered my gaze to my hands, still stained with my brother's blood.

Beside me, Telemachus was speaking in a low, urgent voice to the other handmaids.

'Father told me of an island – Aeaea. A sorceress named Circe lives there. She is feared by men, but Father said she offers sanctuary to lost women. Something to do with Circe not being able to help her niece, so now she helps others. He lived beside the sorceress for a year and saw all manner of women welcomed to her shores. That is where you should go.'

'Why should we believe a word *your father* says?' Actoris spat.

'Where else do you propose?' Autonoë murmured.

'It's worth a shot, surely?' Hippodamia said.

'Who's to say this Circe will welcome us?' Eurynome interjected. 'You say she's a sorceress? She sounds dangerous—'

'I admire any woman feared by men,' Skaris interrupted. 'I say we find the witch.'

'Ask for her hospitality, and by our divine laws she will have to oblige.' Telemachus motioned to the sailor waiting in the rowing boat. 'I have told him the directions my father gave me. They should get you close enough.'

'"Close enough." That's reassuring,' Actoris muttered.

'You must go,' Telemachus urged. 'Now.'

I had been half listening to their debate, my mind wandering listlessly, but now I turned, glare sharp.

'We cannot go yet,' I said.

Telemachus stared at me. 'Why not?'

'Penelope is not here.'

The others shared a look, shifting uncomfortably.

'Melantho—' Hippodamia tried.

'She is coming,' I said. 'I know she is.'

'We have to go—'

'Then *go*.'

An uneasy silence followed. It was Telemachus who broke it first.

'We can wait a little longer,' he relented. 'But only a little while. The rest of you should board the ship now.'

One by one, the handmaids clambered into the small rowing boat. Only Eurynome hugged Telemachus goodbye. The prince tried not to look wounded by this, but I saw the tear he quickly dashed away as we watched the boat glide through the darkness, towards the larger ship waiting just beyond the shallow waters.

'She knew, didn't she?' he said to me after a time. 'My mother knew of Odysseus' plan.'

I sighed. 'Of course she did, Telemachus.'

'And the pirates? Was that her doing?'

I said nothing, but Telemachus seemed to take my silence as confirmation. Through the silvery darkness, I could just make out five shadows in the distance, clambering on to the ship.

'Why did you defy your father's orders?' I asked.

'Because I knew it was what my mother wanted,' Telemachus whispered. 'And she is always right.'

A quietness settled between us, and I felt the seconds spiralling away all too quickly. The rowing boat was empty now, already turning back towards the shore.

But this could not be it.

Our final moment together could not be Penelope in Odysseus' arms.

Come back to me . . .

I closed my eyes and saw my life swirling before me, memories eddying in rich currents of the past. Penelope beat at the core of each one, like an anchor tying me to this world, the pulse that thrummed at the very centre of my existence.

How could I leave her? The idea seemed impossible, like severing a soul from its body and expecting both to continue living.

I heard the shushing of oars and opened my eyes to see the boat drawing up beside us.

'Melantho—' Telemachus began.

'No.' I shook my head. 'I cannot go. I cannot leave her.'

'She would want you to.'

Tears stung my eyes, my nose. 'Not like this. I cannot go like this.'

'You're putting them all at risk by waiting,' he reminded me softly.

It was then that we heard it: a quiver of thunder in the distance. No, not thunder.

Hooves.

We turned in unison to see the Queen of Ithaca breaking through the treeline, her gown billowing behind her as she galloped towards us, forcing her mount faster, *faster*.

My heart leapt as I dashed forward, crying out her name.

'*Penelope!*'

She dismounted and was running to me now, both of us stumbling wildly through the dark, reaching for one another.

'*Melantho!*'

We collided in a desperate tangle of limbs, breaths crashing into chaotic rhythm.

'I'm so sorry.' She gulped out the fractured words. 'I never thought he would . . . I didn't think . . . I'm so sorry.'

I took her face in my hands. 'Did he hurt you?'

'No,' she said. Then her eyes lowered to my throat, tears welling as she traced the angry bruises blossoming there.

'Melantho—'

'I'm fine.'

She reached for my gown next. 'The blood—'

'It's not . . .' My voice caught. 'It isn't mine.'

She met my gaze again. 'I'm so sorry. Your brother—'

'Please. Don't. I can't,' I choked out, shaking my head. 'How did you get away?'

Penelope steadied herself before answering. 'I gave Odysseus my sleeping draught. But it will not last long.'

'Telemachus told us of an island,' I explained breathlessly. 'There is a witch there who welcomes wayward women—'

'Aeaea. Yes, I have heard of it. That is where you will go?'

'Where *we* will go,' I corrected.

Penelope stared at me with eyes so bright they made the moon pale in envy. She took my hands in hers, and I felt the weight of her pain within them.

'Melantho—'

'No . . . No, no, no. Don't do this. Don't you dare—'

'I cannot go with you,' she said, her voice achingly soft. 'Odysseus will never let me leave Ithaca. He would not rest until he found me. I would put all of you in danger.'

'I don't *care*,' I snapped, tightening my fingers around hers. 'Let him come. Let him hunt us.'

'But what of the others? We cannot risk their lives too.'

'We will go separately. We will find our own way.'

Penelope's gaze drifted to where Telemachus stood watching us from a little way off.

'You know I cannot leave him,' she whispered.

'Fine. Then I'll stay with you.'

'If you stay, he will kill you, Melantho. Odysseus must believe you are dead. *All* of you. That is the only way you can be safe.'

A sob swelled in my throat. 'You would really stay with that *monster*?'

'I would.' She nodded. 'To protect you. To protect Telemachus.'

'What if he hurts you?'

'He won't.'

'You saw what he did to my brother—'

'I know, I know.' She drew me to her gently, resting her chin on my head. 'The war has made Odysseus sick, horribly sick. I cannot let him pass that sickness on to Telemachus. I must protect my son and the others beneath our roof. I will not let Odysseus destroy what we've built here.'

'But who will protect *you*?' I wept into her shoulder – furious, useless tears. 'Don't make me do this. Don't make me leave you. I will *never* forgive you if you do. For as long as I live.'

'I know.' She pulled back and smiled at me. 'But you *will live*.'

For a moment, all I could do was stare at her, draped in moonlight and shadows, just as she had been the night we'd met. We had been so very young then, so clueless about the world and all it would take from us.

'I can't lose you,' I breathed.

Tears slipped down Penelope's cheeks as she cupped my face, her touch filled with such torturous love.

'You won't ever lose me, Melantho. I will come for you.'

'When?'

'When it is safe.'

I threw myself into Penelope's arms again, holding her so fiercely, willing every inch of her body to imprint on to mine, so I might always feel the shape of her against me.

The sailor coughed loudly. We were taking too much time.

'You must go now.'

I knew she was right; she was always right. But still I held on tighter.

'Come back to me,' I gasped into her ear.

'I will,' she vowed. 'Wait for me.'

As we drew apart, Penelope's lips grazed mine, just the ghost of a kiss. It was all we could afford beneath the eyes of Telemachus.

Numbly, I turned to walk away, my heart an open, bleeding wound in my chest. Telemachus reached out a hand to help me into the rowing boat.

'Please, look after her,' I said.

He bowed his head. 'On my life, I will.'

All too suddenly, the sailor began to pull at the oars, and I was swept away into the night. I turned to look back at Penelope, a spark of panic bursting in my chest. She was smiling at me, nodding her encouragement as tears slipped down her face. Telemachus took her hand.

When we reached the ship, a ladder was thrown down. Slowly, I hauled myself up, each step feeling heavier than the last. As I reached the top, my body stiffened, my limbs refusing to move. I could not do it. I could not leave her. But then Skaris was there, helping me up on deck, with Hippodamia at my other side. I felt the warmth of their bodies pressing into mine, holding me together.

Once aboard, I staggered to the edge of the ship to see Penelope still standing on that tiny, decrepit harbour. She lifted a hand as the giant oars groaned to life, heaving us towards the endless, beckoning horizon.

I watched until she disappeared into the darkness, the girl who held every piece of my heart.

I will come for you. Her voice echoed through the starless night. A promise. A vow.

Wait for me.

Epilogue

The Queen of Ithaca's handmaids died that day.

That is what the poets shall say.

They will sing of the valiant hero Odysseus, who strung up the unarmed women.

They will delight in the gruesome details of how their feet danced as death squeezed its hand around their delicate, swan-like necks.

They will celebrate Odysseus' triumph, how he single-handedly purged his palace of the rotten suitors and those treacherous slaves. So too will they celebrate his wife's loyalty, admiring her steadfast devotion.

Everybody loves a good, obedient woman, after all.

For the next fourteen years, people will rejoice in Odysseus' mighty rule. They will not question the fact he rarely leaves his chambers or speaks to anyone other than his closest confidants. Nobody will speak of the madness that has infected the king's mind, nor the years Penelope dedicates to trying to cure it. For war does not *weaken* men. No, it makes them valiant and glorious and heroic. *That* is the story people wish to be told.

When Odysseus is finally sent to the world below, people will call his death a 'tragic accident'. It will be Telegonus who takes the king's life, his illegitimate child by the witch Circe. Heralds will tell of how Odysseus mistook his ally for an enemy and was subsequently slain by the son he never had the chance to know. The stories will fail to mention that, in those last years of his life, Odysseus seemed to mistake all allies for enemies.

Once Odysseus passes to the realm below, gossip will spread of the faithful Penelope fleeing to Aeaea. 'Why Aeaea?' people will ask. What could there possibly be for her on the island of her late husband's mistress?

Some will say it was Telegonus who took Penelope there, intent on marrying her. Never mind that Telegonus is the child of Penelope's late husband, or that Odysseus' blood still freshly stained his hands. Some brows will be raised over the fact that Telegonus is younger than Penelope's own son, but those details will, ultimately, be deemed unimportant. For Telenogus is a man, and Penelope a widowed woman, and that is all the justification needed.

And so, when Penelope lives out the rest of her life on Aeaea, people will say it is for love. That part, at least, will be true.

But nobody will ever speak of who awaited Penelope on that isle, who had been waiting there for fourteen long summers. Those details will slip through the cracks of history, like a beautiful, forgotten dream . . .

A woman strides through crystal waters, the waves lapping at her feet.

Beyond her, across the expanse of golden, sun-baked sand, a figure stands, watching. Disbelieving.

For a moment, they can only stare at one another, too afraid to move, in fear that this moment may shatter.

And then, all at once, they are running.

Their bodies are not as fast as they once were; time has taken that gift from them. Yet still, they run with the wild abandon of youth, as if they were children once again, sand spraying behind them like laughter.

Then, they halt, just inches away, both struck by a sudden shyness in the face of all that is between them.

The red-haired woman reaches out; she cannot help herself. She needs to know this is real, that it isn't just another torturous dream the morning will soon snatch from her. With trembling hands, she traces the lines on the other woman's face — some of them familiar, some new, but every detail just as beautiful as on the last night she beheld her.

Her touch is filled with a desperate kind of reverence, fingers trailing over lovely, salt-stung cheeks, down that sharp nose, winding their way to those devastatingly soft lips.

The grey-eyed woman smiles and whispers against her fingertips, 'Melantho.'

'Penelope,' she whispers back.

And they know they are finally home.

Acknowledgements

This book is the definition of 'a labour of love'. There were times when I didn't think I'd ever get to this point, sitting here writing these acknowledgements. It took me a whole year to get the first draft of *Sweetbitter Song* down, and there were times when every sentence felt like a battle. But I kept pushing on, as all writers do, word by word, sentence by sentence, chapter by chapter – fuelled by the support of the amazing people around me – until a story finally began to appear, a story I fell deeply and completely in love with.

I have so many people to thank for making this book possible – those who helped get this story from my brain on to the page, those who shaped and refined those pages into the book it is today, and those who made it possible for that book to be in your hands right now. Words really aren't enough to express my gratitude, but I'm going to try anyway!

Firstly, I want to thank my agent, Jemima, who is truly a ray of sunshine incarnate. Without you, none of this would have been possible and I still count my lucky stars that my email landed in your inbox at exactly the right moment. Thank you for being the first person to believe in me and my writing, and for continuing to champion me every day since. I am so lucky to have such a supportive, lovely and determined agent fighting in my corner. Thanks also to the whole translation team at David Higham Associates, I am so grateful to all of you for all your hard work and for making it possible for my stories to reach readers around the world.

To my editor, Lara, thank you for believing in this book right from the get-go, when it was still just a dreamy vision in my head without a single word written. This was quite a change of tone from *Medea* and *Medusa*, and I am so grateful to you for supporting me in this new challenge, and for falling in love with Melantho and Penelope as much as I have. As always, your thoughtful insights and brilliant attention to detail have helped shape this story into what it is today, and I am so incredibly proud of the book we've created.

To my marketing managers, Sara and Melissa, thank you for all the enthusiasm and passion you have shown each of my books. Your unwavering dedication and drive truly means so much to me and has allowed me to reach and connect with so many readers. You are both an utter joy to work with!

To my publicists, Millie, Ollie and Chloe, thank you for meticulously organizing so many fantastic events. Meeting readers is one of my favourite parts of this job, and I am so thankful to you for creating so many opportunities for this to happen – and for always being such wonderful company along the way!

To the wider Transworld team, thank you for championing me and my books and for working so hard to get *Sweetbitter Song* out into the world. I know so much goes on behind the scenes that we authors don't even see, but I want you to know that I am so appreciative of every single person who has worked on this book!

To my US editor, MJ, thank you for giving *Sweetbitter Song* a home across the pond, and for all your support, enthusiasm and input which helped bring this book to life. I am so thankful for you and the whole Sourcebooks team for believing in this story and allowing it to reach even more readers.

To my husband, Peter, thank you for being there for every step of this journey, patiently listening to each of my 'I-can't-do-this' meltdowns and then picking me up, dusting me off, and gently setting me back on my path. You always know how to keep me both grounded and motivated, and your copious morning coffee and cinnamon-bun deliveries have helped fuel about 90 per cent of this book. I love you endlessly and am so grateful to have a husband who believes in me so completely.

To my sister, Holly, thank you for helping me shape this idea into something coherent, back when it was just a chaotically written synopsis on my laptop. Thank you also for being one of the first people to read this book and for offering your insightful, helpful feedback. This story explores the beauty and power of sisterhood, and I have you to thank for showing me, from an early age, what it means for women to support, encourage and uplift one another – so, thank you.

To my parents, Gilly and Simon, thank you for being my (self-proclaimed) number 1 fans. This is always the hardest paragraph to write in any book, because how do I summarize everything you have done for me in just a few sentences? You have believed in me from the very beginning, encouraging me not only to dream big, but to go out and make those dreams a reality. I feel so very lucky to have parents who support me so utterly and completely, travelling hours and hours up and down the country just to cheer me on at my book events (even though I am certain you must be bored stiff of hearing me talk about my writing by now!). Sometimes this career can be a lonely one, as so much time is spent just me and my laptop, but with parents like you I never have to worry about feeling alone, because I know you are both always right there, just a phone call away, ready to listen and talk whenever I need you. You really are the best.

To my friends (you know who you are!), thank you for all the love and light you bring into my life and into my writing. As I said above, an important theme in this book is sisterhood, and I am so very lucky to be surrounded by such wonderful women who have taught me what friendship truly means. Also, a special shout out to Jess, Nat and Ellie for being the first of my friends to read this book and for being so excited about it!

One of the highlights of this career is having the opportunity to meet other writers whom I hugely admire, and I just want to take a moment to thank all the incredible authors I've had the honour of meeting over the past couple of years, either through sharing panels or at events or even just connecting with online. Thank you all for being so kind and welcoming and for continuing to inspire me day after day.

Lastly, to my lovely readers, whom I can never thank enough. I believe a book isn't truly finished until it is read, so thank you for being the final piece in *Sweetbitter Song*'s story, for bringing this book to life in your minds and hearts. Thank you, also, for trusting me to take you on another journey into the ancient world. Together, we've ventured into the legendary lair of Medusa, battled monsters beside Medea on the Argo, and now, here we are on the rocky shores of Ithaca, falling in love with Melantho and Penelope. I am so excited for all the future stories we have yet to share together, and I am eternally grateful to you for being part of this adventure!

About the Author

Having secured a first-class honours degree in Classical Literature and Civilisation at the University of Birmingham, Rosie Hewlett has studied Greek mythology in depth and is passionate about unearthing strong female voices within the classical world. Rosie currently lives in Buckinghamshire with her husband and is now a full-time author, spending her days lost inside her favourite stories from mythology.

Rosie's first traditionally published novel, *Medea*, was an instant *Sunday Times* bestseller and her self-published debut novel, *Medusa*, won the Rubery Book of the Year Award in 2021.

rosiehewlett.author
rosiehewlett.author
rosie_hewlett